The Trial Match

RENÉE ARONIS

To my best friend, Scott.
Thank you for being the best of husbands
and the best of friends!
I love you more every day!

Other Books in this Series:

Meet Your Match
Striking of the Match
Broken Match
The Perfect Match

CONTENTS

Chapter One

AFTER THE STORM

Erin Elliott stood at the door of her London home long after the police car drove away with her husband, David, in the back seat. Their newborn daughter Juniper was screaming in the nursery, and Erin's heart was pounding in her chest as panic began to grip her mind. Finally, the baby stopped crying, and she could think.

Oh my God! What do I do now? Call his lawyer… start there. The adrenaline was wearing off, and her mind felt fuzzy. It was hard to concentrate, and moving was suddenly exhausting. "Kitty!" she yelled as she turned and saw her housekeeper standing behind her, holding the infant in her arms. "Oh, Kitty!"

"A'right, mum, let's 'ave a fink. I reckon you should ring 'is solicitor to start," she said.

"Do you know his name? I don't remember if I've ever heard him say what it was."

"Search 'is desk. I'll 'elp ya."

"Thank you, Kitty. I can't think straight."

They went into David's office, and Erin lost it. She began crying and was having a hard time trying to compose herself. Kitty lay the three-week-old, swaddled tightly in a blanket, on the large maple desk. She then held her employer and friend, allowing her to cry on her shoulder.

"Did you see what happened? Did you see what *Detective Chief Superintendent asshole* Dawson did to me?" Erin said, her voice shaking.

"No, all I 'eard were Mr. Elliott and 'im 'avin' a row."

"He… touched me, Kitty. He made David fight to protect me, and then arrested him for it."

"'Ee touched ya? Ya mean—"

"Under my skirt, yes," Erin said as she opened and shut the desk drawers.

Kitty covered her mouth in shock. "No—"

"Here it is! Mr. Archibald Hartwell the third Esquire. Holy Moses, my hands are shaking so hard!"

"It'll be a'right; you'll tell the judge what 'at man done to ya, and they'll allow our Mr. Elliott ta come 'ome. You'll see."

Erin sat in David's office chair and dialed the number on the attorney's expensive-looking business card, using the landline phone. A woman answered and listed several names, including Hartwell.

"Hello? May I please speak to Mr. Archibald Hartwell… the third?" she asked, feeling like a little girl.

"May I ask your name, please?" the woman asked.

"Um, this is Erin Elliott, David Elliott's wife. It's… urgent."

"Yes, ma'am, I'll connect you."

Erin waited, shaking and in shock. She wanted to tell her mind to shut up as the events of the previous hour rolled around in her head.

"Mrs. Elliott? This is Archibald Hartwell speaking. What's happened?" he asked kindly.

"He's… David has been… arrested! They just took him away," she said and began to weep, trying not to start bawling.

"Arrested? On what charges?"

"Assaulting an emergency worker and resisting arrest, or something like that, but he was only trying to protect me since the officer was… assaulting me… sexually. He… David… was being held by two officers… men, and he was struggling to stop him. Please help us!" she said, beginning to cry harder.

"Oh, dear! Do you know the officer's name?"

"Detective Chief Superintendent Clive Dawson. He was in cahoots with Susannah and sent her love letters. David put them in a safe deposit box, but I don't have the key for it."

"Mr. Dawson was the officer who entered your home without a warrant last year, was he not?"

"Yes, that was him. Oh no! I... have the Fertilis Defect, and David is my match! If they take him away, I'll start having episodes again! Oh, please, please help us, Mr. Hartwell!"

"Now, now, calm down. I'm sure he'll be home soon. Usually, with cases such as this, they allow the suspect to go home with strict limitations as to where he's allowed to travel until the trial, if it even goes that far, which I highly doubt will be the case. I will get to the bottom of this, Mrs. Elliott, don't you worry," he said, sounding confident.

"Thank you, Mr. Hartwell, I'm... just afraid he'll get hurt. Mr. Dawson seems like a violent person, and he might beat David up or have someone else do it for him."

"Alright, I will check on that as well. There will be a plea hearing tomorrow, and I'll contact you when I know the time. Please tell me the best number to ring you."

Erin gave him her cell number and hung up just as Juniper started crying again, which made her milk begin to flow. "Damn it! He'll get back to me," she said to Kitty. "Alright, Junie, just give me a minute," she said, knowing the baby couldn't understand her.

"'At's all 'ee said, then? 'At's it?" Kitty asked, clearly distressed and upset as she handed Juniper to her.

"Follow me," Erin said, carrying the baby out of the office. "He said there will be a plea hearing tomorrow and that they usually allow suspects to stay at home until their trial, so he should be home soon," she explained as they went up to the nursery to feed Junie. "I hope he's right!"

That evening, the landline rang. "Hello?" Erin answered, hoping it was good news.

"Ach, ma darling," David said, sounding frightened.

"David! Are you okay?"

"Aye, as of now. There will be a plea hearing tomorrow at ten in the morning. I'm not sure what tae plead, though."

"Oh, David, I don't know, either."

"If I plead guilty, it'll be admitting to the world that I've done something I didn't do… intentionally, anaway. It'll go on ma record, and—"

"You didn't do anything wrong, so I guess you should plead not guilty, though that'll mean a trial. I'd say listen to Mr. Hartwell."

"I want tae fight et, but I'm terribly frightened."

"I would be too! I'm terrified that they'll put you in jail for a long time! I already miss you, what will I do if they—"

"Archibald told me not tae worry about that, and you shouldn't either. I love you, Erin, and whatever happens, I'll never stop, a'right?"

"Oh, David! I love you so much! I'll never stop loving you either! I—I miss you! Take care of yourself, and I'll be there tomorrow," she said, knowing the call would soon be over.

"If I do end up in prison, please… try tae bring… things tae help me… meanin', uh, gifts for the officers, if yeh ken what I mean by that. I may not be able tae speak openly to yeh after this, so please remember."

"Oh, okay, but… I hope it doesn't come to that, my love! Oh, God, I don't wanna say goodbye! I love you!" she said, beginning to panic.

"Aye, ma time is up now. I love yeh as well! Kiss ma Junie and yourself—"

The line went dead, and she covered her mouth. "Dear God, please keep him safe!" she prayed as she cried.

An hour before supper, her mobile phone rang. "Hello?" she answered.

"Hello, Mrs. Elliott?"

"Yes."

"This is Archibald Hartwell."

"Is he okay? Will they send him home soon?" she asked, unable to hide her fear.

"I've spoken to him on the telephone. He's told me he's not hurt, though I'm not inclined to believe him. He verified what you told me, and I will be at the hearing tomorrow morning. Are you aware of that?"

"Yes, David called me. Will you please send me the address in a text when we hang up?"

"Of course. I will speak to you in the morning, and hopefully I'll know more at that time."

"Okay, thank you," she said, feeling like a little girl, scared and unsure.

"You're welcome, goodbye."

"Goodbye," she said and ended the call.

That night, after feeding Juniper, Erin ate alone at the dining room table, though she wasn't hungry. She then made sure to pump extra breast milk for Kitty to feed Junie while she was at the trial. Later, she went to bed alone but didn't sleep well.

Though she was exhausted, her mind wouldn't stop replaying everything that had happened over and over. Then, as soon as she'd fall into a restless sleep, Junie would start crying, and she'd have to get up.

In the morning, Erin flew through her usual routine and had a hired car pick her up early for David's plea hearing. Traffic was horrendous, but she made it to the courthouse and passed through the security check with ten minutes to spare. As she approached the door to the courtroom, a white-haired, older man wearing a smart suit addressed her.

"Mrs. Elliott?" he asked, and she turned to him.

"Yes?"

"I am Archibald Hartwell, David's Barrister. I'm afraid you've missed the hearing—"

"What? But I'm early!" she cried, panic and anger gripping her heart. "Did I get the wrong time?"

"No, but it was rescheduled to an earlier time at the last minute. It was a stroke of luck that I was here and learned of the change only moments beforehand," he said, then led her to a bench. "I'm afraid I have some rather unpleasant news."

"Really? What—"

"They will not be releasing David on bail. He'll be on remand until the trial is through."

"Trial? So, he plead not guilty?"

"Yes, he did. The Magistrates decided that the case was too serious for them to rule on and have sent it to the Crown Court. Dawson has convinced the higher powers that David is sure to run to America since that is where you are from. He referred to the fact that after his search of your home last year, you promptly left the country."

"But that's ridiculous! We'd already planned that trip before—Why would we run because of an assault that was so minor there wouldn't even be bruises... after being provoked? That's ludicrous!"

"I agree, but my hands are tied. I'm very sorry," he said sincerely.

"Can I... visit him? Is he allowed conjugal visits if his wife is sick?"

"I'm afraid not, not where he's being held now. There will be another hearing in two weeks, and if he's sentenced to do time, I'll fight so you'll have that privilege, though I'm sure this will be counted as time served, and he'll be home soon afterward."

"Two weeks?" she said with a gasp. "But I need several treatments each week! A whole week is stretching it, a lot! Please... keep that in mind, okay?"

"Alright, that's good to know." He placed his hand on her shoulder and gave her a warm, caring smile. "Do you need anything? A ride home, perhaps?"

"I... I guess so," she said, looking around the area, somehow hoping to catch a glimpse of her husband.

"I wouldn't worry too much, my dear; I'm sure it will all be over soon."

"I didn't get to see him. Will you... please tell him... that I love and miss him!" she said, unable to keep her tears of disappointment back.

"Of course, Mrs. Elliott, I'll do that."

"Okay, thank you." She took a packet of travel tissues from her purse and wiped her face.

"Follow me, and we'll arrange transport for you."

Erin was sent an email the following day, asking her to bring David a suit to wear for court. Thankfully, it included a detailed list of things to gather as well as where to find them in his closet. She was also told where the key to the safe deposit box was and asked to go to the bank and retrieve the love letters from DCS Dawson to David's former wife, Susannah.

It took a few days, but she finally managed to get everything together. She dropped them off at Mr. Hartwell's office, hoping to ask him how David was doing, but he was in court and would be gone all day. Sad and exhausted, she got back into the hired car, praying her husband would be home soon.

Chapter Two

A CASE IS BROUGHT AGAINST HIM

Those two weeks seemed to last a year. Exhaustion and shortness of breath had become Erin's constant companions, though she didn't have an episode. She hoped that maybe the hormones involved in her recent pregnancy and breastfeeding would somehow help keep it from happening, though she knew that wasn't likely.

Finally, the day came for the pre-trial case hearing, which was the only one she could attend before she gave her testimony. She arrived at the courthouse an hour early, trying to stay calm, thankful the media wasn't there to hound her. When an officer unlocked the doors, she entered and sat where the man told her to.

Forty minutes later, the room was packed, and several official-looking people entered through a door behind the judge's bench. A man in a black robe, who wore white bands that resembled the tails on a bow around his neck like a tie, stepped forward. "All rise," he said. "All parties in the case of the Crown vs David Peter Elliott."

Erin watched as her husband was led in with manacles on his wrists and ankles. He was so handsome in the suit she'd brought him, but he looked scared out of his mind, though he was trying to hide it. She wanted to wave and get his attention as he scanned the room looking for her, but she felt it wouldn't be appropriate.

Finally, he saw her, and her heart leapt. "I love you," she mouthed, and he nodded, one short nod. He was led to a seat facing her and then told to stand in front of the judge, an unfriendly-looking man who wore a short wig, a violet robe with lilac facings, and a red sash over his left shoulder. David looked pale, and she could see him trembling ever so slightly.

"Are you David Peter Elliott?" the court clerk asked.

"Yes," David replied.

"David Peter Elliott, you are charged with the assault and wounding of an emergency worker whilst resisting arrest. The particulars of the case are that on the tenth of March, you knowingly assaulted one of His Majesty's police officers whilst you were being arrested. You have pleaded not guilty."

"Correct," he said.

"You may be seated," the clerk said.

There was a lot of activity, and then the court clerk stood before them once more. "The trial for David Peter Elliott is set to begin on Monday, one week from today," he said, then a man came to take David back into custody. Erin's heart was beating hard in her chest as she watched them take her best friend, lover, husband, idol, and healer away. When he turned his head to look at her, his eyes unable to hide his fear, she blew him a kiss.

"Mrs. Elliott," Archibald said, approaching her after the courtroom had cleared out. "I will be petitioning the Judicial Conduct Investigations Office to request a different judge, as I'm not sure I trust this one to grant us a fair trial. I want to assure you that I and my firm will stop at nothing to see David a free man as soon as possible." Erin sat hard on the chair she'd been seated in, and the older man held out his arm to support her. "Are you quite alright, Erin?"

"I need… a treatment, Mr. Hartwell. This isn't a fake disease that has managed to find an excuse to include sex. My symptoms are coming back, and it won't be long before I'm having full-blown episodes again," she said.

"What happens to you when you have an episode? It is paramount that I give the judge as much detail as possible if I'm going to secure conjugal visits for you."

Erin told him how her form of the disease caused a decrease in the surfactant that keeps a human's lungs from sticking together and that when she has an episode, she stops breathing completely, though her muscles try with all their might to bring air in. "It's not like holding my breath, either; I cough all the air out of my lungs, and they stick together, then I pass out from lack of oxygen and literal exhaustion.

"My last episode lasted around a minute and twenty seconds, and I woke up in hospital three days later. Another symptom, along with the lead-ups, is exhaustion. I have a newborn baby, and in a few weeks, David's children, whom I've never had to care for on my own, will return to my home. When I don't have treatments, I can hardly take care of myself, let alone an infant, a nine-year-old, two twelve-year-olds, and a sixteen-year-old! I need—"

"Alright, my dear, I will fight for you. Now, do you need help getting home today?" he asked.

Erin wanted to say no and that she could do it herself, but she was just so tired. "I think I do," she said quietly, glad David couldn't see her suffering like that.

Chapter Three

WHAT ABOUT EASTER BREAK?

On March twenty-fifth, fifteen days after David had been arrested and only about a week before his trial was set to start, Erin was still living moment by moment. Thinking too far into the future was impossibly scary for her.

When she was finished feeding Juniper, she saw a notification on her phone. It was a reminder that the next day was the start of Easter break and that she was supposed to pick the kids up from school.

"Good night nurse!" she said out loud. "How am I going to do that? Junie has to be fed every few hours, and it takes three just to get there!" With a heavy heart, she descended the stairs and found Kitty setting the table for supper.

"Aww, 'ello, mum, what can I do for ya?" her housekeeper said brightly.

Erin couldn't help but sigh as she pulled out the chair at the head of the table and sat heavily, feeling completely overwhelmed. "I don't know if there's anything you can do. I'm supposed to pick the children up from school tomorrow, and I don't know how I'll manage it."

Kitty cocked her head to the side, then began rubbing her chin, and if Erin hadn't been so worried, she would've laughed at how comical she looked. "I reckon you've two options, mum," Kitty began.

"Okay, and what are they?"

"You can fetch them yourself, and I'll mind our Junie, or you could contact the school and 'ave 'em sent 'ere on the train. Wouldn't be the first time 'at's 'appened. 'At's the way it were wiv' the o'ver school, mum. I reckon 'ere's a scheme for 'at very 'fing if ya was ta ring 'em and ask."

"That's brilliant, Kitty! I forget how amazing public transportation is here. I'll call them now," she said and looked at the clock on the mantle. "It's getting late, but I'll try, and if no one answers, I'll leave a message."

She unlocked her phone, found the number, and thankfully got through to the office. The staff member she spoke to assured her everything would be taken care of and not to worry. After she was told the arrival station and what time the train would arrive, Erin felt an enormous weight lift off her shoulders.

The train was only five minutes late the next day. Erin had taken a taxi, which was waiting for her, as she could hardly keep her eyes open. She sat on a bench near the platform while she waited for the children to disembark. Her head began to bob every few seconds and then snap up again, waking her with a start.

"Mummy?" she heard, and as if in slow motion, she lifted her head. Her new nine-year-old daughter Rosie was standing before her, along with her three brothers, looking at her with frightened eyes.

Trying to snap out of her fog, Erin shook her head and smiled at her children. "Oh! Did I fall asleep? I'm sorry, baby girl," she said, hoping to ease her fear. "Did you have a nice train ride?"

Rosie leaned in for a hug, and then Charlie, who was eleven, did the same, while his twin brother, Daniel, recounted nearly every detail, including what each of them ate and how many times he'd used the toilet. The eldest boy Peter, at sixteen, was tall, thin, and handsome, like his father. He rolled his eyes at Dan and then flashed David's amazing smile at her, which made her heart ache.

"Hiya, Mum, ya a'right?" he asked, which was a standard greeting in England.

"Good night nurse, I've missed you!" She stood and wrapped her arms around him. He let go of his suitcase and hugged her tightly.

"Oi, Erin, let's get a move on!" Dan said impatiently.

"Don't be cheeky!" Peter said, turning toward his brother, and ignored the insulting hand gesture that followed.

"We'd better get going. I saw the taxis where I came in… this way, I think," she said, suddenly feeling turned around and flustered.

"The taxis usually stand out here," Peter said, then pointed toward another exit.

"Oh, yeah, that's the one. Sorry, guys, let's go." The blood rose to her cheeks in embarrassment.

"It's alright, Mummy," Rosie said sweetly and held her hand. "I get lost in train stations sometimes as well."

"Yes, and if you'd stay close to me and not dawdle behind, it wouldn't happen as often," Peter said.

"I know," the girl said sheepishly.

"I can't wait to tell Dad—" Daniel began, then put his head down.

"Dan!" Peter scolded, but Erin went to the young boy and put her hand on his shoulder.

"It's okay, Dan. Things are gonna be different with your father gone, and there will be lots of stuff to get used to. We'll have to learn together, but I think if we keep our chins up, we'll be okay in the end, right?" She looked at the others, hoping for affirmation.

"Yes, Mummy, but… I'm going to miss Daddy… a lot," Rosie said as they reached the taxi.

"Me too, darling girl. Now, go on and get in."

As she shut the door, Erin noticed a large sign on the side of a bus stop, one she'd seen many times. On it, David was standing against a white background, smiling and looking impossibly handsome while holding a mobile phone in front of him so you could read the screen. It read, 'I do, so should you,' in a word bubble like a text message. *I miss you, darling,* she thought and took a moment to collect herself before getting into the front passenger seat.

"I can't help it, Peter!" she heard Rosie say from the back, sounding distressed.

"Shush!" Peter hissed in reply.

"Alright, now, we don't need any angry words, okay? When we get home, we can have a talk and get everything out in the open. Right now, let's just allow each other… I don't know… the space to feel what we feel, alright?"

There was a collective, "Yes, Mum," from the children. Then she heard Rosie sniffle, and it took all her willpower not to cry with the young girl.

Finally, the driver pulled over in front of their house. Exhausted, Erin thanked him as they got out of the taxi, then she shut the door. "Oh! My purse!" she cried and turned, watching the car pull away from the sidewalk. "Damn!" she said before she could stop herself.

"Oi! Stop!" Daniel and Charlie yelled, waving their arms and following after it, trying to get the driver's attention.

"Never mind, boys," Erin said, but then the car pulled over and stopped. The twins ran to it and spoke to the driver, who had his window down. When Erin reached them, they had her purse and were grinning like they'd saved the day.

"Here ya are, Mum," Charlie said, smiling brightly, while Daniel held it out to her.

"My heroes," she said and took the bag. "That saved me a lot of headaches, thank you."

Charlie wrapped his arms around her middle and held her tightly. "You're welcome," he said.

"Cheers," Dan said, then ran to the large, wooden front door. He tried to open it but found it locked.

"Sorry, guys, but we started locking it after your dad… well, just to be safe," she said and fished a keychain out of her purse, again thankful she had it back.

"May I do it, Erin?" Dan shouted in his excitement.

"Yes, but please lower your voice; Junie may be sleeping, and she's not used to a lot of noise and ruckus in the house."

"Yes, Mum," he said and smiled at her with full dimples as she handed him the key. He put it into the lock but was having trouble getting it to turn, so Charlie tried to help. "I can do it, ge' off!" he yelled as it finally turned and the door flung open. The two boys practically fell into the foyer, arguing loudly, while Peter scolded them.

Erin looked up and saw Kitty on the stairs holding the baby, her eyes wide. Startled by the sudden commotion, Juniper began wailing at the top of her lungs, which made Erin's milk drop, drenching her top in seconds. "Boys!" she said, having to raise her voice over the crying. "Uhhh!" was all she had the energy for. She dropped her purse and rushed up the stairs, taking Junie out of Kitty's arms. "Okay, sweetie, alright, it's okay. Mummy's here, and I'll feed you. Shhh."

She could hear Peter still scolding them as she reached the nursery and shut the door. Her top and bra stuck to her as she tried to remove them, and Juniper screamed. Wanting to do her own screaming, she sat in her nursing chair and tried to get the pillow in place while also trying to find something to soak up the milk from her leaking breasts.

It was frustrating trying to get the baby to latch on while at the same time reaching for a burp rag a few feet away on the changing table. Junie was too upset to latch on, and Erin needed help. The children passed the door, clearly trying to be quiet, but she could hear Rosie crying, which brought on tears of her own.

A few minutes later, Kitty knocked and stuck her head into the room. "May I 'elp ya a'tall, mum?" she said and then saw the state of her. "Aww, a'right, be back in a tick." The door closed, and within moments, she returned with a soft towel, a dry bra, and a clean top.

Junie was finally nursing, but Erin was cold, wet, and sticky. All she could do was cry and shake her head when Kitty asked if there was anything else she could do.

"Don't you worry, mum, fings'll get easier wiv time, you'll see. I fink Daniel and Charlie 'ave learnt their lessons and won't do 'at again. Our Junie must learn 'at she's not the only one what lives 'ere, and the sooner the bet'er, don't ya agree?"

"Aye," Erin whispered as she rocked the baby and tried to calm herself down.

When Juniper was done nursing and being burped, Erin laid her down for a nap, longing for one herself. Instead, she trudged up the stairs to the children's rooms and gently knocked on Peter's door. "Can I come in?" she asked and poked her head into the room.

"Yes… of course you can. I'm sorry about Dan and—" he began, but Erin put her hand up to stop him.

"We've already had this conversation, remember? *You* are not responsible for your siblings."

Peter smiled at her from his bed, where he was sitting with a book propped up on his knees. "I remember, but old habits are hard to shake, innit? Are you alright? I feel gutted over what's happened," he said, then closed the book and set it next to him, springing forward to sit on the edge of his bed with all the energy of a teenager.

"I'm fine," she said, but added, "…mostly," when he gave her a doubtful look. Smiling, she laid her hand on his cheek and kissed his forehead lightly. "Don't you worry about me—Yes, I know, you can't help it, but your worrying won't do much to help, though I do appreciate how much you care. Now, what do you say to a family meeting here in your room?"

"I don't mind at all. Would you like me to gather everyone for you?" he asked and stood.

"That would be very nice, thank you," she said and closed her eyes as a wave of exhaustion fell over her.

"Mum? Are you certain you're a'right? You seem so tired. We can do this another time if you need a rest." He pulled out his desk chair and set it next to her. "Please, have a seat."

"Thank you, my dear boy. You're so thoughtful, and I'm so glad you're my son," she said, her emotions trying to get the better of her. "Go on and find your brothers and sister. I'll wait here. Please don't look so worried; I'll try to explain everything to you."

"A'right, Mum, just relax." Peter hurried out of the room, and soon she heard each door open, then soft voices speaking.

Charlie and Daniel were the first to join her, both looking guilt-ridden and contrite. "Oh, my boys, come here," she said and opened her arms to them.

Charlie nearly ran into them, but Daniel came to her much more slowly and didn't hug her.

"I'm truly sorry for being loud, fighting with my brother, and frightening Juniper," Dan said, his head hung in shame.

"I'm ever so sorry as well, Mum. Please don't be cross with us. We'll both be better behaved from now on, won't we, Dan?" Charlie said as Rosie entered the room, followed by Peter.

"Yes, we will, I promise!" Dan said.

Erin wanted to cry her eyes out over their sincere apology. She motioned to Rosie to join the hug, and the young girl began to cry as she did. "Please forgive us, Mummy!" she said and cried even harder.

"Hush, now, my darling. I'm not angry, and there's nothing to forgive. I didn't ask you to come in here to scold you; I just wanted to have a little talk. Go on and have a seat; there's a lot that's changed since you went back to school, and I think it would be good to get everything out in the open."

The children found seats, either on the floor or the edge of the bed, and then looked at her, waiting. "I want you to know that we can talk about your dad anytime you want to. He didn't do anything wrong, and I'm sure the jury will see that and send him home soon. Until then, I'm afraid I'm going to need all the help I can get from you."

"Of course, Mum, what do you need?" Peter said.

"To be honest, I'm not sure. Here's the thing; as you know, I have the Fertilis Defect, and your dad is the person who can help me with its symptoms. Now that he's not able to, they'll come back, and—"

"Are you going to die?" Rosie said, wide-eyed and looking terrified.

"Don't interrupt, Rosie!" Peter said.

"Sorry."

"No, I won't die, but it makes me very tired, and sometimes it's hard for me to breathe. It's hard to explain, but the disease makes me—Oh, dear, it's just too much to explain now. When I have an episode, I can't breathe, but it doesn't last very long. Sometimes, after an episode, I have to sleep for a while, so you may have to help Kitty and Francie if they need you."

"A'right, Mum, we will," Charlie said, and the others nodded in agreement.

"I know you will, thank you. Now, is there anything you want to talk about? Do you have any questions?"

The children looked at each other and shrugged.

"Nothing? Well, I want you to be sure to come to me if you think of some—"

"I already have a nickname at school!" Dan said with glee.

Erin couldn't help but smile at him. "You do? And what is it?"

"All the lads call me Rot now."

"Rot? Do I want to know why?" Erin said while the others either shook their heads or rolled their eyes.

"It's on account of my feet; they smell worse than any of the other lad's! It's a stonkin' name, innit? There's a boy named Lobes because of his ears sticking out so far, and another boy is called Runs because of his nose being runny on the first day. There's a boy one year ahead of me who's called Fiz Wiz. Wanna know why?"

"No!" Peter said, and Erin shook her head, though she couldn't help but laugh.

"His birth name's Milton Fitzgibbon, which isn't any good at all, right? Well, everyone called him Fitz, and then it became Fiz. Somewhere along the line, somebody added wiz, and now it's Fiz Wiz. That's a stonkin' name as well, innit?" He looked up at her as she shook her head.

"I guess so—"

"Oh, and there's also Trolly and Bogie and Toots—"

"Don't interrupt, Daniel!" Peter said with a heavy sigh.

"And Trout!" Dan finished despite his brother's correction.

"I'm glad you like your nickname, but it might be wise to change your socks more often, don't you think?" Erin said.

"And lose my name? Are you mad? Not a chance!" he said passionately.

Chapter Four

TESTIMONY DAY ONE

A week later, David was led into the courtroom as before. Once again, several people entered from the front of the room, and the court clerk stepped forward. "All rise," he said, and everyone stood. "All parties in the case of the Crown vs David Peter Elliott."

After the indictment was read, there was a lot of legal talk and arguments from the Prosecution on excluding some evidence and on who would be called to testify. The judge disallowed the love letters from Clive to Susannah, saying they weren't relevant to the case. He also denied conjugal visits, based on the fact that they were not customary or conventionally in use in the United Kingdom.

When that was settled, the jury was led in and then seated. As the jurors were sworn in, David tried to pay attention to the proceedings but couldn't help worrying about his wife. Once the jury was instructed and had taken their oath, the Crown Prosecutor stood to give her opening speech.

She spewed her tale of a pampered, privileged, spoiled, drug-addicted celebrity who had been violent to his former wife and felt he was too important to be arrested. Generalizations, assumptions, and lies were flung out of her mouth as though they were the truth. They were told a scenario and then assured that it would be proven to be true when their case was tried before them.

Next, Archibald Hartwell stood and addressed them, giving them actual facts of the day in question and the truth about David's lifestyle and behavior. He told them they'd be shown evidence that DCS Dawson was a crooked cop and that the whole event was set up because of his desire for revenge. He then closed his statements and resumed his seat.

The Crown Prosecutor began to present her case by calling their first witness. David watched as Officer Baker was called and then sworn in. The wigged woman stood and looked at her notes, then at the young man. "My name is Zoey Franklin, and I represent the Crown Prosecution. Will you please tell the jury what you experienced at Mr. and Mrs. Elliott's home on the tenth of March this year?" she asked.

The young officer said that he'd arrived at the house, and things seemed alright until they tried to arrest him. "Soon as we took hold of 'im, Mr. Elliott begun flailin' and carryin' on like a lunatic. It took all my strength ta hold 'im, then he went all men'al like, kickin', scratchin', and punchin' us."

"Were you harmed during the assault?"

"Yeah, I were. 'Ere, and 'ere," he said, pointing to his upper arm and wrist.

"I'd like to submit Exhibits A through C, which are on pages two and three of your packet," she said to the jury. "They are photographs of the injuries sustained to Officer Baker on the day in question." The jurors were given a moment to view the evidence, then the questioning continued.

Throughout his testimony, the man was visibly sweating, and his eyelids fluttered while his eyes darted to the right and up, then to the left, appearing for all the world like an actor who'd forgotten their lines. He made very little eye contact with the jury, mainly looking to the prosecutor or any other ally in the courtroom for support or encouragement, it seemed. After both the Prosecution and the Defense were finished with their questioning, the relief on the man's face was plain when he was told he could leave the stand.

The next witness was Officer Kent, the other officer who'd held David. Once he was sworn in, the prosecutor asked, "In what way did David Elliott harm you?"

"Right, 'ee jammed 'is elbow into me ribs, and I were bruised for over a week," he said.

"I'd like to submit Exhibit D, page three in your packet. Please continue, Officer Kent."

"Right, then 'ee tried ta 'ead butt me, but I were quicker than 'im, innit? Though 'ee busted my lip up in the struggle, like. 'Ee were tuggin' and jerkin' 'is body all over, and it were 'ard ta keep hold of 'im," he said, moving around as if re-enacting the scene for an audience.

"Was Detective Chief Superintendent Dawson molesting or attempting to rape Mrs. Elliott?"

"Naw, 'ee weren't, though she were fightin' 'im as though 'ee were. 'At's why she 'ad ta be 'eld down, innit? 'At's when Mr. Elliott become belligerent, like."

"Why do you suppose she was fighting him as though she thought he was going to molest her?"

"Reckon it's anyone's guess, ma'am. DCS Dawson 'ad just begun ta inform 'im of the charges against 'im when she begun the Barney, like. DCS Dawson tried 'oldin' 'er 'imself, but wiv her bein' so 'eavy like, 'ee weren't able ta do it alone."

"And what do you mean by Barney, for those unfamiliar with the term?"

"Right-o, it means trouble, innit?"

David felt his face getting hot, both from the overemphasis of her size and because of the blatant lies the boy was telling. *Don't react, let it go!* he reminded himself.

When the officer was finished being cross-examined by Archibald, they took a recess for lunch, though David wasn't hungry, being too worried about Erin.

—

Though she wasn't allowed into the courtroom, Erin was at the courthouse that day. Being a witness, she decided to be there in case things progressed faster than they thought they would. She also just wanted to be near her husband, even if she couldn't see or talk to him.

Just being in the building was more comforting to her than sitting at home, worrying all day. During the lunch recess, Archibald came into the witness room to tell her how things were going. As she sat at a table listening to him, she could feel her breath catching, though she was trying not to panic.

"Are you quite alright?" he asked, looking at her peculiarly.

She tried to answer but nothing came out, so she stood, clutching her throat, then began coughing. There was nothing she could do as she looked into his worried eyes and then fell forward against him.

Shocked, he cried out, "Call for an ambulance; she's not breathing!"

She was still conscious and wanted to tell him not to do that, but then the stars appeared, and everything went black. When she opened her eyes, there were people crowded around her, some looking worried and some standing back, taking photos. From across the room, she heard someone say, "I'll ring 999."

"No, please don't do that!" she croaked, so everyone stopped what they were doing and turned to see who'd said that. "I'm okay now, I just need to go home."

Archibald sat hard on a chair, having to catch his breath. He asked that everyone calm down and then spoke to her gently. "You gave me a fright; are you sure you don't need to be taken to hospital?"

"I'm sure; the episode is over now. I just have a headache and need to rest. If someone could call me a taxi or—"

"I'll ask my assistant to deliver you to your home," he said and helped her up onto a small sofa against the wall. "I must return to the courtroom now, so my assistant will come for you shortly."

"Please, if David finds out about this… I'm sure he will, but please make sure he knows I'm alright and that it was a minor episode and not to worry," she said, aching all over.

"Yes, of course I will," he said and then rushed out the door.

—

News of Erin's episode hadn't yet reached David, so Archibald decided to wait until after court was adjourned for the day to tell him so he wouldn't sit there worrying. He could tell, though, when the judge came back into the room, that he knew what had happened and that he wasn't at all happy about it. There would be words later, he guessed.

Chapter Five

PANTS ON FIRE

Before David knew it, court was back in session, and he wondered what would come next. The prosecutor stood and said, "I'd like to call Detective Chief Superintendent Clive Dawson to the stand."

The hulk of a man stood on the witness stand and was sworn in. He looked to be irreproachable, putting on a facade of innocence. "DCS Dawson, please tell us why you were at the Elliott residence on the tenth of March this year?" she asked her witness.

"I had information which led me to believe that there were drugs and laundered money in his home. I served his maid the warrant and entered the house," he said.

"Were you hindered in any way during your search?"

"We were not."

"And did you find evidence of there being anything illegal in Mr. and Mrs. Elliott's home?

"We did not."

What? They didn't even do a search that time! I can't believe this! David thought.

"Will you tell the court who it was that gave you the information?" the prosecutor asked.

"Yes, it was Susannah Elliott, shortly before she… died," he said, feigning grief.

"And what did she tell you he had?"

"She called me late one evening, quite distressed. She explained that her husband, David Elliott, had been high on cocaine and, in a rage, began beating her because she wouldn't… perform her marital duties with him. She told me she knew where he kept his drugs and that if anything were to suddenly and unexpectedly happen to her, I should investigate the matter."

"She died of an Anorexia Nervosa-related heart attack in Edinburgh, in front of witnesses. There was no evidence of foul play; what made you think it was suspicious enough to raid her husband's home?"

"She was less than thirty-six years old; she should not have died of a heart attack. I stand by my decision and only wish I'd been granted the warrant sooner, before he'd had the chance to dispose of the drugs and money." He put his head down and slowly shook it.

"In your own words, can you tell the jury what happened in David Elliott's home on the tenth of March this year?"

"Yes, I'd be glad to. I received my warrant and brought with me four of my younger officers to the Elliott home. I chose them so they could have more real-life, on-the-job experience; I never imagined *any* harm could possibly come to them. Had I known, I would never have put them in that situation.

"A woman, their maid, opened the door. I showed her the warrant and was allowed to enter the home."

"Do excuse me, DCS Dawson," the prosecutor said, and Clive nodded. "Please note Exhibit F, page six in your packet, which shows the warrant. Thank you, please continue."

"We began our search, and when we finally got to the kitchen, Mr. and Mrs. Elliott appeared. David Elliott then yelled at me, saying, and please do excuse my language, 'What in the fuck are you doing here? Get out of my home!'"

David was livid, as he hadn't said anything even close to that. The man was making the whole thing up, and there was nothing he could do about it.

"I informed him that I had a warrant and that my officers and I were there to search the house for drugs, etc., which he didn't like, because he came at me. As luck would have it, Officers Baker and Kent were there to hold him back. It was then that Mrs. Elliott decided to have a go, so I had to restrain her as well. I was able to take hold of her hair and maneuvered her so that she was pinned over a nearby table. She refused to relax, so I had to hold her there until my other two officers were available to help me."

"And did either Mr. or Mrs. Elliott say anything whilst this was taking place?"

"Yes, Mrs. Elliott was screaming that I had no right to hold her husband and asked if I had any idea who he was. She also threatened to bring me to court and such nonsense."

"Did Mr. Elliott say anything?"

"Oh yes, he did. He didn't care for me holding his wife down, so before Officers Sprot and Woodward took over, he pulled and strained against Officers Kent and Baker whilst threatening to kill me if I didn't unhand her."

"He threatened your life?"

"I highly doubt he could manage anything, but yes, he said something to the effect of, 'Unhand her, or so help me, I'll kill you, Dawson!'"

The judge's eyebrows shot up, and he turned to Mr. Dawson. "If Mr. Elliott assaulted and wounded your officers whilst resisting arrest *and* threatened your life, that is a much more serious offense." He wrote something in his notes, then looked at the prosecutor. "Please continue."

"Thank you, my Lord," she said to the judge, then turned back to Dawson. "I have no further questions for you, but if you will please remain on the stand, my learned colleague for the Defense will ask you some further questions."

Mr. Hartwell stood and stared at Mr. Dawson. The man glared defiantly back at him, his lip curled in contempt. "I am Archibald Hartwell, and I represent the defendant. Why did you enter the Elliott's home without a warrant on the fifth of July last year?"

"I do not recall doing so—"

"This case concerns the tenth of March and what Mr. Elliott did at *that* time. Please do stick to *this* case, Mr. Hartwell," Judge Aldrich interrupted.

"Yes, my Lord. Is it true that you were in love with Susannah Elliott and were hoping to run away with her, but she told you that she wanted to get David out of the way first?"

"What? Are you... that's ridiculous—" Clive spewed, his face red with embarrassment.

"Did you not write love letters to her, claiming your love for her and your desire to be together?"

"I do hate to stand, my Lord, but it seems as though my esteemed colleague is confused as to whom it is on trial today," the prosecutor said.

"I agree and would suggest you get to the point," the judge said.

"As you wish, my Lord," Archibald said. "Did you manufacture the situation *in question* to set David Elliott up because you knew Susannah Elliott wanted to be rid of her husband and because you were angry that she died before you were able to run away with her?"

Dawson's eye was twitching, and the tops of his ears were turning dark red. He looked at his counsel as if for help, but she was reading her notes. "Never! I… would never!" he floundered.

"You would never what, precisely? You would never rid a wife of her inconvenient husband or become angry that you weren't able to run away with her before she died?"

The prosecutor stood but didn't say anything. "I suggest you change your line of questioning, Mr. Hartwell," the judge said, sounding quite impatient.

"Of course, and I apologize, my Lord. Exactly how long did the search of the Elliott's home take on the tenth of March?"

"I'm not sure *exactly*, though I'd reckon approximately two, two and a half hours for a house of that size."

"At what time did you arrive at David Elliott's home on that day?"

"I believe it was around one o'clock in the afternoon."

"And what time did you leave with Mr. Elliott in custody?"

"I believe it was around half three in the afternoon," Clive said.

"Well, that's interesting. I'd like to call your attention to Exhibit G, page seven in your packet. This is an affidavit from Miss Kitty Jones, the Elliott's housekeeper. She is the woman Mr. Dawson said was handed the warrant. It clearly states that DCS Dawson arrived at 1:09 pm. It also states that he left the residence at 1:30 pm. Twenty-one minutes does seem a bit too short for a thorough search, as you've already said."

"The girl is lying," Clive said with a scowl.

"I thought you might say as much; thus, I have included Exhibit H, on page eight, which is the telephone records of my office, and Exhibit I, on page nine, a sworn affidavit from my secretary, Natasa McGeegan, stating that Mrs. Erin Elliott placed a telephone call to me at 1:37 on the date in question.

"I spoke to Mrs. Elliott myself. She told me at that time that David had just been taken away by you, Mr. Dawson. Now, you've already testified that you were at the Elliott residence for between two and two and a half hours, but witnesses tell a different story."

"Perhaps I arrived at eleven, not one. It must have been written down incorrectly in the log," Dawson said.

"That *can* happen, I suppose, though it did *not* happen on the tenth of March. I would like to refer you to Exhibit J through M, on pages ten through thirteen. They are sworn affidavits from four of the photographers who followed David and Erin Elliott when they took their infant daughter on a walk that day."

The jury and Clive were given time to review the pages before Archibald continued. "As you have read, they all verify that the couple left their home between eleven thirty and eleven thirty-five and then returned between twelve twenty-nine and twelve thirty, making it impossible for you to have performed a thorough search on the day in question. It also reveals that you've committed perjury to this venerable judge and made a mockery of the court."

He then turned to Judge Aldrich and said, "I move to dismiss this case, my Lord. There was obvious foul play, and the primary witness has perjured himself—"

"I am not prepared to do that just yet. I admit that your evidence *is* compelling, but I will hear the testimony of every witness before I make up my mind. Now, are there any more questions for this witness?"

"No, my Lord," Archibald said, then he and David looked at each other in disbelief.

"Thank you for your time, Detective Chief Superintendent Dawson. You are excused," the judge said, and Clive was allowed to walk away. There was quite a lot of discussion in the courtroom, so court was adjourned for the day.

Judge Aldrich called Archibald to his chambers and told him, in no uncertain terms, that behavior such as Mrs. Elliott's would not be tolerated and that he believed she'd faked it either for attention, to get her way regarding conjugal visits, or to stop DCS Dawson's testimony.

Mr. Hartwell tried to persuade him that he'd witnessed it and that she most certainly wasn't faking anything, but the judge told him that if it happened again, there would be serious consequences.

Once David was delivered to his holding cell, Archibald went to him and told him what had happened to Erin earlier.

"Is she a'right?" he asked, standing to his feet. "Was she taken in an ambulance? Because that won't help her!"

"She's alright, David. My assistant took her home. She started breathing before there was even time to call for an ambulance and said that it wasn't a bad episode. I'm afraid the judge isn't happy about the scene she made, believing it was feigned."

"But that's ridiculous! How can he say… do that? Did yeh not give him an affidavit?"

"I did, from two doctors and a specialist. He's bound to punish you for some reason."

"But he's no' punishin' me, he's killin' ma wife! Yeh must do somethin'."

"I'm doing everything I can, truly I am, David. Now, we must be prepared for your testimony tomorrow," he said, but David shook his head.

"What's the point, Archibald? Yeh said et yerself, this judge isn't likely tae give me a fair trial. Mebbe I should change ma plea tae guilty and have et done with?"

"Don't give up, David, we're fighting, and we should be able to win."

When Archibald had gone, David was furious about everyone lying on the stand, though he was too worried about Erin and all she was dealing with to think much about that. What he was incensed about was the idea that the judge would think she was faking her symptoms. He felt so helpless and hopeless that all he could do was pray.

Oh, God, please help ma wife! Please keep her safe and give us justice. He prayed as he paced the small room, hoping she'd be able to rest.

She'd been able to speak to Archibald before she was taken home, so perhaps it truly wasn't a bad episode this time, he thought. That should've made him relax a bit, but all he could think of was that her next one was going to be bad, and with the way things were heading, it was unlikely he'd be freed by then.

Martin Green was not sitting idle while waiting for his plan to unfold. He was acquainted with several semi-reputable journalists whose stories were regular tabloid headlines. He knew many of them would sell their souls for the intel he had about the case against David; all he had to do was wave the carrot and wait for the best offer to appear. After a few phone calls, he sent some well-worded emails, then waited.

It was a job, trying to learn what made Kieran Aldrich, the judge assigned to the case, tick. Martin discovered that this would be one of, if not the last, case for the retiring man, so he hatched a scheme to sway him somehow with disinformation by vilifying vague, conveniently unnamed celebrities who, it appeared, had evaded justice. He learned that the judge had a habit of stopping at a newsstand every day on his way to the courthouse to buy a copy of The Telegraph and a roll of Rowntree's Fruit Pastilles.

This particular stand used large placards to advertise the best headlines, so he paid the owner to post a few fictitious ones that were loosely based on true stories of celebrities misbehaving, such as:

**WELL-KNOWN RAPPER ACCUSED OF
BEATING HIS PARTNER!**

**ACTRESS CAUGHT SHOPLIFTING
IN HARRODS!**

**CONSTABLE THRASHED IN ALLEY BY
OUT-OF-CONTROL ACTOR!**

Next, he found every article he could in which an 'expert' explained why sex treatments for the Fertilis Defect couldn't actually be effective. Then he searched out every scandal or protest involved in or about the disease, not bothering to verify anything. He had new headlines, fashioned by a talented spin doctor, posted every day whilst the trial took place, making sure it was in the most prime location.

Finally, though Martin never attended the trial, he made certain that, along with the everyday tabloid journalists, the most vicious reporters were also there to sensationalize everything that was said. Normally, photographs and videos were not allowed in the courtroom; however, he managed to secure special permission for images and short videos to be taken and once approved, released to the public. The trap was set and baited; everything was sure to work in his favor, so he sat back and enjoyed the rush of anticipation.

That night, while trying to rest in bed, Erin made the mistake of looking up news about the trial on her phone. She opened one of the first articles she saw that read:

DCS TESTIFIES OF DAVID ELLIOTT'S RAGE-FILLED RAMPAGE DURING ARREST.

Under the headline was a photo of David in the courtroom, smiling. Erin knew he'd been smiling at her during the pre-trial, but the way it was being used made it appear as though he was unrepentant and callous. She scrolled to the article and groaned as she read,

> *Detective Chief Superintendent Clive Dawson testified at Crown Court today that David Elliott, of* Future Explorations *fame, threatened his life and beat a young constable, leaving him bloodied and bruised whilst being arrested in his London home…*

Her heart was racing, and she, herself, wanted to rage, so she put her phone down, not daring to finish the article.

Chapter Six

CIRCUS

Though she ached from head to foot, Erin entered the courthouse the next day with her head down. Apparently, the media had learned about her episode and now acted as if they cared, prowling at the front doors, waiting for her like she was their prey. Bombarding her with questions, they followed her from the car she'd hired, all the way into the building until security made them leave.

If things went as planned, she would give her testimony that day. Fear and nerves only worsened her aching and strained muscles. The night before, Archibald and his team spoke with her in a video chat, where she was given basic witness prep, including instructions on what to say and what *not* to say. Her mind was racing, trying to remember everything she'd been told.

She went through security, the same as each time she'd been there before, and was led through the building to the witness suite. Before the day of her testimony, she'd been allowed to sit in the room and wait, but now that she was on the witness list, a gentleman with a clipboard greeted her and took her name.

Seeing an empty table, she took a seat, feeling vulnerable and exposed. She wanted to pace the floor, and caught herself wringing her hands several times, before she sat on them to keep from doing it. Waiting was the worst part, and she just wanted it to be over.

A woman approached her and introduced herself as Polly, a volunteer from Witness Services. "We are independent of the legal system. Our job is to offer support and information and to answer any questions you may have. Do you have any questions for me?" she asked as she sat in a chair next to her.

"I can't think of any right now. I'm so nervous!" Erin said and took a shaky breath.

"That's completely normal, Mrs. Elliott. I'm here to guide you through what may be a difficult time and experience. If you think of anything, please ask."

"Okay, thank you, Polly."

Using laminated cards with images of the courtroom, Polly explained how the court system worked and told her what it might be like to give evidence. "It appears you've not given an official statement, then?"

"I don't know… I told David's barrister what happened over the phone, but I don't think I gave an official one," Erin said, flustered and wishing she was more prepared.

"It's alright, dear; not everyone does. If you had, we would simply go over it to refresh your memory. It's not a test, and you were there, correct?"

"Yeah, I was there."

"Then you should do fine. It's nothing but nerves messing about with you," she said with a warm, sympathetic smile. "Now, have you thought of any questions for me?"

Erin wracked her brain, trying to think of what she should be asking, but it was empty. "I can't think of anything. Honestly, my mind is a total blank, which is terrifying! Good night nurse! What if I can't remember anything when I'm up there? Oh, Polly, what if I freeze?"

"Don't fret, love, just take your time, and you'll be alright. There's no need to rush; you're allowed time to think things through should you require it."

Erin took a deep breath and tried to calm her racing heart. "That's good to know. Thank you for your help, I feel a little better now," she said.

"If you think it will help, I will sit with you until the court usher comes for you."

"Yes, please! That would help me a lot, just in case I come up with a question." She sat with her eyes closed, trying to remember what had happened that horrible day. Everything was jumbled up in her mind, and it was difficult to keep it all in order.

Her most vivid memory was when the officers led David out of the house; she could visualize every detail of that. David had been wide-eyed, and her heart had beat so hard it felt like it would escape her body. Without thinking, she pressed her fist to her chest, feeling her heart rate quicken again with the recollection.

"Mrs. Elliott? Are you alright?" Polly asked just as the door opened. A man dressed in a white shirt, tie, and black robe stepped into the room and approached them.

"Mrs. Erin Elliott?" he said.

"Yes," she replied.

"Hello, I'm one of the ushers. You're wanted in court now; would you like to follow me?"

"Yes… okay." She turned to Polly and tried to smile. "Thank you for— Oh, wait, I thought of a question. When I'm done with my testimony, where do I go?"

"You may leave the building, come back to this room to wait, or you may join the public gallery."

Erin sighed. "Okay, good. Thanks again," she said, then followed the usher through the building until he stopped at a closed door. He opened it, then bowed toward the judge as he entered the room ahead of her. It seemed to her like everyone in the courtroom was watching her as she stepped in and was led to the witness box, where she sat in the provided chair.

David was sitting in the dock next to a security guard. He was trying to remain calm and collected, but she could tell he was upset. The sight of him made her heart skip a beat; she longed to hold him and tell him she'd be okay and that she *was* okay. Instead, she tried to give him a reassuring smile.

The prosecuting attorney sat at a table between her and him, writing on a tablet, and didn't look up. Archibald sat to her left and smiled encouragingly at her. The usher returned and asked if she'd prefer to swear on the Bible or other holy book or use a non-religious affirmation.

"The Bible… please," she said, so he lifted a black book from a side table and held it out for her, along with a laminated card that had the oath she was meant to say typed out on it. She read the card out loud, and the usher stepped away again.

The judge then turned to her; she could almost feel his suspicion and wariness toward her as he told her to direct her answers to the members of the jury, who must hear her answers clearly. He then instructed her to speak slowly enough for him to take notes, what to do if she didn't understand a question or know the answer, and that if she couldn't remember, to tell him so.

Archibald stood and asked her to state her full name to the court, which she did. Then he said, "I'm going to ask you some questions on behalf of the defendant. David Elliott is your husband, correct?"

"Yes, he is."

"And you and your husband live at the same address, correct?"

"Yes, we do."

"On the day in question, were you in the room when the alleged assault took place?"

"I was," she said.

"Please tell us, in your own words, what took place in your home on that day."

"Mr. Dawson entered our home along with four male officers. We, David and I, heard a commotion, so we came downstairs to find out what was happening. Mr. Dawson was heading toward the kitchen, and David asked him what was going on as we followed him. Mr. Dawson ordered two of his officers to hold David, then Mr. Dawson said that he was arresting him, but he didn't finish."

"He didn't finish?" Archibald said.

"Yes, he didn't tell him what he was being arrested for at that time."

"What time of the day was this?"

"It was at about one fifteen in the afternoon."

"Thank you, please continue."

The two officers took hold of David by his arms, then Mr. Dawson began to… do… inappropriate things to me while David was forced to watch."

"What inappropriate things did he do?"

"He tried to kiss me, but I turned my head. He didn't like that—"

"I am afraid I must object, your grace, on the grounds that this information is conjecture," the prosecuting attorney said.

"You are correct," the judge said. "Please limit your statements to only what you experienced, and please do not guess what others may or may not have thought or felt."

"Yes, sir, I'm sorry. Uh, he, Mr. Dawson, began kissing and sucking on my neck and earlobe after pulling my hair. I struggled to get away from him, so he yanked on my hair really hard and got me unbalanced enough to turn me around so that I was facing the breakfast table, bent over it. He then held my head against the tabletop and… lifted my dress. Then, he… touched me… between my legs… over my underwear."

She took a shaky breath, remembering the cool air on the back of her legs and being mortified that he was touching her large, thick, menstrual pad. "I heard him unzip his trousers, and then David shouted for him not to touch me. I was yelling, too, for Mr. Dawson to stop.

"I continued to struggle, so he told the other two officers to hold my arms out to either side of me. He then stood behind me… facing me, and there was a lot more yelling. Mr. Dawson acted as though he were going to rape me. He pretended to pull his penis out of his slacks, though I don't think he actually did it.

"David didn't know that and broke free from the men holding him. At that time, Mr. Dawson zipped up his trousers and finished stating the reason David was being arrested. He then took David away in handcuffs."

"Are you telling us that a Detective Chief Superintendent in His Majesty's police force tried to molest you and then act as though he were going to rape you in front of your husband?"

"He *did* molest me when he tried to kiss me on the mouth and then started kissing and sucking on my neck and earlobe, and then when he touched me… between my legs without permission," Erin said, disgusted at the memory. She hadn't had time to think about it after David was taken away, and then later chose not to.

"Did you hear your husband, at any time, threaten Mr. Dawson or any of the other officers with death or bodily harm?"

"He did not."

"Did you, at any time, see or hear David Elliott hit, punch, kick, or in any way harm anyone in the room with you?"

"I did not; he's not a violent man."

"Do you believe your husband capable of harming a police officer, or do you think he would do so for any reason, a'tall?"

"David Elliott would never purposefully harm a police officer," Erin said, trying to keep from being emotional.

"Approximately how long were Mr. Dawson and the four officers in your home?"

"Only about twenty to thirty minutes."

"You and the defendant are asking the court for conjugal visits, although they are not a standard option here in the UK. Mrs. Elliott, will you please briefly explain to the jury why you are in desperate need of conjugal visits with your husband?"

"I have the Fertilis Defect, and the only treatment for its symptoms is intercourse with a man who has been medically matched with me. David is my match."

"And why is it vital that you continue your treatments with your husband?"

"Because the disease causes me to stop breathing until my body can produce enough surfactant to keep my lungs from sticking together. It's not like holding my breath; I cough out any reserved air, then my lungs stick together, and I pass out from lack of oxygen and literal exhaustion. The longest episode, during which I couldn't breathe, was approximately a minute and twenty seconds. If an episode lasts much longer than that, I'll either have permanent brain damage or could even die."

"Are there other symptoms of the disease?"

"Yes, I become exhausted and unable to function doing ordinary tasks, but I… we have a newborn baby who needs care, as well as David's four children, who also need my time and attention. I must be able to exist in their world and care for them and myself," she said as she gazed at each person on the jury, pleading for their compassion.

"Thank you, Mrs. Elliott, I have no further questions for you, but if you'd like to remain seated, my learned friend for the Prosecution will have some questions in cross-examination," he said and resumed his seat.

The prosecutor stood, looked at her notes, and without looking up, said, "I am Zoey Franklin, and I represent the Prosecution. Please tell us what was happening in the room at the time your husband was accused of beating the police officers, Mrs. Elliott."

Erin looked at Archibald and then at the judge. "Please answer the question," he said.

"I just told you what—"

"Let me rephrase the question; what did you *see* happen that day?" Ms. Franklin said.

"I… told you that the officers took David by the arms and—"

"What did you *see* after DCS Dawson allegedly turned you to face the table?"

Erin knew she was in over her head; she could feel herself begin to sweat, and her face was burning.

"Isn't it true that you saw nothing of what took place behind your back?"

"Well, yes, but… I could hear—"

"Do you expect us to believe that your new husband, David Elliott, father of your newborn child, would never harm a police officer, even if he believed his wife was in danger of being raped?"

"Yes, that's—"

"Isn't it true that he *could* very well have assaulted one or both of the police officers holding him even though it was impossible for you to see him do it?"

"He *wouldn't*—"

"What was your husband doing whilst being held by Officers Kent and Baker? Was he relaxed or fighting against them?" the wigged barrister asked.

"At first, he allowed them to hold him, but when Mr. Dawson started assaulting me, he began to struggle against them, but there was—"

"So, you admit he was resisting arrest?"

"He hadn't been charged yet. Mr. Dawson hadn't told him what he was being arrested for. David was provoked into struggling; he, Mr. Dawson, wanted David to fight so he'd have something—"

"You don't know that—"

"...to charge him with—" Erin said, having to raise her voice.

"This court will come to order!" the judge said. "Defense, you will keep your witness under control."

"Yes, my Lord," Archibald said and made a hand gesture, telling her to calm down.

"So, the defendant *was* struggling to free himself from the young police officers. You testified that you saw him doing so before you were turned away, so it *is* possible that you merely did not *see* him assault Officers Kent and Baker, correct?"

Erin closed her eyes and took a deep breath; she knew she was trapped, and nothing she could say would fix anything.

"Please answer the question, Mrs. Elliott," the judge said.

"What is… please repeat the question."

"Is it at all possible that, once you were turned away from your husband, he assaulted Officers Kent and Baker?"

"It's *possible*, but—"

"No further questions at this time," the prosecutor said.

Erin glanced at her husband sitting before her in his suit. He looked terrified but also as though he were trying to appear strong for her. He gave her a tiny nod and clearly tried to smile, but his mouth only managed a straight line.

"I would like to question the witness further," Archibald said, and the judge agreed. "Whether or not it's *possible* that he could or couldn't have assaulted the officers, based on your intimate knowledge of your husband's constitution and temperament, are you saying, as a character witness, that you believe it unlikely that he'd intentionally harm the young men?"

"Yes, sir, that's exactly what I'd like to say." Erin's eyes filled with tears. "He's not a violent man. I've seen him when he's very angry, and at no time did he lash out physically or threaten to harm anyone."

"I have no further questions," he said and took his seat. She glanced at her husband, feeling flustered and fearing she'd done more harm than good by her testimony. That time, he did manage a genuine smile and gave her a short nod.

The judge then turned to her and said, "That completes your evidence. It is important that you not talk to anyone about what you've told us until the trial is finished. Thank you for coming today, you may now go."

Erin stood and stepped off the platform, feeling a bit shaky and light-headed. She took a seat in the public gallery and tried to slow her breathing and racing heart. When he was finished taking down some notes, the judge called a recess for an early lunch.

Erin went to the food cart and ordered a cup of tea and a sausage roll, though she wasn't very hungry. A small table opened up, so she sat there, checking her phone for messages. Archibald approached her and asked to sit beside her. "Of course," she said and sighed, fearing he had bad news.

"Now, now, don't lose heart."

"But I feel like I messed up and made things worse!"

"You did quite well, Erin," he said. "You told the truth and were able to inform the jury of what they needed to hear. It'll be okay; there is very little chance he'll be made to do time for elbowing someone. They'll most likely consider this his time served. Relax, dear, it will all be over soon."

Chapter Seven

DAVID'S TESTIMONY

After lunch and when court had resumed, Archibald stood and said, "My Lord, I would like to call Mr. David Peter Elliott to the stand." Erin watched David cross the room, being led by an usher. She could tell he was nervous, though he was doing a good job of hiding it.

David chose to give his oath on the Bible and read aloud the laminated card held out for him. "I swear by Almighty God that the evidence I shall give shall be the truth, the whole truth, and nothing but the truth." Judge Aldrich turned to him and repeated the same things he'd said to her, then Archibald informed David of his intentions and began his questioning.

"Mr. Elliott, have you ever taken illicit drugs?"

"Never, not once," David replied.

"Have you ever purchased cocaine?" Mr. Hartwell asked.

"No, I haven't."

"Did you ever violently lay your hands on or abuse your former wife, Susannah Sutcliffe Elliott?"

"Never."

"Do you know why your former wife would tell DCS Dawson that you had?"

"I honestly don't know. I thought I knew her, but I reckon I didn't, after all," he said, sounding calm.

"Was the tenth of March the first time DCS Dawson searched your residence for drugs?"

"No, he came to my home on the fifth of July last year whilst I was working. My wife, Erin, was home at the time and rang my mobile to inform me he was there."

"And what happened that day?"

"My wife told me that DCS Dawson had entered our home without a warrant, though she did ask tae see one before he entered. I rushed home and found him and his officers turning our house inside out, though I didn't know why."

"How long were Mr. Dawson and his officers inside your home on the fifth of July?"

"Nearly three hours from the time Erin rang me until they left."

"On the tenth of March, was there another search of your property conducted by DCS Dawson?"

"No, there wasn't. Mr. Dawson and four male officers entered my home using a warrant. He began to charge me, though he didn't finish the charge until much later."

"Why do you believe he did that?"

"Because I hadn't done anything illegal. Once he'd provoked me, he finished informing me of the charges I was being arrested for."

"How did Mr. Dawson provoke you on the day in question?"

David recounted everything that had happened in detail.

"So, you, your wife, Mr. Dawson, and his officers were all in the kitchen, then?"

"Yes, well... that is, two of his officers were in the kitchen with us at that time."

"What happened next?"

"He, Mr. Dawson, lifted my wife's skirt and... put his hand between her legs."

"Did you actually see Mr. Dawson put his hand between your wife's legs and touch her in a sexually inappropriate manner?"

"I did."

"And what were you doing whilst all of this was happening?"

"I was trying tae get to my wife and stop what he was doing to her."

"So, were you pulling and straining to free yourself from the grasp of the two officers who were holding you?"

"Yes."

"Did you say anything?"

"I said something like, 'Don't touch my wife,' though I'm not sure exactly what I said."

"Did you threaten Mr. Dawson's life in any way?"

"No, what good would that do? I'm not foolish enough to believe I could manage tae do him any harm."

"What happened next?"

"He was holding ma wife's head down on the table… she was struggling, trying tae get away from him. Then, I heard him unzip his fly, so I told him no' tae touch her." David was clearly upset as he recounted the events of that day. He closed his eyes briefly and was breathing hard. His brow was furrowed, and Erin thought she could see tears welling up in his eyes.

"Take your time, Mr. Elliott," Archibald said.

David nodded and then swallowed hard. "As I said, Erin was struggling, so he yelled for the other two officers tae join us and hold her down."

"And did they?"

"Yes, they held her arms out, crucifixion-style, whilst he… he began taking his… penis out of his trousers, preparing to… to rape her," he said as several tears fell swiftly down his face. He swiped them away angrily and sat with his eyes closed.

The courtroom was silent as David tried to regulate his breathing. Archibald held out a box of tissues, which he took once his eyes were open. "Again, take your time, but when you're ready, please tell us what happened next."

"I pulled with all ma might tae save my wife from that man; any man would do the same. I reckon that whatever I did in that moment was cause enough for Mr. Dawson to charge me, because he zipped his trousers, turned to face me, then finished what he'd started earlier, saying '…assault of an emergency worker… with intent to resist arrest.' He then put handcuffs on me and led me out of ma home."

"Was there anyone else home when this took place?"

"Yes, ma housekeeper, Kitty Jones was there, but I didn't see her after we entered the kitchen."

"At what time did Mr. Dawson arrive at your home that day, and how long was he there before you were handcuffed and led outside?"

"I wasn't looking at the time, but Erin and I had just returned from a walk with our newborn daughter, so I reckon he arrived at around one o'clock. I don't know the exact time he led me out, I was quite distressed and didn't look at the clock, but he wasn't there long, perhaps half an hour, I'd guess."

"So, you're saying that DCS Dawson and his officers were not inside your home for two and a half hours on the tenth of March this year?"

"That is correct."

"Thank you, Mr. Elliott, I have no further questions at this time, but if you will please remain seated, my esteemed and learned colleague will question you next," Mr. Hartwell said and resumed his seat.

The prosecutor stood, and after informing David of her intentions, began her questioning. "Isn't it true that you abused your previous wife, Susannah Sutcliffe Elliott, whilst binging on cocaine and alcohol and that the reason you assaulted constables Baker and Kent was because that is what you do—"

Archibald stood, revealing his silent objection, but the judge spoke up. "I would like to know the answer to the question. Please, do take your seat, Mr. Hartwell." Clearly stunned, the Barrister stood for a moment while David sat, gaping.

"Please answer the question, Mr. Elliott," the judge repeated.

"I've never done–"

"It's a yes or no answer, Mr. Elliott."

"What are you asking me?" he said.

"Isn't it true that you abused your previous wife, Susannah Sutcliffe Elliott, after binging on cocaine and alcohol and that the reason you assaulted constables Baker and Kent was because that is what you do when you don't get your way?"

"No, that's not—"

"Isn't it true that you hid cocaine from your previous wife, Susannah Sutcliffe Elliott, in your London home?"

"No."

"Did DCS Dawson attempt to molest or rape your wife during his first visit?" the prosecuting attorney asked.

"No, he did not, though my children were home at that time."

"Whilst he was turned away from you, did you actually see, with your own eyes, DCS Dawson remove his penis from his trousers?"

"No, I didn't, but I heard the zip—"

"If you didn't see him, then you do not know whether he did, in fact, do it or not, correct?"

"Correct."

"According to your testimony a few moments ago, you admitted that on the tenth of March this year, you were guilty of resisting the officers who were holding you, correct?"

"In order to—"

"Again, it is a yes or no question."

"Yes, but only—"

"You said, and I quote," The woman looked at her notepad, clearly reading word-for-word what he'd said. "'I was trying to get to my wife and stop what Mr. Dawson was doing to her.' Then, when Mr. Hartwell asked if you were 'pulling and straining to free yourself from the grasp of the two officers, who were holding you,' you answered 'yes,' correct?"

David was clearly stunned as he answered, "Yes."

"Whilst you were resisting arrest, you weren't in any way being mindful of the two young officers, and—"

Archibald stood and said, "My Lord, I believe my learned colleague has forgotten quite an important aspect of what occurred on the day in question. The defendant had not yet been charged; thus, it would not—"

"Yes, yes, I will allow your semantics, Mr. Hartwell. Please rephrase your question, Ms. Franklin," the judge said, sounding put out.

"As you will it, my Lord," she said. "Isn't it true that whilst you were fighting against the two young officers holding you, you weren't in any way mindful of them as you, quote, 'pulled with all my might to save my wife from that man; any man would do the same. I reckon that whatever I did at that moment was cause enough for Mr. Dawson to charge me.' Whatever you did in the moment included elbowing, kicking, and scratching them in your zeal, didn't it?"

"I did not do any of those things," David said.

"And yet you just said that whatever you did was cause for DCS Dawson to arrest you, correct?"

"I said that, but—"

"If that is the case, Mr. Elliott, then you would have done any or all of those things," she said, then paused for effect. "I have no more questions for the witness at this time."

The judge turned to David and said, "That completes your evidence. You may now leave the witness box."

As David returned to his seat, Archibald stood. "I wish to make an application of no case to answer, my Lord," he said. "The Prosecution has not provided enough evidence to prove that my client has committed the offense and any actions which may have caused minor injury to the officers were set up or perhaps even faked and therefore illegal."

"I disagree, Mr. Hartwell. Please prepare your closing statements," the judge said.

"Yes, my Lord," he said softly, plainly stunned but unable to challenge the decision.

"We will now take a twenty-minute recess."

When court resumed, the prosecuting attorney stood and addressed the jury. "This is the case for the prosecution. I urge you to review the solid evidence provided to you, which clearly shows, as even Mr. Elliott himself admitted, that he resisted the officers who were doing their job on the tenth of March this year.

"I also submit that none of the scenarios that allegedly took place in his kitchen happened as stated. I propose that Mrs. Elliott was furious that someone would try to arrest her celebrity husband, which is the reason she was struggling against Mr. Dawson. All Mr. Dawson was trying to accomplish by holding her to the table was to keep her from hindering his duty that day.

"As we have heard from the young officers, Mr. Dawson was not molesting Mrs. Elliott. Any alleged improper act of molestation are simply in the minds of Mr. and Mrs. Elliott, brought up to defame one of His Majesty's officers. I'm sure you already see that this is a case of a privileged celebrity who believes he is above the law and shouldn't be punished for his actions.

"I am confident you will see past his fame and lies and hold him accountable for what he's done." The prosecutor then returned to her seat.

"Defense, you may now address the Jury," the judge said.

Archibald stood and turned to them. "Why was Mr. Dawson at the Elliott home on the tenth of March if no time was given in searching the home? If no drugs were found, or, might I add, even looked for on the day in question, why did Mr. Dawson begin stating the charges for David's arrest long before he finished?

"You have heard Mr. Elliott and his wife, Erin, testify to the brutality of Mr. Dawson, including that he lifted her skirt and put his hand between her legs. That in itself would cause any person to struggle in order to rescue their partner from the assault, whether they *saw* him remove his penis from his trousers or not. Mr. Dawson's behavior toward Mrs. Elliott that day, without question, would be cause enough for Mr. Elliott to believe that she was in danger of being raped.

"I submit that the whole affair was a set-up to give him an excuse to arrest and make an example out of my client without any reason other than revenge or spite. The prosecution would have you believe that David Elliott is at fault for what occurred in his home, but I submit to you that it was a vindictive, defamatory attack manufactured by Mr. Dawson, a crooked cop who didn't get what he wanted and now aims at punishing my client for it.

"David Elliott is not a criminal; he's a father of five and a loving husband who was forced to try and defend his wife from Mr. Dawson's assault. Please do not allow his mischief to pervert the law in this way. Thank you," he said and resumed his seat.

The judge then called a recess, giving the jury time to come to a decision. Erin watched her husband as they stood, waiting for the judge to leave the room. She longed to go to him and encourage him that there was no way a random panel of regular people would find him guilty.

David glanced at her, and she could tell he was trying to keep his chin up, but his eyes betrayed his fear and doubt. "I love you," she mouthed. He gave her a short nod before the officer approached him, and he was led away.

Only an hour later, everyone was called back to the courtroom, as the jury had reached their verdict. Erin resumed her seat and watched the guard lead David back in. Deliberating for an hour was bad news; it generally meant they'd found him guilty, but she held out a fleck of hope that they'd all thought him so completely innocent that the decision was an easy one.

The jury was led back into the room, looking somber. None of them raised their heads very far and didn't look in David's direction at all. The Court Clerk instructed everyone to stand for the judge and then waited. They were told they may be seated, and Erin held her breath, praying for a favorable verdict.

"Would the foreperson please rise," the Clerk said, and a man in the front row of jurors stood. "What is your verdict for the charge against David Peter Elliott of assaulting and wounding an Emergency Worker?"

"Guilty," the man said boldly.

"And what is your verdict for the charge against David Peter Elliott of resisting arrest?"

"Not guilty."

"And what is your verdict for the charge against David Peter Elliott of threatening the life of an Emergency Worker.

"Guilty," he said and then returned to his seat.

A murmur went around the courtroom, and Erin's heart pounded with panic when she saw the judge's slight smirk as he sat at his bench, nearly gloating. He then asked David to rise. "My sentence is severe, but I have good reason for my decision.

"Firstly, celebrities should *not* be given special treatment, and you are *not* above the law, Mr. Elliott. You should *not* be allowed to evade your punishment in *any* way. Assaulting and wounding an emergency worker is a serious offense and has a maximum sentence of five years.

"Threatening to kill DCS Dawson compounds your actions, thus elevating your sentence by two or more years. These are both aggravating circumstances that have been taken into account in my decision. Despite that, I am bound to take into consideration several mitigating circumstances that have decreased the severity of my sentence.

"The assault and subsequent wounding of the constables consisted of a single blow; the assault was an isolated incident; you seem to have been of good character before this incident, and you are the primary carer for your dependent relatives. As for the threat to kill Mr. Dawson, though it is not an excuse for threatening another person's life, especially that of an Emergency Worker, you testified to the fact that you truly believed, whether the threat was real or imagined, that your wife was in danger. Accordingly, I am sentencing you to four consecutive years in prison."

The whole room gasped, and Erin's heart sank as terror began to rise inside her. She felt light-headed as Archibald stood and addressed the judge, saying, "My Lord, I'd like to petition the court, again, to grant conjugal visits to David and Erin Elliott, based on the fact that she suffers from the Fertilis Defect and must be treated for the disease."

"We've already been through this, Mr. Hartwell. Conjugal visits may be common practice in *America*, but they are not compulsory in *this* country," he said, making the whole courtroom gasp again.

"My Lord, her condition requires treatments specifically from David Elliott. If she is not allowed those treatments, she very well could die. Would you allow us, once again, to submit evidence supporting the validity of—"

"Submissions must be on my desk first thing tomorrow morning, including at least two Medical Practitioner's notarized testimonies stating that Mrs. Elliott is in true mortal danger," the judge said, his mind clearly made up. Then he turned to the jury and said, "Thank you for the service you have provided. Your jury duty on this case is over, and you are free to go."

The bailiff gave the order for the court to rise, and Erin stared in disbelief at her husband and their solicitor. It was a legitimate nightmare, and she felt sick. As the judge left and David was led away, she stood in stunned disbelief, her ears ringing and her mind reeling. Unable to wrap her head around the outcome, and not knowing what to do next, she slumped numbly into her seat and remained there until Archibald came to her.

The room was empty as he helped her to stand, then gently led her into the atrium. They sat on a bench, and he held her as she cried. "We will fight this, Erin," he said gently. "We will appeal the case until it is overturned. I'm thoroughly shocked and disgusted at the abuse of justice that has occurred today."

There wasn't anything to say, so she nodded, then sat with her elbows on her legs, leaning over, trying not to vomit.

"Do you need assistance to get yourself home?" he asked.

Again, she nodded, so he took out his mobile phone and ordered a car for her.

Chapter Eight

ERIN'S PHONE RINGS

Erin was gutted. She'd just returned from the last day of David's trial, and she couldn't wrap her mind around the fact that a jury had actually believed Clive's lies and found him guilty. *Four years!* she thought bitterly as she locked the old, heavy, wooden door to their home and dropped her purse on the floor. *I'll never survive!*

Her phone began to buzz in her pocket since she hadn't turned the sound up after the trial. She fished it out and nearly started bawling when she saw who it was.

"Mom!" she cried after answering the call.

"Oh, baby girl!" Liz said.

Erin wept. "But how did you know?"

"I was watching the live feed on the internet."

"Four years! They… he… the judge gave him four years for nothing! He was… just trying to… rescue me, Mom! How will I—"

"Shh, it'll be okay, baby. I've been doing some research, and from what I've read, he'll only have to serve half that. What did his lawyer say?"

"He said he'd ring me, but even if that's true, it's still *two* years! He's gonna miss raising Junie, and I'll be a single mom to *five* kids! Well, that is if I don't suffocate to death without treatments. I don't know what to do, Mom!"

"You're so strong, Erin; you'll just have to do the best you can and document everything as Junie gets older. As for the treatments, I just don't know. Could there be… another match out there some—"

"NO! Are you kidding me? That's *not* an option!" Erin said, outraged at the mere idea.

"Alright, it was just a thought. I'm so sorry, honey. I know it's gotta be really hard to think of the future right now, but Dad and I are here for you. If you need anything, just let us know, okay?"

"I just need David."

"I know, baby, but you can do this! You didn't survive this long just to end up losing your battle now!"

"Yeah, I know you're right, and thanks for calling me. I really needed to hear your voice," she said and suddenly felt very tired. "I'm gonna take a nap if Junie will let me. I love you, Mom."

"I love you too, my baby. Sleep well," Liz said and ended the call.

Erin climbed the stairs and heard Kitty singing to Juniper in the nursery. Her voice was sweet and loving, and she silently thanked God for her help. She didn't want to disturb them, so she sent a quick message to her housekeeper.

> E: *I'm home. Bad news. Going to nap*
> *now. Thank you for all you do! Love*
> *you.*

The door to her and David's bedroom opened and closed silently as she slipped inside. She was far too tired to worry about taking her clothes off, so she lay on top of the duvet, pulled David's pillow to her, and breathed in his faint scent. Then she cried herself to sleep.

Erin woke and groaned, knowing she would have to make an effort and act as though everything was okay for the children's sake. The bedside clock read 4:57, which meant supper was only half an hour away. The last thing she wanted to do was sit and try to eat; to be the grown-up seemed like too much to expect of her.

There was a light knock on the door, and she said to come in, so Kitty opened the door, carrying Juniper, who was beginning to fuss. "I reckon it's feeding time," she said and waited for Erin to stand.

"Okay," she whispered resignedly and made her way to the nursery. When she was in position and comfortable, Kitty handed the baby to her and waited to make sure everything went well. A lump formed in Erin's throat as she croaked, "Thank you."

"I take 'at ta mean Mr. Elliott were found guilty, then?" Kitty asked softly and knelt in front of the nursing chair.

Erin's eyes filled with tears as she nodded her head but couldn't speak. Kitty took her hand, held it to her heart, and squeezed it. She could see that her emotions were getting the better of her, too, before she stood and left the room.

It took nearly all her willpower for Erin to go downstairs that night. The children were already in the dining room when she entered and sat at the head of the table. She cleared her throat and with the calmest voice she could muster, said, "I'm not sure how to say this, but… your father was convicted today and sentenced to four years in prison."

Rosie gasped and began to cry, then Charlie's face crinkled up, and though it seemed like he was trying not to, tears began falling down his pale cheeks. Dan sat in his chair with his mouth open and his brows knit, and Peter stood, looked around the table, then turned, facing away from everyone. No one spoke, and after a few minutes, Peter turned back, his eyes red, and took his seat again.

"I'm sorry if I'm not very good company tonight, I'm just really sad and… I'm not sure what to do."

"But that's not fair!" Dan yelled, then put his napkin to his eyes and began bawling. Charlie was next, and then Rosie's cries became louder before she stood and ran to her, wrapping her small arms tightly around her neck.

Somehow, Erin kept it together; she felt numb, and it seemed, at that moment, like she'd never be able to cry again. She pulled her daughter onto her lap and stroked her strawberry-blonde hair while shushing her gently. Kitty came into the room with the soup and began serving silently, though her eyes were red when she left.

"Alright, my darling, let's try to eat something. We'll just have to figure things out as we go, okay?"

Rosie nodded, then stood and returned to her chair. Everyone stared at their plates, and only Erin took a spoonful of her soup, hoping the others would take her lead. After the first course was brought out, Charlie said softly, "May I please be excused? I'm not hungry."

"May I as well?" Rosie said, then Daniel looked at her, clearly wanting to know the same.

Erin took a deep breath and let it out slowly. "Yes, you may," she said and accepted a kiss on the cheek from each of them. Peter stayed and tried to eat his roast pork, but his bites were small, and he seemed to be chewing for a long time. "You don't have to stay, Peter. I'm not hungry either."

The young man raised his head and looked at her. His next words were so heartfelt they made her soul ache for him. "I'll not leave you, Mum. I don't know why, but I'm afraid you'll… perhaps hurt yourself if I do. I know that seems overly dramatic, but I feel that you shouldn't be alone just now. May I stay with you?"

Feeling immensely weighed down and out of control, she closed her eyes. She hadn't planned on hurting herself, and wondered what would cause her son to think that about her. "Yes, you may stay, but I'm not going to hurt myself. I know that won't help anything. You guys need me, and it would be pretty dumb to jeopardize your trust and safety that way."

"All the same, I'd like to be near you right now, a'right?"

"Alright."

The rest of the evening was quiet. Everyone was in their own head and kept to themselves. Daniel went up to his room, and when Erin and the rest of the children climbed the stairs at bedtime, they heard noises that sounded like things being thrown and Daniel yelling, "It's not fair! It's not fair!" over and over.

When Erin opened his bedroom door, she found him punching his pillow and crying. Every toy he owned was scattered over the floor, many of them broken. "Oh, Dan!" she said, and before she could try to navigate her way to his bed, he sprang up and ran to her, tripping and falling over the mess.

He landed in her arms, and she held him as he wailed, still saying, "It's not fair!"

"I know, baby boy, I know." She sat on the floor and rocked him. His body radiated heat, and chunks of damp, sweaty hair stuck to her face and neck while tears and what she guessed was snot ran down her front.

"I… I want my dad!" he said after taking a long, shaky breath and then started to calm down.

She was struggling to keep her composure, also wanting to rage and throw things. "I do too, sweety. Now, why don't we go to Peter's room, and I'll read to you?"

He shook his head and crawled off her lap. "I'm not in the mood for that tonight," he said and then seemed to realize what he'd done to his things. "I'm… sorry for making a mess, Mummy. I'll clean it up before bed."

"Okay, baby. I don't really think I'm in the mood to read tonight, either. I think I'll just tuck you all in and say goodnight instead. Why don't you clear a path and clean up in the morning?"

The boy looked utterly worn out and exhausted. He nodded and started pushing things out of the way with his foot, then got into bed. She bent down, kissed his forehead, then covered him with his blanket.

"Goodnight, Mum," he said, sounding only half awake.

"Goodnight, Daniel, sweet dreams."

On Wednesday night, the landline began to ring. The children were tucked in, and Erin had just put Juniper to bed when she heard Kitty answer with, "*'ello, Elliott residence.*" There was a moment of silence, and then she heard her say, "*Yes sir! I will,*" followed by shoes running through the house.

There was only one person she called 'sir' in that way, so Erin ran down the stairs and met her in the foyer on her way to David's office.

She picked up the receiver, her heart beating hard in her chest. "David!" she cried.

"Aye, love; I've only three minutes, but I wanted you to know that I'm at Estabrook Prison, and I'll send visiting orders as often as I'm able. I love you so much, ma darling."

"I love you, too! Oh, David, four years? That might be a life sentence for me. What will we do?"

"I don't know, but we'll think of something. Please kiss my darling Junie and the children for me. I'm gutted, and—" He dropped his voice and said, "terrified, if I'm honest. Please… visit me and… dinnae leave me." His voice broke, and then he cleared his throat.

"Of course, I'll visit! I'd come every day if they'd let me, and I'll never leave you, my love! I am yours for—"

"Sorry, darling, but my time is up. I love you with all I am! I… love you!"

"I love—" she began, and the line went dead. "…you too," she finished in a whisper. She put her head down on her crossed arms and sobbed until Kitty came to her and touched her shoulder. "What are we gonna do? He got *four* years! And I can't remember the name of the prison he said he was at!" She reached out and held Kitty, who had knelt before her.

After a while, Kitty leaned back and touched Erin's cheek. "It'll be a'right, Erin. One 'fing I knows about prison is 'at 'ee'll not serve the whole four years. I reckon 'ee'll be out in two. Two years is far too many, but we'll put one foot in front of the over and find a way, Mum, you'll see. I reckon yer barrister will be doin' all 'ee can ta fight for yeh as well… and, well, I'm 'ere for ya, Mum. I'll not allow you ta… give up, not on my watch. I'll be strong enough for the bo'f of us, a'right?"

"Oh, Kitty, I love you so much! I'd never survive without you! Thank God you didn't quit when Susannah was so horrible to you!" She took a deep, long breath and let it out slowly. "Okay, I'm not going to panic… well, not much," she said and helped her housekeeper and friend to stand. Kitty then helped her up, and they hugged. "I'll call Mr. Hartwell tomorrow and find out where David is and how everything works from here. Thank you for your never-ending strength."

David sat shivering in his cell on Wednesday night, his forty-sixth birthday, sore, bleeding, and terrified. He'd been transported to Estabrook prison that afternoon, accompanied by none other than Clive Dawson himself. After a few punches were thrown, a gut feeling told him that until Erin began bringing 'tokens of their appreciation' in the form of bribes, beatings and perhaps worse may become a regular occurrence.

Hearing Erin's beautiful voice had helped to calm him a bit, but it hadn't lasted. His face and side aching, he tried to center himself and not panic in the new environment. He heard other new inmates talking loudly to themselves, and one seemed to be crying.

There was something unnerving about the solid metal door slamming shut with him inside that was terrifyingly final. Though there was no way for him to know the time, his internal clock was ticking slowly, counting the seconds... so many long seconds. Men shouted, and there were other noises, some loud and some whisper quiet, but all of them new to him.

He'd been in countless hotel rooms over the years, none of them exactly the same, so he'd hoped to be able to imagine he was in one that night, but no matter how hard he tried, it didn't work. After what seemed an eternity, all the lights went out, and he lay in his cot, having to constantly push down the panic that wanted to make him rage and cry. Instead, he began praying for the safety of his family and for his own protection.

Chapter Nine

A DIFFICULT START TO THE DAY

In the morning, Erin lay in bed crying, not knowing what to do, not wanting to move, and feeling utterly hopeless. She had no control over anything and felt completely alone without David there. Her phone dinged, and she wanted to ignore it, but then it dinged again, so she reluctantly rolled over, picked it up, and swiped the screen, seeing two messages from her best friend, Lily Graves.

> Lily: *OMG Erin! The tabloids and even the network news here are saying that David was found guilty and put in jail for beating a police officer. Is that true? I can't believe he'd do that! What happened?*

> L: *Do you need me to come there to help you… with anything? School will be out soon, so I could stay with you for a while in June or July if you want me to?*

Erin cried even harder after reading her friend's offer. She wanted her to be there right then, to hug her and tell her everything was going to be alright. Her eyes were blurred, and she couldn't see as she started swiping an answer.

> Erin: *Oh Lily! I dont know what too do. Hes in piston for 2 yards for assaulting an office, but he was force too do it. The judge wouldn't give confocal visits. What will I do? I can't stop craying. Id live it if youd come her! I'll ask D's secretary to make assignments. Thanks you for offering. It meals alot.*

A few moments later Lily replied.

> L: *I'll be there! I assume you meant conjugal visits, and that's just horrible! I don't know what you can do about that! I'm so sorry, Erin! I wish I was there now to hug you. It will be okay. I love you!*

> E: *I live your too! I miss your!*

Erin sent a message to Tina right away, asking her to set up a flight for her friend in mid-July. She then sent Lily's email and mobile number so they could work it out. Tina replied telling her she was on it, and the news made her feel a bit better.

"Good Friday, ha! I don't see much good in it," Erin said as she read the email she'd gotten from the prison system on Wednesday, April eighth, which was David's forty-sixth birthday. She was upset because she should've been able to have her first visitation with him that Friday, but according to the email, there would be none because of the holiday. *Now what?* she thought bitterly and laid her head on her folded arms atop David's desk. Though she wanted to cry and rage, she didn't have it in her, which turned out to be a good thing because there was a soft knock on the door.

"Mummy, may we come in?" she heard Rosie say.

She sat up and tried to put on a happy face. "Of course." The wooden door swung open, and then Rosie and Charlie stepped timidly into the room. "It's okay, come in. What can I do for you, my darlings?" she said and held out her arms for a group hug.

Rosie looked at her brother after their embrace, and he cleared his throat. "Well, we were wondering if we'd be going to Edinburgh for Easter this year? It's what we normally do, anyway."

Erin sat back on the soft, leather chair and sighed. "I haven't even thought about it. There's been so much going on that—Well, I guess we should, shouldn't we?" Both children's brows were furrowed with concern, and she sighed again. "Don't worry, I'll ask Tina if she can make some last-minute arrangements, and it'll be a good thing. It's healthy to get out of the house sometimes, right?" she said with a faint smile, trying to convince herself.

"Okay, Mummy," Rosie said, though she still seemed worried.

"We don't want you to be burdened or... have you think we *must* go, it's just that we were discussing it and weren't sure if you knew about—"

"And I'm so very glad you did!" she said, interrupting Charlie. "Those are the kinds of things I need to know. Thank you so much for bringing it up, and I really do look forward to it. You both look so anxious, but it's all good, okay? I promise."

"Okay, Mummy, and I'm glad. Millie makes the best roast lamb!" Rosie said, her smile brightening Erin's day.

"And her hot cross buns are scrummy, as well," Charlie added cheerfully.

"I've never had roast lamb or hot cross buns, so that's something else to look forward to."

"You've never had either of them?" Charlie asked, his eyes wide.

"Never?" Rosie added.

"Never."

"You'll like them, I promise," Charlie said, and Rosie nodded her agreement.

"Let's tell Peter," Rosie said, and both children gave her a kiss on the cheek before hurrying out the door.

Suddenly the room was too quiet, so Erin sent a message to Tina and then decided to follow the kids, hoping to find something to do together.

Later that morning, Peter joined Erin and his siblings at the park. He'd suggested it, hoping to give his mum a rest. He thought she looked tired as she sat on a bench in the shade of an enormous Castanea Sativa tree while Juniper dozed in her pram. It was hard to keep from watching her, though he was meant to be playing a bit of footy with his brothers and sister.

At his second howler, Daniel swore at him, and the ball rolled toward a bench under a Quercus Robur tree, where an old lady was sitting. As he approached, she squinted at him and started talking. "My dear boy, has anyone ever told you that you look just like a young David Elliott?" she asked.

His siblings yelled for him to return the ball, so he kicked it back to them, and they abandoned him, playing a few yards away. He felt awkward, not being fond of talking to strangers since they usually had ulterior motives involving his dad. Despite that, he'd been taught not to be rude, especially to the elderly, so he nodded. "Yes, ma'am," he said politely with his head down.

"I'm giving you a compliment," the woman continued. "He's a handsome man! Been having a hard time of it though lately, but perhaps you're not aware of that," she said, and Peter sighed softly.

"I'm aware," he said, wanting to hide his face. He wasn't ashamed of his father; he knew his dad had done nothing wrong, but the tabloid coverage of the trial had brought unwanted attention to him since he did look just like him.

"Are you related to him?" the woman asked, which was a step too far over the line in his being polite vs. keeping his private life private, and he wasn't going to answer her.

"I'm sorry, but I must find my mother. It's been nice talking with you," he lied. Two of the many things he'd learned about being the child of a celebrity were not to let people know you were one and to never give out personal information.

He'd experienced firsthand how, just when he thought he'd gotten to know someone and a mutual comfort level had been reached, the moment they learned that he was David Elliott's son, they acted differently. Sometimes they would become shy, not knowing what to say, or would suddenly want to know every detail about what his father was really like and whether he was this or was he that. It was worse than ever between his dad's name being in the spotlight again and starting at a new school, and he thought it was better that people didn't know.

The only outsider who had ever acted cool and normal around them from the start was Erin. She was one of the most interesting and wonderful adults he'd ever met, and he felt so sad for her, having to be separated from his dad, especially with the new baby. It wasn't fair, and he'd pounded his pillow many nights because of it after the trial was over. He wished he could help her, to be the 'man of the family' until his dad was home again, but he had school, and he didn't actually know what that meant anyway. Not feeling much like playing football, he decided to sit with her for a while.

"What kind of tree is this?" she asked, looking up into the branches as he approached.

"It's a Castanea Sativa."

"Duh! I knew its *Latin* name, I just couldn't remember its *common* name, silly," she said and smiled up at him.

He laughed, enjoying her sense of humor. When he didn't answer, she looked at him with her eyebrows raised. "Sweet Chestnut, innit?" he said.

"Right! It was on the tip of my tongue, thanks. I noticed you speaking to that older woman just now—"

"I didn't tell her anything about us or who my dad is!" he said quickly. "She asked, but I know better than to—"

"Hold up there, cowboy. All I was gonna say is that I'm proud of you for speaking to her and listening. Many people your age are rude or impatient with the elderly," she said.

"Oh, well, that's how I was taught... by Dad and Millie, not my mum. Mum was always worried one of us would... I don't know, tell someone our address or telephone number," he said with a short laugh, then bent over the pram and let Junie grab his finger. "Hello, Little Sprout," he said, using the nickname he'd given her on the day she was born. He smiled at her, completely head over heels for his new baby sister.

"You can pick her up if you'd like to."

He raised his eyebrows at her. She was so little, and he hadn't been allowed to pick up or hold his other siblings, so he didn't know how to do it properly. Sure, he'd held Junie a few times, but only when someone handed her to him. Lifting her seemed like it took skills he didn't yet possess. "I don't know—"

"I'll help you," she said, then stood and reached into the pram, lifting the seven-week-old baby out, easy as that. She set her on his lap, and Junie cooed at him.

"She's so small," he said, feeling awkward and wishing he'd get the hang of holding her.

"Yes, but you won't break her," she said with a gentle laugh. "Just don't drop her, and you'll be fine." She showed him how to hold her so that her little head was in the palm of his hand and her back was on his forearm.

If he rested his arm on his lap, it would be easy to see her and touch her using only one arm. She looked up at him for a while and then fell asleep again. They sat watching the younger kids running around the park with the ball in companionable silence until Erin sighed, which made him turn to her. "Mum?"

"I just wish I had energy like they do, that's all. To be a kid again, you know?" she smiled at him and tousled his hair. "No, I guess you don't know… yet. Someday you'll understand, but try to stay a kid for a while longer, okay?"

"Will do," he said just before his stomach growled, setting Erin's off as well.

"I guess it's lunchtime, then. Give Junie to me, then run and tell the others it's time to go, please."

"Yes, Mum," he said and looked at the sleeping baby on his arm. "Ah, I'm not sure how to—"

She smiled at him and stood, reaching for her. He sat, trying to figure out the best position, but she laughed and lifted Juniper out of his arms, easy-peasy. "You'll get the hang of it the more you do it," she said.

Peter stood, and once the baby was back in the pram, he kissed Erin's cheek and ran to fetch his siblings.

After lunch, she checked her phone and saw a message from Akshara Anand, the television actress and contestant on *Strictly Come Dancing*, whom she'd met at her Bollywood party the year before.

> A: *Oh, Erin! I saw the news today and cannot begin to tell you how sorry I am for what you're going through. Please promise that you'll reach out if you need anything, anything at all. Akshara x*

She responded:

> E: *Thanks for the kind thought. I promise I will. Take care, my friend.*

The rest of the day was a blur. The children were very well-behaved, though they seemed to be walking on eggshells a bit. Erin did her best to engage with them and be available, but when the exhaustion set in, Kitty managed to keep them busy so she could rest.

Guilt began to plague her, making her believe she was a horrible mother, and she vowed to do more with them after a nap. When she woke an hour later, even more spent than before, she promised herself that the next day would be different. As soon as she checked her phone, though, her heart dropped.

There were three messages from Tina about the trip, each more urgent than the last. Essentially, the gist was that she needed to know more details, though she ended up booking them using the information from their previous trip to Scotland. They would be leaving the next morning, Good Friday, though she'd managed to find enough seats in business class.

The seats weren't all in the same area, but Tina explained that often people would change seats if asked politely and that the children were used to flying alone, so it should work out just fine. As far as the return date was concerned,

she had booked them as open tickets so she could choose their return date. She sent a message to Kitty, asking her to help everyone, including her, pack.

At supper, the children were excited about going to their gran's house, and the meal was filled with chatter about what they were looking forward to and what Erin should expect. At bedtime, the children came to her for a short bedtime story and a goodnight hug and kiss. She didn't want them to see her crying all the time, but she couldn't control the tears as she apologized for not spending more time with them.

Her heart ached as they each tried to assure her that they understood and that she shouldn't worry about it. Kitty followed them upstairs for any tucking in that was needed, so Erin got into her pajamas and fed Juniper. Once the baby was in her crib for the night, she took her phone out of her pocket and noticed a new message.

Marvin Brunet? Why is that name familiar? she thought until she read the first few words of the preview. "Champ!" she said out loud and opened it.

> Champ: Mon amie! *I have seen on the news that your amore has been imprisoned! This cannot be true! If there is anything Champagne can do for you, all you must do is ask!*

Erin sat on the side of her bed trying to keep from crying, though it was no use. The tears flowed as she replied.

> Erin: *Thank you for your message, Champ. Yes, it's true, and I am devastated. He was forced into doing what he was arrested for, though we don't really know why. He got the maximum sentence of FOUR years, though he'll hopefully only serve two! It's*

> *unbelievable, but the judge seemed to have*
> *some prejudice against us. Thank you for*
> *your offer, but I really don't need anything*
> *except David.*

She touched send and figured she'd have to wait until morning for a reply. Instead, she saw the little dots begin moving, indicating Champ was typing.

> C: Mon Dieu! *If you change your mind, do*
> *not hesitate to contact me! Champagne is on*
> *your side,* mon amie, *and my thoughts and*
> *prayers are with you!*

Erin took a deep breath and replied.

> E: *Thanks, Champ, that means a lot!*
> *David and I can use all of them we can get!*

She set the phone to 'Do Not Disturb' and put it on her nightstand, then she got into bed and held David's pillow until she fell asleep.

David's first full day wasn't too bad; he kept his head down and tried to stay out of the way of anyone who looked like they might strike. That night after lockdown, however, he had a visitor to his cell. The door unlocked with a loud *buzz,* then a smart *click.* His heart jumped in fear as he stood at attention and braced himself.

The officer who stepped in wasn't tall, but he was built like a tank. David had noticed him right away when he arrived and had been leery of him from the start. The scowl on his face just then didn't make him feel any better. His uniform was straining to its limit, and he thought one of the shirt buttons might go flying at any minute.

The man approached him, saying nothing, so David stared straight ahead, waiting. Looking him over, the officer glared questioningly at him. "You don't seem the type, but you'll have it for what ya did to those young constables," he said, then backhanded him across the face.

David didn't know what to do, though he figured silence was the best plan. The officer seemed to be waiting for something, but when he didn't get a reaction, he grunted and turned away. The adrenalin was getting the better of David; he was beginning to shake, but he didn't want the man to see it.

A short-lived wave of relief washed over him, thinking the officer was going to leave, until suddenly, boots squealing, he turned back and punched him hard in the stomach. David couldn't help but double over in pain. "I believe a 'thank you, officer Guthmann,' is in order," he said calmly and waited for David to recover.

"Th-ank you, officer… Guthmann," David managed after straightening up.

"With pleasure. See you again tomorrow," he said and left the room.

David held his stomach and groaned but refrained from saying anything just in case someone heard him and it made things worse. *I've a week and a half before Erin can… rescue me from this. Please, God, keep them from doing any real damage, and please remind Erin to bring something for them!* he prayed desperately.

Chapter Ten

HOLIDAY IN EDINBURGH

The next day, they left the house early, hoping they'd get to the airport with enough time so Erin wouldn't feel rushed. Her plan almost succeeded, but they didn't arrive as early as she'd hoped. Tina had gotten them seats in business class, which was great, as Erin had to feed Junie for most of the flight and there was more room there.

Peter managed to keep Daniel in line for her, and she was truly grateful for it. She'd just finished nursing as the pilot announced that they were second in line for landing. Being a holiday, the airport was crowded, and people were more impatient and in a hurry than normal.

She tried to stay out of the way, but it was just too difficult, and they got jostled around more than she liked. The children seemed to understand the importance of staying close, even Daniel, who behaved perfectly. "Remind me when we get to your gran's to do something special for you to thank you for your good behavior," she said just before she finally found Roger waiting for them at the arrivals loading zone.

"Hiya, Erin," he said as the kids hugged him and got into the black SUV. "I'm sorry, love, but ya look a wee bit stressed."

"More than a wee bit, Roger. I'm glad to be here and out of there, she said, pointing to the terminal, then buckled in Junie's car seat with Charlie's help.

"Aye, and we're chuffed you're here as well," he said, then opened the front passenger door for her.

"Ach, et's so good tae see yeh, Erin," Millie said as she and the children entered the house. "Where's our wee Juniper, then?"

"Peter has her in the—" Erin began, but just then, Peter arrived carrying the car seat, and Millie made a noise that was something akin to a screeching owl.

"Ach, ma wee gairl!" She bent over the seat, then stood and smiled at Peter. "I'll have that if yeh dinnae mind," she said, and he handed her the seat. "Yer gran's been on pins and needles waitin' for yeh, ma lovely one."

"Allow me to take her out for you," Erin said, then quickly unfastened the harness. She lifted the baby out of the seat and handed her to Millie, who took her and cradled her in her arms, then walked away from them, speaking softly to her.

Peter smiled at her and then went back out to the SUV. She could hear Milly and Annis talking in high voices to Juniper, and she sighed, happy to be there. Soon, a stampede of dogs tore through the house, followed by a melancholic eleven-year-old boy named Daniel. The dogs jumped and yipped, eager to play, but Dan clearly wasn't, which seemed to confuse the pups. Gurty stayed close to his side as they exited through the back door.

The soft, cozy bed in her and David's room was calling to her, so she climbed the stairs, happy to have a place to escape. When she opened the door, a million memories flooded her mind, and she had to catch her breath. Pushing them back again, she took most of her clothes off, got into bed, and fell asleep, clutching David's pillow.

She woke to a knock on the door, then heard Millie's tender voice telling her that supper would be ready in thirty minutes. It was difficult to leave her comfortable haven, but she somehow managed it and put her clothing back on. She'd slept for quite a while and knew she'd have to feed Juniper before she got to eat.

As she'd predicted, the baby was getting fussy, so she quickly took her into the sitting room and began feeding her, hoping to have her fed and burped before supper was on the table. She almost made it, too. Annis had just finished the prayer when she stepped into the dining room. Peter sprang from his seat and brought the car seat to her so she could put Junie into it.

"Thank you, Peter," she said, enjoying the smile he was giving her. "Also, thanks, Millie, for waking me early enough to get her fed. Maybe try for forty minutes next time."

"Will do, love," she said.

"Will you be attendin' Good Friday services with us tonight, Daughter?" Annis asked.

"Oh, I didn't think of that. I didn't bring anything to wear to church," Erin said.

"A'right, though I do hope ye'll join us on Easter Sunday, even if we must go out and find yeh something tae wear," she said with a gentle smile.

"Yes, of course I'll come with you, but we may *just* have to go shopping."

"May I come?" Rosie asked.

"May I as well?" Charlie added, both of them looking excited.

"I don't see why not," she said.

After a delicious supper of fish and chips with hot cross buns, Annis, Millie, Roger, and the children walked to the Kirk. Erin was already asleep when they got back home.

The next morning, Rosie and Charlie were chomping at the bit, excited to go shopping with her again. At the breakfast table, they were almost giddy, asking her all sorts of questions.

"Will we be going to Multrees Walk?" Rosie asked.

"I'm not sure; I've never heard of it," Erin said.

"It's the *only* place our mummy would even *think* of shopping in Scotland," she retorted, sounding quite snobbish.

"Well then, if that's the case, maybe I'll skip it," Erin said and watched Rosie's eyes grow wide. "I only mean that I won't be spending thousands of dollars… I mean pounds on a designer dress. I saw a few stores at the Waverly Mall when I was there last time, so I think we'll start there, okay?"

"Yes, Mummy," Rosie said solemnly.

"Now, now, no need to be glum. We're gonna have a good time no matter where we go, right?"

"Right!" Charlie said brightly, and his sister nodded.

"I'll join you if yeh don't mind," Annis said. "I need a new pair of shoes." Millie shot her a look that made her cheeks bloom pink, and Erin figured it meant that she already had enough shoes.

After breakfast, Roger delivered them to the mall and dropped them off on Princes Street. Millie had offered to watch Juniper, and Erin had managed to pump some milk for her so they wouldn't be rushed. The building was packed with people doing their last-minute Easter shopping.

Erin bought a flowing, pale green, floral wrap dress with a pretty, cream-colored knit cardigan and two tops Charlie picked out for her. Rosie got a new hair tie and shoes that were very similar to the ones Annis bought. Charlie got a new tie and slacks.

The rest of the day was spent using markers and paint to color and decorate Easter eggs, which Erin thought was odd. She had to explain that in America, most people used dye and vinegar to color white eggs and that most eggs sold in American supermarkets were white. "We also don't really decorate them; we mostly just color them and leave it at that."

"If they're not decorated, how will you know which egg is yours in the egg roll, silly?" Dan said.

"Don't be cheeky," Millie scolded him.

"What's an egg roll?" Erin asked and then laughed. "I presume you don't mean from a Chinese restaurant."

"Do you mean Chinese takeaway?" Dan said.

"Yes, that's what I meant. Perhaps they're called spring rolls here. Anyway, what is an egg roll, then?

"Oh, it's a brilliant game, Mummy," Rosie said.

"All the kids in the village roll their decorated egg down a hill, and the one that reaches the bottom unbroken wins," Charlie said.

"It's stonkin'! Three years ago, I was given a chocolate egg when mine won. I'd painted Gurty on it, and it was brilliant!" Dan said.

"That was the year Daddy painted mine," Rosie said with a weak smile.

"Goh! I remember that year!" Peter said. "Dad was being cheeky and tried spinning a raw egg on the table. It spun out of control and landed on the floor, taking three more with it. Millie was sore with him and had him clean up the mess."

Millie smiled at him and touched his shoulder. "Aye, and he did a fine job of it, as well."

"He painted a robin on mine," Rosie said.

About an hour before supper, Roger left to pick up his partner and Fertilis Defect match, Tilly Maxwell. When they arrived at Owlgate, Erin saw her get out of the SUV, looking tired, and then she watched as they headed straight up to his flat above the garage. She knew Tilly would be getting a much-needed treatment. *What I wouldn't give...* she thought.

Forty-five minutes later, just as Millie was laying out the meal, the two entered the dining room, laughing, in love, and untroubled. Erin was happy for them, and yet she still felt a twinge of jealousy since they were allowed to be together while she and David were not. Tilly saw her and squeed, rushing to her, then waited for her to stand so she could give her a hug.

"Oh, Erin! I think about you all the time! It's so unfair! How are you?" she said, then saw Juniper lying in a nest made from several blankets in David's old highchair. Roger had found it in the garret, and Millie had scrubbed it to within an inch of its life.

"Oh! She's so adorable! She looks just like—" she cocked her head to one side and then the other, "...well, like you both! I can't decide. And look at that beautiful ginger hair! I love it!" She laughed lightly as she touched the baby's head, then looked around the table. "Hello, children, it's good to see you, too!" she said.

They all said, "Hello, Tilly," in unison, which got a laugh from everyone at the table except Millie. Millie made a noise, letting everyone know that they should shut up and sit down.

"Sorry," Tilly said quietly, and everyone sat at their places.

After supper, Roger started a fire in the saucer, and everyone gathered outside on the patio. Annis mentioned that when she was young, some people would make an effigy of Judas Iscariot, the apostle who betrayed Jesus, and burn it like they do Guy Fawkes on the fifth of November.

"Oh, that's horrible!" Erin said.

"But he betrayed our Lord," Annis said.

"Yes, he did, but we don't really know the *whole* story, do we? I mean, perhaps Jesus asked him to do it, like Dumbledore asked Snape to kill him instead of Drako, right? If Judas *hadn't* done it, it wouldn't have happened the way it needed to happen and at the correct time, right?

"I mean, wasn't Jesus all about forgiveness and compassion? Peter denied him, and the others fled, didn't they? Aren't we all guilty of something or another, and to think that the only thing a person might be remembered for, for all eternity… or at least the last two thousand years, would be their biggest mistake is horrible to me.

"I mean… what if… David's imprisonment is the biggest thing he's remembered for? It's… just not… fair," she said and stood, unable to keep from breaking down as she stumbled into the house. She began heading up the stairs but stopped a quarter of the way up and sat, face in her hands, bawling.

After a few minutes, she heard someone come up the stairs and join her, but she didn't look up. A large, warm hand touched her shoulder, and she knew it was Roger. The story of how his wife had died because of the young boy and his toy bow and arrows came back to her, and she buried her head in his shirt, sobbing.

"I'm sorry for ruining the night. I don't know what's wrong with me, and I don't know why I said all that. I've never thought of that before; it just all came out," she said, allowing him to hold her.

"Ach, I reckon they were wise words. You've a point there; we shouldn't judge Judas, or anyone, for that matter. We weren't privy to what truly happened, and I reckon I'd rather believe he did the Lord's bidding and that he found forgiveness on the other side.

"Another thing I love about yeh, Erin, is yer ever-loving heart. Yer ability tae find the good and lovely things in people. Et's a real gift, yeh ken?"

"I can't find the good in everyone," she whispered. "I don't think I'll ever be able to forgive that horrible Judge, or Susannah, or Clive, or Bran or... or any of the people who've done such terrible, mean, selfish things to David when he hasn't done anything wrong... nothing!"

"Aye," Roger said, then Peter came around the corner of the stairwell, his eyes red, and sat a few steps down from them.

Soon, all four children were sitting with them, though no one said anything for a long time. "I'm sorry for making a scene, children," Erin said gently.

"I also don't want Dad to be remembered for going to jail," Peter said, and his siblings nodded solemnly.

"I'm sure he won't be, my darlings. I'm sure this will all be forgotten before long. I don't know what came over me out there," Erin said, then took a deep, cleansing breath. "Let's go back out and enjoy the fire, alright?"

Peter sat beside her on the bench seat, and the family sat in a slightly awkward silence. Soon, the tension in the atmosphere began to ease, and she started noticing how Roger and Tilly touched each other often, how they smiled and teased, obviously in love. They were perfect for each other, and she was glad they'd ended up together.

Watching them was bittersweet. She missed that connection with David and began to feel sorry for herself, until she realized how the time she was spending with them was making the time away from him feel like it was going faster. She decided to suck it up and chose to have a good time.

"Are you alright, Erin? You seem sad. Are you... thinking of Dad?" Peter asked her quietly, which made her want to cry.

She took hold of his hand and leaned against his arm. "I was. You're so observant. I'm glad you're so caring."

They listened to the crackling fire and the night sounds for a while longer before Annis and Millie decided to go indoors. "Come now, Children," Millie said, and though they were reluctant, they followed her into the house after a hug and kiss for Erin.

"May I stay for a while longer?" Peter asked.

"I don't see why not, I mean, aren't you *technically* an adult at sixteen?" Erin said but didn't like the sound of it once it left her mouth.

Peter smiled brightly and seemed well pleased with himself. "Thanks, Mum, though I'll be back in a tick, I need a wee," he said, chuckling as he stood and followed his siblings into the house.

"Roger, can I ask you a stupid question?" she said when Peter was out of earshot. Tilly was asleep with her head on his shoulder, so she spoke quietly.

"If et's comin' from you, Erin, I rather doubt et'll be stupid," he said with a grin.

"Well, I heard someone say something, and I'm not sure I understand it. I'm pretty sure it was vulgar, though," she said and suddenly didn't want to mention it to him.

"Aye, nothin' I've no' heard, I reckon," he said, giving her a sideways glance.

"I heard someone say, 'I'd like to roger her,' and I'm not sure what that means. I mean, it sounds pretty straightforward, but I don't want to presume anything, you know?" she said and blushed, though she didn't know why.

Roger gave her a slightly sideways nod in recognition of how his name had been used. "Aye. I've been told tha' a few hundred years ago, the word roger meant a... well, an erect penis, and then, no' so many years ago, et became a quick way tae say… well, tae roger someone would be tae have sex with them. I hope they didn't say tha' tae you!" he said, sounding like he'd be upset if it had been.

"Ha, not likely! Someone said it about Tilly," she said and laughed as his eyes grew wide. "I'm just kidding. It was in London a few weeks ago. A pack of neds were ogling a beautiful woman in the park."

"And et wasnae you, then?" he asked again.

"No, Roger, it wasn't me," she said, feeling her cheeks grow warm again, understanding full well what he was trying to say. Peter came back out looking tired yet determined to stay up with the adults. "How'd you get the name 'Roger,' anyway? It's not a Scottish name, is it?"

"I dinnae think many parents stick tae trad names anamore. I'm named for ma grandfather on ma mother's side; he was French.

"Other than... what you just mentioned, what does your name mean?" Erin asked, not wanting to say it in front of Peter.

"I dinnae ken, really," he said.

"Famous spearman," Tilly said, apparently not actually asleep after all. "I looked it up and thought it was fitting."

Roger blushed, and Erin laughed. "Oh, I see, so that's why it also means, umm, yeah," she said, and laughed even harder.

"I'm not following. What else does it mean?" Peter asked with a puzzled look on his face.

"Et means... uh, member," Roger said.

"Member?"

"Aye, yer, member... yer, willy, yer tallywacker, dobber, knob, trouser snake, yer... peter," he said and then sat gaping at the young man. "Ach! I'm sorry."

Tilly sat up and stared at Roger, and Erin didn't know what to do. Peter knit his brows together and thought for a second, then he smiled. "So, in a way, our names mean the same... thing?" he said, completely unperturbed by Roger's faux pas.

"I reckon... in a way," Roger said.

"That's a'right then," he said. "And don't forget John Thomas." He laughed as the three others breathed a sigh of relief and joined him.

Chapter Eleven

EASTER SUNDAY

In the morning, everyone was up and ready to go early. Between services there was a hot breakfast followed by the day's festivities, such as an egg roll. They walked to the kirk for breakfast, where Erin met several parishioners and the minister, a kind, humorous man with pure-white hair.

After breakfast, they sat in the old kirk and enjoyed the opening hymns. Then the minister called the children up to the front of the sanctuary, where their decorated eggs were laid out. He held one of them up and asked whose egg it was. A girl of about seven lifted her hand.

"So, Meghan, what is your egg meant tae be?" he asked.

She looked at the congregation, and a woman nodded encouragingly to her, so she looked up at the minister and said, "A wee baby lamb."

"Well done," he said, then lifted another one. "And whose egg is this?" A boy of about five lifted his hand. "And what is et meant tae be, George?"

The small boy blushed and turned to his mother. She stood and said, "Father Christmas." The whole congregation laughed. "Et's been his singular focus since early December."

"Et's lovely, George, and I can see the resemblance now. Well done." He lifted a bright yellow egg next, and a girl of about six smiled up at him. "Is this yours, Lucy?" he asked, and she nodded. "Your duckling is delightful."

"Thank you, though Mummy helped me quite a lot," she said.

"Well done, Mummy Murphy," the minister said, which got another laugh and a round of applause. "Now, this one is nice; whose is it?"

Rosie beamed and lifted her hand. "It's mine."

"Ah, Rosie Elliott. You've done a fine job; it's a blue tit, isn't it?"

"Yes, it is, thank you," she said happily.

"Now, whose is this?" he asked and held up a very well-done representation of a hedgehog.

"It's mine, Minister," Charlie said.

"Well, well, it's quite striking, ma lad. Well done."

"And this one must be Daniel's," he said and lifted a similar looking one, though it was darker.

"Yes, and it's a porcupine," he said proudly. "It was our new mum, Erin's, idea. She helped me find an image for inspiration, but I painted it all myself."

Everyone looked at her, and she felt exposed as her cheeks flushed pink. The minister smiled at her and then at Dan. "Well done, Daniel. Et's nice having someone who cares about you to help with things like this, isn't it?"

"Oh, yes! Erin is stonkin' good fun," he said and smiled at her, showing off his deep dimples.

"I'm happy for you and your family," the minister said and then began telling them that the egg roll, which would follow the service, represented the stone that was rolled away from the tomb of Christ. The children were sent back to their parents, then he continued with his message. He spoke about the hope we have of forgiveness and eternal life because of the sacrifice of Jesus.

The message was well said and ended with encouragement from Deuteronomy 31:8, which says, *"The LORD himself goes before you and will be with you; he will never leave you nor forsake you."*

When the service was over, the minister walked to the doorway and spoke to his parishioners as they left the kirk. Erin was tired and just wanted to go back to Owlgate and take a nap, but there were too many things on the agenda for that to happen. As they got to the door, the minister shook her hand.

"What Daniel said today touched ma heart, Mrs. Elliott. I'm glad tae know how fond your new family is of you. Et's not always the case, and I'm happy for you and David," he said.

"Thank you, I'm so grateful for my new children; they're a true gift, and I love them all dearly!" She then lowered her head. "Uh, if it's not too much to ask, would you please keep us in your prayers? I… we would really appreciate it," she said, fighting back the urge to cry again.

"Ach, I already have been since the day I learned about et, dear. Things'll come round right, I'm sure of et," he said kindly.

The family followed the other congregants up the hill to the community gardens in the shadow of Arthur's Seat, where there was a small orchard and quite a few chickens underfoot. The children scampered up the hill a bit further and found a spot to begin the egg roll. The minister stood at the bottom of the hill, ready to officiate the event.

Many of the parents joined the smaller children and helped them get things started. Erin stood at the bottom of the hill, wishing for Roger's walking stick that unfolded into a small seat. She cheered as the children began pushing, rolling, and nudging their decorated eggs toward her and the other waiting families.

In the end, it was Lucy's egg that made it the furthest, then Rosie, and finally, George's Father Christmas took third place. Lucy won a large chocolate egg filled with Freddo frogs, while Rosie and George each won a Cadbury Caramel egg. Dan was quite disappointed, but he was a good sport.

Juniper had slept during the service and was a perfect dream for the rest of the activities as she was passed between Annis and Millie, but as they started walking home, she began to fuss. The last thing Erin wanted was for her milk to drop, so she did her best to hurry, trying to keep the pacifier in her mouth. The house smelled amazing when they got home, and as her stomach growled, she took Juniper upstairs to be nursed right away.

After all the fresh air and exercise that morning, she was exhausted and wanted to nap, but she didn't want to be late for lunch. Once the baby was fed, Erin put her down to sleep, and though her bed was calling her name, her stomach was much louder, so she went downstairs, arriving at the table right on time.

They were served leek and carrot soup, roast lamb, boiled baby potatoes, gravy, peas, and simnel cake for the pudding. Everything was so good that she ate too much and regretted it afterward. At that point, a nap was unavoidable, so she trudged up the stairs, wishing someone would give her a good push. Junie was still asleep, so she got undressed and fell into bed.

She dreamed she was in Upper Lake Park, in Port Washington, standing on the edge of the bluff, looking out at the Breakwater Light. A storm was coming in fast, the wind was rising, and the sky was growing dark. Large, turbulent clouds were rolling toward her, and the churning waters of Lake Michigan began battering the already crumbling breakwater walk that led to the tall, white beacon. Her hair whipped her face, and cold rain stung her skin. In the distance there was a figure standing on the plinth, but she couldn't make out who it was.

Suddenly, like a tunnel-vision close-up, she could see that the figure was David, surrounded by water with the Breakwater Light towering over him. He was looking at her, and she raised her hand to him, reaching out, longing to protect him. Then, an enormous wave rose, and the angry water swallowed him up.

"No!" she cried and sat up in bed, gasping for air.

Juniper was awake and grunting, clearly filling her diaper. Shaken, Erin got up and dressed, then used the bathroom, changed the baby's diaper, and brought her downstairs.

"Whatever is the matter?" Annis said when she entered the sitting room. "Yeh look as though you've seen a specter."

"I had a nightmare, but I don't want to talk about it," she said. Her mother-in-law reached out for the baby, so she handed her over and noticed she was shaking. "Would you mind if I took a walk before supper?"

"I don't mind at all," Annis said and touched her trembling hand. "Are yeh sure ye're a'right, dear?"

"Honestly, I don't think I'm going to be alright until David is home. I just need some fresh air and a distraction right now."

"Gran, do you know where Erin—" Peter said as he was coming into the room. "Oh, hello, Mum, ya… a'right?" He frowned and went to her. "What's wrong? May I help you at all?"

She couldn't help but smile at him and shook her head. "I'm fine, I just had a bad dream. Are you busy? Would you like to take a walk with me?"

"I'd really like that," he said, his face bright and happy.

"Good then, let's go."

Erin grabbed her jacket, and they left out the front door. It was a sunny day, but an occasional chilly breeze had them looking for shelter. They ended up at Doctor Neil's Garden, sitting on a bench with hedges around it that helped cut the wind.

They sat quietly for a while, listening to the swans whistling and chirping at each other on the loch. "What's that yellow building over there?" she asked, pointing to an octagonal tower near the water. "I've noticed it before but never thought to ask."

"That's Thomson's Tower; it was built for the Duddingston Curling Society in the nineteenth century. That's all I really know about it, but there's more information near the door. Would you like to head over there?" he said.

"Sure." She accepted his hand to help her up, then followed him toward the building. "So, why were you asking where I was at the house?"

"Right, well—" he began, then stopped walking and began pacing and biting his nails.

"Oh, wow, is it that serious?" she asked.

"Erin... I mean, Mum."

"Yes, Peter?" she said, having no idea the enormity of what he was about to say to her.

"I've made a decision, and I hope you can see why I've decided what I have and that... well, that I'll have your blessing, although my mind is already made up on the matter."

"That doesn't sound good. What—"

"Please hear me out, a'right?" he said, and she reluctantly nodded.

"I'm going to leave school early so I can be here for you... whilst Dad isn't. I can still qualify for uni without the last year of school, I'll just have to work harder and perhaps attend an extra year, but I want to do this for you and for Dad," he said and looked at her.

Erin was so stunned, upset, and yet touched, she didn't know what to say. She stared back at him, blinking and trying to form an argument against it in her mind. "I can't tell you what that means to me, Peter, but—" she began.

"I'm not changing my mind," he said stubbornly.

"I'm trying my best to be respectful to you and not discount what you want to do, but, Peter, what is it you think you'd be doing for me and your father by not finishing school? I mean, I won't be hurting financially if that's what you're thinking."

"Well, there won't be a... man around to... protect you or watch after you. I know that's incredibly unfeminist of me, I mean... I don't know. I'm meant to be the man of the family whilst Dad is gone; shouldn't I be here for you?"

"I'm sure you've thought about this long and hard, and it's not been an easy decision, but I don't think you've thought through all the angles." She could see the conflict in his young features and knew she had to tell him the truth. "I'm going to tell you something, and I don't want you to be hurt by it... and I know it makes me a horrible mother, but... I need time away from you and your siblings.

"I love you all more than I ever imagined I could, but I feel so much stress to be there for you when you're all here. Stress makes my disease worse for me, so, when you're at school, I'm able to breathe and relax a bit. I don't mean to say that I don't want to be with you, not at all, I wouldn't trade our time together for anything, but with your father gone, there's more on me.

"I have to make hundreds of decisions... ones that I'd otherwise be able to confer with him about or that you'd just ask him instead of me, but now it's just me. It breaks my heart to tell you that; it's been one of those things I thought I'd never tell anyone, but I have to tell you now. Please don't tell the others; they'd be upset, maybe," she said and started to worry a bit since she wasn't able to read the expression on his face.

"I didn't think about that. I reckon I thought you'd be lonely and could use someone here to help you and for you to talk to. Someone to share the load with you, but you have Kitty and Francie for that, I suppose," he said and began pacing again. "Oh, Mum, I thought this was the right thing to do."

"I'll talk to your father about it when—"

"No! I mean, please don't do that. I'd rather tell him myself if that's a'right with you?"

"Okay, I was planning to bring you with me when I visit your father during your next Exeat. Why don't you talk to him then? He can give you some good advice and tell you what he'd like you to do, okay?" she said, and Peter nodded, dropping his head.

"Yes, Mum." He stepped up and hugged her tightly. "I... want to help you. I can see how tired and worn out you are, and... I feel as though I should be doing something."

He pushed himself away from her and looked her in the eyes, suddenly very serious. "If you need anything, if there is anything I can do to help you... ever, I will drop everything and be there for you. Anything, Mum! Please promise you'll ask me for help if you need it," he said as though it were life or death.

Do I really look that worn down? she thought. "Okay, I will. You look so frightened, my darling; everything will be okay, I promise… good night nurse, I can't promise that, can I? I have no control over it, but you're far too young to be so worried!"

She looked into his dark blue eyes, which seemed to have all the cares of the world in them, and shook her head. "Oh, Peter, you are the dearest boy a mother could ask for, honestly. Your willingness to sacrifice your education, knowing how much it means to you, is the best gift in the world. Don't think that I don't appreciate it. I love you so much, thank you."

Peter nodded, then he bent down and kissed her cheek. He took a deep breath, turned, and walked away from her toward the tower. It was difficult, but she managed to keep it together. They spent at least an hour longer in the garden before Erin got a text from Millie saying that supper would be ready in forty-five minutes.

They hurried back to Owlgate, and after another long hug, they went their separate ways. She found Junie, who was fussy and ready to eat again. As she carried her upstairs, Erin melted, finally able to mourn the loss of Peter's childhood.

That night, they ate a lovely supper, though it was much lighter than lunch had been. Juniper had the hiccups during the whole meal, which had everyone laughing. After supper, Roger had to take Tilly home, and Erin went to bed early.

On Thursday, Juniper's two-month birthday, the family packed up their things and said a tearful goodbye to the residents of Owlgate. They'd had a lovely time, but Erin's first visitation with David was the next day, and then the children had to be taken back to school on Sunday. Roger delivered them to the airport, and before she knew it, they were back home again.

Chapter Twelve

FIRST VISITATION—APRIL SEVENTEENTH

The day was overcast and looked like it might start to rain on Friday, April seventeenth, as Erin drove into the car park of Estabrook prison and shut off the engine. She'd had the choice to wait two weeks, which would balance the bi-monthly schedule, or visit the week after Good Friday, though she'd then have to wait three weeks after that for the next visitation. She had decided to come early rather than wait since she wanted to bring the 'gifts' for the officers guarding him as soon as possible, and she really needed to see him.

The largest of the many imposing brick buildings loomed before her as she sat in the car staring at it, trying to will her body to stop trembling. She'd never been inside a prison before and didn't know what to expect. Of course she'd seen visitation scenes in movies and television, but this was real life, and she'd heard that the place didn't have the best reputation.

She'd gotten there early just to make sure she wasn't late, and her Passport for identification, David's prisoner number, and visiting orders were tucked away safely in her purse. A van pulled up near her, and a woman got out, checking her reflection in the tinted window. Then a man came around to the front of the van holding a large camera. They started walking toward the main door but didn't go inside.

Two more vans pulled up, and the same thing happened, although that time, both people were men checking their reflections. Before long, there was a pretty sizable group of them jostling and pushing to find the best spot outside the doors. *I wonder what that's about?* She checked her hair in the vanity mirror and unbuckled her seatbelt, then she put her purse strap over her head to wear like a messenger bag.

Next, she grabbed the bag containing a bottle of expensive whisky and a carton of cigarettes from the passenger seat, hoping it would be helpful in some way to David, and got out of her car. The SUV chirped as she touched the little button on the handle to lock it. As she started walking up the drive to the entry doors, she heard someone say, "There she is!"

Erin looked behind her, thinking there must be someone else they were talking about. All of a sudden, she was surrounded by vulture-like reporters, pecking out questions and sticking their microphones and video cameras in her face, which instantly turned bright red.

"Is it true…"

"How long has it been since…"

"Have you really been denied…"

"How are you coping…"

All she heard were the beginning of their questions, but it didn't matter, she wasn't about to answer any of them. Suddenly, someone was lifting the bag out of her arms, and she heard, "Let me help you, Mrs. Elliott."

"Wait! Stop!" was all she could say over the din of the reporters.

Several of them were speaking to the cameras, saying something like, *"I'm here outside Estabrook prison as Erin Elliott enters for the first visitation with her husband, David Elliott, who was convicted of…"*

She was being elbowed and shoved and was getting angry. Finally, an officer came out the door and rescued her, taking the bag, which she could see had been opened. When they got into the building, she had to lean against the wall for a few seconds to get her bearings and was so glad she hadn't brought the baby.

"The bag… what's in it… is for… you and the others… to thank you for… all you do," she said quietly. The officer nodded and waited patiently for her to collect herself, then he led her to the person she needed to give her information to. Once she had gone through a metal detector and cleared, she was taken into a room with several other people already waiting to be let into the visitor's room. They stared at her, making her want to leave and never come back.

At two o'clock, they were allowed to enter the room, where David was already sitting at one of the tables that were bolted, along with the chairs, to the floor. He was wearing a grey sweatsuit and white sneakers. His head was down, and it didn't seem like he wanted her to see him at all as she sat on the other side of the table, not knowing what to expect.

She wanted to hold him and kiss him, but he seemed unaffected by her presence in the room and wouldn't lift his head. "David?" she said tentatively. "Are you alright?" It wasn't at all like her husband to act that way, and she was afraid there was something seriously wrong with him. "Look at me, please!"

He shook his head.

"I... love you," she said at last when he didn't move or make any noise. "Please talk to me. What happened to you?" He sat still, not making any reply and hardly even acknowledging she was there.

Did they drug him? she thought wildly, and tears sprang to her eyes. "If... if you're not going to look at me or even talk to me, then why am I here? What are you hiding?"

He didn't answer her; he only shook his head.

"David, if you don't look at me, I'm leaving, and I won't come back," she lied. There was no way she'd be able to stay away from him; she just needed him to react. She then noticed a tear fall from his eye and hit the table with a tiny splash. "Are you... being... hurt in here?"

He shook his head again, but there were more tears.

She was getting frustrated and angry, not understanding his behavior at all. "Goddammit, David, *lift your head!*" She didn't shout, but it was loud enough to make him know she was serious, and if she got kicked out, then what was the difference anyway? He lifted his face, and she saw that his eye was green and yellow, the remnants of a black eye, and his lip had clearly been split and was still a bit swollen. "Oh my God! David! What happened?"

He shook his head, looking miserable. "Humph, Clive had the *honor* of escorting me here on Wednesday," he said softly. "Yeh look bonnie, love."

"Will you hold my hand?" she asked, swallowing hard to keep from crying, and laid her hands on the table in front of them. "And why won't you hug me?" He lifted his hand from off his lap, and she saw that it was bandaged up. "How—"

"Ma hand ended up in the way of a few blows. Dinnae fash, he'll not be back, and et's already healed up… mostly. But I dinnae want tae talk about that now. I didn't want yeh tae see me like this."

"Are you sure he won't come back? What if he makes it a habit?"

He shook his head dismissively. "Tell me about our wee Junie."

He was clearly changing the subject, so she went with it. "Juniper is so sweet! She's been smiling a lot; she coos and is starting to lift her head off my chest when I hold her. Her hair is growing out curly and flaming red."

Another tear fell silently from his chin. "I'm missin' et all again, Erin. She'll be half grown when—" he said and then shook his head. "Did yeh bring the things I asked for… for the officers?"

"Yes, I did, but they already took it." They both knew it was his best chance to stay safe in there.

"I dinnae care, as long as et helps me. How are you, ma darling? I worry about yeh all the time; are yer symptoms worsening?" he asked.

"I'm fine," she lied. The truth was, her symptoms were back, and she could feel the same old lead-ups and exhaustion she'd lived with most of her life. "Don't worry, I'll be alright. I'm sorry I missed your birthday, darling," she said, trying to change the subject. "I wish we could have celebrated it. I thought about you and—"

"Thank you, but dinnae change the subject. If… yeh need et… of course ye'll need et… but… get help. I'll… support yeh," he said, but Erin could tell by the look on his face that he wasn't sure he'd be able to.

"I'll be fine," she said again. "I'm not going to seek treatment from someone else, David, I'll just… have to live with it again until… you get out. It's only what… twenty-four episodes? I've lived through hundreds of them.

"Erin, please promise you'll get help. You were in hospital three days last time… just say yeh will, darling," he implored her.

"Fine, I'll talk to the doctor, alright?" She wasn't going to fight with him about it there.

"Good. Are yeh a'right for spendin' money? My accountant will pay all the bills, but ye'll need cash as well. Can yeh access our—"

"I have plenty of money, David. I… don't have the…" she wanted to say 'strength,' but decided against it, "…time for shopping or… well, anything. I haven't tried accessing our accounts yet. I feel like people stare at me everywhere I go. To walk into the bank and give them my name would be… difficult right now. I have the accountant's number, so if I have any trouble, I'll call him."

Her chest felt heavy, and she knew an episode was fast approaching. She tried to breathe as regularly as she could, but the constricting in her chest made her either want to take very deep or very shallow breaths, and it was difficult to regulate. A wave of exhaustion seemed to cover her like a nice soft blanket, and all she wanted to do was lay her head down and sleep.

"Erin?" she heard from somewhere far away, and she was jerked awake by David squeezing her hand. "What's the matter, darling? Yer breathin' seems labored; are yeh… havin' lead-ups?"

It took a lot of energy to speak, and she tried several times, but nothing happened. She raised her eyes and saw his bruised, worried face. "Yes," she managed and could feel the urge to cough. "I love—" she whispered as she started coughing in earnest. She tried to stand, but the table and chair wouldn't move, so she lay forward on the cold metal table, hearing a terrible commotion all around her.

"Erin? Help! Please, she's having an episode!" He grabbed her, but suddenly, a guard was pulling him away. An alarm was sounding, and then everything went black.

Chapter Thirteen

A DOCTOR'S AUTHORITY

Erin woke as she was being wheeled into the emergency room of a hospital. She was sore all over, and it took a moment to comprehend where she was and what was going on. "David?" she gasped as she tried to sit up and catch her breath.

There was a plastic mask over her mouth and nose, and someone was squeezing a ball, sending bursts of air over her face. She tried pushing the hand away, but they just went right back to it. "Stop!" she cried out and turned her head. "I'm fine! Where's David?" she asked before she thought it through. "Never mind," she whispered, remembering he was in prison.

The EMTs and nurses were all talking, and then the lady was back with the mask. "Just stop!" she yelled, making everyone look at her. "I'm fine now. I have the Fertilis Defect, and I had an episode. I just need to rest, so stop fussing over me! Didn't you read my bracelet?" she asked then remembered that she'd taken it off so the metal detector wouldn't sound.

"There wasn't anything—" an EMT began, but she cut him off.

"I took it off at the prison. Didn't David tell you what was wrong?"

"The prison went into lockdown; we didn't speak to anyone named David. The Fertilis Defect? Alright, we'll find a doctor who specializes in that. Just sit tight," a man said as she was wheeled into a room and the curtain was drawn. A woman was sitting at a swiveling laptop and began asking her questions.

"Can yeh tell me yer name, love?" she asked.

"Erin Mar… I mean, Elliott," she replied, angry that she couldn't seem to remember to say her new name.

"Erin Elliott? Well then. And what's your date of birth?" Erin answered all her questions, wanting to sleep. Another nurse came in and put a plastic bracelet on her wrist, then a little clamp was put on her first finger to measure her oxygen levels.

A nasal cannula was fitted, the tubes running from her nostrils over her ears, then a blood pressure cuff was placed around her arm, and she was told it would go off every fifteen minutes.

"And what's the doctor's name who's treatin' you?"

"I… don't really have one here yet. I can give you the name of my doctor in America… oh, and my OBG… I mean midwife—" she began but was interrupted.

"Dr. Jill Westin; I'm her doctor. Hello, Erin, what happened?" she asked, and Erin wanted to cry.

"Oh, Dr. Jill, I'm so glad you're here! Please tell them that I'm fine," she said as the nurse started an IV in her arm.

"It's nice to see you, too, but I'm not sure you're fine. I'd like to talk to you about what's going on with you."

"I'm nearly done," the nurse said when the IV was in place. She used a handheld scanner to scan a code on Erin's bracelet, and then the woman and the nurse left the room.

"I had an episode; it's no big deal," Erin began, but Dr. Jill slid the glass door closed and stood at her side.

"So, you're not getting treatments, I take it?"

Erin thought that was a really stupid question. "I'm not allowed conjugal visits, so no," she said, trying not to sound snotty or bitter.

"David will be away for at least two and up to four years, correct? You're going to have to find a way to get the treatments you need if you're going to raise Juniper and David's children, Erin. It isn't just going to go away. Have you looked into a temp—"

"NO! I can't do that! I won't!" she wailed. She began sobbing and clutching her sides in pain, her muscles sore and exhausted from the exertion of her episode.

Dr. Jill put her hand on Erin's shoulder and allowed her to get it out. "I'm afraid you don't have a choice. If you don't seek a temporary match, you risk hurting yourself or one of your children.

"I see this one wasn't so bad, but the next one could do real damage to you. I'm going to recommend that you talk to a doctor about setting up a treatment appointment. We will try to find a match for you right away. There are many new methods now—"

"New methods? Ones that don't involve having sex with a stranger?" she interrupted.

"Well, no. It still involves—"

"Then I'm not going to do it! Are you going to force me to? Can you force me?" she asked, feeling betrayed.

"I can't force you to go to the treatments, but I can force you to see someone who can explain your options and try to convince you that you need to do it, if not for yourself, then for those you love," Dr. Jill said passionately.

"How do you think David will feel knowing I'm sleeping with someone else? He's told me to get help, but I know he won't be able to deal with it! I can't put him through that!"

"What if you go blind and can't see your husband's or baby daughter's face anymore, Erin? We don't know yet how age affects the disease; what if the surfactant doesn't replenish in time and you die? Would you rather David have to mourn your loss or work through a medical procedure?" she asked, and Erin sighed.

"Fine, I'll talk to the doctor, but I need to go. Our children will be going back to school on Sunday, and I've got to take them there. Wait, where's my car—"

"You're too weak to drive, and you know it. I want you to rest now. You may leave tonight."

Erin's temper and stubborn streak were trying to gain full reign over her, and it was difficult for her to put them down, even though she knew Dr. Jill was right. "Fine! You... don't... understand!" She was measuring her breathing the best she could and trying not to start crying again.

"I under—"

"No, Jill, you don't. I've been thrown into this life… into this family, and I'm so grateful for it, but this will… could… make David shut down or stop being able to love me anymore. I vowed never to cheat on him, and I'm learning to trust that he won't cheat on me. What if this ruins everything, and he starts justifying… why it's okay to… flirt and then—" The hot tears rolled down her face.

"I don't have those answers for you, Erin. You're right; perhaps I don't understand completely, but anyone who looks at the two of you can see that he's head over heels for you. In fact, if I could root for any couple to make it through something as difficult as this will be for you both, I'd… well, I'd bet everything I have that you two will, and you'll be stronger in the end," the doctor said candidly.

Erin took a deep breath that made the muscles in her chest ache and looked at the woman who was probably ten years her junior. "Okay, fine," she said resignedly. "I'll stay, and I'll see the doctor." She shook her head as she allowed her words of encouragement to sink in. "And… thank you for what you said. I needed to hear it."

"You're welcome. I'll check on you before my shift is done." She wrote something on the clipboard she was holding, scanned Erin's bracelet with a scanning gun she took from a bracket on the wall, and then left the room.

Erin slept until a woman wearing plain clothes stepped into the room and woke her. "Mrs. Elliott?" she said and gently touched her hand.

"What… where am I? Oh… wait… now I remember," she said, feeling groggy, and looked up at the small, slender, dark-haired woman.

"My name is Portia, and I'm here to schedule an appointment to discuss your replacement treatment partner and to answer any questions you may have."

Her hackles rose at the woman's choice of words, and she shook her head vigorously, wide-eyed and angry. "Replacement? No! I will not—I can't do this!"

"Oh, I'm sorry, Mrs. Elliott, that was a poor choice of—"

"I don't care what Dr. Jill says, I won't do it! I love my husband too much, and this will—"

"Please, calm down, Mrs. Elliott. I misspoke, and I apologize. This appointment is simply to talk about your options, not for an actual treatment, and I'm afraid I must get you scheduled before you'll be released from—"

"Fine then, just pick something and let me go home." Erin was determined to cancel any appointment she was given, so it didn't matter to her what time or date it was.

"Oh, right, well—Will Wednesday at ten o'clock work for you?"

"Yes, that's fine," she said and started taking off the nasal cannula.

"Please wait, Mrs.—"

"Listen, I know you're doing your job, but I have an infant and four children at home who will be going back to school… what day is it today… Friday? They go back on Sunday. I don't have the luxury of sitting here, no matter how tired I am or how adamant Dr. Jill is about forcing me to go to your appointment. Please, just let me go now," she said, tears rolling down her face.

The woman placed her hand on hers and looked into her eyes. "I will tell the staff that you may go, but I want you to know that I'm on your side. Perhaps that sounds a bit trite, but I am. I do care and cannot imagine how difficult this must be for you… this whole situation is more than any woman should be asked to bear, but I reckon you're stronger than most women."

"But it doesn't matter how strong I am, don't you see? David won't be able to take it, and I can't break his heart like that!"

"But you must fight! If you choose not to have treatments, you're allowing that…" She looked around the room and whispered the next few words, "naff wanker of a judge to win! Please don't allow that to happen, Erin. You've too many people on your side who are rooting for you and your husband to thrive."

She squeezed Erin's hand and smiled at her. "Perhaps you're not aware, but there are people… groups, sites, and forums out there, filled with people who are outraged by the injustice of what's happened to your husband."

"There are?"

"There are, and we… they won't rest until something is done to remedy the situation, whether that means the case is overturned and he's released early or simply that you're allowed conjugal visits. It's vital that you stay healthy until we, I mean they, can cause a change. Yes, you may have to break down and receive treatments from another man, but it'll be worth it to stay alive, won't it?"

Erin studied the woman's face, presuming she wasn't supposed to be sharing so much with her, and sighed. She closed her eyes and hung her head. "Thank you for saying all that, I know you're sincere, and I'll think about it. I hope they are able to do something, but it's hard to imagine it making any difference.

"David and I both have demons to slay in our personalities, and I truly think the dragon might defeat him if I seek treatments elsewhere, no matter what he thinks. I know for a fact that I would die... at least on the inside, if the tables were turned and he had to have sex with another woman."

A shiver ran through her at the mere mention of it, and she shook her head, trying to remove the thought from her mind. "Let's just hope all those people out there can cause a change sooner rather than later."

"Yes, let's hope so," Portia said with a frown, clearly disappointed that she wasn't swayed.

"Thank you for caring so much, and it's good to know that people are taking action to avenge us."

Before she left, Portia handed her a few leaflets and a card that had the appointment date, time, and address written on it.

Erin was finally released from the hospital and hired a taxi to take her to her car. She was tired and sore, but she drove herself home after sitting in the prison parking lot, knowing how close she was to David and wishing she could see him, if only for a few minutes. She sent a message to Kitty, letting her know when she'd be home, and when she stepped through the door, the children ran to her, wanting to make sure she was alright.

"Kitty wouldn't tell us what happened except that you were in hospital. We were worried about you, Mummy," Rosie said, then wrapped her arms around her.

"Yes, we were frightened, Mum," Peter said, fear creasing his young brow.

"Now, now, I'm okay. I just had a small episode, nothing to worry about," she said and accepted the hug from Charlie, though all she wanted to do was sit and rest.

"Francie said you should have a seat in the dining room," Daniel said, taking her hand so he could help her.

She smiled and allowed him to lead her there. The children took their places at the table, though she figured they'd already eaten. "Thank you for—" she began, but Francie entered the room and started serving her.

"Where's Kitty?" Erin asked, since she was the one who normally served at the table.

"I'm 'ere, Mum," Kitty said and helped the cook, though Francie didn't leave when she showed up.

The two women placed many dishes on the table and poured tea, juice, and water, fussing and fretting over her until she put her hands up to stop them. "What is all this? I don't understand."

There was silence for a few moments as Erin looked first at Kitty, then at Francie, who suddenly lifted her apron to her face and began crying. "We were beside ourselves wif worry, Mum," Kitty answered, while Francie nodded, too upset to speak.

Erin knit her brows and touched her cook's arm, as that was all she could reach. "Listen, it's not that bad. I was even able to drive home... please don't cry or worry about me. It's all going to be okay, you'll see," she said, also having to convince herself.

Midway through a strained, tense supper, Junie began to cry, so she excused herself and trudged up the stairs to feed her. Her top was drenched by the time she got to the nursery, so she closed the door, took off her top and bra, then rolled up a receiving blanket to use as a towel. She was a bit chilly, but she wanted to get it over with.

There was a light knock on the door, and Kitty poked her head in. "Do ya need anyfing, Mum?" she asked and then saw her sitting there half naked.

Without waiting for an answer, she left, then returned a moment later with a warm, fluffy blanket.

"Thank you, Kitty, I don't know what I'd do without you! Well, in this instance, I guess I'd freeze, huh?"

"You're welcome, Mum; now you try to relax, a'right? I'll come see to you again in a bit," she said, and stepped out of the room, closing the door gently behind her.

One of the silver linings to enduring an episode was that it seemed to reset her symptoms, at least for a while. That night, Erin had enough energy to climb the stairs to the children's rooms and was able to read to them. She continued reading *Anne of Green Gables*, then tucked them into bed.

When that was done, she didn't bother going all the way downstairs; instead, she decided to go to bed early. After sending a message to Kitty, she got into her pajamas and, as was her new habit, got under the covers and pulled David's pillow close. That night, she found herself talking to it as though it was him and not a big bag stuffed with goose down.

Chapter Fourteen

READY TO GO

Sunday morning was chaotic, to say the least. If it hadn't been for Kitty and Peter's intervention, they never would have left the house. Daniel was causing trouble by hiding his siblings' things so they had to search for them, thus making more work for everyone.

Rosie had woken up on the wrong side of the bed, so she was grumpy, yelling at Daniel and whining at everyone else. Charlie's fuse was getting shorter every minute with his twin's antics, and his temper got the better of him several times. Everyone's nerves were frazzled to the point of near exhaustion.

Erin and Kitty were at the bottom of the stairs and looked at each other when they heard cries of distress coming from Dan. "I'll see to them, Mum," Kitty said and rushed up the steps.

Though she hated to admit it, Erin was glad she'd have a bit of peace once they were safely back at school. A few moments later, Kitty descended the stairs, trying to hide a grin. She was followed by Dan, who had red eyes and his hand covering his right ear protectively. Next came Peter, who seemed chuffed at having used his authority against his errant sibling.

"And what's this, then?" Erin said, though she thought she had a good idea.

"Seems as Peter stepped in and took 'old of 'is ear, Mum," Kitty said before swiftly leaving the room. Erin could see her covering her mouth in an apparent attempt to hide her mirth.

"I had to do something—"

"He can't tell me—" the boys said over each other.

"One at a time, and please be quick; we need to get going soon," Erin said. "Peter, you first."

The teenager was clearly glad to be chosen first and glared at his brother. "He had to be stopped, Mum. His… shenanigans were out of control, so I took action."

"Shenanigans?" It was Erin's turn to cover her mirth at his vocabulary. "And what do you say in defense of your behavior?" she said, turning to Daniel.

"Bah, I was only having a bit of a laugh. No need to—"

"You hid Rosie's school jumper in the toilet bin! That's not a laugh, that—"

"Daniel!" she said hotly.

"It was under the bin liner—"

"Nanny would've given you a right smack for it," Peter said.

"She's not here, is she, mate?" Dan said, squinting at him.

"Stop!" Erin said a bit more loudly than she'd planned. "Here's what's going to happen. Daniel, you are going to bring everyone's things back to them and quit your games, or…" She had to think of something he would care about, but what? A grin spread across her face, and she squatted before the boy. "Or you'll not have any dessert when you're home for a month."

"A whole month?" he wailed and even stamped his foot. "That's not fair!"

"Don't argue, or your punishment will get worse," she warned. He opened his mouth but wisely decided not to speak. "Peter, in the future, please try to come to me or Kitty before taking action unless you truly must."

"Yes, Mum, I will," he said, then followed his brother up the stairs.

"Oh, and both of you, please hurry up! We have to leave in less than an hour!"

They managed to leave on time, but everyone was tired and somber on the ride back to school. Daniel slept most of the way, Charlie read, Peter listened to music through his earbuds, and Rosie stared out the window. As they got closer, the sun came out, and Rosie smiled at Erin in the rearview mirror.

At school, Peter helped divvy out everyone's bags and even offered to carry Rosie's for her. Erin walked to each of the children's rooms and hugged them before saying goodbye. Rosie's farewell was tearful, though she was consoled with the reminder that there was an Exeat in three weeks, and she'd see her then.

With a heavy heart, Erin pulled into the driveway of Cliff Cottage and parked in front of the cream-colored lime stucco building. The high hedges around the garden obscured her view of the front door, and the towering hydrangea bushes swayed in the wind as if waving hello to an old friend. She sighed as she opened the car door and stepped out into the lovely, warm, spring day, hearing the gulls crying and the wind through the trees.

She wanted to cry too, as the memories of their time living there flooded her mind, like how regal David had looked in his Bollywood costume and how she'd sat with Judi Dench and Johnny Depp on the garden bench, which she noticed as she approached the front door. The rustic wooden gate in the garden wall was barely visible through the leaves and vines and brought back the memory of stepping through it with Ian McKellen.

Asit's car pulled up next to hers, she could see it at the end of the walk, so she stopped and waited for him to join her. "Lovely day, isn't it?" he said brightly, making her smile in spite of herself.

"Aye, it's nearly perfect," she replied and accepted a brief hug and an air kiss on her cheek. "I've missed this place!" Tears smarted her eyes, so she turned and continued to the covered doorway.

"I've missed you and our pleasant conversations, my friend." He put his key into the lock, and the door swung open before them. "After you," he said and stepped aside for her.

"Thanks, Asit." She entered the cottage and saw it was just as they'd left it on that cold February day when she'd been miserable, wanting her pregnancy to be over and done with. "I just need to grab a few things," she said softly, though she'd already told him as much in the email she'd sent him.

"Are you certain about having me store your personal items, Erin? I don't mind leaving them—"

"For two years? No, you shouldn't have to wait for us. I'd take it all with me, except I don't have the room, or honestly the energy, to do it myself. When this is all over with, we'll come get everything or hire mov… I mean, removers to sort it all out. Thank you so much for offering to let us use your office; it's so kind of you."

The tall, older man looked at her sadly and gently touched her shoulder. "Come now, my friend, it's the smallest of things. I'm glad I have the space for it, truly. I will keep it for you as long as you require it; there is no rush or ill feelings, alright?" He smiled at her, making sure she understood.

"Thank you… I just wish—" She shook her head and started for the stairs. "I won't be long."

"Take your time, Erin. I will prepare the tea this time," he said and turned toward the kitchen.

At the end of the open hallway, she saw that they'd left their bedroom door open and stepped inside. Tears clouded her eyes as she thought of all the good times and bad she and David had spent in there. The throes of both passion and despair she'd felt came flooding back to her, making her want to turn and leave them there for better times.

That option wasn't available to her though, so she went to the small dresser and opened the top drawer. Methodically, she took her jewelry and undergarments out of it, laying it all on the bed, and continued until it was empty. In the closet, she found a small empty box, several tote bags, and one of her and David's suitcases.

On the floor was one of his shirts that had missed the laundry basket at some point. She lifted it to her nose and inhaled deeply. It still smelled of him, and not caring if anyone saw her, she sat against the wall and cried, holding it to her while rocking back and forth, feeling gutted.

Before long, she heard Asit call up the stairs that the tea was ready, so she wiped her face with one of the many tissues she'd pulled out of her prepared pockets and made her way to the kitchen. "How are the children and your newest addition?" he asked as she sat at the table.

"They're brilliant; Juniper is growing fast, like a weed," she said, knowing he'd enjoy the gardening reference.

They sat in companionable silence for a while before Asit sighed. "Do you—" he began but then shook his head. "Never mind."

"Do I what?"

He looked at her as if deciding how to word whatever it was he wanted to ask her. "Do you—Is there anything—If there's a way I can help you at all, I—"

"Oh, thank you, but I have everything I need, unless you know a way to break David out of jail," she said and laughed half-heartedly.

"I don't, I'm afraid, though if I could, I'd have already done that," he said with a smile.

"Aye, I know you would, and thank you for asking." She dunked her digestive biscuit into her tea and tried to keep up her brave face.

"Well then, I've some plastic totes for you to use—"

"Oh, Asit, you didn't have to—"

"It was no trouble, truly. They were only partially full, so I consolidated them into one. I will bring them inside and then help you get everything sorted," he said and smiled warmly at her.

"Okay, thank you for being so kind and generous," she said.

An hour later, the totes were full of the things she was leaving there, and Asit was finished lugging them to the small, unused office building. They sat together on the little deck attached to it, which was covered with potted plants. There was a lovely breeze to cool them off while they listened to the bees flitting from flower to flower around them.

"This was nice," Erin said. "Hard work, but it was good to have a friend sharing the load."

"Many hands make light work," he said.

"Yes, and now I have to go, though I'd rather sit here and forget everything else I'm meant to be doing. Junie will need to be fed, and there are a million phone calls I have to make—Sorry, you don't need to know my schedule. Thanks again for your help."

"It was my pleasure, and you're welcome to come visit anytime. I'll keep that chair open and waiting for you."

Chapter Fifteen

SAME OLD SAME OLD

Erin's life was becoming a series of routines. Things to help her get through the lonely days filled with worry and fear about David and what was happening to him in that horrible place. She didn't like routine and got bored doing the same thing over and over, but she found that if she could look forward to little snippets of time coming up in her day, it made it the tiniest bit more bearable.

She and Juniper were getting into a rhythm of waking, feeding, sleeping, and playing, which repeated itself all day, every day. Junie was getting stronger and beginning to show her personality more all the time. She self-soothed by sucking her middle two fingers, and though Erin knew it could ruin her teeth eventually, it was one tiny silver lining in her cloud of despair and anxiety.

Kitty was the only thing that kept her sane. She helped and fussed and did all she could to make Erin's life easier. She often thought about David describing her as 'flighty' and wondered where on earth he'd gotten that from. Susannah, no doubt.

Kitty was the farthest thing from flighty she could think of. She was thoughtful and timely and seemed to have a sixth sense about when she was needed or when to leave the room. She adored Junie and had just as much joy in the little things the baby did every day as Erin did.

She had a new appreciation and understanding for her mother-in-law and Millie finding love with each other. Not that she was suddenly physically attracted to Kitty, but their camaraderie and friendship was helping her through her ordeal, and she could see more fully how something like that could build a relationship much closer than mere friendship.

It was turning out to be a long, unproductive day. Being Tuesday, Francie was gone, and Erin had forced Kitty to take the day off, though she'd protested. Thus, the house felt empty and far too quiet.

She felt utterly alone and wanted, with all her heart, to talk to her mother in person. The more she thought about her mom, America, and her former life, the more she wished she could hang out with her girlfriends at Marcia's cabin.

The thought of checking her Facebook notifications was tempting but also a two-edged sword. The last thing she wanted was pity or cliché platitudes from people who merely felt uncomfortable about her situation and decided to say something. On the other hand, if someone did manage to send something heartfelt, it may bring her to tears, and she'd end up crying all day.

Out of desperation, she thought of sending a message to her friends, and as if on cue, her phone began exploding with notifications. "What in the—" she said and picked it up.

The lock screen preview showed it was from her group of girlfriends, so she closed her eyes and sighed, bracing herself for the onslaught of emotions reading it may cause. Swiping the screen, she had to laugh at the first message.

Fucking Laura: *Thought I'd wait for a while to say anything, and you know I'm no good at finding the right thing to say,* Erin Elliott, *so I'll just start with FUCK THAT ASSHOLE JUDGE!*

Colleen: *Yeah! What in the hell was he thinking? I hope he goes bald (unless he already is under that ugly wig). Speaking of wigs, I hope his gets lice and fleas and chronic halitosis so no one wants to talk to him!*

Good night nurse, I love those girls! Erin thought and continued reading.

> Marcia: *Agreed! I'd like to add chronic gas, the really smelly, 'old guy' kind, like the kind that comes out when he's walking or if he coughs or sneezes!*

> New Laura: *And I hope he never has sex again! Yeah, like he gets kicked in the nads and has to be castrated or something awful! Oh, and incontinence! Yeah, so he has to wear a male diaper!*

> Carrie: *If I could get off work (like that'll ever happen!) I'd go there and do the kicking! Then I'd come to your mansion and visit you!*

Erin laughed so hard she snorted.

> Erin: *I love you guys! I needed a good laugh! I was afraid you'd send sappy stuff, and I really couldn't bear that! It's nice to know that I have you to hypothetically avenge us. It means everything! I was just thinking about you and feeling sorry for myself, of course, as I believe I have the right to do at the moment!*

> Marcia: *I read that he got FOUR YEARS! That's insane!*

> Erin: *Well, yeah, it's four years, but he'll only serve two, though that's far too long!*

Marcia: *And didn't you just have a baby? That must be... wait... sorry... I don't mean to trigger you!*

Erin: *Yeah, her name is Juniper Annis Elliott, and she's the most beautiful thing on the planet!*

She sent one of the photos she'd taken the night before. All the girls oohed and ahhed over the picture, so she sent a few more.

F. Laura: *Wait, you have a fucking mansion? We NEED to see photos!*

N. Laura: *Yeah! Photos!*

Erin: *We don't have a mansion, guys! It's just a row house.*

Colleen: *Photos! Photos! Photos!*

Erin: *Alright, fine.*

She spent the next forty minutes sending them photos of the inside of her house. When they saw the kitchen, there was a mix of reactions.

Carrie: *Fancy, modern kitchen!*

N. Laura: *Ummm, NOT my taste! It's so ugly and, well, just UGLY!*

F. Laura: *I'd rip that fucker apart and put up something pretty!*

Marcia: *Girl! I'm so sorry! That would be depressing AF! I'd NEVER even go in there if I were you! How do you cook anything good in there?*

Erin: *Well, I may not have a mansion, but I DO have the best cook in England! I rarely have to cook, which is so nice! I wish I could have a party here and have you guys come visit me! I'd ask Francie to make a roast joint, mashed potatoes, Yorkshire pudding, and custard tarts for dessert!*

N. Laura: *That was my stripper name.*

Erin: *Huh?*

N. Laura: *Custard Tart!*

Erin groaned and laughed so hard it hurt.

Carrie: *That's just gross!*

Erin: *I love you guys!*

They talked for another half hour, and then everyone had things to do, so she said a sad goodbye and reread everything.

Later that afternoon, Erin heard the mail drop, so she went to the front door and picked up the stack of letters from the floor. There was one from Puncknowle, and she groaned, dreading to know what it was about. *They didn't call me, so it can't be too bad,* she thought, and took it to David's office to open it. Inside, there was a letter on fine, linen paper with the school's letterhead at the top.

> *Dear Mrs Elliott,*
>
> *I am sure you will share my concern that Peter's recent grades have not matched his previously excellent achievements. We of course understand that there have been difficult circumstances at home, and without wishing to intrude too far into the delicate nature of those, I was wondering if you might be available to discuss what steps the school, with your support, could take to help get Peter 'back on track'.*
>
> *The next Exeat weekend is almost upon us and provides an ideal opportunity for us to meet if you are able to arrive early? Would one pm be possible?*
>
> *I shall assume this is acceptable unless I hear otherwise from you.*
>
> *Kind regards,*
>
> *Dr. Donald Dingledine - Deputy Head (Academic)*

Donald Dingledine, huh? That's one of the best names ever, she thought with a smile, then set the letter on her lap and sighed heavily, ashamed that she didn't know Peter's grades were suffering. *I don't know what to say to him.* Though she would rather have ignored the situation, she knew it was too important to do that, so she set a reminder on her phone, then spent the next hour scrolling on Instagram, which she found herself doing far too often.

An ad caught her eye for high-quality prints on canvas with optional brush strokes added to make them feel more like real paintings, and she had to check it out. It wasn't anything new, but she decided she had to have some of them, so the rest of the day was spent searching and downloading photographs, excited to see how they would turn out.

Chapter Sixteen

SCHOOL MEETING

Time seemed to fly, and before Erin knew it, two and a half weeks had passed, and it was time to pick the children up from school for an Exeat weekend. Kitty was tasked with watching Junie, and though she was exhausted again, Erin drove the three hours down to Dorset.

With a heavy heart, she stood in the car park of Puncknowle Academy, gazing up at the beautiful Bath Stone building with some kind of rusty-orange stone used as an accent around the windows and doors, which made it pop beautifully. It had once been a grand summer home to a wealthy eighteenth or nineteenth-century family. She couldn't remember all the history she'd been told when they'd toured the grounds the year before, but there was something to do with the land being owned at one time by the founder of the White Star Line.

No use putting it off, she thought and walked up to the cathedral-like entryway, the interior flanked on either side by built-in wooden benches and a mosaic border of black and white marble checks around the edge of the floor, making it look like a carpet. She stepped through the enormous, arched, wooden doors and went through the vestibule.

Having only been inside the main building once before, she tried not to gawk at the expansive leaded glass windows that allowed the midday sun to brighten the open, carved, wooden staircase, which she viewed through intricate, scalloped, gothic, sandstone arches with marble support columns.

After speaking to a receptionist and signing in, she was given a bright-red lanyard to show she was a visitor. On the way to Dr. Dingledine's office, she was led through several grand rooms with the most beautiful, delicate molding and decorations on the ceilings that made her want to stop and examine them more closely. Clearly, the woman she was following had gotten used to the grandeur of the place and did not allow for the indulgence.

They walked down a long hallway that on one side had rows of cases filled with trophies and team photos. On the other hung ornately framed portraits and photographs of former headmasters. The last picture was of the current headmaster, Dr. A. Povey, who had a genuine smile and seemed like a caring person.

They reached an open door and entered an office that also had decorative plasterwork on the ceiling, as well as more tall, leaded glass windows. She was asked to take a seat and told that Dr. Dingledine would join her shortly. Erin thanked the woman and then stood, studying the moldings and carved plaster trims.

In the window alcove, the coffered pattern of the small ceiling was a Moroccan trellis design, with shells or similar embellishments at each inner point of the raised enclosures. At the top of each shell was a bouquet or spray of tendrils, some with roses, thistles, or other flowers she couldn't identify. Over the top edge of the window, on the outer wall, was a plasterwork border of entwined ribbons filled in with what appeared to be bunches of grapes, roses, wheat stalks, pomegranates, and other flowers that may have been irises.

Losing all sense of time, she was startled when a man said, "Aren't they lovely? When I started my career here, I often found myself straining my neck to examine the decor of this old place."

She turned and smiled at the older man, who wasn't much taller than her. He had a jolly face with rosy cheeks, and ears that stuck out just slightly too far to be fashionable. He was nearly bald, though he tried in vain to cover it with a comb-over of nearly pure white hair.

"It's rare to find decor like this in America; well, at least in Wisconsin, where I'm from," she said and shook his outstretched hand.

"Doctor Donald Dingledine, it's a pleasure to meet you, Mrs. Elliott," he said and motioned to a chair on the far side of his desk. Once she was seated, he took his seat.

"It's nice to meet you, too," she said.

"Could I just start by saying how much I appreciate you coming in to see me today? I do find it always so much easier to have these sorts of discussions in person, face to face, you know, rather than talking to a computer monitor. I'm afraid I'm a bit old-fashioned in that regard."

"I understand, and I'm happy to be here," she fibbed.

"Now, Peter's grades, just to put a little perspective on things, are still good, and I could name a few of our pupils who would be quite happy with those results, but they aren't reflecting Peter's full potential, which is what we always try to achieve for all of our students."

"I'm… glad to hear it. I mean, Peter is so bright, and we want him to do well."

"We've also noticed a change in his demeanor. He has always been fairly outgoing, mixes well with the other boys, and enjoys his sport, particularly fond of cricket, it seems."

"His father played cricket in school, and I know he's wanted to play, but there was, well, a problem with communication while he was at the last school… anyway, I'm happy he's able to do it now."

"Actually, our sports master thinks he could make a rather good fast bowler and make it onto the first team next year," he said, becoming a bit more animated, but then he cleared his throat and smiled. "But my apologies, I'm starting to digress. Mr. Clapperton, his house master, tells me that Peter has become somewhat withdrawn.

"There was an altercation with another boy last week, as well. Nothing serious, of course, or we would have let you know, but it was out of character for him. So, what with that and his grades starting to slip, I thought it might be wise to have an early discussion with his parents, try to nip whatever it might be in the bud, so to speak, before things become too serious."

Erin sighed and began playing with an errant string hanging from her purse, which she was hugging on her lap. "Thank you for reaching out to me about Peter's grades and behavior. I want to help, but I have to be honest and tell you that I don't know anything about raising teenagers, and I'm not sure what I can do. I'm new to this whole mother thing and feel like I'm just treading water most of the time."

She stared at the edge of the desk, feeling lost and overwhelmed. "I'm sure you've heard about what our family is going through right now? Oh, wait, I think you mentioned it in your letter."

"Well, I did, of course, see some of the news coverage. I don't normally take much interest in that sort of thing as a rule, but as it was to do with one of our boys, then of course one has to."

"Yeah, it's hard not to see it. Seems like it's everywhere. The thing is, Peter told me that he's thinking about leaving school early. He said he wants to be there for me now that his dad is away. I don't know where he got the idea from, and I told him I didn't want him to do that. He needs to stay here and finish his education—"

Her eyes filled with unwelcome tears, which she wiped away with the back of her hand. "He's going through so much right now and wants to grow up too fast. I mean, I guess I did, too, at sixteen, but it breaks my heart. I want him to be a kid for as long as he can, you know?"

"Yes, but Peter is a young man now, not a child. There's quite a well-known saying, I don't think anyone knows who first wrote it, but it goes something like, 'Sons may grow into men and grow out of their toys, but in the hearts of their mothers, they are still little boys,' so, of course your feelings are entirely natural."

"Makes sense." She hadn't known Peter when he was a little boy, but she was beginning to understand the heartache of the sentiment.

"That said," he continued, "Peter should definitely stay and complete his exams at the end of the year. Leaving now would certainly be a mistake, although I will admit that wasn't something I knew he was considering."

"I think I've talked him out of it, and we'll see his father tomorrow. Hopefully, David can help him make the right decision." She closed her eyes and shook her head slowly. "Doctor Dingledine, I don't know what to do!"

Her heart began to beat hard in her chest as the panic and stress of the whole situation threatened to overwhelm her. "Does the school have a counselor or someone he can talk to? I mean, I could maybe arrange for him to see someone, but I don't know how I'd schedule that—"

"Don't you worry, Mrs. Elliott, if that's what you want, we do have two counselors here, so we can absolutely get Peter in to see one of them. He is certainly not the first young man who's needed some help to navigate stormy seas in his life, and our counselors have certainly had some excellent results in the past. Just a slight word of caution, though, as he must agree to speak with them. Hopefully, he'll see the sense in that; he seems like a reasonable young man, and I'll have a word with him myself."

"Thank you, Doctor, I'm sorry I'm such a mess."

"No, no, don't you worry, we are here to help. I'm sure that between us, we can get Peter all the help he needs to get through this with some excellent exam results at the end of the year. Now, why don't you go and enjoy some of the kitchen's delightful tea and cake in the conservatory."

He smiled at her reassuringly. "Peter should be in there by now, and I'll be along in a while. Hopefully, there will be a scone left, as I am rather partial to Mrs. Brown's scones, apparently a secret family recipe, you know."

"Okay, and thank you again," she said as they stood. He shook her hand, and she left the room feeling only a little bit better.

The very last thing Erin wanted to do was socialize with a bunch of rich people and their teachers, but she knew it was probably expected of her, so she headed in that direction. The conservatory had a good bit of space, though large double doors that led into the Drawing Room were open, allowing for overflow. Beautiful, ornate cornice moldings seemed to be holding up the high ceilings, and the old oak floor was highly polished and smooth from years of use. Its white painted walls gave the room a sunny and light feel to it.

Along the outside wall were large, wooden-framed patio doors with old-fashioned iron locking mechanisms that went from the top to the bottom of the door, led onto a patio with views over the back of the house. From that vantage point, she could see across the gardens, past the playing fields, and could just make out a small lake, though it was mostly hidden by trees.

Student artwork was displayed in frames on the walls, over the large fireplace, and upon a grand piano in the corner of the room. A staff member was playing softly for the parents, which was quite nice. Against the back wall, opposite the patio doors, tables covered with white tablecloths stood, laden with tea, coffee, and soft drinks as well as an impressive array of cakes and scones served with jam and cream.

Peter was standing near a window, speaking to a teacher. When he saw her, his face lit up, and he beckoned for her to join them. "Hiya, Mum! This is Mr. Dearlove, the director of drama. He's asked if I'd like to try my hand at the Theater Company next term."

"Hello, Mr. Dearlove, it's a pleasure to meet you," Erin said, enjoying the interesting surnames she was encountering.

"Likewise, Mrs. Elliott. Peter speaks very highly of you," he said. "I'm aware that he'll have an opening at the start of our fall term, so I asked him if he'd like to give it a go. Who knows, perhaps the ability to perform runs in the family."

Erin smiled at her son, who was now taller than her by several inches. "I think it's worth a try. You'll never know unless you… give it a go," she said and rolled her eyes at herself.

"Well said," the tall, rather handsome man agreed and put his hand on Peter's arm. "I'm sorry to desert you, but I must speak to Doctor Dingledine. Please excuse me."

"Of course," Erin said, then noticed Charlie, Dan, and Rosie waiting patiently for her to be finished with her conversation. She waved them over and accepted the hugs from Charlie and Rosie.

"Hi, Mum," Dan said in lieu of a hug.

"Hello, guys," she said. "I'm sorry to rush us, but we really should be leaving soon. It's a long drive, and I'll need to feed Junie when we get back. You should go ahead and choose something to eat for the ride home."

Dan rushed to the refreshment table and grabbed a piece of frosted cake. Before she could say anything, he'd already stuffed it into the pocket of his hoodie, and she groaned. Peter looked at her and rolled his eyes, then gifted her one of David's smiles.

When they finally got to the SUV, Erin said, "Okay, I need a nap. Who wants to drive us home?" It was something she'd say to the children on her bus sometimes, just for fun.

"Are you alright, Mummy?" Rosie said, sounding worried, her eyes serious.

"Oh, darling, I'm okay. I was only joking, though it would be nice if Peter could drive—Wait, no, I take it back, I'm not ready for that!" she said and smiled at him.

Chapter Seventeen

SECOND VISITATION—MAY EIGHTH

The next day, Erin pulled into a parking space in the prison car park and turned off the engine. She took a deep breath, trying to relax and make the kids feel a bit more comfortable. She'd been having shortness of breath again and was exhausted, though she tried to hide it. She thought three weeks was too early for another episode, but that's how long it had been in New Orleans, and she'd never been under so much stress in her whole life.

The visiting orders were for her and all the children every time, in case she was able to bring them, and since they were home, she wanted to surprise David. Everyone was quiet, even Juniper, who was sleeping peacefully in her car seat. "Alright, everyone, remember not to engage with the media. Peter, please carry the car seat, and I'll take the... gift... for the officers," she said.

"Yes, Mum," they all replied, and she smiled at them in the rearview mirror. She saw Rosie looking back at her, tears raining down her wee cheeks, and she felt so badly for the young girl. It was hard enough on her; she couldn't imagine how much pain the children were feeling about the whole situation. She blew her a quick kiss and suddenly felt like crying herself.

They opened the doors and piled out. Charlie grabbed the fold-up stroller, while Rosie took the diaper bag, although Erin wasn't sure if they'd be allowed to bring it all the way in. Thinking twice, she had Charlie put the stroller back, and Peter disconnected the car seat, while Erin opened the hatch and grabbed the bag of what were essentially bribes.

As she closed the hatch, she prayed that the reporters wouldn't ask the children any questions, since they had enough to deal with. Dan walked in front of them, pushing and nudging anyone or anything that got in their way, including a guy holding a camera who was obviously a bodybuilder and who could've squished Daniel in his sleep. They were bombarded with questions and heard intros all around them.

"We're here at Estabrook Prison, where Erin Elliott has come for the second time to visit her husband, David Elliott, best known for the series *Future Explorations*. She's brought David's four children from his marriage with supermodel, Susannah Sutcliffe Elliott, who died of a heart attack less than two years ago. She's also brought *their* baby, which was born only a few weeks before David's arrest and subsequent prison sentence. 'Mrs. Elliott, how are you and your family coping with your husband's absence?'"

"Erin, may we see your baby?"

"Just a peek, Erin?"

They finally got to the doors and had to wait for an officer to open them because there were too many people crowded around them. When the doors were opened, they rushed in as the reporters continued their volleys.

"Mrs. Elliott, how are you feeling since you're no longer receiving treatments for—"

The door shut behind them, drowning out the voices, and they all breathed a sigh of relief. "Is everyone alright?" Erin asked before proceeding. They all nodded and looked up at her with large, worried eyes. It was then she realized that none of them had ever been to a prison before and most likely didn't know what to expect.

"Come close," she said, and they made a perfect huddle. "Now, there is nothing to be afraid of in here; the officers will keep us safe. You will need to walk through a metal detector just like at the airport. Then we'll wait in a big room before being brought into the room where your dad will be sitting."

"Will I... be allowed to... hug my daddy?" Rosie said, her little chin quivering.

"Yes, darling, though you should probably walk instead of running toward him. Does anyone else have questions?" she asked and waited. When no one said anything, she started walking down the entry hall and stopped at the check-in window, going through the same process as before.

The security check took longer, as the car seat had to be gone through thoroughly, and a dog was brought around to sniff around Juniper and the children. They managed not to wake Junie when she was gently taken out of her seat, and wasn't fully strapped back in afterward. Again, they were led into a waiting area, where people stared and whispered behind their hands.

The children stayed close, and Rosie held onto Erin's arm as though she was afraid they might be separated while they waited. They heard a noise and saw a guard come to the door. He opened it and told them they could enter.

The children looked around, absorbing everything, especially the high, gymnasium-like ceilings with windows covered by bars way up at the top. A man who could've been David was seated at one of the tables with his head down. *Oh, God, not again!* Erin thought, but then he looked up, and they saw that it was another prisoner, who was joined by a petite woman.

Rosie snuggled up to Erin, the girl's grip on her hand almost painful as they scanned the room. Finally, the tension was eased when they saw David, his face lit up with joy. He didn't say anything until they got to the table, and then it was as if he were a magnet, and the children were all drawn toward him.

"Ach, I've missed yeh," he said as they hugged and cried.

To Erin, it seemed like slow motion as she watched, relieved to see that some of the burdens he'd been carrying were eased, at least for the moment. He looked over at her, smiled, then stood. She went to him, and they held each other for as long as they could get away with it.

"Losh, I've missed yeh, ma love! I've been worried to death since they took you away last time!" he whispered into her ear. "How are yeh feelin'? Yeh look bonnie but tired. Have yeh spoken to yer doctor?"

Junie began to fuss, so she got out of telling him that she hadn't. Instead, she crouched down and lifted their baby, who was only eleven and a half weeks old, then handed her to him. "Say hi to your daughter," she said, changing the subject. She was still fussing, so she asked Rosie to get her pacifier.

David held her and nuzzled her face with his nose. He kissed her cheeks and then her tiny hands. "Ach, Erin! She's so wee! I can't believe how perfect she is," he said, then returned to his seat.

"Dad, what's it like in... here?" Dan asked, and everyone stared at him, wanting to know the answer.

"It's verra boring and loud most of the time, but sometimes et's too quiet, and yeh can't avoid yer thoughts. I worry so often about you, your mum, and our wee Junie. I can't begin tae tell yeh how I long for yeh all. Are yeh behavin' for your mum? What am I sayin'? I know yeh are! Do yeh like yer new school?"

"Yeah, Dad, it's cracking! I like it much better," Peter said, and the others agreed.

Erin knew they didn't want to talk about school, and they all grew quiet, not knowing what to say. She watched them and wanted to start a conversation but was suddenly too tired and couldn't think of anything. All she could think about at that moment was having David hold her once more. *Just the feel of his skin might revive me,* she thought and was startled awake when he touched her hand.

"Erin? Darling, are yeh a'right?" he was saying, and she had to pull herself out of a deep sleep.

How long was I asleep? It felt like just a second or two. "I'm sorry, David, what'd I miss?" she said, trying to be lighthearted about it.

David furrowed his brows and spoke quietly to Peter, who nodded and motioned for his siblings to follow him. She watched them walk over to the snack area and frowned. "They'll be back," he said and took her by the hand. "Ye've not seen yer doctor, have yeh?" he said, nearly scolding her.

She felt defensive, wanting to shut down and not talk about it, but that would only ruin the visit, so she shrugged. "I will, I've... been busy," she said, telling a half-truth. She had been busy, but that wasn't the reason she hadn't done it.

After leaving the hospital, she'd canceled three appointments with the doctor she was supposed to see. "Why are you pressuring me? I don't want to find someone else for treatments! I... want to wait for you! It's almost like you want me to—" She was too exhausted to argue any longer, so she squeezed his hand and laid her head on them.

"Ye're sick again, I can see et. I dinnae want yeh tae have tae do et either, but... yeh need tae be healthy for our bairns and for yerself," he said gently.

Erin wanted to be petulant and stamp her foot, but all she could do was hold him and cry, knowing he was right but not wanting to admit it. "I... miss you. I miss your touch and your kisses. I need you, not someone else!" she said a bit too loudly.

"I'm sorry, David, I know you're right, but I don't want to! Also... I'm afraid you won't be able to handle it. You might be able to in theory, but once it happens, it'll be different. I'm afraid you'll see me differently, or... I don't know... things will change, and not for the better."

"Aye. I reckon you're right, et would be different—" he began, but she cut him off.

"I keep thinking about when I told you what happened with Bran... I mean, how you reacted. I don't want to go through that again, and I don't want you to have to either."

Erin felt David stiffen at the mention of his cousin and doppelganger. Bran had raped her while David was at his former wife's funeral, and he'd not taken the news well. "Aye," was all he said at first. "I'm... so ashamed of tha', darling."

"I know you are, but I had no part in that. This... would involve me choosing it; it's a million times worse, and I can't bear to imagine your fury once you're out of here after I've done that."

"I reckon there's no winning, is there? But you HAVE to do it, or... or something bad will happen. I'll jest have tae deal with et. I'd rather tha' than for you tae... well, I dinnae wanna say et. Please, please see the doctor this week," he pleaded.

Erin nodded reluctantly. "Alright, but remember that I don't want to do it, and I love only you forever!"

"Aye, I will," he said as the children returned to the table.

They would have two hours together, and Erin couldn't help but think that it was plenty of time to have a treatment. Then she thought that it would also be enough time to take a nap... while David watched the—

"Erin?" David looked extremely worried as he gently shook her, and she knew she'd have to talk to her doctor, whether she liked it or not.

"I'm sorry, David; maybe I'll have someone pick us up, and I can come back for the car another day," she said, hardly able to keep her eyes open. She also felt that familiar tightness in her chest and knew she was in for a big episode... soon. She tried to stay awake but would find herself jerked out of sleep by David's energy flowing through her as he touched her hand.

"Peter... you should tell your father what you talked about with me the other day," she said.

Peter looked at her, then at his father, and hesitated. "Go on, son, what is et?" David asked.

"Well," Erin heard him say, then woke with a start from David speaking quite loudly.

"Ye'll do no such thing!" he barked.

"David!" she said, panting, as she'd been startled awake. "Please don't yell at him! He's trying to be helpful, and you need to think about what he's willing to sacrifice for me... us before you get upset. I... don't want him to do it either, but please take a minute and be kind to him... about it. Keep talking... I just need a few... minutes... to—" she said.

David woke her again. "They've given the five-minute warning," he said.

"What... did I miss? Oh no! I'm so sorry," she cried.

"It's a'right, Mum, I'll tell you about it later," Peter said.

David motioned to his children to draw near. "I love yeh. Please dinnae forget tha'. I'm sorry I can't write to yeh from here. I'm no' allowed tae have much paper, but I think about you every day, and when I return home, I'll make sure tae spend all the time I can with yeh." Rosie began to cry as she said goodbye.

"I'm so sorry ye're goin' through this. I wish I could fix et," he said, and Erin saw tears in his eyes. They all hugged, and he took Junie out of Peter's arms. "I love yeh, ma wee Junebug. Dinnae forget yer daddy," he said, then laid her in her car seat.

He stood and grabbed Erin, who had managed to stand, then pulled her close. It would be another two weeks before they saw each other, and it was almost too much. "I love yeh, and I dream of yeh all the time. Remember your promise, and... thank you for your love... and for being a great mum and wife."

—

"Elliott!" the guard barked, indicating that he should finish up his goodbyes. He wanted to kiss Erin so badly and thought of doing it anyway, but he'd been warned on the day he'd arrived that if he did, he'd be punished severely and could even lose the privilege of visitors permanently. He sat on the chair and watched his family walking away.

The children were crying as they left the room. Charlie turned to run back to him, but instead, he panicked. "Dad!" he yelled, which made David stand. The officer nodded, and the boy was allowed to give him one more hug.

—

Erin could see both of them shaking and speaking to each other. Finally, David let go, wiped his face with his sleeve, and waved to his family. Charlie then returned, and another officer shut the door behind them.

The waiting room was silent since all the other visitors had gone. From the other side of the door, Erin could just make out the squeaking of rubber boots on the polished concrete floor. It sounded like a basketball game in a school gymnasium, and she knew the officers were leading David and the other inmates back to their cells.

Now that it was over, she felt guilty, wishing she'd been able to stay awake and alert for the visitation. Peter fastened Juniper into her car seat, and they left the building, feeling depressed and sad. Once they were back at their vehicle, Erin opened her car hire app and ordered a car to bring them home.

The prison wasn't too far away, so she figured she'd come back for it the next day. She was so tired, she found herself dozing, falling in and out of sleep until the SUV arrived, and then she slept the whole way home. After apologizing to the driver, she gave him a healthy tip as they all piled out of the vehicle.

"I'm sorry, children, it's because of the disease... that's why I'm like this now. We'll get through it," she said as they made their way into the house.

"Kitty?" she said when they were all inside and the door was shut, then she turned to the children. "I should probably tell you what to do if I have an episode. You don't need to call for an ambulance, as they won't be able to help me. Just find Kitty or... Francie... and... I'll be okay... it will... pass—" she said and felt her airway tighten. "No! Kit—"

The coughing began, and she saw the fear in the children's eyes as they watched her clutch at her throat and fall to the floor. Peter yelled for Kitty and sent Rosie and Dan to find her, then he told Charlie to call Emergency Services for an ambulance.

"But she just said not to!" Charlie said, sounding like he was about to cry, then everything went black.

Erin woke on the sofa in David's office, sore and weak. The lights were low, and she could hear nothing but the occasional sound of a car's tires passing the house on wet pavement. "David?" she said, then remembered that he wouldn't be there. "Peter? Kitty?"

"I'm right 'ere, mum," Kitty said, coming into the room with something in her hand.

"Where are the children? I want to—" she began, but Kitty shushed her gently.

"Never mind that now, mum, they're a'ready back at school," she said and came to kneel beside her. "It's Monday afternoon, and I 'ad a car take 'em back on Sunday."

Erin was gutted. She tried to sit up, but she was too weak. All the muscles in her chest and back ached. "Oh, Kitty, I'm so sorry! I'll pay you back for the fare. They... you shouldn't have had to deal with this... it's not fair to you. Are they... the children alright? They must've been terrified!" she said.

"They were frigh'ened, mum, to be sure, but they'll be a'right. They seen 'at you were breaven again, and—"

"Junie! Oh, God, Junie! But I didn't pump any milk... how did you feed her?"

"Well, I found a formula sample in the fings ya brought home wif ya from 'ospital. I fed her 'at when I couldn't wake ya, then, you fed her mostly... after that. You was leakin' so bad, like, an' Francie said you'd dry up if ya weren't feedin' 'er, regular, like, so I'd come in to wake ya. We'd get 'er into position, and I'd 'old 'er to ya, then I'd wake ya again and change sides. I fig'erd you'd remember doin' 'at, mum."

"No, I don't remember anything except seeing the fear in the children's eyes and poor Peter trying to take charge. Oh! And I left the car at the prison! I'm going to have to pick it up!"

"Come now, I've bought some bone broff for ya ta eat. Francie says I'm ta force it down your froat if ya won't take it. Let's get ya sittin' up a bit, a'right?" she said sweetly and patiently.

"Alright, Kitty, thank you," Erin said, wanting to cry but knowing that it would hurt too much to do it. "Dr. Jill gave me the phone number of a doctor—"

"I have it 'ere for ya, mum. You shou'd ring 'er when we're done," she said, and Erin nodded.

When she was done with her broth, Kitty brought in her cell phone, and she called the number. She was able to set up an appointment for the next day to find a temporary replacement match.

Chapter Eighteen

ERIN YIELDS

Erin sat in the waiting room, weak, shaking, and wanting to vomit. She decided it would be best to hire a car to take her to the clinic so she could drive herself home from the prison afterward.

The nurse called her name, checked her weight and height, then led her to an exam room to get her vitals. When that was done, the woman asked why she was there, even though she'd explained it briefly on the phone when she'd made the appointment. She had to explain the situation again, including that her symptoms had returned.

Tears rolled down her face and the fit, young nurse looked at her with compassion. "Dr. Wilcox will be in shortly, Mrs. Elliott; hang in there."

Erin thought of the stupid poster she'd seen every day at an office she'd worked at many years before. On it was a kitten hanging from a tree limb, with the caption, 'Hang in there.' *Fuck hanging in there and fuck that kitten! I just want David back, and I don't want to be doing this!* she thought miserably. *And fuck the fucking judge too!*

Knowing she was going to start sobbing at any moment, she began pacing but was too tired and weak from the episode to keep that up. When the doctor came in and shook her hand, she cringed, knowing that it must be sweaty and gross.

"Hello, Mrs. Elliott, I'm Helen Wilcox. I see that your match is... not available right now, so you're in need of a replacement," she said kindly.

Erin was so worked up she couldn't speak. All she could do was nod as more tears fell off her chin. The doctor reached over, grabbed a box of tissues from the small desktop, and handed them to her. She took one from the box, blew her nose, and winced in pain as it strained her chest muscles.

"I... don't *want* to find one, I *have* to. Also, I need a *temporary* match, not a replacement—" She broke down then, sobbing and trying to collect herself, but she couldn't. Everything hurt, her whole body, heart, and mind. She wanted to crawl into a hole and die. *This shouldn't be happening.*

"Alright, I understand. I can't say I've followed your husband's case closely, though I do know about it. Seeing that you're married, and on the basis of your disease alone, you should've been allowed conjugal—"

"The... judge wouldn't allow conjugal visits under ANY circumstances," Erin interrupted. "No one can understand why."

The doctor frowned and shook her head. "I think you should try to get the ruling overturned, especially in your circumstance!" she said vehemently, but Erin shook her head.

"We've tried, but something is being held against us or him, though we don't know what it is. All we're told is that conjugal visits aren't done here, that's it. All I know... is that... even though I'd rather die, I need... treatments, and soon. I was hoping I could live with it, but I had a very bad episode on Friday, and now I'm endangering my infant and children's lives... it's... I'm... they're not safe anymore."

"I wish I knew what to do to help you legally, but there is a silver lining. You do have another match, and he lives in London, which is rather miraculous. Most women have only one, or the other one lives too far away to make regular treatments practical," the doctor said.

Erin stood, knowing she was going to be sick and possibly pass out. Seeing her reaction, the doctor took out an emesis bag and handed it to her just in time for her to throw up in it. She leaned against the examination table to keep from falling.

"Alright, dear, let me help you to the chair."

"I just want my husband," Erin whispered and was sick again in the blue bag she was holding. The retching hurt her body horribly, but she wasn't able to stop it.

The doctor rubbed her back and waited for the heaving to stop. "Would you like us to set up a visitation with the man here before you make an appointment?" she asked, and Erin looked at her.

"You do that now? I... I don't know. I don't know what would be worse, knowing who it was, or—Oh, God!" she said, and the heaving started again. "Maybe I can... live with it... for another—"

"Two years?" the doctor said gently. "No, I'm sure you couldn't. There are options now where it isn't necessary to see the person. It's facilitated by medical professionals at a surgery specifically designed for those who don't want to know who is giving them their treatments. It's quite basic and involves a curtain that wraps around an exam table. You can either use a rear-entry position or use the stirrups without ever seeing the person involved," she said.

Erin frowned; that option seemed like the best one, though it was still horrible, no matter how it was done. "I guess... that would be better," she said and sat on the plastic chair next to the exam table.

"You may also choose things such as whether or not he's allowed to talk to you or whether either of you is given each other's first names."

Erin's eyes grew wide. She was quickly becoming overwhelmed and needed to make it stop. "Okay! Stop! This is too much... too real. I... don't care! I just need a treatment. Please make the arrangements and... and… let me know. I... have to... go," she said as panic set in. She stood and felt the whooshing in her head, then saw the familiar stars as darkness covered her eyes.

She woke with a nurse standing over her. "Alright, Mrs. Elliott, let me help you up. Doctor Wilcox had another appointment, so I was sent to help you. Would you like any water?" she asked.

Erin shook her head. "No, I just want to go, thank you," she said.

"A'right then, up we go," she said as Erin got up off the floor. "I have some paperwork for you with the time and date of your first treatment." The nurse looked at the paper and read the date. "Let me see, it's... nine days from now."

Erin couldn't breathe and was glad she hadn't driven herself there. "Could you please help me get a car to pick me up here?" she asked and sat on the chair to unlock her phone and open the car hire app with shaking hands.

"Of course I can," she said sweetly. The nurse typed everything in and hit 'schedule.' "Should be here soon. Now let me help you find a seat in the waiting room."

"Wait! Good night nurse! Contraception! I... I don't have any!" Erin cried out, panicking again.

"A'right, a'right... I'll talk to the doctor, wait here," she said and left the room. Quite a while later, she returned with a syringe. This is called Birconti; it will last for three months and only takes a week to become effective."

She'd heard of the drug but didn't know anything about it. The nurse administered the shot, then, after helping her stand, handed her the paperwork with the appointment information on it.

"You'll have to come back here or go to your usual GP to get your next dose... well, until your original match is available again, unless you don't want to get pregnant, then you should stay on it until you do. Just... don't put it off, or it will stop working," she said delicately.

Erin nodded, and the nurse helped her out to the waiting room. The driver was standing just inside the door; they could tell he'd been waiting for a while, so she assisted her to the car as well.

"Thank you for your help," Erin said. "You've been a Godsend."

—

"It was my pleasure, Mrs. Elliott. Take care of yourself," she said as the driver got in and she had to close the door. That poor woman! Married to David Elliott and being forced to sleep with someone else! *It's not fair; not fair at all!* she thought sadly as she walked back into the surgery.

Erin thanked the driver for waiting and gave him a ten pound tip, then she had him drop her off at the prison. She drove herself home, and as soon as she was through the door, she headed straight upstairs to the nursery, not caring if she woke the baby or not. Lifting the tiny bundle out of the crib, she sat with her in the chair David had bought for them only three months before. She rocked and cried until she felt as though she would die because of the pain she felt in her heart.

Kitty came to the door, then stepped in and knelt before her. "What happened? Didn't fings go well?" she asked gently.

Erin looked at her much-loved and trusted housekeeper and couldn't hold it in. "I... have to—Oh, God, Kitty! I have to start getting treatments from a stranger until David comes home. How am I going to do it? The first one is set for nine days from now!" she said and held little Juniper tightly, kissing her tiny cheek and sobbing.

—

"Treatments meanin' sex, correct?" Kitty asked, wanting to make sure she understood the severity of the situation, and Erin nodded.

"David won't want me back after this!" she said. "I don't know what to do! I don't want to do it, Kitty! That fucking judge! Why wouldn't he allow David and I to—I don't understand it!"

"None of us can, mum, but you'll get frew it... you've got'en frew so many o'ver fings," she said, trying to encourage her employer but more importantly her friend. "Let me take Junie for ya and go 'ave a nice long sleep. I'll come get ya for supper, a'right?"

—

Erin didn't want to let go of her and David's child; she wanted to hold her every minute he was gone, but she was incredibly tired. "Alright." She handed her the sleeping infant and watched as she lay Juniper in her crib, then she took the hand Kitty offered to help her stand. "Thank you," she said and hugged her tightly.

Kitty led her to bed and helped her off with her clothing, tucking her in as though she were a child, then left the room. Erin cried herself to sleep, wishing she could talk to her husband, wishing she could see him, and wishing, most of all, that she could make love to him.

David lay in his cell, thinking about Erin and Juniper, wishing he could do something to help her. He knew she'd have to break down and find someone to give her treatments until he was released, and it made him sick, completely gutted. She'd told him she wouldn't do it the first time she'd visited and only agreed to call her doctor because she was doing so poorly at the last visit.

She was a stubborn woman, but he knew that no matter how much she didn't want to, she'd eventually have to if she didn't want to die, become blind, or lose some of her brain function from lack of oxygen. He'd witnessed two very bad episodes, and he knew they would only get worse.

Sex with another man was hard enough to deal with, but it was the fear that she'd fall in love with the other person, as she'd done with him, that kept him awake at night. *Oh God, please don't let that happen!* he prayed again, as he did every night while he sat in his prison cell.

There wasn't anything he could do, so there he sat every day, praying for Erin, Juniper, and his other children's safety as well as his own. He knew he was a target for sodomite attacks, and so far, he'd avoided them, though he knew it was only because she brought bribes when she came. It was the cigarettes, cigars, and bottles of good whisky that kept the officers close.

He never saw anything she brought, as they divvied it up long before he had a chance to see it. That was most likely the reason he hadn't been given a roommate yet, either. They wanted the gifts to continue, so they accommodated him as best they could, he just hoped it lasted his whole internment.

He couldn't lay on his bed any longer, so he got up, took out one of his precious pieces of paper and his only pencil, and started writing to her. He told her of his love and that he would still love her, no matter what she had to do for her disease. Though he wanted to tell her just what he wanted to do with her, sometimes sexually, he knew that wasn't wise.

Instead, he mentioned the little everyday things he missed, like holding her hand and sitting next to her on the sofa to watch something on the telly. He wrote of wanting to play with his baby daughter, how he longed to hold her, and reminisced about talking to her while Erin was still pregnant. Then he ended it with, '*Please be patient, and know that I love you more than my own life, David x.*'

He put his head down and tried to hold back the tears, knowing she'd not get to read it unless he could keep it safe until her next visit. She wouldn't be back for two weeks, so he knew it would most likely get taken away from him before then. He didn't know who took them, and though he kept them in his pocket or under his mattress, they would inevitably disappear before he could give them to her.

Chapter Nineteen

AN UNEXPECTED VISIT

"Do come in, Mrs. Elliott!" Erin heard Kitty say on Monday after the doorbell had been rung. "I'll find Mrs.... Elliott—"

"Mother? What a nice surprise," Erin said as she came down the stairs and saw her mother-in-law, Annis, standing in the foyer.

"Hello, dear, I hope I'm not interrupting anything?"

"Nope, come in, and we'll have tea," Erin said and glanced at Kitty, who nodded.

"I had business in London and thought I'd stop for a visit. How are you, daughter?"

Erin's cares seemed to overwhelm her at that moment, though the last thing she wanted to do was show such a strong, capable woman, one she admired so much, her weakness. She smiled and shrugged, willing her tears back, at least until Annis was gone. "I'm... alright," she said, though it came out in a whispered croak.

Annis took her hand and smiled sweetly. "Aye, I understand, love." She looked around the room. "Where shall we take our tea?"

Feeling the warmth of the older woman's soft hand was breaking down her resolve, and Erin felt the prick of hot tears come to her eyes. She couldn't speak, so she shrugged. Annis squeezed her hand and started toward the kitchen just as Kitty returned.

"I think tea in the sunroom would be lovely, do you agree?" she said, and Erin nodded, thankful that someone else had made the decision for her.

"Yes, mum, I'll bring it in directly," Kitty said, her voice filled with compassion.

Annis led Erin to the sunroom, and before they sat, she pulled her close and held her without words. Erin lay her head on her husband's mother's shoulder and wrapped her arms around her, weeping. "Ach, ye're a strong woman, Daughter, but I ken yer strength is bein' tested to ets limit. I hope you know I'm here for yeh, whenever yeh need me?"

Erin nodded but didn't let go right away. "Thank you for coming. I'm so glad you're here!" she whispered.

"I'm pleased tae hear et; I've missed you and ma newest granddaughter," she said. "Speaking of her, where's our wee Juniper, then?"

Erin let go of Annis, and they sat before she replied. "She's sleeping. I'd just fed her and put her to bed before you rang the doorbell."

"Well then, is there anywhere you'd like me to take you after tea? Perhaps the salon, or are you in need of any clothing? I think it might be nice for you to get out of the house for a bit, don't you?" Annis said and looked at Kitty, who'd come in carrying a tray with the tea set and a plate of small scones and small dishes filled with raspberry jam and Devonshire cream. She exchanged glances with Annis in a way that seemed a bit conspiratorial to Erin.

"You two are up to something—"

"Never, mum, though I agree 'at you should 'ave a fink about gettin' outta the 'ouse wiv Mrs. Elliott."

Erin knew she must feel strongly about it for her to say something so bold to her employer. "I wouldn't know where to go or what to do," she said. "I guess a haircut would be nice. I haven't had one in years. I could also use a new bra and summer shoes, but that'll take hours! Junie will be up in less than an hour."

"Now, you know I'll care for our Junie, mum," Kitty said, wearing a wide grin.

"Et's settled then," Annis said and took a bite of her scone.

When they were finished with their tea, Kitty returned to take the tray. Annis smiled at her and said, "Kitty, please thank Francie and tell her that her scones rival Millie's, which is a true compliment!"

"Yes, mum, I will," she said.

It was genuine work for Erin to get out of the house. She was exhausted, though she did her best to hide it. Also, having never been to a salon in London, she had to trust Annis to choose one.

After a search on her mobile, Annis discussed what she'd found with her, then made an online reservation and ordered a car to deliver them there. "Thank you, Mother," Erin said as they waited. "I've had so much to do and so many things on my mind that I wasn't even thinking about taking care of myself."

"Aye, I thought as much, and I'm pleased I can help. I'm afraid you've been thrown into a whirlwind; a new home, family, city, country… it would be difficult for anyone, but now that David isn't here, I reckon the difficulty is multiplied."

"Yes, it really is," she said and decided not to add the returning symptoms of the Fertilis Defect to her list.

The car dropped them off at a salon that seemed much more posh than she'd hoped. She felt run down and out of place, especially standing next to Annis, who was always perfectly and impeccably put together. While they waited, Erin flipped through a hairstyle magazine and watched the slender young women leaving the place, looking lovely.

"Erin?" A middle-aged man with a perfect tan, ice-blue frosted waves, and a pencil-lead-thin beard said. She stood, and he eyed her, scanning her full length before he smiled and led her to his chair. "My name is Raphael. And what are we doing for you today?"

"Hello, Raphael," she said and sat in his chair while he took her hair out of the clip she'd tucked it back with, then he touched and fluffed her frizzy, outgrown mop. Embarrassed and blushing, she shrugged. "Can I be honest with you?"

He raised his eyebrows and returned her shrug. "If you'd like."

He seemed a bit impatient, so she tried to stay calm. "As you can see, I've not had my hair cut in a long time…" she slumped a bit in the chair and sighed. "I'm not usually quite this blunt, but I just need to be right now, and I'm sorry for it.

"I know you're used to beautiful young people who know what they want, but I just moved here and… got married to a man with four kids… and just had a baby. My husband was… well, he's not home right now, and I also have the Fertilis Defect. I'm exhausted, and I just want to have a nice time with my new mother-in-law and feel a bit better about myself.

"I really hope you can give me a little compassion and pretend I'm not a middle-aged, overweight… I don't know, blight on your beautiful day." She cast her gaze to the floor in front of her and closed her eyes. In the silence that followed, she heard footsteps and looked up, finding Annis standing next to her.

"Sorry if this is unwelcome, but I saw a style in here that I thought would be flattering on yeh, dear," she said and turned to Raphael, holding out an open book.

"Yes, I agree," the man said, and Annis turned the book toward her.

"What do you think?"

Erin looked at the page and frowned. "I love it, Mother, but… it would take a lot of straightening and product and… work for my hair to do that."

Raphael began to caress his chin thoughtfully, then he smiled and waved his hands as if to dismiss her concerns. "I have the solution, just trust me, okay?" he said.

"Okay," Erin said, smiling at him and Annis in the mirror.

An hour later, her hair was cut and styled perfectly. Raphael had given her detailed instructions on how to use the four styling creams he'd recommended, depending on whether she wanted to straighten it or leave it to dry naturally. Her head felt lighter, and so did her heart. "I love it, thank you so much!" Erin said and handed him a fifty pound tip.

"It was my pleasure, Mrs. Elliott, and please tell your husband we're on his side, a'right?"

"You know who I am? But—"

"I sussed it out. I hope you're feeling a bit better now?"

"I am, I really am," she said and stepped up to the sales counter, where Annis was.

"Thank you, Mrs. Elliott," the cashier said and handed her a receipt.

"Did you… but, Mother, you didn't have to—"

"Et's my treat, Daughter, now let's go, we're burning daylight," she said and touched a strand of Erin's hair. "It's perfect, thank you, young man."

Raphael smiled and seemed to bow slightly. "My pleasure, madam."

They stopped for lunch at Fortnum and Mason, where Annis insisted on paying. She had the chicken, and Erin had the pork. It was a relief to know that at least her hair looked good as she sat in the overpriced, fancy restaurant.

The rest of the day was spent shopping for necessities and trying on far too many shoes. In the window of a stationary shop, Erin saw figurines in the shape of families holding each other. There was one of a mother and son that made her gasp since it looked so much like her and Peter.

"Oh, Annis, look at these," she said. "I'd like to see what else they have. Do you mind if we go in?"

"I don't mind at all."

They were able to find a figurine that looked similar to each of her brood, hugging a mother with dark hair, like hers, and then Annis showed her a catalog with hundreds of choices that could be special ordered. "Oh, this is perfect!" she said. It took a long time, but she managed to create one depicting the whole family, including Juniper and David, and placed her order.

She'd had one of the best days, but Erin was exhausted when the car returned them to the house. It felt like she was sleepwalking as she opened the large, heavy front door and took off her shoes. "Thank you, Mother, I needed a day out, but now I need a nap," she said with a well-timed yawn.

"Yes, I imagine you do, love. I've had a lovely day as well. You go on up tae bed, and I'll say ma farewells to our wee Juniper."

"Thank you for coming to see me; I'm so glad you did. You're always welcome," she said and hugged her mother-in-law tightly.

"Ach, thank you, Daughter, and I'll see yeh next month for the gala."

Erin groaned, remembering when she and David had been invited to the fundraising gala for Thistledown, the treatment center his cousin, Bran, was being held at. He'd been adamant that he wouldn't attend, but Annis had brought up the idea that if he didn't, perhaps Bran would be let out early. Honestly, it didn't make sense to her, but she didn't know how things like that worked there.

Whether it was true or not, the idea had caused David to change his mind, and the tickets had arrived earlier that month. She was *not* looking forward to the event, but it seemed she didn't have much of a choice. "Aye, Mother, see you then." She climbed the stairs, nearly fell into her bed, and was asleep moments after her head hit the pillow.

Chapter Twenty

THE DREADED TREATMENT

Thursday morning came, like any other day, but it was the ninth day after Erin's doctor's appointment, and as the sun rose, the thought of what she had to do filled her with dread. An extra half hour was spent in bed until she finally made herself get up. She showered, got dressed, and did her hair without feeling, glad for the numbness.

The last thing she wanted to do was to feel; she just wanted to roll over, take her medicine, come home, and try to forget about it. Noticing the paperwork from the clinic sitting on the bathroom vanity, she read the appointment sheet to find the exact time and address of the place she was supposed to go to. In a daze, she stepped out of the bathroom, having already forgotten what it said.

Then, like a zombie, she walked into the nursery and fed Junie as if it were a routine instead of something she looked forward to every day. Forty minutes later, and right on time, Kitty came into the room, looking happy. She smiled at her as though it were any other day; like it wasn't the end of the world, and as if her heart hadn't shattered into a thousand bits, ready to be ground into the carpeting.

Kitty took Junie, and Erin sighed. After looking at the time on her phone, she made her way downstairs and ordered a car. Then, she went to the kitchen, hoping for a cup of tea, only to remember it was Francie's day off, so she'd have to get it herself. The electric kettle was already full of water, so she flipped the switch and took a mug out of the ugly concrete cupboard.

After digging a tea bag out of the stainless-steel container they were kept in, she plunked it numbly into the mug that read, 'I heart EDINBURGH' on it and waited for the water to boil. *I don't have time for this!* she thought and flipped the switch on the kettle to stop it. Leaving the mug on the counter, she headed out of the grim, lifeless kitchen Susannah had designed and went to David's office.

She sat on his leather desk chair, spinning aimlessly, smelling his scent and remembering the times they'd spent in there together. From the top desk drawer, she took out one of the alligator tooth keyrings he'd bought in New Orleans when they'd first met and kissed it. *I love you, David!* she thought miserably.

The shadow of a car appeared through the window as it pulled up to the front of the house. Its dark outline landed half on the bare wall and half on the bookshelves she'd spent so many hours staring at over the last two and a half months since David had been taken away. Replacing the key ring in the drawer, she stood, still numb.

It was a habit for Kitty to take Juniper on a short walk in the pram after her breakfast in good weather, and she usually joined her, but not on that day. Kitty was leaving the house when she got to the front door, so Erin grabbed her purse, followed her out, and locked the heavy wooden door behind her. After kissing her darling baby girl, she gave her Eskimo kisses and told Kitty she'd be back soon.

She watched them walk away, then got into the waiting car and tried not to think of anything as they made their way through London to her destination. The driver pulled up to a plain, unremarkable building, and Erin hesitated before handing him a fifty pound note. "Uh, I don't know exactly how long I'll be, but if you could wait for me, I'll pay you for your time," she said, knowing she wouldn't be in a good state after what was going to happen in there, and wouldn't want to wait around for another car.

"Sure fing, love, I've nofin' ta do anaway. Take yer time," he said.

Erin thanked him, got out, and stood staring at the clinic door, desperate to run away. Instead, she climbed the three concrete steps and entered the building. Just inside the door was a sign listing multiple businesses, including a car insurance company and travel agency, of all things.

She located the clinic, then found the door, up two floors in the elevator, then at the end of the hall. Clearly designed to put their patients at ease, the reception/waiting room was cozy, and the young receptionist greeted her kindly as she approached. After telling the woman her name, she was given a clipboard with a stack of paperwork and told to wait until someone came for her. Among the many pages was a form asking for her preferences.

The privacy curtain was a must, and she didn't want either of them to know each other's names. She wasn't sure about whether or not to let her match speak, thinking it might be necessary sometimes, so she allowed it, hoping he wouldn't. They even wanted to know her choice of positions, but that was too overwhelming, so she left it blank.

When she'd filled out as much as she could take, she brought the clipboard up to the desk and returned to her seat. She had just turned off the sound on her phone when a nurse in pale blue scrubs came in and called out her first name, though there wasn't anyone else in the room. Trembling a bit, she stood and tried to smile at her.

"Hello, Erin, I'm Wendy, and I'm going to try to make this as comfortable for you as I can, alright?" she said as she led her to what looked like a small, cozy bedroom.

"Thanks," she whispered.

Wendy turned on the lights as they stepped in and quickly dimmed them since they were quite bright. "Please, take a seat," she said and sat on a small rolling stool that she took from the corner of the room. "I've read your file, so I know why you're here today, and I understand that this must be traumatic for you."

"Just a bit," Erin said ironically.

"I truly sympathize with your situation, and I don't want to rush you, but as fair warning, you'll have to do it eventually, so it may be better to get it over with, so to speak, though it's all in your timing. Now, before we begin the tour, do you have any questions?" Wendy asked with a grin.

Erin sensed she was sincere, and her candor was helpful, which made her feel a tiny bit better. "Okay, umm, will you be watching—us?" For some reason, she had a mental image of being in a room with a two-way mirror while people watched them from above in an elevated room.

Wendy smiled at her and shook her head. "No, we won't be watching. There's a call button next to the bed that you may press if you need help or feel unsafe. I will come in to help you if you or your match hit the button—no one else, only me. Are you okay with that?" she asked.

"Yes, I like that plan." Truthfully, she felt relieved. The last thing she wanted to do was worry about who might come through the door if she needed something. "I... didn't know which... position to choose—Do you have any... I don't know, suggestions?" she asked nervously.

"It's up to you, really, but I reckon laying on your back is technically easier as far as entry goes. The rear entry position can be slightly more awkward and requires more... touching and direction to find the vagina and not have it hurt," Wendy said without the slightest hint of embarrassment.

"Makes sense. Okay, thank you, that helped a lot," Erin said and gave her a weak smile.

"Good, now, allow me to show you around."

They stood, and Erin was shown a small remote control attached to a cord that was plugged into a panel on the wall. It had several buttons; one was a large red oval that said 'CALL' in the center. "I guess that's the button I use to call you?"

"Yes, and that one is for the lights over the bed." She pointed to a slider with a light bulb icon above it. "This one is for sound; you can choose from music, crashing waves, or white noise if you'd rather not hear your match," she said, raising her eyebrows.

Erin swallowed hard and looked at the slider with a speaker icon above it. "Okay, I guess crashing waves?" she said as a question.

Wendy smiled. "That's the one I'd choose, except you must take into account what the sound of water can do."

"Makes you have to pee... right. I guess it's white noise, then," she said and almost laughed. "You're good at your job, Wendy. I feel much more comfortable with you helping me. I don't reckon you'd like to stay and hold my hand during the treatment, would you?"

She was joking, but Wendy smiled, not laughing. "If that's what you need to get through it, I will."

Erin nearly started crying. "Oh, I see, it's very tempting," she said quietly, looking down at the bed.

"Wouldn't be the first time, if I'm honest, though I'm not meant to say that."

Erin smiled but didn't say anything.

"Alright, your match is in another room, so—" Wendy said.

"He's… already here?" Erin interrupted, trembling and wanting to run away.

She must have looked frightened, because Wendy put her hand lightly on Erin's shoulder and looked her in the eyes. "I will be just outside this room if you need me, Erin," she said reassuringly.

"Okay." She started to feel a bit calmer, though a tear slid down her cheek before Erin could wipe it away with her hand. "Better to get it over with," she said, quoting what Wendy had said earlier, and closed her eyes.

"You'll be fine. Now, I'm going to leave the room. Get undressed so that you're comfortable, your slacks and pants must be completely off. When you're ready, sit or lay on the bed, then close the curtain." Wendy pulled open the curtain, which wrapped all the way around the bed, then explained that there was extra fabric added for her legs, showing her how it parted at the proper place so that the man wouldn't have to lift it for the treatment.

"Once it's in place, hit the call button. I will come in with your match and help him if he needs me to. He will most likely be nervous and scared as well, so it may take a few minutes and even a few tries to be successful, so please be patient."

Erin remembered how nervous she and David had been when they'd met. "I understand," she whispered. Wendy left the room, and Erin took a deep breath. *You have to do it! Just rip the band-aid off so you can go home and try to forget about it.*

She took off her bottoms, folded them neatly, and placed them on the small chair next to the door. Then, she got onto the bed and put her feet into the stirrups, feeling utterly exposed and vulnerable. She wished she actually had the guts to ask Wendy to stay and hold her hand, but she couldn't do that.

The white noise could wait, at least at first, but she dimmed the lights a little bit more, just so it wasn't as glaring. Finally, she held her breath and pushed the button. Trying to steady her breathing, she focused on not panicking, especially when she could hear Wendy and the man talking as they approached the door.

"What if—" he began to say, and Wendy cut him off.

"I'll be right outside the room if you need help with anything. There's a call button within your reach if you need it, remember," she said.

Erin wondered where his button was. She hadn't seen one, but her thoughts were interrupted by the door opening. The shadow of Wendy and the man appeared, vague and floating, as the curtain moved with the breeze the opened door made when they walked in.

All she could tell about her match was that he didn't seem to be very tall. Wendy showed him where his call button was and then talked about the opening in the curtain as though she'd already gone over everything with him in the other room. When she asked if he had any questions before she left, Erin's stomach dropped, knowing they'd soon be alone.

"No, I don't, and Thank you for yer help," he said in a Scottish accent that sounded only slightly different from David's.

She was kinda glad he was Scottish because it would make it easier to imagine it was her husband and not some stranger having sex with her. The door opened and closed as Wendy left the room, and Erin swallowed hard, feeling like she might be sick.

"Right," she heard the man say quietly, then he addressed her. "I want you tae know I've… never done this before, and… I dinnae want yeh tae be uncomfortable or, erm, anathin', so… uh, please tell me if yeh need me tae… I dinnae ken, do somethin'… different, or anathin'," he said sweetly.

Erin felt a lot less scared, at least. "Okay, I'm sure it'll be fine," she said and then shook her head, wishing she'd kept her mouth shut. She could see his figure moving on the other side of the curtain as he got undressed, and then, suddenly, she felt him standing between her legs, which made her gasp. "Woah… fuck!"

"I'm sorry—I didn't mean tae startle yeh," he said.

Just get it over with. "It's okay, just, please—I don't mean to sound rude, but please, just… get on with it—" she said, and her voice broke, so she stopped talking. Her breathing got deeper and heavier as she tried not to cry.

"Right," he said.

She could feel him positioning himself in order to enter her, and she held her breath. Then, as soon as he touched her, she felt a powerful energy run through her, which made her whole body tingle with unwanted excitement. He entered her slowly, which was a good thing.

"Oh!" she said and sat up a little as she felt how large he was. Then, as he began to thrust, she had to stop him. "Please," she said, "Please, not so… deep."

"I'm sorry. I'll back off," he said and tried again.

The energy flowing through him was different from the one she shared with David; it was stronger and less comforting, though not unpleasant. After a few misstarts, he found a depth she could handle and started to thrust. Her body began responding to him, though she didn't want it to and tried not to make any noises.

Though she wanted to be silent, it felt so good that she began gasping when she found herself climaxing. "Oh, oh!" She couldn't hold back the exclamation as her body released, and she realized just how much she missed sex. She assumed he'd finish quickly, like David had at first, but he didn't.

Not knowing what to do, she tried to relax and wait for him, but he just kept going, bringing her slowly back to the point of orgasm a second time. This time, he also shuddered and moaned, and she felt his cock pulsing as it released.

Out of breath and panting, she didn't know what to do next. *Is there an etiquette to this?* It had felt so good, but she didn't want to say that; she didn't even want to admit it to herself.

He pulled out and allowed the curtain to fall back into place, then, she watched the man's shadow as he cleaned himself off and put his clothes back on.

"For what et's worth," he said softly, "tha' was… verra, verra nice. Thank you."

Erin didn't know what to say. "Uh, yeah, it was," she ended up saying, and he walked out the door. She tried to go back to being numb, but her mind continued rewinding the memory of it all, playing it back, over and over again. *Holy Moses, now what?*

She was supposed to lie still for as long as possible after a treatment, for everything to soak in, so she lay there, willing her mind to go blank, before eventually realizing that she was imagining what he looked like. After about twenty minutes, there was a knock on the door.

"Erin? Are you alright?" Wendy asked.

Erin didn't know what she was, but it was far from alright, though she couldn't say that. "Yes, just letting everything soak in. I'll be out in a minute or two," she said and sat up.

I don't need this! FUCK! Why couldn't he have been terrible? She got off the exam table, cleaned herself off, got dressed, and then opened the door.

Wendy smiled at her from the hallway. "Not so bad, right?" she said.

"Not so bad," Erin repeated, feeling utterly miserable as she walked into the hall.

"Is something wrong?" Wendy asked.

Erin tried to smile and pretend she was fine, but as soon as she opened her mouth, she started sobbing. Wendy stopped her and waited until she'd calmed down a bit. "What happened? Your match seemed to think everything went well?"

Once she could speak, she began pacing in the narrow hallway. All the doors were open, so she didn't think anyone would hear her. "Oh, it went well—too well. It was too good! I don't want it to be amazing; I want it to be functional only!" she said and started wringing her hands.

"He was sweet and kind and made sure I was comfortable. I don't want him to be amazing either! I want him to do a job so I can live again, but of course, he's gotta be wonderful. God dammit! I… can't start to have feelings for him! I can't and that's it!" she said wildly.

"Calm down, Erin. Who said anything about feelings? It's far too early to talk about—"

"No, it's not!" Erin interrupted. "David and I were saying we were falling in love within three days of meeting! I… I felt the energy with this man too— It wasn't like it is with David, but it was there, and it was… pleasant. I can't… I can't! Fuck!" She was desperate to see her husband, to hold him and kiss him. "I need to go."

She rushed through the waiting room and hurried out of the building, panic gripping her heart. Not seeing the hired car, she scanned the area wildly.

Finally, the vehicle pulled up beside her, so she opened the door and got into the back seat.

She needed to see David, but she wasn't sure whether or not they'd let her do that unannounced. "Excuse me? Uh… do you know… anything about prison?" she asked the driver, and he frowned.

"You fink I've been to prison, do ya?" he said, and she thought he was getting angry.

"No! That's not what I meant. My… husband is, and… I need to see him. It's an emergency," she said and couldn't stop herself from crying. "Do you… think they'd let me have a visitation?"

The driver looked at her in the rearview mirror and sighed. "Naw, I'm afraid they won't love," he said. "Me brover served Her Majesty's pleasure, many years ago, now, and they wouldn't allow anaone, not even 'is mum, ta visit 'im except durin' visitin' hours, and you're ta have your visitin' orders with ya, as well."

Erin nodded, unable to speak. He handed her a small box of tissues, and she blew her nose. "Alright then, please take me home," she said quietly and closed her eyes. Then she pulled her knees in and curled up against the door with her forehead on the window.

—

"Do ya… need a doctor?" The driver asked as it looked like she was in pain.

She shook her head and whispered, "No."

The man could see her whole body shaking and pulled over. "Can I… help ya, ma'am?" he asked, feeling sympathy for her. "What's the emergency, then?"

"Humph. You don't want to hear my troubles," she said between staggered breaths.

"Try me."

"Alright then," she began. He listened as she told him that she had the Fertilis Defect and then explained the whole story about her husband being arrested, which meant that she had to go to another man for treatments and that the guilt was tearing her apart.

"You say ya have to see another bloke for treatments? Well, what are the treatments, then… that ya feel so guilty about 'em?"

The woman shook her head as more tears flowed down her face, landing on her neck. "Sex. I had to have sex with a stranger today. I didn't want to, but it's the only thing that works."

"Cor blimey! 'Ee… didn't hurt ya, did 'ee? B'cause if 'ee did, I'll take you ta hospital—no charge; I'll not abide a man mistreatin' a woman! I'll help ya call the po—" he said, getting angry.

"No, he didn't hurt me, in fact… that's what I feel most guilty about. He was sweet and gentle and… well… I wish he'd been terrible or something instead."

"I see. I reckon 'at would be hard to deal wif, but does your husband know ya had ta do it?"

"Yes, he knows I'll have to… eventually, but he doesn't know it was today."

"Well, if you're after my advice, I'd say you're bet'er off not goin' to 'im in this state. Ee'll be feelin' awful 'bout it, and if he knows you've just done it… well, it'll be quite upsettin' for 'im, don't ya fink? Let him have a few more nights peace b'fore he knows it's happened. Trust me, as a married man, hen, it's bet'er that way."

—

Erin could see his point and nodded. "That makes sense, I guess. Thank you, I needed to hear that," she said.

The man pulled away from the pavement and took her home in silence. The meter read £125.50, but he cleared it before she could pay. "Never mind 'at. Give me twenty quid, and we'll call it even, a'right?"

She took a fifty pound note from her purse and handed it to him, since he'd waited so long for her. "Thank you so much. I'm sorry for the waterworks," she said, but he shook his head.

"No worries, ma'am. Just glad I could make ya feel a bit bet'er. Goodnight."

"Goodnight," she said as she got out a few numbers down from her front door. She was relieved now that much of the burden had been lifted from her shoulders. His advice had helped her more than if she'd been able to see David that day.

—

The driver shook his head as he pulled away from the woman. He'd figured out who she was and wished he could help her somehow. *How could the judge do 'at to 'em?* he thought.

Louis left the clinic in a daze. He'd never felt anything like that before and didn't know how to react. He'd actually felt her orgasm—twice. He'd also felt something else… a kind of pulse… a focus of something extremely powerful coursing through him.

More accurately, he felt it through his cock and through his hand when he'd grabbed her leg for leverage. It had been intoxicating, and it hadn't stopped until he pulled out of her and backed away. They had given him a prescription for something to help him become erect if he thought it would help, but he didn't want to use it, not unless it was a problem. After that appointment, he knew he would never need it.

I wonder what her name is and what she looks like? he thought as he drove home, and then again later that night as he got ready for bed. It was while he lay in his lonely bed, waiting for sleep to come to him, that he wondered, *What would et be like tae kiss her?*

Chapter Twenty-One

THIRD VISITATION—MAY TWENTY-SECOND

The next day, at her third visit with David, Erin was beside herself with anxiety and wanted to vomit. The night before, she'd written to him, pouring her heart out, begging him to forgive her, but she was relatively sure he wouldn't get it. She arrived early and fought her way through the reporters as usual, that time carrying two boxes of fine cigars in the bag, hoping it would be just as effective as anything else she'd brought.

The air was close in the waiting area. She could smell the remnant odor of smoke on the other people waiting to see their loved ones as well as the oniony smell of body odor from the man standing next to her. Keeping her head down, she didn't make eye contact with anyone.

It was none of their business who she was visiting or whether or not she was 'Erin Elliott,' so she waited in silence until the officer opened the visitor's room doors and allowed them to enter. Scanning the inmates, it took a while before she found David, sitting at a table on the far side of the room.

All the emotions she'd felt after her recent treatment washed over her, and she thought she'd collapse with the weight of the guilt she felt once more. She tried to keep it together as she walked toward him, and he stood when she approached.

The energy of their connection was so strong, and she couldn't take it any longer. She wrapped her arms around her husband, knowing they weren't allowed to hug for too long, but she held him and smelled him. He smelled like an institution, but she could almost smell his scent and didn't care; it was him, her true love, her soul mate.

"I'm sorry! I won't do it again. I—I'm sorry. Please keep loving me! I won't ever do it again, I swear!" she said and started bawling, sobs racking her body as she held onto him, needing his touch.

—

He didn't need to ask what she'd done; he already knew it, and his heart felt like it was breaking. "Erin, ma love, yeh must do et again if yeh wanna keep yerself healthy and able tae survive this. Yeh ken et as well as I do, and yeh also ken I'll love you forever; we're an ever fix-ed mark, remember?"

"Look at me," he said, feeling himself losing it as well, and lifted her chin. "Ach, yeh look bonnie. Yer hair looks verra nice! I've missed yeh, darling!"

—

"I didn't want to do it, David, but I had a really bad episode the day we last visited you, and I had to. The children witnessed it, and Kitty helped me through it, though I was unconscious by then. Kitty said that from what she could get out of Peter, it lasted well over a minute.

"I was out for two whole days, and I was scared, but I didn't want to, I swear it! I love you and don't want to do it again. Please forbid me! Please tell me not to!" she begged, fully aware she was making a scene but also knowing that would be the only thing to keep her away.

"Ach, I can't do that! I want to, believe me, ma heart's burnin' up tae think of et, but I dinnae want you tae stop breathin' long enough that yeh... die because of ma selfishness. I couldn't live with that," he said gently.

Erin nodded, but she was beside herself. "I'm afraid!" she said, her eyes wild. "I'm... terrified! I... felt... the energy with him, too. It was different than ours, but... and I don't want to feel anything... I want to be numb! David... I'm so scared! Please... you have to... you have to forbid it!" She was panic-stricken with desperation, wanting him to tell her not to go back.

He wrapped his arms around her again and didn't speak for a long time.

"Elliott!" one of the officers warned, and they had to let go.

"I can't... say et. I... won't say et. I love yeh so verra much, ma darling. You must continue the treatments," he said at last and turned his head when she tried to kiss him. "I'm not allowed tae kiss yeh, ma love, and et's the hardest thing tae do right now, but if I ever want to be able tae hold yeh again whilst I'm here, I must obey my rules."

Erin had seen several other inmates kiss their wives and sweethearts, but they couldn't, and she didn't understand. "Another rule that only you have to follow? That's ridiculous, don't I bring—"

"Shhh, darling, I reckon et's the price I have tae pay for special protection. I dinnae ken, but I was told explicitly that I'm not allowed."

Erin nodded, dropping her head. There was more silence as they both sat, facing each other. "How is everyone? Our bairns? Our Junie?" he asked, unable to hide the pain in his voice.

"They're all doing well. I think Charlie grew two inches since his last Exeat weekend; Dan's gonna have a helluva time catching up. Peter looks and acts more mature every time I see him, and, actually, so does Rosie. They've been so sweet and helpful to me. I love them so much, David, though I always feel worn out when they leave.

"Our Junie is the sunshine of my life; she's growing every minute! I think she's already started teething. She tries to bite down sometimes when she's nursing and drools constantly. She makes the most beautiful sounds though, little noises that tear at my heart and make me miss you terribly," she said and put her hands over her eyes.

—

David's heart was breaking. He wanted to scream out of frustration and anger at the injustice of it all. He watched his wife sitting before him in so much pain and having such a hard time coping, and he wanted to kill that judge.

His prison sentence was bad enough, but to punish her as well was unthinkable. She was the one Clive Dawson had assaulted; she should be getting special treatment, not having to stretch herself as emotionally and physically thin as she was, but there was nothing to be done about it.

"I… wrote to yeh. Did you—" he began but didn't finish. He knew she wouldn't have received them, as his letters were always taken before he could put his address on them, let alone find a stamp.

"You did?" she said, tears rolling down her face. "I haven't gotten anything yet. I also wrote to you. Did you get mine?"

He shook his head and closed his eyes, wanting to yell and make a fuss, but he knew that would only get him beaten up. He wasn't allowed to question anything; he had to take whatever he was given and shut up about the things he wasn't.

"How are you feeling, darling? I… mean… do yeh think et'll help yeh?" he asked.

—

"What?" she said. "Oh, the treatments… I don't know." If she were honest, she'd say that even though it had only been twenty-four hours, she did feel a little better. She had a bit more physical energy, but emotionally, she was at her lowest, so they almost canceled each other out. "Maybe."

"As long as et's… worth it. If et's working, then yeh must continue."

She nodded and sat silently for a while, trying to order her thoughts. "Half-term break begins tomorrow, then Rosie turns ten at the end of next week. I don't know what kind of party to give her or… if I'll even have the energy to come up with anything. I feel so bad, David! I should be there for them, doing things like birthday parties. Ten is a big step… double digits!"

"Ma wee girl is nearly ten already. I've missed everathin', Erin! Please kiss her for me and tell her I love her. Tell her I'll be thinkin' of her on—" he hesitated, then flushed, clearly ashamed that he didn't know which day it was.

"On Thursday, darling, May twenty-eighth. I'll tell her… that is if she's not terrified of me," she said, and he frowned at her.

"I'm not following—"

"They watched me have an episode without anyone else there to help. They couldn't find Kitty right away, and I saw the terror on their faces, David. They're going to be timid and worried, just like you were after you witnessed one. I didn't even get to talk to them before they left for school since I was still out of it."

"They'll be—" he began, but Erin felt a surge of adrenaline hit her.

"No! I have to snap out of this fog! I have to do something for our daughter's birthday! Wait, Peter's birthday is the week after hers, isn't it? I'll get Kitty to help me. I don't know if they have any friends in London, but I'll order a cake, or ask Francie... yes! Oh, and I'll get balloons and hats, and... I hate clowns, so… ooh, maybe a really good magician or a puppy! Yeah—" she said excitedly.

—

"Woah! I dinnae think a puppy's a good idea, darling," he cut her off, staggered at the sudden change in her.

"Okay then, no puppy. What about a cat?" she said and laughed, light and happy.

His heart both melted and burned at the same time, glad she was feeling excited and had a bit of energy again, but also gutted that he wouldn't be there for the party she was talking about. He also knew that her burst of energy was partly due to the treatment she'd gotten from some other bloke finally kicking in.

"Dinnae buy them a cat, either, or ye'll be the one takin' care of et whilst they're at school," he began with a laugh. "And dinnae think I'll be takin' up… the… slack," he said without thinking it through, and all the lightness faded back to grey. The excitement in the air fell to the cold, bland, concrete floor of the visitor's room and shattered.

"Five minutes," one of the officers said.

Erin's eyes grew wide as she stared at him. "I can't... I don't want to do it again! Please! Please forbid me! I'll obey you if you do, David, please!" she implored him once more.

David stood and held her, trying to burn and etch the feeling of her body against him into his memory as vividly as possible. He let her go and put his hands on her face, looking into her wild, half-mad eyes, then shook his head gently.

"I can't do et. Oh, God, Erin, I can't say et," he said, the words tasting like bile coming out of his mouth. No matter how much he wanted to do it, he knew he had to be the strong one at that moment. "I love yeh more than ma own life, darling. Please be patient and keep lovin' me."

"David!" she said, clearly panicking that their time was up. "I love you so much! Please—" she said.

"Kiss her and make it quick!" the guard said gruffly.

David pressed his lips to hers, and it was as if they melted together. He wanted to keep her, to smuggle her into his room and keep her there, all to himself. The guard tapped his baton against the table, and he knew it was the signal telling him to stop.

"Dinnae worry, Erin. I love yeh, and I always will," he said as a guard came up to her, ready to lead her to the door.

"I love you too, always," she said, and he stood, watching her walk away. He glimpsed her mouth the words, 'thank you,' to the guard who'd allowed the kiss, and he gave the slightest of nods in her direction.

Earlier that morning, David had woken up drenched with sweat because of a nightmare. "No!" he'd cried as he was ripped out of the dream by the morning bell. He'd gotten dressed and tried to force it out of his mind, but the more he pushed, the more vivid it became.

In the dream, he could see Erin's face smiling at him. She was holding their baby and had just handed her to him when his perspective changed. He then watched as another man took Junie, bouncing her on his knee and speaking softly to her. Erin leaned in and kissed the stranger, still smiling, looking so happy and carefree.

He'd fought back the tears and anxiety all day until nearly two o'clock when the officers came to get the inmates who had visitors. When he saw Erin enter the room, muttering to herself and wringing her hands, he knew what had happened. He was torn to shreds on the inside, both at what it meant for him and, even more, from how he could tell she was dealing with it.

He could see she was falling apart, beside herself, and grieving for him as well. Then, as she begged him to forbid her to go back, he could hardly stand it, knowing it was because she'd enjoyed the treatment, and the guilt was eating her alive. Miraculously, he'd managed to hold himself together, faking a calmness that would've earned him a BAFTA.

The feel of her in his arms was glorious; he could smell her hair and wanted with his whole being to kiss her, so when the guard told him he could, he wasn't about to waste any time. Her lips on his were like a healing balm, like a magic potion, giving him a bit more sanity and patience to wait out his sentence.

That evening, as he lay on his bed, the dam broke, and he cried, begging God to help him cope and asking Him to keep other men away from his family.

Chapter Twenty-Two

HALF-TERM ALREADY

Thankfully, Erin's energy was only improving because of the treatment, so picking the children up in Dorset again on Saturday wasn't as difficult as before. She was looking forward to spending time with them and listened to CDs of some of her favorite music on the way down, which made the time fly. The party would be on Saturday, so she and Kitty had made simple invitations for Peter and Rosie to give to their friends.

She decided to skip the conservatory and met the children in their quarters. Peter was talking to a good-looking boy as she walked in, and when introduced, she learned his name was Max. When she gave Peter the invite, he smiled and handed it directly to his friend.

Peter said he'd meet her at the SUV, so she left to find his sister. When she got to Rosie's room, she saw her daughter sitting on a bed next to a young girl. After a warm greeting, Rosie introduced her friend as Cassie, and she was given the invitation in a similar manner to Max.

Cassie thanked her, and the girls giggled, clearly excited about seeing each other later in the week. After the girls hugged and said goodbye, Rosie followed Erin to retrieve Dan and Charlie. The boys were waiting for her, so they all headed to the parking lot.

Erin felt alive and free again, and though she knew it wouldn't last very long, she was determined to make the most of the energy while she had it. On the way home, they listened to music and sang along at the tops of their voices without a care in the world. They were sharing unity and love together without fear of judgment or keeping up some pretense of public image.

It was pure joy, and all the resentment of having to drive such a great distance to pick them up so often faded. She hadn't even realized she was feeling that way until it lifted, and she began to realize what a gift it was for her and them. It was a time to make memories and bond, and she was grateful beyond comprehension.

"So, I had a few ideas about our skits," Erin said when they got home. "I thought maybe we could work on them this week. What do you think?"

"Yes, I'd like that!" Charlie said as Rosie bounced on her heels in excitement.

"Sounds like fun," Peter said, and Dan just shrugged, though he was smiling.

"Do you have any ideas for what to do together?" she asked.

Rosie looked at Charlie and gently nudged his arm. "Go on and say it," she said, but he seemed hesitant.

"What is it?" she asked, wondering what could be so intimidating that he wouldn't say what it was. He looked at Dan, then back at Rosie, and she figured it out. "Okay, I see. Dan?"

The boy had clearly not been really listening and turned to her when he heard his name. "Huh?" he said, his eyes wide as if he thought he was in trouble for something. "What'd I do now?"

Erin laughed gently and touched his face. "You haven't done anything… yet," she said cryptically, which made his eyebrows go from high on his forehead to down in a heavy frown, which made her laugh even harder. "Oh, Dan, you're so funny. What I need from you is to be kind and not tease… take the piss out of your brother for what he's going to suggest, okay? Do you think you can do that for me? If not, I'd like you to leave the room."

Confusion made his face contort again as he seemed to be computing the information he'd received. Suddenly, his face lit up in a smile as he went to his brother and put his arm around his shoulder. "I can't be bothered about what *he* wants to do, if I'm honest, but I'll tell you what I'd like to do."

Everyone looked at him, knowing he could say anything. "And what's that?" she asked, having a hard time holding in her amusement.

"I'd like to make Francie pop a whole bag of popcorn, cover it in butter… or even better, make half of it into toffee popcorn. I'd like to drink all the fizzy drinks I can do until everything I say comes out as a belch, then I'd like to watch every… *quality* film we have in the media room."

"Wow, Dan, some of that sounds like fun. Perhaps we can *ask* Francie to make some popcorn, and I'm not sure what you'd consider a *quality* film, but if there's one we can all agree on, I'd really like that. Now—"

"Right, well, if it's all the same to you, I need a wee," he said, then left the room.

"Well, there really is never a dull moment with him, is there? At least it was an amusing moment this time," Erin said. "Now, Charlie, what was your idea?"

"Err, well, I thought we could do up the nursery. It's a bit boring, innit?"

Erin raised her eyebrows, surprised at the suggestion. With everything going on, the nursery had taken a back seat regarding things to do. "That's a really great idea! I'd love to hear what you'd like to do in there. Rosie… Peter, I'd love your input as well. I've ordered canvas prints of some recent photos; perhaps we can find more to put in there."

Charlie's face was beaming, and Rosie giggled excitedly. Peter smiled and shrugged one shoulder. "I reckon that project isn't for me, but I'm sure you'll do a brilliant job," he said, then headed upstairs to his room.

"Alright then, there's no time like the present, right? Now, where to start?"

The trio poured over websites and decided to spend the next day shopping.

Sunday was spent shopping with Charlie and Rosie, and though they offered to allow Dan and Peter to join them, they declined. At least a dozen baby emporiums and department stores later, a corner of the nursery was piled up with boxes and bags filled with their treasures, and Erin was shopped out. She could tell that the treatment was already starting to wear off, so she was determined to finish the project as soon as possible, knowing she wouldn't have the energy by the end of the week.

After supper, Francie made toffee popcorn, which Erin learned was the same as caramel corn, and they all headed to the media room. It turned out that Dan's idea of a *quality* film was the exact opposite of what everyone else thought, so there were some strong words when it came to choosing one. In the end, they managed to come to a compromise.

Halfway through the movie, Erin fell asleep and awoke to Peter touching her shoulder. "Wake up, Mum, it's over," he said, bestowing David's smile on her.

She'd been dreaming about the first time they'd met in New Orleans and, truthfully, would rather have stayed in it instead of waking. "Oh, right, sorry," she said and accepted his hand up. She felt a bit dazed and wanted to go straight to bed, though she knew that luxury wouldn't be afforded to her.

Once the children were put to bed, read to, and tucked in, Erin went through the routine of feeding Juniper before dragging herself to her room. As she lay holding his pillow, she opened her phone's photo gallery and tried not to cry as she swiped through the pictures of David and her new family, smiling and happy.

Part of her was starting to think that the whole thing, being married to David Elliott and having had his baby, was imagined. That one day, her previous nightmare would come true, and she'd wake up with Todd standing over her, telling her she was delusional after all. Scrolling through her photos helped ease her anxiety and fall asleep a bit more peacefully.

On Monday, Erin and the children decided to work on their skits. They had come up with quite a few really good ones she knew David would love. She wished she had enough energy to sew more costumes for them but was well aware of her limitations.

Peter found a snake bracelet meant to go with a Cleopatra costume and a sleeveless white t-shirt that he paired with jeans and white sneakers. He wet his hair and slicked it back, then sang "Crazy Little Thing Called Love," by Queen.

Erin promised to order him a fake mustache and a black studded cat collar to complete the Freddy Mercury ensemble.

One of the best was where Charlie played a ventriloquist and Dan played his dummy. They had a bit to work on with timing, but even as it was, everyone was rolling on the floor, laughing so hard it hurt. Dan's face was so expressive, and as soon as Charlie would look away, he'd roll his eyes or pull a face that was truly hilarious.

On Tuesday morning, with the help of Peter's height, Erin, Charlie, and Rosie began decorating the nursery by putting up pale green wallpaper with a pattern of light blue stripes and scattered bunches of old-fashioned flowers wrapped in gauze and a pink ribbon. Peter and Erin scrubbed the top half while Charlie and Rosie scrubbed the bottom half of the walls, then they watched a YouTube video before having to go to the hardware store for more supplies.

Eventually, they got everything measured up and leveled out. It took all morning, but working as a team, they finished two walls just before lunch and decided that would be enough. After lunch, Peter left them to it, and they hung the coordinating drapes, then they took turns pounding little nails into the walls for pictures and art.

Finally, since they couldn't find an electric drill and thus couldn't put up the little hooks and shelves, they removed the bedding and changing table pad and replaced them with the ones they'd bought. The room was lovely, and as they stood back to admire it, Erin turned on the new, small revolving lamp, the shade having holes in it shaped like clouds that danced around the walls.

After supper, they invited the whole family, including Kitty and Francie, to have a look-see, and it was a great hit. Francie had to get back to the kitchen, but everyone else sat in the nursery and played with Juniper until bedtime. She smiled and babbled and bounced herself in her bouncy chair, flailing her arms and legs.

It was one of the most bittersweet times in her life. She recorded it on her phone with photos and videos, but her heart ached that David wasn't there to experience it with them. At one point, while Daniel was holding her, Juniper latched onto his cheek like a lamprey for at least two minutes. Erin laughed until she cried and very nearly peed herself.

That night, she wrote David a letter, telling him about their wonderful day, crying through the whole thing. Tears blurred her eyes and splashed onto the paper until she had to stop because she couldn't see to write anymore. She addressed it, stamped it, and set it next to the door, ready to be sent in the post the next day.

Wednesday afternoon, she received the canvas prints, which turned out beautifully. With the children's help, she hung them around the house, mainly in her room and the nursery. Then, the family poured over all the pictures Erin could find on her phone, on David's laptop, and in a few albums and framed photos she found in his office.

After ordering far too many prints, she showed them all the paintings and art the children had sent David from school over the years, which she'd found in his office. They laughed at the primitive nature of most of them and recounted their memories from when they'd made them. She asked them to write out, or dictate to her, short descriptions, ages, and memories for each piece, then ordered mats and frames for them, planning to paste the papers onto the back of each.

Thursday was Rosie's tenth birthday, and though they would be having a party on Saturday, Francie made her a special dessert, and they sang "Happy Birthday" to her. After supper, she got to choose a movie, and again, Erin fell asleep halfway through it. The treatment was noticeably wearing off, and she just hoped she'd be able to hang on to a bit of energy until Saturday night.

Chapter Twenty-Three

A TWENTY-SEVENTH BIRTHDAY PARTY

Erin knew planning two birthday parties, one each for Rosie and Peter, was out of the question, so she'd decided to throw a joint party and add the two ages together, which equaled twenty-seven. She'd asked Kitty to help her plan it, and Francie was asked to make a cake, which she knew would be the best in London.

Peter's friend, Max Neely, and Rosie's friend, Cassie Bateman, responded and would be staying overnight. She presumed their guests would be used to elaborate parties, which she wasn't prepared for, so she was determined to make up for it by planning something fun and engaging.

After their guests arrived, Erin led them into the sitting room, where she and Kitty had hung streamers and colorful balloons, and Junie was placed in her bouncy chair. When she was a kid, Erin's best friend, Mindy, had a party where her mother had taken a game of 'BINGO' and changed the letters to 'MINDY.' Erin decided to do the same and changed theirs to 'ROSIE' since 'PETER' had two 'Es' in it.

She was amazed at how excited everyone was, even the older boys, with the simple game. They played for over an hour, winning small prizes when one of them would yell, "BINGO... I mean, ROSIE," and laugh, sometimes hysterically.

Rosie won a small rubber unicorn that went on the end of a charging cord to keep it from fraying. Cassie chose a black candle shaped like a skull and crossbones that Erin had thought one of the boys would choose. Dan won a dog-shaped cord protector, and Charlie and Peter won round, metal-rimmed sunglasses; Charlie's was black and Peter's brown.

The only prize left was a face mask cream that looked like marshmallow fluff. Max was a good sport about winning it, and before long, the kids began putting it on themselves, even the boys. Erin took dozens of photos of them wearing pale pink fluff on their faces and wondered how she'd get it off the sunglasses Peter decided to put on while wearing the goop.

They were all sent upstairs to wash it off while Erin and Kitty put the game away. "I fink 'at were a perfect game, mum," Kitty said, still laughing at the sight of them.

"Who knew! I hope they like the rest of the activities as much," Erin said.

"I reckon they will."

The children came back downstairs, laughing and talking, and were led into the kitchen, where there were seven stations similar to *The Great British Bake Off.* Francie made them roll up their sleeves and put on frilly, flowery aprons, which the boys laughed about and the girls loved.

They were made to wash their hands, and then Francie stood before them to teach them how to make bread. Erin was certain more flour ended up on the floor and tables than in the loaves; however, at the end of the lesson, after a thirty-minute intermission to allow the dough to rise, each of them had mixed, kneaded, and formed their own small loaf of bread.

The plan was that Francie would bake them, so they'd be ready to eat at supper. Surprisingly, they all asked to be allowed to bake it themselves, so they were told to come back in forty minutes, giving each loaf a second rise.

Erin thought the gift opening would last about that long, so everyone returned to the sitting room and sat on the floor near the gift table. Rosie went first and opened a plush robe with a hood that looked like a unicorn head. It had a silver horn and purple mane that ran almost all the way down the back, and the ties had little black hooves at each end.

Rosie squealed with joy over it and wore it for the entire gift opening. "Thank you, Mummy! I love it," she said after giving her a hug.

Peter's turn was next. He opened an instant print digital camera that printed on sticky paper so he could put them up wherever he wanted. He took a selfie with Erin, one with Max, and finally a group photo. "It's really cool,

Mum, thanks!" he said, and she was glad she'd thought to get several refills of the paper since he was going crazy taking photos of everything.

They opened the gifts from their friends next. Rosie got a magnetic dart board and a diary with a lock and key from Cassie. Peter got a fancy drone from Max that must have cost a pretty penny.

The next two gifts from Erin were meant to be opened at the same time. They each got a lamp of the moon; Peter's was black, and Rosie's was cream-colored. They were incredibly detailed, and Rosie begged Erin to turn off the lights so she could see hers in the dark.

It glowed beautifully, revealing all the craters and features of the moon, while Peter's looked quite different, like a negative. The light areas were dark, and the dark light. He and Max were enthralled with it, turning the globe around and around, examining it carefully.

They each got a clock with no numbers on it, where Erin had written things like, 'Wakey, wakey eggs and bakey,' at seven o'clock; 'Ring your mum,' at six, and 'Time for bed,' at nine, etc., which they really liked as well.

Not wanting the twins to feel left out, she decided to give all her children the figurines she'd found while shopping with Annis. She wasn't sure how much Peter would like his, as it was a bit cheesy and sentimental, but she couldn't resist. To keep it a surprise, she had them open their gifts at the same time, on the count of three.

Rosie's was a mother and daughter that looked very much like her and Erin. A small card inside read: 'I'm so blessed that you're my baby girl. Love, Erin.' The young girl sat staring at it, while her brothers examined theirs.

Charlie held his and smiled at her tenderly. His card read: 'I'm so thankful to have you as a son. Love Erin.' Dan frowned when he realized it wasn't a toy, until he noticed that the boy on his looked like him, too. His card read: 'You are so special to me, and I'm chuffed to be your new mum. Love Erin.'

When Peter opened his, he sat examining the small statue, turning it around in his hands. His card read: 'I'm so proud of you. You're a fine young man, and I'm blessed to bits that you're my son. Love Erin.'

"I know it's a bit girly, Peter, but it just looked so much like us that—" Erin began, but she didn't get to finish. Peter took a deep breath, let it out, and went to her, holding her tightly, and then Rosie and her brothers joined him. "Oh my! I take that to mean you like them, then?" she said.

Charlie hugged her for a long time, and Dan gave her a quick squeeze, then a grin, showing off his dimples. "It's crackin', Mum! Thanks!" he said.

"Yeah, thanks, Mum, I truly like it," Charlie said before they returned to their seats.

"You're welcome," she said and could feel her neck was wet where Peter's face was buried.

Rosie wasn't as subtle and was crying with her head on Erin's knee. "Thank you, Mummy! It's... perfect! I love it so much! This has already been the *best* birthday of my *entire* life!" she said passionately.

Peter wasn't ready to let go yet, and Erin didn't want him to be embarrassed in front of his friend, so she took action. "Will you help me in the kitchen for a minute, Peter?"

He nodded, and she led him out of the room so he could express himself privately. Instead of the kitchen, she took him to his father's study and waited for him to speak. "I'm sorry for behaving like a baby," he said and hugged her again.

"You're not behaving like a baby, darling; what is it?"

"I agree with Rosie. This has been the *best* day, Erin, I mean, Mum. Our mother wasn't one for celebrating us *or* our birthdays. This statue means a lot to me, and I'm also blessed that you're my mum now. I... well, I love you a lot. Thank you for this party... and knowing I didn't want Max to see me crying and trying to cover for me."

"I love you too, my sweet boy, and you're welcome." He took another deep breath and blew it out. "Now, wipe your handsome face, and let's check on your bread," she said. Peter smiled David's smile at her and took a tissue from the box on the desk. He blew his nose, then they walked out of the room together.

Francie had come to get the others only a few minutes earlier, so when they entered the kitchen, there was a lot going on. They each put their loaves on a large baking stone, still on the brown parchment paper they'd allowed them to rise on. Their names were written on the paper so there'd be no confusion. Peter was the last to add his, and then it was time to wait.

Erin had thought of another silly game for them. She called it, 'Pin the Tail on Barbie's Horse.' She'd found a small poster of Barbie riding her horse named Dixie, so she made several tails out of curling ribbon. The poster was hung on the wall with mounting putty, and she used double-sided tape for the tails.

One of the children was blindfolded, spun in place, and was then meant to stick the tail onto the horse. The one that landed closest to the tail on the poster won. The boys were really good sports about playing what Erin thought of as a little girl's game, but they seemed to have just as much fun as Rosie and Cassie.

Peter's tail landed on Barbie's stomach, Rosie's on Dixie's hind leg, Dan's was stuck to the horse's eye, and Charlie's looked like it was riding in the saddle behind Barbie. Max ended up with his where Dixie's genitalia would've been, and Erin figured he'd been peeking. Charlie's tail was the closest, so he won a full-sized inflatable guitar, which seemed to be the one they all liked best, though Erin had to convince him to wait until later to blow it up.

The bread was finished baking just after they were through with the game, so they returned to the kitchen. Francie allowed them each to use a pizza peel to slide under their loaf and then set it onto a cooling rack. The house smelled amazing, and everyone's mouths were watering, wanting to rip into the little balls of yeasty goodness.

Erin took photos of each loaf and wished there was a way to record smells so she'd be able to revisit the atmosphere in the house just then. Finally, Francie herded everyone out of the kitchen and had them sit at the long dining room table, while Kitty started serving the meal.

They had roast beef, gravy, new potatoes, and roasted broccoli with garlic and parmesan cheese. Instead of Yorkshire pudding, they spread butter on their own homemade bread. Erin was given Francie's demonstration loaf and was thankful, since it was delicious.

After supper, Kitty brought out the cake, which even Erin hadn't been allowed to see beforehand. Everyone was speechless, struck dumb by the impossibly cool and incredibly beautiful cake Francie had made for them. Erin had imagined she'd make a half-and-half cake, teen boy stuff on one side and tween girl stuff on the other, but it was so much more.

It wasn't a large cake, though it was three layers high. The bottom layer was like something out of Hobbiton, with four different colored round doors, each bearing a plaque with one sibling's name on it, small round windows with transparent caramel window glass, and little picket fences with flowers poking through them.

There were hyacinths, foxglove, hydrangeas, lilacs, and hollyhocks growing lush out of crushed chocolate wafer cookie dirt. Birds, bunny rabbits, foxes, bees, butterflies, and kittens played and peeked around beautiful little flowerpots, wee hedges, and climbing vines in the garden as well.

The second tier had a picket fence all the way around it, with ivy and morning glory climbing it. There was a homemade seed packet with daisies on it that read, '*Elliott Seeds*' and a small plaque that read, '*Happy 10th Birthday, Rosie,*' which was nestled in a rose bush covered with pink flowers.

The topmost layer was shaped and painted like a galvanized water can surrounded by moss that was climbing the walls of the can. A spray of roses, peonies, lily of the valley, bleeding heart, ivy, and sweet potato vine burst forth from the hole in the top. The side of the can read, '*Happy 17th Birthday, Peter.*'

It was quite literally a work of art, and no one wanted to cut it. Erin took photos and videos of it alone and with the children. Kitty held out a few slender, tall sticks and pushed them into the cake, making everyone gasp. Then she struck a long fireplace match and lit the sparklers, making it rain down stars and fireflies. Erin took more video and then turned out the lights. It was magical as they sang "Happy Birthday."

When the sparklers went out, Erin turned the lights back on and saw that Rosie was crying. The young girl ran out of the room, and Erin was worried until they heard a protesting Scottish woman being forced to join them. "Are there more sparklers, Kitty?" Rosie asked.

"Yes, but—" Kitty began.

"Please do it again! Francie needs to see it, too!" she said, sniffling.

Kitty left the room, and everyone began talking at once, telling the cook how brilliant the cake was. When Kitty came back, she took the used-up sticks out and replaced them with new ones. She lit them, and once again, it was magical.

Erin turned out the lights, and the lightning bugs returned, illuminating bits and pieces for just a second before they were replaced by other ones. "My dear Francie," she said, "This cake is the most beautiful, imaginative, delightful thing I've ever seen. It's an absolutely jaw-dropping, amazingly perfect cake. You are the birthday hero!"

She started singing "For She's a Jolly Good Fellow…" and everyone joined in, applauding at the end. "There's only one problem," she continued. Francie, who had been smiling and blushing, suddenly looked scandalized.

"I can't cut it! Can you?" Erin asked Peter, and he shook his head. She asked everyone in the room and then handed Francie the knife and cake server. The cook smiled and began dishing out perfect wedges onto the family's good china dessert plates.

The bottom tier was chocolate cake with a layer of whipped cream and fresh strawberries. The second was marble cake with whipped cream and raspberry filling, and the watering can was mocha cake with coffee-flavored whipped cream that had little bits of white chocolate in it.

"Oh, how I wish your dad was here!" Erin said suddenly and had to turn away to hide her tears. All four of her children went to her and hugged her. "Good night nurse, Peter, you look so much like him. It brings me joy and breaks my heart every time I see you. I'm sorry, I don't want to ruin your party, but it just hit me how much he'd have loved this."

"Mrs. Erin, mum," Francie said, and Erin turned to her. "Ah'll be savin' half of each layer in the deep freeze, so et'll be here when our Mr. Elliott returns. Ah'll be sure tae wrap et up well and box et, so et willnae be ruined. And, so help me, if et does become freezer burned, ah'll make yeh another one, grander than this, a'right?"

"Thank you, Francie, I love you!" Erin said and gave her a hug, though she didn't seem too comfortable with it.

"Ach, and I care deeply for yeh, as well. Now eat yer cake," Francie said, only smiling for a split second before she was all business again.

Chapter Twenty-Four

SITES OF LONDON

"Alright, people, we need to get ready to go," Erin said when everyone was finished eating their cake. She was tired and needed to feed Juniper, but she had to get them ready first. I'm gonna feed the baby, and then we have an adventure to go on, so please take your things to your rooms and be ready to go in... forty minutes. Peter, please ask Kitty to come get me since I might fall asleep, okay?"

The young man smiled at her and went to find Kitty straight away as Erin carried a fussy Junie upstairs. She managed to stay awake while feeding her on the first side but fell asleep for most of the second. There was a knock on the door, and Kitty appeared.

"It's time ta wake up now, mum. The children and the limousine are waitin'."

"Oh dear, Kitty, I'm not sure this was a good idea. I'm knackered!" Erin said and handed the sleeping baby to her. "I'm gonna need some strong coffee!"

"Francie's 'fought of 'at. She's prepared a cup for ya a'ready, mum."

"What would I do without you two? Wait, don't answer that, I don't want to know! Thank you!" she said, then got herself together and went downstairs. The children were looking out the windows at the stretch limousine idling in front of the house. Rosie came to her and handed her a travel mug, smiling brightly.

"Thank you, darling. Let me get my things, and we can go. Peter and Max, you may tell the driver that we'll be out in a few minutes; the rest of you, wait here."

Erin had Rosie hold the cup again while she grabbed her spring jacket. The coffee would be too hot to drink for a good half hour or more, so she took the mug, told the rest of the children to go out to the car, then ran into the kitchen. She poured some of the steaming brew into a big ceramic mug and swirled it around to cool off before downing it like a shot of booze.

Then, she ran to the bathroom, knowing she'd have to go halfway through the tour anyway. Finally, she seized her coffee, grabbed her purse, and left the house, out of breath and sweating.

The chauffeur smiled at her as he opened the door and tipped his cap. "Good evening, ma'am," he said.

"Thank you for your patience," she said and got into the back seat with the excited children, who were changing radio stations with the volume turned up high.

Erin tried to deal with it but couldn't. "A'right, I hate to be the adult here, but choose something and turn it down, or please turn it off," she said over the din of yelling kids and ever-changing, thumping music.

"Sorry, Mum," Peter said and turned the volume down, keeping it at the station it was on.

"Thank you."

The driver was told to take them to the London Eye and then give them a tour of the most exciting parts of London at night. They opened the sunroof and poked their heads out, though Erin wouldn't let them ride like that for more than a block. There were chocolate-covered strawberries, Malteasers, and wine gums, as well as sparkling juice served in champagne flutes to give the effect of adult-like luxury.

Before she knew it, she was gently shaken awake in front of the London Eye. "Oh, I'm sorry, guys! I guess I'm just an old lady now!" she said as they all piled out of the limo and walked toward the attraction's entrance to wait for their private box to come around.

A few people stared at them, and some spoke to each other behind their hands, but only one person approached them. "John Thomas?" a young woman said, making everyone in their group turn around, embarrassing the girl, who turned bright red. When she saw Peter up close, she realized he wasn't

David, and her eyes grew wide. "Oh! I thought you were... but you look so much like him! I'm sorry."

"It's a'right. I get that a lot, actually. Cheers," Peter said.

The poor girl went back to her family but continued to stare at him. Erin was proud of her son for not being rude to her, then she overheard the boys talking.

"Your dad's ledge, but you're too generous, mate! Save it for the minted ones! She's as skint as they come!" Max said, and Peter frowned.

"Don't be daft, mate! If she's choong, what difference does it make?"

"If she's not minted, I can't be arsed, mate. I have standards, innit? She was clapped, anyway."

"Rubbish, and you're a proper toff! But shut it, or my mum'll be vex," Peter said.

Max looked at Erin with a smile. "Your stepmum's a cracker!" he said quietly, leaning close to Peter.

A smile lit up her son's face as he looked back at her. "Yeah, she is!" he said and then looked away.

"This party's ledge, mate! I reckon it's on account of your dad doin' porridge that she's splashed out on it, innit?"

"Wind your neck in, mate!" Peter said and nudged him hard on the shoulder.

Twenty minutes later, they were in their private box, moving slowly up into the sky. The views were incredible, and the lights on the Thames sparked and glistened, appearing wavy and distorted. The buildings, old and new, were lit up and shone beautifully in the night sky.

They could see forever, and Erin was glad it wasn't foggy that night. She watched the excited kids go from one end of the car to the other, pointing out landmarks and trying to find their house. It had been just under a year and a half since she and David rode on it together, though it felt like years.

Thirty minutes later, they stepped off the exaggerated Ferris Wheel and found their waiting limo. Erin was utterly spent and longed for her comfortable bed, but they still had the drive around town. The last thing she remembered was driving around Trafalgar Square and then waking up back at her front door.

"Oh no, I missed it all! I'm so sorry!" she said as she got out and tipped the driver. "I *am* an old lady! Please tell me you had a good time, at least?"

"I've had a lovely time, Mrs. Elliott," Cassie said as they entered the house.

"I have as well," Max said.

"Yes, Mum, it's been perfect! I don't know that you'll be able to top it for Charlie and Dan," Peter said.

"Oh dear, I won't be able to do another one this year, boys. I'm so sorry. It may have to wait till next year, or... even... the year after, when your... father is... home," Erin said to the twins, feeling terrible about it, though it seemed like she'd never have energy again. "Are you all able to get yourselves to bed? I'm afraid I've overdone it, and—"

"Are you going to have another episode, Mummy?" Rosie asked, and at that, all the children, except Max and Cassie, gathered around her in a circle. They looked terrified but organized, and she was shocked at their bravery and composure.

"Oh, my sweet, darlings! No, I'm not going to have another episode. I'm just very tired, that's all, I promise. Did you plan this?

Peter took her hand and stared at it. "Yes, Mum. We were unprepared and frightened last time, so... we sorted out a plan. If any of us thought you might be having an episode, we'd surround you to make certain you didn't fall and get hurt. I was chosen to speak to you... to let you know you're safe. Dan would find you a pillow, Charlie would find an adult, and Rosie would administer the breath of life if we agreed it might help."

"Come here." Erin held out her arms to them. "Thank you," she whispered and held them. Even Dan allowed her to hug him for a moment before he wriggled out of the huddle and stood a few feet away. "I'm so proud of you, and I hope you'll never have to implement your plan. You're all so unbelievably wonderful, you know?"

"You should go to bed now, Mum. We'll be fine," Peter said.

"Okay, but no sneaking around the house at night. I think Francie's begun sleeping with a chef's knife under her pillow now that your father isn't here at night to protect us. I wouldn't want her to think you were an intruder!" Erin said and smiled at their worried faces.

"Yes, Mum, we'll stay in our rooms," Charlie said, and the others nodded in agreement.

In the morning, they had French toast made with the remnants of their homemade bread and were then free to do as they pleased, as long as it wasn't so loud as to wake or startle Junie. Peter was excited to have his friend over and was kind enough to invite his brothers to hang out with them.

Dan joined them for a while, but he wasn't interested in cars or pretty girls, so he played in his room. Charlie opted to hang out with Rosie and Cassie. They listened to music and played with Junie until she became fussy. Finally, after lunch, it was time to pack up and drive back to Puncknowle.

Since they all went to the same school, Erin took Max and Cassie back with them. Kitty watched Junie for the day, as there wasn't enough room for her, plus it was a long, stressful day, being stuck in a car seat for at least seven hours.

When Erin finally returned home, she was knackered, but she had to feed Junie and sit for a proper supper, though she could've skipped it and gone right to bed. It was getting harder and harder to keep the exhaustion away, and it would be another four days before her next treatment, which she dreaded and looked forward to in equal measure. She just hoped she'd make it that long without falling apart.

Chapter Twenty-Five

THE SILENT TREATMENT

Once again, Erin lay on the exam table, the curtain drawn around her, waiting for the man she'd been with two weeks earlier to come through the door. She heard Wendy greet him in the hallway. *"Hello, Louie, how are you today?"*

"I'm a'right, though ma name's pronounced Lew-iss, no' Lou-ee," the man replied.

"Right, I knew that," Wendy said, sounding a bit flustered. *"Sorry, but I looked at your name on my clipboard and… well, I have an uncle whose name is spelled the same way, and he's called Louie. He's French, though."*

"Ach, I'm no' French," he said with a laugh.

FUCK! I didn't need to know his name! Erin thought, then heard the door open and shut. "Don't even talk," she said as he entered the room. "Please, don't say anything. I'm going to call you David because that's my husband's name, and I'm going to pretend you're him, so… just don't say anything unless you absolutely must."

She heard a little grunt that sounded a bit like, "Aye," come from behind the curtain and then heard him undressing. Suddenly, he was in position, and she gasped as he entered her, amazed that he managed to penetrate her at the same comfortable depth he'd found before. When it started feeling good, she whispered, "Oh, David, I love you! I'm sorry! I love you, and I miss you!" She continued to say that and other similar things, then cried as she felt her body reacting to the stranger.

—

After listening to her crying, and muttering things he could no longer understand, Louis stopped moving. "Are yeh a'right?" he asked quietly, not understanding the change in her from the last time they'd met.

"What? I'm fine... please just… get on with it. I want it to be over with. I need it to be done. Please hurry up!" she said, sounding unhinged.

He pulled out, stepped back, and ran his hand over his scalp. "I cannae do et with yeh cryin' and carryin' on like tha'. I feel as though I'm raping yeh. Can yeh turn on the speakers, at least?" he asked, having lost most of his erection.

He then wondered how he'd manage to get it back. There was a blue pill in the pocket of his jeans, and he thought of taking it as the sound of white noise filled the room. But when he returned to the end of the bed and touched her leg to get his bearings, a jolt of energy flowed through his body, making him hard again.

—

Erin felt the jolt as well. Her leg twitched, and her clitoris was instantly aroused, making her want him to touch it and roll it around on his tongue. She longed for him to enter her again and raised the volume on the white noise, panting as he pressed his cock against her ready vagina.

As he slid effortlessly into her, she thought, *Oh, David, please forgive me,* and felt her body release in one of the most powerful orgasms of her life, one that caused her to arch her back and cry out in pleasure. He wasn't far behind her that time, and she heard him moan as he came inside her.

—

The woman didn't turn down the white noise after he pulled out, but Louis could hear her crying as he cleaned up and got dressed. It broke his heart to hear her like that; he wanted to comfort her but couldn't. Instead, he left the room with his head bowed, feeling bleak.

Louis had arrived at the clinic that morning, looking forward to the treatment. Wendy greeted him in the hall, and everything felt the same. The only difference was that his confidence was much improved compared to the fortnight before.

He'd opened the exam room door, expecting his match to be quietly waiting, as she had been before, but the whole atmosphere of the room had changed. It felt almost hostile, and before he could say anything, she told him not to and that she would be calling him David. He'd been confused but thought she'd warm up to him a little once he got started, except she didn't.

In fact, the conditions continued to get worse as she cried and begged 'David' to forgive her. Finally, he reached a point where he couldn't go on. He wondered what could've happened in those two weeks to cause such a complete change in her.

He drove home a bit dazed and shaken up. It had been the second most amazing sexual experience of his life, but it was bittersweet. She'd been beside herself, calling out to her husband, and her grief tore at his heartstrings.

"Wait!" he said out loud as he pulled into the car park behind his terraced house. He rushed inside and went directly to the kitchen table, where a pile of junk mail and newspapers had begun to accumulate. He found the previous week's tabloid, which his housemate was always reading, then flipped through the pages until he found what he was looking for and read:

Dear Erin,

I've been tormented by nightmares in which you find someone else to replace me, and I can hardly stand it! I miss you so much it physically hurts.

It's been at least two months since we last made love, and I'm sure you're beginning to suffer again. I wish I were there to help you! I long to hold you again and make love to you more than I can tell you.

I can't believe or understand why the judge was so unmoveable about conjugal visits! When I get out of here, I'm going to fight for new laws for those needing treatments and those giving them! This isn't fair to you! Punish me if they need to, though I've done no wrong, but there's no need to torture you! Though, I reckon doing so does, in turn, have that effect.

I hate the very thought of it, darling, but I understand that you must find a match while I'm away. I only wish we'd had the time to find someone trustworthy while we were together. Please, my love, I know it'll be hard for you, but don't wait too long, though I know you will. I don't want you to suffer.

I'm suffering here without you~ needing and desiring you with my whole heart! I long for you and think of you and Junie every second I'm awake, and I often dream of you at night as well. Give the children my love! I miss you all so very much! Please don't forget me, Erin. I know it sounds daft, but the fear of that haunts me.

Please be patient and know that I love you more than my own life,

David x

Louis closed the paper and set it down. *It can't be her,* he thought. He found all the tabloids printed since David Elliott had been, in his, and it seemed everyone else's, mind, set up and sent to prison. Everyone knew he'd been framed or somehow forced to act in order to protect something or someone. He began reading the letters from David to his wife, Erin, which had started appearing in the tabloids soon after the verdict had been read, not bothering to put them in order.

Dear Erin,

I can't breathe in here sometimes. I see how the other inmates look at me, and I've started to become paranoid they're plotting something, or that the sodomite predators will get to me. Please continue bringing the things you do!

I believe it's the only reason I'm being guarded as well as I am.

I dream of you nearly every night, and I've never felt so empty. Oh, God, I need you! Please give my love to the children and Junie! She's not going to know who I am when I finally get out of here, and it breaks my heart.

Please be patient, and know that I love you more than my own life,

David x

Dear Erin,

I dreamed you decided not to visit any more, and I need you to know that I wouldn't be able to stand it if that happened! I must see you, even if I can't kiss you. You're what keeps me alive in here. Please bring Juniper if you can on your next visit. I want to see her sweet face next to yours.

I've managed to get more paper to write to you, but I'm not meant to have it, and I hope they don't confiscate it! I don't have enough to write to the children, so please tell them how much I love them and how I wish I could write to them and want to see their sweet faces so badly. Please tell them all the wonderful things we'll do together when I come home, then tell me what you've told them, so I can look forward to it as well.

I long for you so much! I want to hold you and touch you and make love to you. Don't stop loving me! I need you!

Please be patient, and know that I love you more than my own life,

David x

Louis was gutted when he finished reading the letters, written for David Elliott's wife's eyes only and were now being shown to the whole country and maybe even the world. He wondered if Erin ever wrote to him, and if she did, was he allowed to read her letters? He determined that he'd be more gentle and accommodating to the woman he was treating, whether she was Erin Elliott or not.

Chapter Twenty-Six

FOURTH VISITATION—JUNE FIFTH

Erin arrived at her fourth prison visitation and again had to wade through the sea of reporters as she tried to get to the large double doors of the jail. The men and women holding microphones and mobile phones spewed their questions at her, as they always did.

"How are you coping…"

"Are you having symptoms?"

"Will they release your husband early?"

"How is your baby?"

Once again, an officer came out, took the goodies she'd brought, and helped her to the door. He opened it for her, then disappeared with the bag as she made her way to the visitor's check-in counter. "Erin Mar—I mean Elliott, to see David Elliott," she said. She was still getting used to using her new surname, and if she was tired or stressed, which she was both that day, she'd slip up.

The woman at the counter waved her through to security, where she had to walk through a metal detector and only had to take a few things off that time. She'd wanted to bring Juniper, as she had the second time she'd come, but didn't think she could manage both the baby and the bag of bribes, not with the reporters in the way. She'd bring her the next time she had the children along and hope the reporters wouldn't be there.

They won't keep coming every two weeks for the whole two years, will they? she thought.

She waited a good fifteen minutes before being allowed into what was known as the 'visits' room. As she got near, she noticed that David's hair had much more grey in it, and his face looked gaunt. He had dark bags under his eyes, and he looked tired.

"David! Oh, darling," she said as he stood, and she wrapped her arms around him. "Are you okay? You look... sick or... something."

He didn't answer, he just held her with his face buried in her hair. "Ach, Erin, ma love! I've missed yeh terribly!" His energy flowed through her as he put his hand on the back of her neck.

"You're too thin; are you eating?" she asked as they sat at the table bolted to the floor.

"I eat when I'm hungry," was his noncommittal answer.

"What's wrong? I can tell there's something you're not telling me," she said.

He sighed and gave her a weak smile. "Do yeh need anathin'? Are yeh able to access our bank accounts? I worry about that," he said, clearly trying to divert the conversation.

"I'm fine, David. I don't need anything like that. Please tell me the truth, why are you so thin?" she asked again.

He closed his eyes, and his face began to turn red. "I can't eat... sometimes... knowin' ye're with another man," he snapped in a terrible hiss. "There, does that make yeh happy?"

Erin felt a bit stung and hung her head. "I understand. I thought it was because you were being mis—" she began, but he took her hand.

"I'm sorry, but yeh dinnae understand, no' fully. Do you remember how yeh felt when yeh thought I was havin' an affair with Emily? Yeh ken now I wasn't, but what if yeh kent I had tae, and there wasn't anathin' you could do about et?"

"I see, and I get it, but remember how angry you were when I stopped taking care of myself? You can't just stop eating for two years! I need you! I literally can't and don't want to live without you. Please, David, try to take care of yourself. If you can't do it for yourself, then do it for me, Junie, and your family," she pleaded.

—

He put his hand on her cheek and sighed again. "I dreamed that because I couldn't go tae the gala for Thistledown they let Bran out," he said, and saying it out loud suddenly filled him with fear. "You don't think et was a prophetic dream, do yeh?"

"I'm planning on going to the gala. I don't think you should be afraid of—"

"I'm terrified Bran will be released, or escape, and come tae find yeh! In the dream, I could see him at the door of Owlgate. You wouldn't let him in, would yeh, Erin?" he said, panic gripping his heart.

"Let him in? Of course not," she said. "The gala is in two weeks; they won't let him out before then, and I'm sure Oscar knows that you're in jail and can't come to it. Please don't be afraid."

He nodded, though his hands were trembling. "I know I'm overreacting, and ye're right, I'm sure yeh are, but after the dream, I can't get et out of ma head; I can't sleep, and eating is even more difficult. I… imagine you asleep in our bed and tha' bawbag somehow gettin' into the house and... hurting you... without me there to protect you."

—

"I'm—" she began, but he spoke over her.

"You lock the doors every night? You should lock the bedroom door as well, and... make sure the windows are shut and locked. He may try tae get in that way," he said as if Bran had already been released.

"I do, but—"

"And Kitty knows tae lock hers, and Francie as well?" he continued, making Erin afraid that he was losing his mind.

"David, my darling, I'm safe, please believe me. He's still locked up and can't hurt me. Plus, I'll be leaving town for Edinburgh next week," she said, not knowing how to reassure him.

"But I saw him come to the door of Owlgate! Yeh can't stay there! Yeh may be in danger if yeh do. What if he hurt our Junie as well? He knows how tae get intae Owlgate, Erin. He'll hurt yeh if—" He put his hand on his chest and gasped as though he couldn't breathe.

She could tell he felt helpless and out of control. "David, please don't do this to yourself. Calm down, my love. Look at me, I'm right here, and I'm safe. I'll tell Roger about your dream, and he'll make sure I'm okay, alright?" she said.

He looked into her eyes as he nodded again, taking deep breaths. She saw several tears of frustration and fear fall down his face, and she wished she could help him. "Maybe you should talk to someone. Isn't there a therapist or—"

"I'm not talkin' tae anaone in here," he snarled, his face becoming hard and angry.

Erin frowned and put her head down, not knowing what to say after that. "What's happening to you in here, David? What have they done to you? You... seem like you're becoming a different person," she said quietly.

He didn't say anything for a long time, and she was beginning to think he wasn't going to. She looked up at him and saw that his face was red and the vein on his forehead was starting to pop out. She felt like she was watching Bruce Banner turning into the Hulk before her eyes, and it scared her. She wanted to run away and hide, but she only had two hours with him twice a month, so she wasn't going anywhere.

"What have they done to me?" he whispered intensely, spitting as he spoke. Erin's eyes were wide, and tears fell onto the table as she saw her husband struggling to keep his composure enough to not be taken back early. "They've—" he began and must've seen the tears, now pouring from her red eyes, because he paused.

"They've taken you away from me, and I dinnae wanna live without yeh," he continued, his voice much softer as his face returned to normal. "I ken I sound like a ravin' lunatic, but I can't control anathin' in here. I'm afraid all the time!

"I'm terrified ye'll be hurt by something or someone, or... that... ye'll fall in love with your new match, and ye'll not want me anamore. But I can't do anathin'! I can't even talk tae you or write yeh. Have yeh received *any* of ma letters?" he asked, so sad.

"No, I haven't. Have you gotten any of mine?" she asked, and he shook his head. "I'm not going to fall in love with my temporary match. You have to believe me. No matter what, you will always have my love, and no one will ever take it away."

He frowned at her, suddenly seeming to be angry again. "So, yeh dinnae have *any* feelings for him then? Yeh don't... enjoy your treatments?" he spat.

Erin felt as though he'd slapped her in the face. "I... don't have feelings for him, except—" she began.

"Except he gives yeh what I can't. He's the one who satisfies you in bed now," he whispered so that only she could hear him, making them both want to be sick.

"Except for gratefulness to him for helping me." She was so stunned that her ears were ringing. She wanted nothing more than to get up and walk away, but she did her best to imagine what he was going through and sat tight, putting her head down and closing her eyes.

"When was your last treatment?" he asked, sounding calm, but she was afraid to answer.

"What? Why are you asking me that? Does it matter?"

"Answer me," he demanded in a strong whisper.

"David, I don't see how—"

"Answer me."

"Thursday," she said quietly.

"Thursday," he repeated. "Yeh mean yesterday?"

She nodded, feeling ashamed and belittled. "Aye, but—"

"And what are yeh goin' tae do for treatments whilst in Edinburgh then?" he asked, sounding condescending and mean.

She felt humiliated, but it wasn't anything she didn't already feel about herself in the situation. "I'm going to ask him to travel there for me... if there's a—"

David's eyes grew wide. "Yeh can't be serious?" he interrupted quite loudly, and she really did want to hide. "And jest where shall he stay, then, Erin? Will yeh be puttin' him up in a hotel so you can be together—" he began, but then put his hand over his chest again and started crying.

Erin sat watching him torture himself, and there wasn't anything she could say to stop it.

"Answer me!" he said and slammed his fist on the table.

"Elliott! Once more, and you're done!" one of the officers said with authority.

"Answer me," he said again, but this time he was quiet and frighteningly intense.

"No… I mean… I'll offer to pay for the trip and… lodging, but we'll be meeting at a clinic, not a hotel room, David. You don't understand how—"

"No, I don't understand how you can… be with him… and not… not want tae… leave me," he said. He was shaking and crying, his head down on the table, cradled in his arms.

"I'll cancel them. I'll… I'll just not have them anymore. I can live without them, and you can't handle it, so… I'll just let him know that I won't be needing any more treatments," she said, knowing she wouldn't be able to manage without them but needing David to feel better, somehow.

He didn't speak for a long time, then he shook his head. "No, you can't do that," he said without lifting his head. "I'm sorry for behavin' this way. I jest can't keep the thoughts of et out of ma mind. Yeh… dinnae ken how terrified I am, Erin.

"I jest know ye'll come here one day… tae visit me, only tae inform me ye're gonna stay with him and leave me, jest as you had tae do with Todd, and I'm at the end of ma tether. Et's eatin' me alive!" he cried.

"I don't know how to reassure you that that won't happen. I don't feel like that toward him at all, not at all. I love you with my whole heart, David. You are my dream come true. I won't leave you, and I won't fall in love with him. I swear to you before God that it won't happen." She placed her hands on his forearms and then pulled one of his hands out to hold.

"You didn't think ye'd fall in love with me, but yeh did," he said pathetically.

"I fell in love with you on the first night we met. If I were going to have a problem with… him," she almost said his name, "I'd already be in love with him, and I'm not. Not in the slightest," she said, and he looked up with red eyes and kissed her hand.

"Ye're sure? Ye're no' lying tae me just tae save ma feelings?"

"I'm sure, and I'm not lying. It's only you, forever," she said and marveled that he could be who he was and still be so scared and insecure. "David? Don't you know who you are to me? Don't you remember how I looked at you at the Bollywood party? You're my King... my Prince David, remember? Do you really think I'd give you up for someone else? You're my fantasy and everything I've ever wanted.

"I don't understand... well, I guess I do understand. Like you said, I'd be beside myself if you had to have sex with some other woman... but... please, my darling, please believe me that I love only you. No matter what I'm forced to do to remain healthy, you're the one I'm staying healthy for."

"But... yeh ken the real me now, not the famous me, and—"

"I love the real you more than I could've ever imagined loving the famous you. YOU are the you I love."

"I'm sorry I spoke tae you that way! I dinnae ken what comes over me sometimes. Yeh don't deserve et, ma darling. I dinnae want tae push you away, and tha's all I'm doin'!" he said, sounding miserable again.

"No, you're not. I'm doing my best to understand, and I promise I won't come here telling you I don't need you anymore. I'll need you forever. I was going to tell you about the birthday party. Do you want—"

"Yes! Oh, darling, here I am ravin' and bein' selfish! Please tell me all about et!"

"Kitty and I managed to put together a fun little party. Did you know that neither Peter nor Rosie have ever had a birthday party? That was one of the saddest things I'd ever heard! I also learned that they don't have *any* friends in London, either? I just can't believe that! They don't have many friends at their new school yet, so they each invited one."

She told him all about the party and the amazing cake. "Kitty lit sparklers on the cake, and we sang Happy Birthday. I have pictures on my phone, but I wasn't allowed to bring it in with me. I'll get some printed to show you next time. I also have a short video of us all saying that we miss you and love you." She then told him about the children's plan in case she had another episode.

—

David smiled as he heard her recount the events of his children's party and was blown away by their foresight, but when she was finished, he bowed his head. "I'm glad you were able tae do that for them, darling. I can't help but feel sad that I wasn't there," he said.

He knew their time that day was running out, so his constant companion, panic, reared its ugly head again. "Erin, please! Be aware of where you are and… keep the house locked tightly! Also, please do tell Roger—"

"Five minutes, wrap it up!" the officer said, and their hearts sank.

"About ma dream, and… and… don't stop… lovin' me! Dinnae… leave me!"

They stood and held each other, both crying now.

"I miss you so much. I won't leave you, David, I need you! I'm sorry I won't be able to come to the next two visits, but I'll be here for the one after that, I promise!"

"I cannot live without yeh. I feel as if I'm suffocatin' in here. I'm not a criminal!" he whispered, unable to hide his fears.

—

In every television show or movie Erin had seen, the inmate had kept his composure, except for a fit of rage, perhaps, but she could tell David was losing it, and it broke her heart.

"Time's up," an officer said, and all the visitors stood to say their goodbyes and began leaving the room.

Erin blew him a kiss as she walked away. She went to the lockers, grabbed her purse and keys, and left the building, feeling gutted.

One lone reporter had stayed that whole time, and the cameraman stood at his side, recording her, red-faced and crying. They started to follow her, asking questions as she trudged, blinded by her tears, to the SUV, until she turned on them and gave them the finger. She got into her car, shaking and enraged. As soon as the door was shut, she put her head on the steering wheel and bawled.

A week later, the children had another Exeat, thankfully the last one of the term, and she longed more than ever to move closer to the school. The three-hour drive was becoming a real chore, especially when it fell a week after a treatment. Though she was thankful for them, they didn't last long enough.

Riddled with guilt, she decided to have them take the train that time and picked them up at the station. Their train arrived later than the last one, so it was already suppertime when they got home. Junie was happy and playful that night, so after they ate, they sat in the sunroom and played with her until she had to be fed, and then it was bedtime.

Chapter Twenty-Seven

A DAY IN THE LIFE

Erin was ripped out of a sound sleep by a knock on the bedroom door on Saturday morning. She could hear heavy rain hitting the windowpanes, then saw a bright flash of light, almost immediately followed by a loud crack of thunder that startled her. A scream pierced the air, and the next knock was more urgent than the first.

"Mummy!" Rosie cried in distress.

"Come in, baby girl," she replied. The door opened, and the young girl entered with Daniel at her heels. "Are you sc—" Another flash of light and crash of thunder cut her off, so she patted the mattress next to her.

"I'm frightened by storms, Mummy," she said and hugged Erin tightly.

"I understand," she said, then looked at Daniel to see if he'd admit to the same fear. He shrugged and put on a brave face until the next thunderclap rattled the windowpanes, then he hurried to join his sister under the covers. Expecting Charlie and Peter to join them, she waited a while, but there was no sign of them, so she gave up on it.

"This reminds me of *The Sound of Music*."

Rosie cocked her head to the side, clearly not understanding her reference. "Is that a song?" she asked.

"No, well... yes, I mean, maybe, but it's a film. Haven't you seen it?" she asked, shocked.

"I don't think so, but I'd like to, Mummy," she said and smiled at her.

"Yes, we'll have to watch it soon! You'll love it! It's about a nun, well, a soon-to-be nun, who becomes a nanny to—"

"Oh, we didn't like our nanny!" Daniel said, interrupting her.

"Dan! Don't interrupt!" Rosie said.

"Well, they didn't… I mean, the children in the film didn't think they'd like her either, but—Well, I won't spoil it for you, but you'll like it."

That afternoon, Erin found one of Daniel's sweaters, or jumpers, as he would call it, on a chair in the sunroom. She decided to take it upstairs to his room for him, though after two flights of stairs, she was out of breath and second-guessing her decision.

As she headed down the hall to the room Dan shared with Charlie, she passed Rosie's room and heard her talking to someone. The door was ajar, so she opened it a wee bit more and watched her, sitting on her small chair, chatting away to someone she couldn't see. "Knock, knock," Erin said, and opened the door a bit wider. "I heard you talking to someone, and I was hoping to be introduced."

Rosie smiled and blushed. She knew that at ten, she was too old for imaginary friends, but she also knew that if anyone would understand, it would be Erin. "Do come in," she said quite formally. "Mummy, I'd like you to meet my friend, Gretchen. Gretchen, this is my new mummy, Erin. I know you will get along very well." She was relieved when Erin smiled at her.

"Hello, Gretchen, it's a pleasure to meet you!" she said, holding her hand out for a handshake.

Rosie giggled and pretended to cover her friend's ears. "Gretchen doesn't have hands; she's a chicken," she said and put her hands down.

"Oh! Pardon me!" Erin began bobbing her head like a chicken pecking the ground, which made Rosie laugh so hard she fell off her chair. "Cheep, cheep, boock… cluck. I'm a bit rusty on my Chickenese, but I think I said, 'It's nice to meet you,' though I might have said, 'You have big feet.' Let's hope it's the former and not the latter." She then helped Rosie to sit up on her chair again.

"You're the funniest person I know, Erin... I mean, Mummy."

"Well, thank you! So, what secrets were you telling our friend, Gretchen, here?" she asked and sat on the end of her bed.

"Nothing important, really." She then looked down at her extra fluffy purple carpet and lowered her voice. "Except that I miss Daddy... a lot, but I'm used to not seeing him, so it's not that bad." Something dawned on her, and she looked up at Erin with sad eyes. "You must be very sad, Mummy! You're not used to being away from him."

—

Erin was delighted her new daughter still had an imagination, but she hadn't expected her to say anything like that. A lump started to form in her throat, so she swallowed it down and smiled sadly. "Aye, Rosebud, I do get sad a lot, but... actually, I do something similar to what you do with Gretchen," she said, not believing she was admitting that to her.

"You do?" Rosie asked, clearly shocked.

"I do. When I get really, *really* lonely, I... well, I pretend your daddy's pillow is him as I'm falling asleep at night. I talk to him about my day and about you and your brothers. About how you're doing and what crazy thing one of you did that day." She smiled at the young girl, who was listening intently.

Rosie smiled back and went to her, wrapping her slender arms around her neck. "I didn't know adults did that! I thought it was something I was meant to grow out of. At least that's what... my mum would've said." She sat next to her with her head down.

"My mum wouldn't have played along like you just did. She'd have told me to 'grow up.' It makes me happy that you have an imaginary friend as well. Oh, and now you're friends with Gretchen, so that makes two, doesn't it?"

"I guess it does, but you should know that it's not good to rely on imaginary friends and not have any real ones. I don't think it hurts to imagine there's someone you love in the room with you when you're lonely, just as long as you don't suddenly start to think they're really real. That's something people need to see a special doctor for.

"I'm glad you have Gretchen; chickens make nice friends! Do you know that someday I want to have a bunch of them... chickens, I mean. I want to move out to the country and have a little farm with chickens and geese... maybe a goat or two.

"I also want you and your brothers to have a place to play. To climb trees and explore, like I did when I was a kid," Erin said, having a feeling Rosie would like to hear about that.

"You climbed trees when you were my age?" she asked, wide-eyed. "Will you teach me how to as well, Mummy?"

"I look forward to it every day, darling girl. I've dreamed of it since I was your age, you know, to have a little girl and teach her the things I know. One of the great things about growing up is teaching younger people how to do cool stuff.

"That reminds me of something. When I was your age, we had bright red poppies growing in the back garden. One day, my daddy was outside, and he called me over to him."

"What did he want?" She was clearly excited and looked expectantly up at her.

"He'd seen an *enormous* bumble bee on one of the poppies!" Erin said, and Rosie's eyes grew huge!

"Oh! Did it sting him? Or you? I'm afraid of bees!"

"No, baby girl, it didn't sting either of us. He brought me up to it very slowly and crouched down, then he stuck out his finger and touched it!"

"No!" she said.

"Yes, he did. He petted it gently, like a cat, only with one finger, then he said I could do it, too, and *I did*. It was soft, and it didn't hurt me or fly away. It let me touch it, and I learned something important that day."

"What did you learn?"

"I learned that it's good to have respect for things that can bite or sting you, but that when you are with an adult who knows what they're doing, sometimes you can do things you never thought possible. I wouldn't just go around trying to pet bees, but sometimes, big bumblebees get tired and need to rest.

"They will crawl around and are docile enough to pet. I've even seen videos of people who have let them walk on their hands. My dad was really good at things like that. He'd pick up earthworms, frogs, and salamanders for me to look at and touch. I wish you could spend more time with him."

"I love Grandpa Frank! He's a very nice person. He's funny, like you, and I had loads of fun when we explored the land he and Grandma live on. I hope we can go back there soon! Peter told us all about what happened when he taught him how to drive. He had a brilliant time. I'm ever so glad they came here at Christmas and… the wedding. Do you remember dancing to the Christmas songs?"

"Yes, I do! That's something I'll never forget," Erin said. They sat quietly for a while, but thinking about her parents and the wedding was beginning to make her sad. "So… I think it's time to change the subject. You told me you don't like ballet; what do you like to do?"

Rosie glanced up at her and scrunched up her face a bit, as if either trying to think of something or perhaps whether or not she should tell her what it was. "It's not that I don't like it, really. I like to dance, but I don't want to be on stage… performing. I get nervous, and my palms begin to sweat. I'm terrified I'll forget what I'm meant to do and embarrass… the family. I'd much rather play the piano, though only when I'm alone."

"Really? That sounds wonderful—Wait, is there… a piano here?" Erin said, mentally scanning all the rooms in the house, trying to think if she'd just missed it.

"No, Mummy didn't want to encourage me. She wanted me to be a prima ballerina and made me practice endlessly when we were home on holiday from school."

"That makes me sad, Rosie. I believe kids need to have play time."

"I didn't have time to play with Gretchen. I'm glad you didn't scold me—"

"Scold you? For playing with your imaginary friend?"

"Yes, Mummy didn't like it," she said simply and put her head down.

"Well, my sweet baby girl, I'm your mummy now, and I say you don't have to do ballet any longer, and you may play with your friends, real or imaginary, whenever you like. We grow up too fast as it is; play while you're a child and then play when you grow up."

"Thank you, Mummy!" Rosie said and hugged her tightly.

"You're quite welcome. As for a piano, we'll have to see about that."

"That's alright, I can wait. Anyway, there's a piano at Punk I'm allowed to play sometimes. I… love you, Mummy, and I'm happy Daddy married you!"

"So am I, baby, and I love you too. Hey, I have an idea. Would you like to write a letter to your grandpa and grandma? I know they would love to hear from you, and I'll ask the boys if they'd like to as well."

"Oh, yes, please!" Rosie said excitedly. "Do you think they'll write back?" she asked, and Erin could sense her trepidation, clearly remembering how she and her brothers had hoped for a letter from her dad for so long and rarely got one.

"I know my mom will, and I'll ask her to make sure Dad does, too. Now, let's find some paper."

Erin put Dan's sweater in his room, where he was pestering Charlie, who was trying to read. She convinced them both to meet her downstairs in the study to write a letter to their grandparents. Then, she found Peter with a book of plants and herbs open on his lap. He had his earbuds in and jumped when she touched his shoulder.

"Bloody—you startled me!" he said and took the earbuds out.

"Come with me; we're gonna write letters to my mom and dad," she said. He closed his book and stood, already taller than her. She put her hand on his head and pushed down. "Stop that!" she said sternly, and he raised his eyebrows in confusion. "Stop growing up! You have to hit pause so your dad doesn't miss it!"

"I'll see what I can do," he said, smiling down at her as she ruffled his hair.

They descended the stairs and met in David's office, where Erin found some stationary and several pens and pencils. "But what shall we write about, Mum?" Charlie asked, making her smile.

"Well, you can tell them how much you *adore* me! Yeah, that's good. Tell them how *blessed* you are that I've become your mummy. Tell them about our adventures and even sad things, if you want to. Tell them how we visited your father and that you miss him… whatever your hearts' desire, my darlings. They will love to hear about your lives, and no one ever sends real mail in the post anymore, so it'll be a treat!" Erin said.

"This paper doesn't have lines on it! I don't like it at all! Dan said after an apparently poor start and crumpled his sheet up. It was fine, expensive paper, so Erin picked it up and flattened it out.

"Dan, just do the best you can on this page… wait, I have an idea. I need a ruler and some lined paper, please. Dan ran out of the room to find what she'd asked for, while Erin found a thin black marker in the desk.

"What are you going to do, Mummy?" Rosie asked.

"It's a surprise," she said. Dan came back a few minutes later with a meter-long stick and a notebook. "Wow, thanks. I'm not sure this will work for what I need, but I'll think of something."

She ripped out four sheets of lined paper and stacked them up as best she could, so the lines were the same. After another search through David's desk, she found a clipboard with a straight edge. "This'll work!"

She traced the lines of the notebook paper so that they were dark black and thick. When all four pages were marked, she showed them that if they put the unlined pages over them, they could see through it, and their letters would look neat and tidy.

"You're a genius, Erin… I mean, Mum!" Charlie said, and Rosie nodded her agreement.

"What can I say? Maybe you should tell them *that* as well!" Erin laughed and laid a piece of paper on the desk in front of her. She unscrewed the cover of a weighty, expensive-looking fountain pen and gently tapped her temple with it, deciding what she wanted to write.

> *Dear Mom and Dad,*
>
> *I hope you enjoy these letters from the kids… that is if I can get them to finish them. They've been so wonderful since David's been gone! I'm so proud of them!*
>
> *I just met Rosie's imaginary friend, Gretchen, who is a chicken. I made the mistake of trying to shake her hand and had to be corrected. My bad! I know I fought you with each lesson in Chickenese, but now I'm so glad I learned*

it! I only wish I'd paid better attention so I could remember more!

I wish you could come visit us! I miss you both so much! I'm trying to keep my spirits up, but it's really difficult most days. When I spoke to Annis last week, she asked about you and told me that she sends her love and hopes you're doing well.

Well, I'd better check on the kids' progress now. I love you both! Hug each other for me! Oh, Mom, I know you'll do it, but please make sure Dad replies to each of the children. It'll mean everything if he does!

Love,

Erin
Xoxo

She sighed, missing her parents even more after that. The children seemed fully absorbed in their letters, so she watched them for a while. Finally, Peter stood and handed her his neatly folded stack of paper.

"Wow! How many pages is this?" she asked.

"Uh, four, I think," he said shyly.

"May I read it, please?"

"I'd... uh, prefer you didn't, if that's a'right?"

"Yeah, sure, that's okay. I'll put it in the envelope then."

He smiled down at her, then bent over and kissed her cheek. "Thanks, Mum. May I go back to my room now?"

"Of course, and thanks for participating with a good attitude."

He shrugged his shoulders. "It was fun, actually. See you at supper then," he said and left the room.

Rosie was next to hand her two flat pages, covered with doodles of butterflies, flowers, and hedgehogs. "Oh, Rosie, that's lovely!" Erin said and smiled up at her.

"You may read it if you'd like," the girl said, then kissed her cheek.

"Thank you, I will!" Knowing she might be interrupted, she decided to wait until everyone was finished to start reading it.

Charlie was next; he handed her one sheet, written on both sides. She noticed his handwriting was uncommonly legible for an eleven-year-old boy and was about to mention it when Dan approached them, impatiently waving his stack of paper.

"Wait your turn—" she began, but he practically threw them on the desk.

"You should read it! Some of it's stonkin'! Oh, I forgot and wrote on the lined paper at the end, sorry," he said and ran out of the room.

She and Charlie watched him leave and then looked at each other. Erin raised her eyebrows, and Charlie smiled. "You get used to it," he said and turned to go.

"Wait, may I read yours?" She could see what looked like conflict in his eyes, but he shrugged.

"If you—"

Erin put her hand on his shoulder. "I won't be upset if you don't want me to, don't worry," she said. She pulled him to her for a hug and stroked his hair before letting him go.

"Thanks for that, Mum. In that case, I'd rather you didn't."

"Okay then, I won't. You don't have to agree to something every time I ask, you know?"

"It's become a habit, I suppose. If I didn't—"

"With your mum… yeah, I figured, but as I just told Rosie, I'm not her, so I hope you learn to be your real, wonderful self with me."

He smiled at her and leaned in to kiss her cheek. "I am, and it's a good feeling."

Once everyone was out of the room, she sat at David's desk and picked up Dan's letter, shaking her head. *How is that possible*, she thought. Every page was crumpled, dog-eared, or both. The first page was relatively neat, showing he'd at least tried.

Hi granpaw and granmaw,

Erin said I have to rite a letter to you, so I will because I like her. My dad is in jail now, so she has to take care of us without him.

Have you been in jail? My dad said it's no fun. I miss him, but I'm used to that. I miss you as well, and wish you would come for a visit. If you came here I'd show you my bedroom and take you to the park where we play football and cricket. We played quoits there once, but that's a kid game.

We are now at a new school in Dorset called Puncknowle Academy. Everyone calls it Punk and I think that's banging, innit? I don't have any new friends yet. Charlie told me it's becuse I don't bathe enough and I smell bad. I can't help it if I smell bad!

I herd Charlie likes a girl! I don't think she knows Charlie exists, so that just proves it doesn't matter if you smell bad, or use to much nasty collone, innit? Anyway, I found two hairs on my chest last week and Charlie doesn't have any at all!

I hope you write back to me. I don't think you will becuse we all wanted our dad to rite to us before he met Erin and when our mum was alive, but he never did.

Granpaw, did you see that stonking snake again? I wish I had it at my new school so I could let it go in the canteen and all the girls would scream and drop their food on the floor! Then, everyone would try to run out and they'd slip and fall and would be covered in food! Then EVERYONE would smell bad, not only me!

Uh oh, I'm riting on the lined paper Erin made for me so I could follow the lines on the posh paper. I reckon it doesn't matter as I'm finished anyway.

Your favourite granson,

Dan Elliott
Age 11, ALMOST 12

Erin laughed so hard she had to wipe her eyes with a tissue before reading Rosie's.

Dear Grandma and Grandpa Wallace,

Mummy thought it would be nice if we all wrote to you. I think it's a lovely idea. I hope you're healthy and happy! I miss you very much. I hope we can see you again very soon.

I'm doing well except that I miss my daddy. He can't be home now, but Mummy has been so much fun! She's good at playing. And she didn't scold me for talking to my imaginary friend, Gretchen. I'm very glad she's here! And I'm happy that Daddy married her and that she is our Mummy now! I love her very much!

I know Mummy loves us all very much and I know you love us as well! Now that Daddy is away, Mummy is tired a lot so we try to be very good. Well everyone except Dan tries to be extra good and not be loud or bother her very much.

We got to see Daddy where he's living now. It is a very scary place with scary people. He is made to wear ugly clothes as well. The tea there is revolting! Dan upset me by asking Peter dreadful questions about what might happen to Daddy whilst he is there. It made me cry. Dan often makes me cry because he doesn't think before he speaks. That's what Peter told me.

I always try to think before I speak because I don't want to upset anyone by what I say. I know Mummy does that as well. I want to be like her when I'm an adult.

I wish I could give you a hug right now!

Love, your Granddaughter,

Rosie Elliott
Age 10

Erin sighed and lovingly touched the childish handwriting. *The poor thing! It must be so hard for them!* she thought and then added to her letter.

> *P.S. I just read Dan and Rosie's letters (Peter and Charlie asked me not to), and my heart hurts for them. They are so sweet and go out of their way to be helpful. I know Peter is struggling with wanting to be the man of the house, but that's far too much to put on a kid. I tried to talk to him about it, but it's so difficult… everything is difficult right now.*
>
> *I hope you're able to understand Daniel's letter with his misspelling and slang. If you have any trouble, just ring—oops, I mean, call me for a translation.*
>
> *The latest news is that—Oh, Mom, I had to find another match, and I'm devastated, but I have to be able to take care of the kids and myself, so I didn't have a choice. I don't know what to do. David said I should do it and that he'd be okay, but that's not true! He's not able to cope, and I don't blame him.*
>
> *I'm afraid he's not going to be able to let it go and forgive me! What if he leaves me? I want you to tell me what to do, but I know you don't have any more answers than I do. I just needed to vent and let it out.*
>
> *I love you both so much!*
>
> *Erin*

Sunday was a beautiful, warm day, so the family went to the park, which had become their habit when the weather was good. Erin sat on the bench under the sweet chestnut tree again while the children played football, though she'd have called it soccer. Junie was resting in her pram, happy to be shaking her little rattle and sucking on her two middle fingers.

Peter was the first to join her on the bench, smiling and out of breath. He leaned over the pram and smiled down at his little sister. "Hello, little sprout, are you enjoying the lovely weather?"

Erin helped him lift her and got him situated so that he could engage with her. He put his hand to her mouth and let her suck on the end of his pinky, then laughed when she grabbed it, pushed it into her mouth, and tried to bite it.

"Oww! She bit me!" he said.

Erin nearly rolled on the ground laughing. "Good night nurse!" she exclaimed and took out her cell phone. She found the YouTube video, *'Charlie Bit My Finger,'* and had him watch it, though it didn't amuse him much. "I know you think I'm a nerd, but it was a thing, trust me," she said, still laughing.

The rest of the children came running when they saw her laughing so hard and gathered around Peter, playing with and talking to the baby. Erin couldn't help herself and opened the camera on her phone. She took a short video and then a few pictures, wishing she could show them to David.

"May I hold her?" Rosie asked, and Erin told her she could, but she needed to be sitting first. She sat on the ground in front of the bench, and Erin explained to Peter how to hand Junie to his sister. He was so overly careful that Dan grew impatient and, like an expert, took her out of his brother's hands and gently laid her into his sister's.

Erin was amazed. "Where did you learn to do that?" she asked him, to which he shrugged.

"Dunno—I've seen you and Kitty do it loads; it's not difficult," he said, then started cooing at her and making her laugh with his big smile and lively dimples.

"Oh, Dan, you're a natural!" she said.

Rosie soon got tired of holding her, and Charlie said he wanted a go, so Erin asked Dan to hand her over, which he did beautifully. After that, it was Dan's turn. He sat on the bench next to Erin and lifted his sister up, facing him, then gently twisted her from the middle, dangling her feet in the air.

Then, he easily set her facing away from him and bounced her on his knee, making her squeal. A soccer ball came rolling toward them, and just like that, he got up, held Junie on his hip, and kicked it back without even thinking about it.

"My dear boy," Erin said, shocked and delighted, "you are going to make some woman very happy someday, and you're gonna be a great dad!"

He rolled his eyes and handed Juniper back to her so he could run and play with Charlie, who had joined the kids whose ball had rolled to them earlier. She watched as they ran and yelled, knowing what to do and where to go. Memories of the times they'd come to the park with David the summer before flooded her thoughts.

She smiled down at Juniper, who looked so much like a mixture of her and David it made her heart confused, not knowing whether to laugh or cry. Taking a ragged breath, she sighed and watched her children. Though she was knackered, she wasn't about to leave until the kids had played themselves out.

Half an hour later, the boys and Rosie came back, looking tired but happy, flushed with playing and running. Her heart swelled, and she felt so blessed to have them as her bairns. "I'm hungry," Dan said, and everyone else joined in, saying they were too.

Erin put the baby back in the pram, and they walked home. She didn't want to admit it, but she could tell it had been nine days since her last treatment, and she looked forward to the one scheduled for that Thursday. It meant nearly a week of freedom from exhaustion and being able to breathe freely once more. That night, she wrote David a letter, recounting the lovely time they'd had in the park that day.

Chapter Twenty-Eight

THIRD TREATMENT

Louis stopped at a florist on his way to the third treatment. He felt sad for the woman he was treating, both for her situation and because things hadn't gone very well during their last appointment. Wanting to cheer her up, he picked out a single peach-colored rose, then asked the florist to cut the stem short and tie a light blue ribbon on it.

It was chilly and drizzling that day, so he'd brought a flannel shirt with him, though he hadn't planned to use it. When he arrived at the clinic, he suddenly felt stupid having the flower with him, so he carefully wrapped the rose in the shirt before entering the building.

"Good afternoon, Louis," Wendy greeted him cheerfully when she saw him in the hall. She then opened the door for him when Erin pushed the call button. He walked into the room with trepidation, not knowing what to expect from his match that week.

"Umm," he heard from behind the curtain, "I need to apologize to you, Louis," she said humbly. "I was in a bad place last time, and I'm really sorry I spoke to you so rudely and acted... like an idiot."

He was pleasantly surprised to find her in a better mood. "Right, I understand. I... was told, when I agreed tae do this, tha' yer permanent match was... unavailable, and tha' I was jest fillin' in. I cannae imagine how difficult tha' would be for you, sae please dinnae worry about et," he said.

"You should know that I overheard Wendy say your first name last week, which was one of the reasons I was so upset. You see, I didn't want to know it, but now that I do, I think it's only fair to tell you mine. I'm Erin, and I want to... well, thank you for helping me," she said, her voice starting to break.

"Ye're welcome, Erin. I'm glad I can help yeh, truly," he said, wishing he could open the curtain and smile at her or see what she looked like. Now that he knew she must be Erin Elliott, he knew he could look her up online, but it wasn't the same, so he decided not to.

He unwrapped the rose and laid it on the neat pile of her clothing on the chair. Then he thought she might read more into it than he meant and was angry that he hadn't thought to write a note or something. Between the talking and worrying about the *stupid* note and the *stupid* idea about the *stupid* flower, he wasn't very hard when he got undressed, but he approached her anyway.

As he parted the curtain, he could see her pubic hair and a bit of her creamy-white inner thigh. When he put his hand gently on her knee, even through the fabric, he felt a surge of power flow into him that made him almost painfully erect. He could hear her start panting and wanted to touch her; he longed to explore her with his fingers and, even more, his tongue.

Instead, he took hold of himself and guided his cock into place, rubbing his head up and down along her folds to make himself wet enough to enter her easily. She was very wet, and when he ran his cock over her clitoris, she cried out, revealing that she was ready and perhaps even desiring him.

He slid into her and immediately felt her contracting before he had done anything. Gasping and moaning, she said, "Oh! Oh!"

That made him so hard, it almost hurt to move it, but the feeling of pleasure far outweighed any pain at that moment. He wanted to touch her breasts, to kiss her thighs and her mouth. Again, he felt her pulsing and gasping for breath as she climaxed a second time for him.

He thrust as deeply as he could without hurting her, wanting to pound himself into her all the way and feel her thighs against his hips, then he felt it. "Ach, Christ! I'm gonnae—" he said, as his body shuddered, and goosebumps ran up and down his entire body. "Ma God!" he said, not wanting to say too much, though he was overwhelmed with a satisfaction and release like he'd never known in all his years.

"Yeah, I know," she said simply, still panting.

"Thank you," they both said at the same time and couldn't help but laugh a little. He pulled out of her and was about to mention the rose, but she spoke up first.

"I need to ask you something, Louis," she said as he was cleaning up and getting dressed.

"Aye," he said.

"Do you ever visit Scotland? I mean... Edinburgh?"

"Well, I havnae been there for a long while, why do yeh ask?"

"There's an... event I have to attend, and I... want to stay with my husband's family, but I'll need at least one treatment while I'm there. If you're willing to travel for me, I'll put you up in a hotel and pay for your travel costs, whatever you need," she said. "Oh, wait! Are there even clinics like this up there? Shit! Why does this have to be so difficult?" she said impatiently.

"Well, I have friends there, so yeh willnae need tae put me up anawhere, and I quite enjoy the train. Aye, I'd be willin' tae do tha' for yeh," he said. "I dinnae ken if there are treatment surgeries there, but I know someone who might." He carefully laid his shirt over the rose, then hit the call button.

Wendy came rushing into the room. "What's wrong?" she asked, out of breath.

"I'm sorry tae worry yeh, but we have a question. Are there surgeries, such as this, in Edinburgh?" he asked.

"I imagine there are. I'll find out for you, sit tight," she said and left the room.

"Well, this isn't awkward at all, laying here with my legs in the... stirrups... and only a sheet... between me and the, uh, rest of the world," Erin said, after a long stretch of silence.

The thought of it made him feel awkward as well. "Aye, I reckon... et—" he began, but then Wendy came back in with a sheet of paper in her hand.

"There's a location in Leith and one in the old town. I've written out the addresses for you. Were you asking for a friend, or—"

"I want to stay with David's family, and Louis said he'd be willing to travel there for me. Can we set up an appointment at one of them, please?" Erin asked. "Either one is fine with me. I'll be staying pretty much right between the two, but I love the Old Town, so I guess I'd choose that one, although it truly doesn't matter to me."

"I love the Old Town as well, so I suppose that's where I'd choose unless there's not anathin' available, then Leith is just as good," Louis said.

"Alright, then I'll schedule an appointment for two weeks from now in Edinburgh. I can make two if you plan to stay for that long," Wendy said helpfully.

"I'm not sure, I mean, I couldn't ask Louis to come back like that," Erin said.

"Ach, I'll jest stay if yeh need me to," he said nonchalantly. "I work for maself, so I can do what I want, and ma housemate will tend the cat whilst I'm away."

"I—" she started to say, but he cut her off.

"Jest schedule two appointments, please," he said.

"Alright, then I'll email you the times and dates," Wendy said and walked out the door.

"Thank you, Louis. It means a lot to me," Erin whispered, sounding more than a little choked up. "I could really use some time with... my family... right now."

"Dinnae worry, love," he said, and then remembered the rose. He lifted his shirt and looked at it, lying on top of her clothing, and almost changed his mind. "Right, Erin?"

"Uh, yeah?" she said.

"It's my turn tae ask... well, tell yeh somethin'. Yeh see, I've brought yeh... well, somethin', but... I dinnae want yeh tae read anathin' intae et. Et's jest because I felt heartsick about... last time and I wanted tae cheer yeh up a bit, tha's all," he said, rubbing the back of his head and feeling like it was a horrible idea in hindsight.

"Oh, um, well, thank you, although... I don't think it's a good idea to start... getting things for each other and all that, but... it's nice of you to—" she began but then seemed to change her mind. "Just please don't do it again," she said quite firmly.

"I'm sorry... I don't want to be rude, especially after you've been so accommodating, but I... can't... and you can't... Don't you understand? I can't... start to... like you! I'm married and desperately in love with my husband. I don't need to complicate things by... thinking about you... more than—Please, I beg you, try to understand and take pity on me!" she said with real anguish.

"Aye, ye're right, and I'm sorry. I'll no' do et again," he said, then turned around and looked at the curtain, wishing for X-ray eyes. "Goodbye, Erin, see yeh in Scotland in two weeks."

—

Erin heard the door close and sighed, she could tell he was a kind, thoughtful man. *Too kind and thoughtful,* she thought. She was already heading down a slippery slope and would have a hard time trying to gain back any lost ground in the feelings department if she didn't nip it in the bud right then. It made her come across as a bitch, but what else could she do?

When she sat up and pulled the curtain away, she saw a beautiful peach-colored rose tied with a light blue ribbon on her clothing and nearly cried. After she cleaned up and got dressed, she picked it up and smelled it, feeling the delicate softness of the petals on her lips. She thought about how he felt inside her and secretly longed for them to be his lips on hers, *brushing them lightly across—*

"What are you doing, Erin?" she said out loud and held the demon flower away from her as though it were possessing her. "NO! You're not going there!" she scolded herself and threw it into the bin, along with the tissues she'd used to clean up with.

Chapter Twenty-Nine

OWLGATE WITHOUT DAVID

That afternoon, Erin and Kitty stepped off the plane, Erin carrying Juniper in her car seat, and Kitty with the carry-on luggage. They'd packed light to save time, and Erin knew that either Kitty or Millie would make sure things got washed as needed. The baby had slept most of the way to Edinburgh, which was a blessing, but she would soon be fussy and need to be fed.

As they entered the arrivals concourse, Erin noticed a commotion. Suddenly, she was surrounded by people holding their phones up or carrying cameras, each vying for a good shot of her. "Erin! Are you here to visit David's mum?"

"Erin! How have you been holding up?" the people began saying to her while blocking her way.

"Erin, please stop for a moment and speak to us. I'm here on behalf of other Fertilis Defect sufferers, because we care about you," one woman said.

Erin heard something in her voice that made her stop. "Kitty, will you please take Junie and find a seat while I talk to them?" She could see that her friend wanted to argue and tell her to ignore them, but she nodded and did as she was asked.

"I don't understand why any of you care, not that I believe you *really* do. I know you're after headlines and want me to say something controversial so your careers will take off. I don't even know why I stopped, except that I'm tired, and I want you to get your fill and leave us alone, though I have a bad feeling I'll regret it."

The woman who'd gotten her to stop spoke up, saying, "I reckon it's wise for you to feel that way, Erin, but I'm not a reporter. My name is Nadine, and I started a vlog for women who were born with the Fertilis Defect, where I discuss what the true ramifications of your husband's prosecution means for you *and* them. FD sufferers are frightened, and I believe rightfully so, that the same thing could potentially happen to them. They feel you and David were persecuted with a discriminatory bias, regardless of whether or not he physically harmed anyone, and by not allowing you conjugal visits, the judge has sentenced you as well."

Erin had a lump in her throat and covered her mouth with her hand. The crowd was silent for a moment while she collected herself, then leaned in to hear her response. "I… didn't know about—I guess I didn't think about what it might mean to other women, like me. I… I thought it was something… that would only affect me and David. It makes sense that every judgment sets a precedent, so it could be used to argue for or against someone else in the future."

She looked into the eyes of the woman and then touched her arm. "Thank you for taking up the cause, Nadine. I'd like to speak to you more about this, but I'm afraid my daughter won't be willing to wait for me. Do you have a card so I can reach out to you?"

"I do, and I've written my personal mobile number on the back, along with my email. I would love to tell you more, and possibly interview David when he's released… to raise awareness… that is, if he's willing to do so," she said, and her cheeks flushed as she handed her a business card. "Sorry, I don't want to get ahead of myself."

"That's okay, I'll speak to him about it. Now, I really do have to go," Erin said and could hear Junie start to fuss.

"Thank you for stopping, and safe journeys," Nadine said as the other reporters made way for Erin to reunite with Kitty and Juniper.

"That was amazing," she said to Kitty as she picked up the car seat and headed straight toward the exit. Thankfully, she saw Roger waiting for them. He grabbed the baggage from Kitty while Erin got in, not waiting for him to open the door for her, and immediately started feeding Junie.

—

When Roger got into the driver's seat, he looked in the rearview mirror and saw Erin trying to get the baby to latch on. He could feel his cheeks become painfully red and looked away, utterly embarrassed.

"I'm sorry, Roger; I would normally cover up better, but she's fussy and needs—"

"Dinnae worry, Erin! I can handle it," he said and turned his gaze to the tarmac ahead of them while they waited. "How was your flight?"

"I used to think travel was fun. I looked forward to going to the airport and being on a plane headed somewhere different. Now, I just want to be home and not have to deal with outrageous prices and rude people. I'm so glad to be here with my family," she said, and then reached out to touch his shoulder.

He made the mistake of looking in the rearview mirror again and saw the beautiful scene of mother and child, though this time he wasn't as quick to turn away. "Ach, sorry, Erin, but yeh do look bonnie with yer bairn at yer breast," he said rather candidly, and it was Erin's turn to blush.

"Thank you," she whispered. "You remember Kitty?" she asked, clearly wanting to change the subject.

"I do," he said, and quickly smiled at her in the mirror without looking at Erin that time. "Hello, Kitty, et's good tae see you again."

"'Ellow, sir, it's nice ta see you, as well," Kitty said cheerfully.

"Ach, no need for usin' 'sir' with me, remember? I'm jest the driver and handyman; call me Roger, a'right?"

"You're more than that to me," Erin said. "Just like Kitty, she's our housekeeper, but she's also my friend and support. She's been amazing, taking on the role of nanny when I need her, and I need her all the time! I couldn't manage without her!"

Kitty blushed and shrugged her shoulders. "Aww, mum, it's nufin'. Our lit'le Junie is worf it, ain't she now?" she said, as Erin handed the baby to her and refastened her nursing bra. Kitty put her over her shoulder and started pounding the baby's back until she let out a nice big belch.

"Well done!" Roger said, and though he didn't mean to, he glanced into the mirror again as she switched sides. It was difficult for him not to stare at such a beautiful sight, but he looked away quickly.

—

"I'll only be a few more minutes," Erin said and felt silly sitting in the car while Kitty and Roger waited for her. Finally, Junie was done and was handed to Kitty for another burping. Once she was covered up again and Junie was secured in her seat, they pulled out of the car park.

Eventually, they arrived at Owlgate, where Roger got out, opened the heavy gate, got back into the SUV, drove through the opening, and got out to close it again. He then got back in and drove them to the front steps. "Oh, Roger! It's good to be back!" Erin said as tears of joy filled her eyes.

"Aye, we've missed yeh," he said, and smiled at her in the mirror.

He got out to open the door for Kitty, then opened the door on the other side for Erin. She unbuckled and lifted Juniper out of her seat, then got out and started walking toward the steps, assuming Kitty was following her. However, when she turned to say something to her, she saw that she was still at the SUV, waiting for Roger to hand her their bags.

"Follow me, Kitty, Roger will take care of that… I mean, you don't mind, do you? I mean… you always have before. I've never asked, but is that in your job description?" she said, just then realizing she'd taken his help for granted.

Roger smiled and came around the car to her. "There's no' a job description for what I do, Erin, and I dinnae mind doin' et for you," he said and gave her a hug. "Ye're so thoughtful, love; I appreciate tha' about you. Go on and find Ann and Millie, both of yous. I reckon they're impatient tae see the bairn… and you, of course."

"Thank you, Roger. Make sure you come in and say a proper hello to Juniper, okay?" she said.

"Aye," he said, and returned to the car.

The women ascended the grand staircase that led to the large front door, and Erin decided to ring the doorbell, just for fun. She remembered standing there with David nearly a year earlier, nervous and excited to meet his mother. Back then, she'd felt horrible, thinking no one liked her, especially Millie, the housekeeper, cook, David's former nanny, and most importantly, Annis Elliott's life partner.

The dogs were going crazy, barking on the other side of the door, and Erin could see Millie, in her mind's eye, getting aggravated at them. She took Juniper from Kitty just as the door opened. Millie took one look at them and made a noise like a cat being tortured, or a really old, really squeaky door being opened slowly.

"Ach, ma dear girl!" she said, bawling like a child. "Yer a sight fer these sore old eyes! We've missed yeh somethin' fierce! Come in, come in! Ach, and here's our wee Juniper! Ach, come inside." She pulled Erin into the house and pretty much ignored Kitty, but that was understandable since she hadn't seen the baby for a while.

"Hello, Millie, I've missed you too! Do you wanna hold her?" Erin asked, seeing the look of longing in her eyes. The old woman put her hand up to her mouth and acted like she would decline, but Erin persisted. "I know you want to, and it would be a real help to me. She gets so heavy!" she said a bit dramatically, and then turned to wink at Kitty, who knew what she was up to.

"Oochh! Ye're sae bonnie, ma wee Juniper. Ach, look at yeh! Yer da was no' much begger than you when I became his nanny. He was a bonnie lad as well, aye, he was, ma love," Millie cooed. She fussed over her dress, on how wee and sweet it was, and Erin could tell she didn't really want to hand her over to Roger when he came into the house.

"Where's Mother?" Erin asked. She couldn't quite seem to bring herself to call her Mum, as she thought she would. In her eyes, Annis was too queenly, or something, and it felt more natural to call her Mother.

"She'll be down shortly, I expect. She's gone tae change out of her gardenin' kit, yeh ken?" Millie said, keeping an eye on Roger, whom she clearly thought wasn't qualified to hold such a wee bairn.

"You and David must be so verra proud! She's an angel; and look at tha' ruddy hair! I dinnae recall anaone in the Elliott clan havin' red hair, do you, Millie?" Roger asked with a slight grin, apparently aware she was hovering over him.

"Humph!" she said but didn't move.

"My dad used to have red hair," Erin said and touched one of the ginger tendrils on her forehead. *There was a little girl, who had a little curl, right in the middle of her forehead. When she was good, she was very, very good, and when she was bad, she was horrid!"* she quoted, making everyone laugh.

"One day she went upstairs, when her parents, unawares, in the kitchen were occupied with meals; and she stood upon her head in her little trundle-bed, and then began hoooraying with her heels. Her mother heard the noise, and she thought it was the boys a-playing at a combat in the attic; but when she climbed the stair, and found Jemima there, she took, and she did spank her most emphatic," they heard Annis reciting on her way down the stairs.

Everyone applauded, which startled Juniper, and she began to cry. Erin was about to take her from Roger, but Annis hurried and managed to lift her swiftly into her arms, gently shushing and bouncing her until she quieted down. "I didn't know there was more to the poem than that! My mom used to say it to me when I was growing up, I don't even know who wrote it," Erin said.

"Henry Wadsworth Longfellow, dear, isn't that right, my little sweetums? Aye, et is," she cooed.

Juniper looked up at her grandmother and smiled. "Gwahh," the four-month-old said. "Dadadada." Her little feet bounced and kicked in their stockings as she gurgled and giggled. Then she reached out and grabbed Annis's nose.

"Aww!" The three permanent residents of Owlgate said in unison.

"I'll bring your fings to your room, mum, if 'at's a'right?" Kitty offered.

Erin smiled, watching her family enjoying her daughter. "Okay, I'll come with you." Kitty followed her up the main staircase that wound up the center of the house. She opened the door to David's old bedroom and smiled, noticing that Roger had put a comfortable-looking rocking chair in the room. "That'll be nice," she said as Kitty started putting things away. "You can use the blue room across the hall, the one we used to get me dolled up for the wedding."

"A'right, mum," Kitty said.

Erin went to David's side of the bed and pulled his pillow from under the blankets of the perfectly made bed. She lifted it to her face and inhaled deeply. It didn't smell much like him, though it did smell like the detergent Millie used, which was nearly good enough. She held the pillow and turned away from Kitty, wanting to hide her tears, but soon the trickle turned into sobs, and Kitty came to comfort her.

"It's a'right, Erin, let it out," she said and put her hand on her grieving friend's shoulder.

"Erin, dear, I believe wee Junie needs a new nappy," Annis said as she entered the room through the open door. "Ach! Yeh poor thing." She handed the baby to Kitty, who then left the room to give them privacy and to change the baby's diaper. Annis went to her daughter, who wept on her shoulder until she was able to calm down.

"I don't think I can do this, Mother. I feel like I'm going to lose it. I've… had to find a… temporary match, and it kills me! It's killing David as well, but if I stop the treatments, I could die. I… want to die sometimes." She hadn't meant to tell her any of that, it just poured out of her.

"Of course yeh do, ma dear. I felt verra much as ye're feelin' now when ma Charles died. Et's no' the same thing, but I ken how et feels tae miss yer love and no' be able tae stand et. And you with yer wee bairn tae care for, and then the older children as well. I'd be worrit if yeh didn't feel as though yeh were goin' out of yer mind."

"Mum?" she said softly, feeling like a small child, wanting comfort.

"Aye, love? Let's set for a spell, a'right?"

"Okay," Erin said and sat in the rocking chair. "There's so much… stress. We're not allowed to kiss, even though I've seen other prisoners and their loved ones do it, and I'm scared for David. He's not eating, and he's torturing himself, thinking I'm going to leave him for my temporary match. I don't know how to make him understand that I'll never do that, but—"

"But?"

"Well, visitations have become… almost frightening. He can't help but rage and cry and panic. It stresses me out so much that even with the treatments each fortnight, I'm struggling. I… don't think it's enough.

"When I went back to America before Junie was born, I didn't have a treatment for five days and started passing out, hyperventilating, and couldn't stay awake. How do I tell my husband, the love of my life, that twice a month with another man isn't enough? Oh, Ann, and it's worse when the children are home. I love them so much, and they have been more awesome than I have ever known kids to be, but it's exhausting with both them and Junie. I don't know what to do."

"I don't envy you, Daughter. Ye're between a rock and a hard place, ma dear, and I can't give yeh the correct answer or tell yeh what yeh should do. The one thing I will say is that if et's true ye're no' tempted tae leave him for the other man, then yeh should look after yerself the best yeh can. Yeh can't be a good mother if yeh can't function."

"I agree, but just the thought of telling him makes it hard to breathe." She put her hand to her chest and frowned. "I'm going to try to make it, but I may have to give in, at least while the kids are home for any length of time."

"Aye. I'll expect tae have them for at least a week before they return tae school in September. Yeh needn't do et all yerself, dear, ye've family tae support yeh. Perhaps you should consider… well, I hate tae say et, but for David's health and sanity…yeh might no' mention increasing yer treatments? I'd no' lie to him, mind, but you might jest not bring et up, yeh ken?"

Erin studied her husband's mother's face, considering that option. "That might… work. I'd feel gutted with guilt, but it would save his feelings and sanity, like you said. Thank you, and thanks for listening to me, Mother. I can't believe I told you all that!"

Annis smiled at her and stood, then she bent down and kissed Erin's cheek. When Kitty held Juniper out for her to take, with a fresh diaper and a smile, she laughed. She took the baby from the young woman and said, "Thank you, Kitty."

"I couldn't survive without Kitty, Mother. She's been my… savior, I guess, through all this," Erin said with tears of gratitude in her eyes.

"Aww, g'on," Kitty said and blushed, "It's nice ta see you again, Mrs. Elliott, ma'am."

"That's praise, indeed, young lady! It's a pleasure to see you again as well, dear, and you may call me Ann," she said.

"Yes, mum," Kitty said and shrugged.

"Kitty's only flaw is that she has an aversion to calling anyone she feels is above her by their first name. She only calls me Erin if it's vital to do so, but I'm getting used to it," Erin said with a smile.

"I'm glad our Erin has you tae take such good care of her. How long have you worked for my son, Kitty?"

"Blimey, I reckon it's been five years, now, mum."

"I'm quite sure I've visited David's home within the last five years, why don't I remember seeing you before the wedding? You're clearly an essential part of the household," Annis said.

Kitty looked down and kicked the toe of her shoe over the carpeting. "Mrs. Elliott… I mean… the former Mrs. Elliott din't care much for me, mum. She sent me away when you were meant ta visit."

Annis pursed her lips, clearly irritated. "I try ma best no' tae speak ill of the dead, but I reckon yer service, so tae speak, wasn't meant for tha' evil, wicked woman. Perhaps you were meant tae be the person who helps our dear Erin and ma poor David survive. Et seems tae me ye're doin' a fine job of et so far, and I thank God for yeh," the grand older woman said, making Kitty stand taller and smile at her and Erin.

"Hear, hear! I concur! I couldn't have said it better, plus, everything sounds better with a Scottish accent, anyway," Erin said. "I feel a bit better now that I've gotten some of that off my chest. What time is it? I'm hungry."

"I reckon et's nearly time for tea. I'll jest take this wee bundle down with me then," Annis said and left the room before anyone could object.

"She's an amazin' woman, mum," Kitty said.

"Aye, she's so wise and… I don't know, well-bred. I wanna be her when I grow up," Erin said, and both women giggled.

"I fink ya are a'ready."

"Oh, Kitty, you're so sweet, thank you."

Chapter Thirty

GALA PREPARATIONS

Erin and Annis spent that whole week hunting for the perfect gala dress. They went to every clothier in town before finally finding a long, black, low-cut, high-waisted dress. Erin hoped it would accentuate her top and hide her belly, since her recent pregnancy was still quite noticeable. Next came shoes, undergarments, and finally, a haircut.

She thought she'd have to go to the gala alone since David couldn't come, but Annis graciously offered to be her date, which took a load off her mind. The Christmas dinner at an old supper club, hosted by Todd's employer, had been the fanciest event she'd ever been to, well, that and the Bollywood party, but that was different. She honestly didn't know how to prepare herself, so her mother-in-law was bombarded with question after question about what to expect and how to behave.

"Don't worry, dear, I'll keep a hawk's eye on yeh," Annis assured her on Friday night. "And if yeh feel as though ye're in hot water, excuse yerself and find me."

"I'm terrified they'll tear me to shreds, and I'll end up digging myself deeper into the pit they've prepared to trap me in," Erin said, frowning.

"I've no doubt they'll try, but I ken ye'll make et through jest fine. Yeh already know they'll be lookin' tae find fault, so you can keep yer wits about yeh."

"But what do I say when they ask about David, or, God forbid, Susannah?"

"Ye'll tell them the truth, dear. David didn't do anathin' wrong, and you were here when Susannah died, so you ken the truth of et. You even tried tae save her life, so ye've nothin' tae fear," Annis said and took her daughter-in-law's hand in hers.

Erin smiled, hoping she was right. The Gala was the next night, and she didn't think she'd be able to sleep at all. "Well, I should probably go get my beauty sleep, God knows I need it!" she said, and laughed. "Goodnight, Mother."

"Wait, dear, I've somethin' for you tae wear tomorrow. Come with me."

Erin followed her mother-in-law into the closet of the room she shared with Millie and sat on a small, upholstered chair, waiting to find out what it could be. She watched the older woman move a step stool to one of the high shelves above the many racks and drawers in the sizable room. She opened the door and reached up to what looked like an oversized shoebox covered with a floral design.

"Let me help you," Erin said and stood next to her.

"Thank you, ma dear. I must've shrunk, as I used tae be able tae reach et," she said and smiled.

She stood on the stool, easily took the box off the shelf, and handed it to her. As Annis walked over to her bed and opened the box, Erin imagined moths flying out of it, released from their musty prison, though that didn't actually happen. It did remind her of David, though, and she felt a pang of sadness at it.

She watched as Annis took out several flat, velvet and leather covered jewelry boxes. Next, she lifted a tall, half circle shaped box covered with very old velvet which had faded into a lovely color, close to purple. It had silk ribbon embroidery made up of tiny knots arranged to look like flowers, leaves, and a voluptuous bow, which had all faded as well.

Erin gasped at the beauty of it and covered her mouth with her hand in shock and delight. "Oh, Mother, that's exquisite! What's in it?" she asked. Annis smiled and set it on the bed, then she put all the other boxes back into the shoebox and set it aside. "That's what you were looking for? Oh, Mother!" She could hardly control her excitement.

"I meant tae loan this to yeh on yer weddin' day, but it wouldn't have been suitable with yer dress. Et'll be perfect with yer attire for the Gala, though." She handed Erin the old box and watched her examine the outside of it like a child. "Go on, dear, open it."

Erin flipped the tiny, beautiful clasp, and slowly lifted the lid. "Oh, Ann… Mother, it's beautiful!" Tears rolled down her face, just from being in the presence of something so stunning. Laying on a bed of rich maroon velvet that was much brighter than the faded outside, was a delicate tiara. It was silver, with diamonds and sapphires.

"I'm pleased yeh fancy et, love. Now, get yeh off tae bed, and I'll see you in the mornin'."

Erin set the tiara down in its box and hugged her. "Now I know I'll *never* fall asleep tonight! I'm far too excited! Thank you so much for… all you've done for me," she said and turned away, not wanting her to see more tears.

"Nae, thank you, dear, for all ye've done fer ma son and his wee bairns. Ye're a Godsend."

Chapter Thirty-One

GALA NIGHT

Erin had loved her new dress when she bought it and had been looking forward to wearing it, but when she put it on Saturday night, she started having second thoughts. The front was much lower cut than she'd ever worn in public before, and she wondered what she'd been thinking. There was no time to change her mind, so she fretted and worried as Kitty fixed her hair, attaching the beautiful, antique tiara so that it didn't fall out.

Kitty tried to reassure her that it wasn't as bad as she thought; however, Erin was sure that it was, and she'd be laughed at behind her back or right in front of her face since many of them would be wealthy, entitled, pompous women. She did her makeup with a towel draped over her front, and when it was removed, Kitty gasped. "Cor blimey, ya look stunnin', mum! The only reason anaone might be talkin' about you t'night, is b'cause they're jealous."

"Thank you, Kitty," she said as the two women gazed into the full-length mirror.

When she and Erin were both ready, Annis sent a message to Roger, asking him to bring the SUV around for them. Erin was so nervous, she felt like she had to pee every few minutes, which was annoying. She also kept putting her hand up to cover her cleavage, but after the fifth time, Millie took her hands in hers and smiled at her.

"Ye're a bonnie sight t'night, ma dear. I think we should take a photograph tae mark the occasion." She asked Erin to stand near the piano in the drawing room and used Annis's phone to take a few pictures. Then she asked Annis to join them and took a few more. "Ach, I wish our Davey were here tae see yeh t'night! He'd be beside himself."

—

"Are yeh ready?" Roger said, coming through the door, wanting to know what the hold-up was, but as soon as he saw Erin, he stopped and stared. "Ach, Erin, ye're… pure braw!" he said softly and approached her timidly. He took her hand and kissed it, completely enchanted by her. "I'd be proud if you were holdin' ma arm tonight."

Erin blushed and smiled. "Thank you, Roger. You know how to make a girl feel bonnie."

"Ach! David should be here!" he said passionately, suddenly aggrieved and sorrowful, echoing Millie's comment, which he hadn't heard.

—

Erin's smile fell, and she sighed. "I really wish he was, too," she said and fanned her eyes with her gloved hand.

Annis had also loaned her a lovely necklace, earrings, and a bracelet, which caught the light in the room and made little circles dance on the walls. They began to feel heavy as Erin thought about attending the stupid gala without her husband. She was suddenly resentful toward Oscar for the imagined necessity of her attendance that night. It wasn't fair, she was the one who'd been raped, yet it felt to her as though she were being assaulted again by the fear that if she didn't go, they might let Bran out.

"A'right, ma dear, et's time tae be off," Annis said, looking stunning as well.

Erin had never thought about the fact that her mother-in-law would sometimes need to dress up for formal events. She was wearing a platinum grey chiffon gown with lace accents. Her hair and makeup were flawless, and she looked as elegant, modern, and tasteful as any aging movie star she'd ever seen.

"By the way, Mother, you look simply smashing," she said, and took her hand as they walked out the front door of Owlgate.

After first helping Annis, Roger beamed with pride as he opened the car door for Erin in front of the venue. "Give 'em hell," he whispered and saw her cheeks become rosy. He couldn't help but take a moment to admire her before getting back in and driving away.

Erin followed Annis into the old Scotsman Hotel, not sure what to do or expect. Annis was so sure of herself and led the way so that Erin could copy her. They followed other guests downstairs, through a stunning, marble stairwell and landing, then stepped up to a table where invitations were being taken.

In a large room to her left, she saw wood-paneled walls and hardwood floors. Half a dozen large, round tables were all decked out, looking like floating princesses with long, flowing skirts. She'd always dreamed of attending a real black tie, formal ball but never imagined it would actually happen.

Once their invitations were verified, they made their way into the dining room and found place cards with their names on them. Erin was thankful that their table was near the doors at the back of the room, in case she needed to make a speedy exit for some reason. She placed her handbag on her chair and stood awkwardly, not knowing what to do next.

Having never worn a tiara before, she was self-conscious and touched it, scanning the room in hopes of seeing someone else wearing one as well. She put her hand over her front as she'd done a dozen times since they'd arrived, even more anxious and distressed for not choosing a more sensible gown.

Annis smiled at her and took her hand. "Et's no' as bad as you imagine, dear, and the tiara is lovely. Ye're fretting for nothing," she said.

"I wish David were here; I feel so alone. I'm sorry, Mother, I know you're here for me, but—" she began.

"Ach, I ken jest how ye're feelin', ma dear." Annis patted her hand and then looked over Erin's shoulder. "Chin up, here comes trouble."

"Annis! How lovely tae see you here tonight," a petite woman said, holding out her hands as if expecting Annis to take them. She couldn't have been more than five feet tall and couldn't have worn anything bigger than a size one. Erin recognized her from the photographs of Bran posing as David.

"Sandra—Et's good tae see you as well. Have yeh met my daughter-in-law, Erin?" Annis said, only offering one hand to her and placing the other on Erin's arm.

"Nice to meet you," Erin said, remembering too late that she should've waited to be given the other woman's name first.

"Erin, this is Sandra Campbell," Annis said, ignoring her faux pas.

"Well, look at you! Ye've married our David, haven't you?" she said, dripping with disdain.

"Good guess, since he's an only child and his mother just introduced me as her daughter-in-law," Erin said with a forced smile, giving it right back to her.

"Well played, dear," she said, cloying her with the saccharin in her voice. "She's a bright one, isn't she, Annis?"

"Aye, she is, and I am quite fond of her, so you may retract yer claws, Sandra," she said, and Erin was grateful.

"So… how *is* our *poor* David then? Still in prison, I presume?" she said, and Erin saw red.

Annis gently squeezed her arm to keep her calm and answered for her. "Yeh ken et well enough, I dare say," she said, but then another woman joined them, and introductions were made. "Erin, this is Déserée Davies."

Déserée was quite obviously a fan of plastic surgery. Her nose was pinched so thin that Erin was sure her head would explode if she suddenly sneezed, and her lips were so puffy she wondered if it hurt. She was quite a bit taller than Sandra and was probably about a size four, with grey eyes and brown, highlighted hair, styled impeccably. This woman had also been in the photos with Bran.

"Well, look at you!" she echoed Sandra's comment perfectly.

Erin guessed that was their way of saying, 'bless your heart!' covertly meaning something like, 'look at how fat and ugly you are!' which was what she guessed they were thinking. "Aren't you adorable?" she added. "How is *poor* David faring in that *horrible* place?"

"As well as can be expected for an innocent man," Erin said, really hating the banter.

"Of course, dear, of course," Déserée said, then shot Sandra a look.

"Well, then… I'm in need of the powder room, if you'll please excuse me?" Erin said, needing to get away.

"Of course, dear. I remember all too well how often I had to use the toilet when I was pregnant," Déserée said, and Erin chose to ignore her.

After checking her hair and makeup, Erin left the bathroom and overheard several women talking. "Innocent? Poppycock!" Sandra said. "Clive himself told me what that brute did to the poor young officer!"

"He told me that Susannah once called him whilst David was consorting with the gold digger. She told him that David fancied cocaine and would beat her when he was high," another woman said.

"He told me that, as well. That is what he was looking for in their house. He said Susannah had found David's stash and told Clive that if anything ever happened to her, he should go there and have him arrested. I reckon he didn't find anything, though. David and his new wife probably used it all!" Déserée said.

"*I* heard that after one of David's drug addled tirades, Susannah was so badly beaten that Clive hid her in a hotel room to keep her safe. Apparently, he has a horrid temper," yet another woman said.

Though the gala had just begun, Erin felt tired and worn out as she made her way back to the table and sat at her place, next to Annis. "None of these people are going to be my friends, Mother. I just thought I'd let you know ahead of time," she said.

"Aye, dear, I believe that's a wise decision," Annis said with a smile.

There were three other couples seated at their table, one of which Erin thought she recognized from the photos. She wasn't sure, and it was difficult for her to be polite and not stare. Everyone made small talk until the staff began serving.

First, large bottles of flat and sparkling water with lemon wedges on the side were set out, then coffee and tea were offered. Soup and starters came next, then perfectly plated food, served by smartly dressed, professional, courteous men and women. They brought plate after plate of food, each more lovely and delicious than the last.

The two women she'd met earlier were seated at an adjacent table with their oblivious husbands and two other couples she hadn't met yet. They were close enough for Erin to hear most of what they were saying, when she chose to listen, and she tried not to.

"David's new wife—" Sandra said.

"Yes?" one of the unknown women said.

"Did you notice, she's absolutely licking the plates clean?" she said, and the rest began to snigger.

"I doubt we'll see her in the toilets later," Déserée said.

"Not with that body!" the other woman said to more laughter.

"David has lowered his standards!" Sandra said. Erin didn't want to hear anymore, so she excused herself, but Déserée tried to trip her. "Oh, dear, terribly sorry," she said, not hiding her smile.

Erin caught herself and then lost her temper. "Maybe you're right, maybe David has lowered his standards, but at least he has some, since your husbands apparently don't," she shot back at them, managing not to raise her voice.

Sandra stood and whispered into her ear, "Well! I know a few… intimate details about your husband that would—"

Erin's laugh was easy and confident. "Is that who you thought he was? Sorry to disappoint you. Fun fact: David has a look-a-like cousin who's a junkie and probably has every communicable disease. You and your friends might wanna get checked," she said.

Sandra's eyes widened, so Erin figured the slut wasn't likely to say anything more about it in public after that. The woman didn't have a comeback, so she took her leave and spent the next few minutes in the ladies room trying to calm her temper and her racing heart. When she returned, she smiled at her mother-in-law and felt more confident than she had all night.

Chapter Thirty-Two

AN EARNEST PLEA

When dessert, or what they called the pudding, was brought out, Oscar stood behind a podium at the front of the room to address the crowd. "Good evening to all of my esteemed and, thankfully, wealthy guests," he began in his plea for funds, making his audience laugh. Erin smiled, noticing how uncommon he was, and stopped paying much attention to his words, focusing more on how he engaged the crowd.

His wit, charm, and demeanor won people over, and he seemed to her to be a likable man. She remembered the day he'd come to take Bran away. His presence commanded respect, and his name alone had terrified Bran when Annis had said it over the phone.

That day, he'd made her think of a renegade biker or a character from an apocalyptic aftermath film, but as he stood before them, he looked quite handsome in a well-tailored tuxedo. His long, dark blonde, greying hair was pulled back into a neat ponytail, and his smile was gentle and kind. Suddenly, he was smiling at her, and her cheeks grew warm as it seemed like he'd read her thoughts.

She wondered how a man like him was able to change personas so thoroughly. "He's quite striking when he's not being intimidating, isn't he?" Erin commented to Annis after his appeal for generous donations and his wish that everyone 'mingle and have a pleasant evening.' She knew that mingling, for her anyway, would not make for a pleasant evening at all.

"Aye, verra much so," Annis replied, and Erin thought she might've noticed a hint of a crush in her mother-in-law's voice.

"Ah-ha!" Erin said, teasing her. "Is that a bit more than mere admiration I detect, Mrs. Elliott?" The older woman actually blushed, and Erin laughed as she took her hand in hers. "No shame in that, Mother. You may not be young anymore, but you're not dead! How old do you reckon he is?" she asked.

"He's sixty-two," she answered quickly enough for her to know that she was on the right track.

"Mother?" She looked at her and saw that her face had deepened to a dark shade of rose.

"Dear me! Don't tell Millie! I can't help et, and I'd never do anathin' about et, yeh ken?" Annis said, looking worried and flustered.

Erin smiled at one of her favorite people in the world. "Your secret is safe with me, don't worry, it was just some harmless teasing. He's an attractive man; I'd be surprised if Millie didn't have a slight crush, too," she said.

"Humph, I dinnae reckon she does, dear. She doesn't fancy men, yeh ken?"

"Oh! Right, I see," she said and didn't know what else to say. They sat in silence for a few moments. "Would you like something to drink?

Annis looked relieved and nodded. "Aye, gin and tonic, please," she said, so Erin stood and headed to the bar.

Halfway there, she saw Oscar coming toward her. "Good evening, Erin—Oh, do forgive me, Mrs. Elliott. It's lovely to see you again," he said with a gentle English accent that made it difficult to guess where he was from. He extended his hand, so she did likewise, and his smile was genuine as he kissed the top of her hand.

"Good evening. You may call me Erin if I can call you Oscar?" she said, looking up at the man who had to be at least six foot, five inches tall. "I don't believe I know your surname, which is completely my fault. I should have done my homework." Oscar smiled again. *He does look kind when he smiles*, she thought.

"Of course you may, and my surname is Lincoln, in case you need to use it. I was so very sorry to hear of your husband's injustice, and I do believe that is what it's been. How are you coping, my dear? Are you in need of anything?"

Erin truly believed he was sincere in what he was saying and smiled at him. "Thank you for asking, Oscar. I'm doing alright, I have good days and bad, as I'm sure you can imagine. I have everything I need, more than I'm used to, if I'm allowed to be frank with you.

"By the way, I'd like to personally thank you for inviting us. I realize it's to raise money for the hospital, but I'm so grateful to you for… helping… take care of… Bran," she said, wanting him to remember, and to make sure he knew how she felt so he wasn't released, in case David's fears were warranted.

"I'm glad you've brought that up, actually. I very much need to speak with you about him if you have a moment, although Annis should probably be present for the conversation as well," he said almost as an afterthought.

"Me? You want to talk to me about… him?" she said, afraid he was going to tell her that they no longer had room and would be releasing him into their custody that night.

"Oh, dear, you look frightened! Don't worry, he's still quite well guarded, and you needn't worry about his release, if that's what you're afraid of," he said gently.

Erin smiled, relief washing over her. "That's good to hear. For a moment I thought you were going to tell me he'd escaped," Erin said with a nervous laugh.

Oscar shook his head and then leaned in a bit closer. "Would you and Annis be available to come to my office at the hospital sometime this week?"

"I'm… free all week, except Thursday morning. You'll have to speak to Ann about her schedule," she said, not really wanting to go to the place Bran was being held. A couple who looked to be about her age approached them, obviously wanting Oscar's attention. She thought the woman looked familiar, but she wasn't sure.

"Hello Ralph, Claudia, have you met Mrs. Erin Elliott?" he asked.

Erin smiled, expecting to see the same half-hearted smiles she'd been receiving from everyone she'd met that night upon being introduced. Fake smiles followed by the courtesy handshake, for etiquette's sake, though it seemed their smiles were genuine, at least in front of Oscar.

"No, we haven't, and we've heard so much about you," Claudia said. She was tall and had long, black, wavy hair. Her eyes looked almost black as well, and her makeup was flawless. "It's such a shame about David!"

"Erin, I'm pleased to introduce you to Ralph and Claudia Reynolds," Oscar said. Erin held out her hand, just as she'd done all night, and Claudia took it, like everyone else had done.

"It's a pleasure to meet you," Erin said simply. "Yes, it is a shame about David." She turned slightly to shake Ralph's hand, but he lifted it to his lips and kissed it instead. With sandy hair and blue eyes, he looked a bit like Cary Elwes. He was several inches shorter than his wife, and she took notice of how completely different they looked from one another.

"Your humble servant," he said. His smile was charming, and for some reason, his gaze made Erin blush.

Claudia didn't notice and continued the conversation. "I've known Annis for years; salt of the earth, she is," she said.

"I agree. I feel blessed to have her for my mother-in-law." *Well, at least she's a good judge of character.* Erin thought. "I… imagine you'd like to speak with Oscar, so I won't keep you. It really was nice to meet you." She didn't want to stand around for too long, being a nuisance.

"Yes, I'm afraid we do, but I'm sure we'll speak again soon," Claudia said and shifted her attention to Oscar. Her husband smiled warmly at Erin as she walked away.

Erin turned toward the table, then remembered the gin and tonic, so she headed back to the bar. Many of the guests were leaving the room, and all around her, the wait staff were clearing tables, though it was barely noticeable. When she returned with Annis's drink, she asked where they were going.

"The adjacent room to ma right has a band and dance floor, and to my left is the silent auction."

"Ooh, goody! That'll be fun," Erin said, hoping she'd be asked for at least one dance.

Chapter Thirty-Three

SWEPT OFF HER FEET

Oscar gave her the honor of his first dance of the night, which was a waltz. She saw the women in the crowd gaping at her as she floated effortlessly around the dance floor with him. "My dear woman!" he exclaimed when the song ended and they bowed toward each other. "I must say that you are the finest dancer at this event. I've danced with all but one…" he glanced at Annis, "woman in attendance, and none can compare."

Her face was already red from the exercise, but she felt it deepen at his compliment. "Really? Well, thank you! I'm just glad I managed to keep up with your long stride," she said and laughed. "I'm sure it's completely inappropriate for me to be so blunt, but I think I like you, Mr. Lincoln. You are a brilliant dancer yourself; your lead was impeccable. Thank you for asking me; it's… difficult being—" She couldn't finish, as she didn't want to cry.

"I understand, Erin, it was truly my pleasure. If you don't mind, I may ask you for another before the night is through?"

"I'd be honored, but do ask Annis as well, I happen to know she's had lessons," she said and smiled at him.

The next to ask for a dance was Ralph Reynolds, but she saw more than one man headed toward her, only to turn away once Ralph stepped up.

"Mrs. Elliott, would you be so kind as to honor me with this dance," he asked so formally, she couldn't help but let out a tiny giggle, which made his face fall.

"Oh! Oh, I'm sorry, I didn't mean to be rude, Mr. Reynolds. You were just so formal and… well, sweet, that it tickled me. Please don't be offended; I would love to dance with you."

The handsome man flashed a boyish grin at her and let out his own short laugh, seeming to relax a bit. He led her to the floor for a rumba. "You have a disarming way about you, Mrs.—"

"Please call me Erin, and I'll call you Ralph, alright?"

"A'right, Erin. It's impossible to know exactly what to say to… well, quite a few of the guests here tonight so as not to offend them. I try to cover… how would you say it? Cover all my bases, is it?"

"Yes, that's correct. You don't need to worry about offending me, Ralph, I'm quite easy to get along with as long as you don't outright insult me or my family, that is. Are you friends with… David?" Just saying his name brought a lump to her throat.

"We are acquaintances, really; invited to many of the same events as well as each other's social gatherings and such. I believe that has more to do with our wives, though," he said, and his eyes grew wide. "Oh dear! I've stepped in it, haven't I? I'm terribly sorry for that."

"It's… okay, I understand," she said, trying not to let it sting.

"I've admired him for his career and for how he's handled the attention he's received with… well, everything lately. I admit I tend to cow down in uncomfortable situations and try to blend in with the furniture, if you know what I mean?"

"I believe I do." She'd lost some of her energy, talking about David, and it must've shown, because Ralph frowned at her.

"Oh dear, I've made you uncomfortable, haven't I? I'm always saying the wrong thing. Claudia's forever reminding me to shut my gob."

"No, it's not… you, I just—" her eyes smarted with tears, "I… miss him, that's all," she whispered, and seeing that the song was done, she thanked him for the dance and quickly left the room before anyone could see them fall.

"There you are," she heard Oscar say when she returned, after somehow managing to keep it together.

"Here I am, who was looking for me?" she asked, and the half dozen men standing around the giant who was Oscar, raised a hand or finger to indicate it was they.

"Oh!" she said and blushed again. "I see, what for?" She thought she knew but didn't want to presume.

"We are all looking to sign your dance card, of course," Oscar said. "Do choose one of us for the next dance."

"You're serious? Me? But… okay." She closed her eyes and pointed to a short man with a hilarious ascot. "Well, I guess it's you," she said.

"Acsually, the only danth I'm any good at ith the walth," he said with a pronounced lisp. "If you'll be tho kind asth to thave the next one for me, I'd be honored?"

"Of course I will, Mr.—"

"Mathon, Gregory Mathon, Mrs. Elliott."

"Mr. Mason. You may… well, you *all* may call me Erin," she said, to her admirers, feeling like a celebrity, in a good way. "You have all made my evening, I hope you realize that?"

The next dance was a Foxtrot, so she looked at the men and chose the one who nodded. The following was a waltz, so she danced it with Gregory Mason. She hardly had time to breathe as she was led by so many fine dancers and was delighted to see Annis on the floor with Oscar more than once.

Silvano Sabatini was next; he was in his mid-sixties or perhaps early seventies and dressed to kill. His suit felt like silk, and he smelled delicious, to the point that it was intoxicating. "Mr. Sabatini, you are a divine dancer! Please tell me… my husband's favorite book is Captain Blood; are you related to Raphael Sabatini, the writer?"

"I believe I am, though not a direct descendant, unfortunately," he replied with a thick, though quite understandable, Italian accent.

"What part of Italy are you from?" she asked.

"I stay in Roma at the moment. Have you been?"

"Have I been to Rome? No, I haven't been to Italy at all, though I love Italian food," she said and laughed, knowing that what *she* thought of as Italian food was a far cry from anything authentic. "I'd love to go there someday and experience the real deal."

"You will be my guest, *mio caro*, should you decide to visit *my* country. I will hear no arguments, *bella*," he said as he led her off the floor. He then reached into his suit coat and handed her a linen business card.

"I will just have to talk David into it then," she said, allowing him to kiss both her cheeks. "Thank you again for the dance, it was delightful, honestly."

The next dance would be her last of the evening, and even then, she wasn't sure she'd be able to stay upright for another one. She chose Oscar as her partner before she knew it would be an incredibly fast foxtrot. Therefore, because she had to modify her American ballroom technique to fit international standard, there was no conversation as she flew across the floor. She was completely winded when the music ended, and he kissed her hand.

"Erin, I find you delightful in every way. I am grateful to have had this opportunity to become better acquainted with you and am now slightly jealous of David's good fortune to be able to—" he paused as if trying to select his words wisely, "call you his wife," he finished.

"Wow, thank you, Oscar. I didn't have high hopes for this evening, to be honest, but I've had the best time in a long time," she said, and stood on her tiptoes to kiss his cheek.

Chapter Thirty-Four

A KINDRED SPIRIT AT THE BALL?

As Oscar led Erin off the dance floor, she noticed a tall, slender, elegantly dressed woman with long, perfectly straight red hair, and she seemed to be heading straight for her. She didn't mean to stare, but she reminded her so much of Anne Shirley that she couldn't help it. Suddenly, the woman was looking right at her and though she turned her head, Erin could feel the blood rise to her cheeks. Knowing she'd been caught, she shrugged as she approached her.

"Erin Elliott, I'd like you to meet Lizette Lovelock. She's asked me to introduce her to you," Oscar said.

"I'm sorry for staring, but you look so much like… well, never mind, it's not important," Erin said, feeling stupid and imagined the specter would look down her nose at her in disgust. Instead, the beautiful, freckle-faced woman smiled, revealing perfectly straight, white teeth. Her green eyes sparked, and she took both of Erin's hands in hers.

"You're just as I imagined you'd be, only better! I've heard nothing but 'Erin Elliott this,' and 'Erin Elliott that' since I arrived tonight. You have the divas in a tizzy, so I knew I simply must search you out," she said passionately.

The last thing Erin wanted was to be gawked at and made fun of, so she put on a fake smile and said, "Well, now you've seen me. I'm glad you're pleased." She began to turn away, but Lizette held tight to her hands.

"Wait, you've misunderstood me. I don't always say things the way I mean for them to come out. I'm terribly sorry, Mrs. Elliott. What I meant was that…

oh, my, I'm not sure how to say what I want to say. May I speak frankly to you?"

Erin still wasn't sure whether to trust the goddess in her pale green, flowing gown. "I guess so," she said tentatively.

"Thank you for introducing us, Oscar. I'll speak to you later, alright?" she said, almost rudely, then pulled Erin toward a bank of velvet couches.

"You're welcome—" he said, but they were already several feet away.

"Please excuse me, Mrs.—"

"Call me Erin, please."

Lizette sat gracefully on the steel grey couch, crossing her ankles, then took a shaky breath as Erin got comfortable. "I detest those women, Erin," she began and looked around her to ensure no one was listening to them.

"They hate you because you're an outsider and don't fit in with them, like… Susannah did. Honestly, Susannah didn't at first either, but that's a story for another time. They hate me because, well, honestly, I'm wealthier than they'll ever be, and I don't play their game… any longer. Oh, and the red hair doesn't help, I suppose."

"So, you wanted to meet me because everyone here hates us?" Erin said, thinking it a bit strange.

"In a way, yes. I reckon you must be feeling a bit like a fish out of water, and not only that, a horde of Neanderthal women have taken aim with their clubs, trying to beat you to death," she said and laughed.

Erin couldn't help herself and laughed at the mental imagery. "You're not wrong, I guess, though I hadn't thought of it quite like that. I'm just glad I have Annis to lean on."

Lizette's eyes widened, and a smile lit up her face. "Annis Elliott is a true pioneer when it comes to holding her own in the pack of wolves that are this social circle. I have admired her for years! I've only spoken to her briefly, but she carries herself like royalty, though not in a pretentious, stuffy way. I wish I could be more like her, actually. Having her on your side will go a long way toward keeping the bitches from biting."

"I'm truly blessed that she's my mother-in-law," Erin said, scanning the room for David's mother.

"Yes, Erin, I believe you've won the lotto between Annis and David Elliott. I would hazard a guess that's one of the other reasons the women hate you. Oh, and I saw you dancing with several of the gentlemen here earlier; they won't like that either."

"So… they don't hate me because I'm fat?"

Lizette looked at her and narrowed her eyes. "If we're being frank, and if you will try not to be offended by what I say, I'd say that, yes, they hate you because you're not thin. However, I'm thin and they hate me, as well. They hate everyone who isn't them, and it doesn't matter what reason they give for it. You'll never fit in with them and, in my estimation, that fact should be celebrated."

"Yes, you're right, and I agree, though I'd rather be hated for being thin and rich," Erin said and laughed lightly.

"I think you're too hard on yourself. You've just had a child, haven't you?"

"Well, yes, but I was big before that."

"Let me ask you, have any of the men been rude to you? Have they snubbed you because you're not thin?" Lizette asked.

"Well, no. I don't think so."

"I reckon men don't really care as much as women think they do about all that. Don't get me wrong, shallow men do, and perhaps immature ones as well, but I believe they'd rather have an honest, loving, partner and friend rather than a fake, liposuctioned woman who starves herself and hates everyone and everything, don't you?"

"I guess so."

"You have a way about you, Erin. Something under the skin, something… almost irresistible. Part of that is the honesty of your figure; you're not trying to hide or be someone else, and there aren't many people in this room whom I can say that about. Fake gets old, and you are a breath of fresh air.

"Listen to me! You'd think I had a crush on you!" The angelic creature's cheeks suddenly bloomed pink, and she laughed. "Alright, maybe just a small one," she said and looked into Erin's eyes, smiling.

"You? *You* have a crush on me? But next to David, I think you're one of the most beautiful people I've ever seen! That makes no sense to me, honestly," Erin said and fanned her burning cheeks with her hands.

Lizette leaned in a bit closer and spoke softly. "You can't help who you're attracted to, Erin. I find you alluring and—"

"There you are, Daughter. I was beginning tae worry," Annis said, startling them both and interrupting what Erin would later consider to be a seduction, of sorts.

"Hello, Mother, Lizette was just giving me a much-needed pep talk."

Lizette stood and seemed awkward for the first time. "Mrs. Elliott, it's nice to see you again," she said, and Erin was sure she saw her give a slight curtsy.

"Hello again, Lizette, you look breathtaking tonight. I don't know why we don't speak more often; I find you to be a lovely creature," Annis said, uncharacteristically open and complimentary.

The woman's blush deepened, and that time she did curtsy. "I'm… at a loss for words! I'd very much enjoy your company… any time."

"Let's have lunch, the three of us," Annis said.

Erin and Lizette looked at each other and smiled. "Yes, I think we should plan it now, so it doesn't get forgotten," Erin said. "I leave for London in two and a half weeks, and Thursday is already full."

"Why don't you join us for tea at Owlgate? Are you free on Tuesday?" Annis asked.

"I'd be honored to join you and will clear my calendar to do so," Lizette said eagerly.

"Good, then it's settled. Please arrive between three and four o'clock," Annis said and took the woman's hand. "Ach, I see someone I must speak with, so we'll see you then?"

"Yes, and thank you, Mrs. Elliott." Lizette turned to Erin, almost aglow with anticipation. "Oh, I've just remembered that when we were introduced, you said I reminded you of someone; please tell me who it is," she said, her smile beguiling.

"Oh, well, you look just like how I imagine Anne Shirley, from—"

"Anne of Green Gables? And you remind me of Diana. I think we should be best friends from this point on," she said and grasped Erin's hand in hers.

"Kindred spirits, for sure."

Chapter Thirty-Five

AFTER THE BALL

Erin and Annis spoke to Oscar before they left the Gala and agreed to come to Thistledown on Wednesday afternoon, though neither of them were looking forward to it. They stepped out into the comfortably warm June night and waited for Roger to come close enough to let them into the SUV.

"What a lovely night," Erin said and took her mother-in-law's arm.

"Aye, et is at that," Annis agreed.

Roger got out and opened the door for them, smiling proudly at the two Elliott women. Once he was on the road, he looked in the rearview mirror. "Yeh both look smashing; how was yer night, then?" he asked.

"I had a verra fine evenin', and I believe our Erin did as well," Annis said with a coy smile.

"Is tha' so?" he said with a gleam of amusement in his smile.

"She was the belle of the ball, I'd say," Annis continued.

"Now, Mother—"

"Ach, yeh can't deny et, Daughter. The women hated her, and the men were, quite literally, linin' up tae dance with her."

"Yeh dinnae say? Well, I'm no' surprised. I'd stand in line as well, yeh ken?"

"Oh, Roger, thank you. I did have a wonderful night. I was even invited to Rome, to be one immaculate man's guest!" Annis gave her a look she didn't understand. "What? Is that a bad thing? I… told him that I'd have to convince David—You don't think he meant anything… improper or—"

"I highly doubt et, dear. What was the man's name?" Annis asked.

"I don't remember his first name, but his last name was Sabatini," she said, worried she'd gotten mixed up with a mobster or something.

"Silvano Sabatini?" Annis said, and Roger whistled through his teeth.

"Well, I wouldn't turn him down, even if et *were* improper!" Roger said.

"Roger!" Annis said, and he laughed. "Dinnae look sae frightened, ma dear, he's not a dangerous man. He's hideously wealthy, born into money."

"I heard his family was from Monaco, so no one really knows where it all came from," Roger added.

"It's rumored that he and his family practically own everything in and around Rome. He's quite a big deal."

"Oh. I—I didn't... know," Erin said.

"Ye've never heard of Silvano Sabatini? He's the Richard Branson of Italy, in as far as his wealth and inclination toward dabbling his toes into numerous diverse business pursuits, anaway," Roger said.

"I know who Richard Branson is," Erin said, hoping she hadn't said anything stupid to him.

"An invitation from a man such as Mr. Sabatini is a great honor, Erin. I hate to ask, but how did you manage to come by it?" Annis asked.

"Well, I complimented his dancing and asked if he was related to Raphael Sabatini. He said yes, though distantly, then I asked him where he was from in Italy, and he said, 'I stay in Roma at the moment. Have you been?'," she said, mimicking his beautiful accent.

"Dear me, I imagine he's no' asked tha' verra often, go on," Annis said, clearly dying to know.

"Well, he asked if I'd ever been to Rome, and I said that I'd never been to Italy at all... but that... good night nurse—That I like Italian food and would love to go there someday and experience the real deal. Did I just invite myself? I didn't mean to! I really didn't!" Erin said, feeling like an idiot of an American.

"I don't imagine he'd fall for tha' from someone who wasn't sincere, love. What did he... say tae you?" Annis asked.

"Are you envious, Mother?"

"Me? I should say—Ach, aye, jest a wee bit, I must admit, but only tae you and our Roger," she said with a smile.

"He said I'd have to be his guest, ending with something in Italian that I assume meant 'my dear,' that he wouldn't hear any arguments, and… then he called me… bella. Wow! That's really exciting! I'm glad I didn't know who he was, or I would have been a *real* idiot," Erin said.

"And yeh told him ye'd have tae convince David? Ach, tha's crackin'," Roger said as they turned onto their street. "I cannae wait… I mean, I'd love tae see his reaction when yeh tell him."

"Me too," Erin said, though it was only a half-truth. She didn't want to tell him about the attention she'd gotten that night, afraid he'd be upset about it.

An hour and a half later, after her dress and makeup were off and she'd fed Junie, she sat at the desk in David's room. She stared out the windows at the side garden and the houses along the road outside the gates. The old tile roofs were in shadow, while their windows reflected the light coming from the closest streetlamp.

Dear David,

She wrote, then sighed. While it was happening, she couldn't fully experience the events of the night as she should. However, now that it was over, she wanted to hoard the feeling of being special and desired by those rich, obviously blind, men.

There was also the thought that she didn't want to be made to feel guilty about anything she shared if David became jealous. *Will he? Has he ever acted truly jealous, except over Louis? Well, he was about Roger… oh, and Bran, in a way. Well, I can't help it if he gets jealous, so I'll write what I want to.*

Dear David,

> *I feel a bit like Cinderella after the ball right now.*
> *The gala was interesting in so many ways. The women*
> *were horrible, but I expected that. What I didn't expect*

were the men. The men were sincere and kind and made me feel ~ valuable.

None of them looked down their noses or seemed to judge my size at all. One of them said that I had a disarming way about me. I guess if the only people they encounter are like their wives, I might be a breath of fresh air ~ maybe? That sounds conceited, but you know what I mean.

My dancing skills came in handy tonight, and my dance card was full the whole night through. Oh, and we've been invited to Rome, but I'll tell you all about that another time.

The only thing missing tonight was you, my love. I would have traded all the attention I got from them to have had you to dance with. I would have turned them all away and ripped up my imaginary dance card if I could have had you at my side, my darling.

Nearly all the men I spoke with said how they admire you and hope you're well. They all asked me to give you a 'hello' from them and to tell you that they support you and are 'on your side.' I only cried once, which was an achievement, let me tell you!

I miss you so much, David, and I'm longing for your love tonight. I'm worn out, physically and emotionally, but at the thought of making love to you, I feel like I could do anything. No exhaustion would stop me from accepting you. I'll never be so tired that I turn you away, ever.

If only you could feel my love for you across the miles and through the thick walls and bars of your cell. I'd come to you and touch your face. I'd run my fingers through your soft hair, and then feel the contrast of the stubble on your cheeks and chin. I'd kiss your lips, and then ~ Well, I'll tell you about it in person, not in a letter. I wouldn't want someone else to see it.

Maybe I'll read the rest to you when you get home, which feels like a million years from now. I miss you completely! Please remember how much I love you and that I long for you to come home with everything inside me!

Your loving wife,

Erin

Chapter Thirty-Six

LIZETTE FOR TEA

The first Tuesday in July started off blustery and overcast, though by midday the sun had chased away the clouds and tamed the wind. Erin was excited to see her new friend, Lizette, again, but Annis seemed almost giddy, though she knew how to temper herself enough that only those who knew her well could tell it.

As the hour of Lizette's arrival drew nearer, Erin began watching her mother-in-law. First, she checked the time on the mantle clock, then her hair in the mirror above it. Next, she straightened the clock, and finally looked out the window to see if anyone had arrived.

"I'm not sure the mantle clock is straight enough; would you mind checking it?" Erin said to her after the third time she'd gone through the routine, and giggled when she was rewarded with pink cheeks and a flustered look from being caught.

"I don't know why I'm in such a state," she said and rolled her eyes at herself.

"I don't blame you, really," Erin said and took her hand in order to lead her to the sitting room. "She's the loveliest creature I may have ever seen. It's normal to be in awe of such a demigoddess. Come, sit with me while we—"

The doorbell rang and Annis jumped. "Dear me!" she said and began fanning her face with her hands, her cheeks having grown a shade darker.

Erin laughed lightly. "I'll get it." She opened the door and smiled when she spied the younger woman through the small entryway window, smoothing her ginger locks and checking her breath in her hand.

When she opened the outer door, Lizette jumped and her cheeks bloomed pale, cherry blossom pink, which Erin thought suited her perfectly. She was wearing a cornflower-blue dress with a flared skirt that accented her hair color beautifully. "Hello, my friend! Please come in," she said and then gave her a hug after closing the door.

"Hello, Erin, it's good to see you again," Lizette said, then she saw Annis through the inner door and corrected her posture, becoming, to Erin, a perfectly crafted, life-sized porcelain doll.

"Lizette, my dear! I'm so glad to see you! Please come in and make yourself at home," Annis said before they exchanged air kisses on each cheek.

"There are few places I'd rather be, if I'm honest. Thank you for inviting me, Mrs. Elliott," she said. "Your home is lovely, truly!"

"You may call me Ann and thank you for the compliment. Now, please join us in the dining room."

"I think the house is stunning, too," Erin said softly as they followed Annis to the table that Millie had laid out beautifully. The wedding china, cutlery, linens, and silver tea set, minus the teapot, were spotless and gleaming. A three-tiered serving stand was laden with crustless sandwiches on the bottom, fresh, steaming scones in the middle, and beautiful pastries and frosted cakes on the top.

Small china bowls were filled with Devonshire Cream along with Millie's homemade rhubarb jam and lemon curd. Crystal champagne flutes also stood tall and stately by each plate. To top it all off, a stunning, fragrant floral arrangement, the flowers cut from the garden and the arrangement designed by Annis herself, sat in the center of the table, brightening everything up.

"Oh, this is lovely! It's more stunning than tea at the Balmoral, or even Fortnam and Mason!" Lizette said after she'd gasped and put her hand up to her mouth.

"Pish posh," Annis said, but her face was flushed, and she was smiling brightly.

"I must agree, Mother, it's delightful. You and Millie have outdone yourselves," Erin said, and Annis seemed to tense up a bit.

"Thank you, Daughter. Now, please do be seated."

Lizette and Erin sat across from each other, and Annis sat at the head of the table. Soon, Millie came into the room with the teapot, looking more smart than Erin had ever seen her. She was wearing clothes reminiscent of a servant, and she didn't speak.

Annis nodded at her, and she began pouring out the tea for everyone. Erin wanted to laugh at the show, but she knew it would hurt their feelings and ruin the event. "Thank you, Millie," she said when she finished pouring hers.

A curt nod was her reply, then she set the pot on the silver tray and left the room. "The silver tea set is stunning, Mother," Erin said as they fixed their tea the way they liked it.

"Thank you. They were a wedding gift from Lord Sanderson of Ayot."

"That name sounds familiar," Erin said.

"He owned the White Star Line," Lizette said after taking a cucumber sandwich from the tower.

"Oh yeah, that's it. He owned Pucknowle Academy… well, the house and land, I mean. I'm not sure that he lived in it very long, but it was mentioned in the tour of the school," Erin said.

"I've heard it's a very nice school, Erin, is that where David's children attend?" Lizette asked.

They talked about the school and life in London, then what Erin thought about living in the United Kingdom, in general. It was a lovely meal that filled her up, and she was having a delightful time.

"Wait, where's your baby, Erin?" Lizette asked and looked around the room as if she'd just not noticed her.

"My housekeeper, well, she's also our nanny now… anyway, she's watching Junie," Erin said.

"Are they here?"

"Uh, yeah, they should be upstairs."

"May I see… it? I'm sorry, but I don't know if it's a boy or girl," Lizette said and blushed.

Erin could see her new friend was embarrassed and placed her hand over hers. "No worries, though I'm surprised you didn't know; it's been all over the tabloids lately. She's a girl, and her name is Juniper."

"Oh, that's a darling name! Would it be alright to meet her?"

"Sure, do you mind, Mother?" she asked since they'd have to go further into the house.

"I don't want to intrude—" Lizette began.

"Go on with yeh," Annis said with a smile.

The two women ascended the staircase and found Kitty in Millie's old room, holding Junie, who was fussing and didn't want to take the offered bottle. Erin stepped in, and Kitty said, "Blimey, I'm glad you're 'ere, mum, she's not 'avin' it wif me." Then she saw Lizette and gasped. "Oh, I'm sorry, I di'n't know—"

"Don't worry about it, I'll take her, Kitty," Erin said and turned to Lizette. "Do you mind if I feed her in front of you?" She then lifted Junie and when Kitty stood, took the seat she'd been in.

"I don't mind," she said, though she looked a bit nervous about it.

"Go on and have a seat, this'll take a little while." The baby was beginning to get quite upset by then, and not wanting her to begin crying in earnest, Erin lifted her top and unfastened the nursing panel near the strap, exposing her engorged breast.

"Oh!" Lizette said and looked away, red-faced.

"Come on, Junie baby, you know what to do," Erin said as she coaxed her to latch onto her nipple with Kitty's help. Finally, she did, and Erin breathed a sigh of relief. "Thank goodness!"

When she glanced over at Lizette, she noticed the woman watching her with what seemed like awe and wonder. "Goh, Erin! That was fascinating, but why do you seem so relieved? Does it… hurt?" she said and then covered her mouth. "Oh, I'm sorry if that's too personal or—"

Erin laughed and glanced at Kitty, who returned her knowing smile, then left the room. "You're fine, and there's very little you could ask that's too personal or that I'd be offended by, so you don't have to worry about that. I'm relieved because if she begins to wail, I start to leak… like gush, and it makes a mess. I just really didn't want to have to change clothes again today."

"Again? Is it that bad?" Lizette asked, wide-eyed.

"It happens all the time. I'll be glad when I'm done breast-feeding, but she needs all the good stuff I can give her… isn't that right, Junie? Yes, we want you to be healthy, don't we?" she said, switching from talking to Lizette to the baby, who was making little grunting noises as she drank.

"How often do you have to feed her?"

"Oh, every few hours, though she's beginning to sleep through the night now, aren't you, baby girl?"

They fell into a companionable silence while Erin rocked, and Lizette watched. Erin's eyes began to grow heavy, but then Junie was finished on the first side, so she was lifted to Erin's shoulder. She tried to refasten her bra, but the latch wouldn't catch. "Good night nurse, this thing isn't cooperating."

"May I… help you… a'tall?" Lizette asked softly and stood, then she approached Erin and leaned over her.

"Oh, sure, just try to get the little plastic—" Lizette smelled of flowers and spice, and her touch was light as she lifted the clasp and held the strap of her bra, taking her time. Junie began to whimper a bit, so when everything was back together, Erin quickly patted her back, hoping she'd not get too upset.

After a nice little burp, Erin went through the same routine on the other side, and everything went well. "Whew, that's a stressful thing! With nursing, everything has to be done quickly, though *Junie* gets to take her good, sweet time." She smiled at Lizette, who still seemed a bit nervous and shy about watching her. "I'm sorry if this is uncomfortable for you, but sometimes I don't have a choice on waiting, you know?"

Lizette smiled warmly at her and shook her head. "I wouldn't have missed this for anything, Erin, it's beautiful. If anything, I feel as though I should thank you for allowing me to be here."

"Maybe I should charge admission," Erin said with a laugh. "Oh, that might've sounded inconsiderate… I'm sorry if it did. What you said was so sweet and—"

"Don't you worry, I'm not offended."

When Junie was finally finished eating, thoroughly burped, and laid down for a nap, the two women went back downstairs. The table was cleared, and they found Annis in the sitting room, doing a crossword puzzle. "There you are, I thought perhaps you'd gotten lost," she said with a smile.

"Well, if I hadn't pulled Lizette out of the hole in the floor, she'd have been lost forever! Then, we found a wee, hungry Brownie bairn, and I fed her on the hearth. I reckon that appeased the lot of them, and they allowed us to leave, isn't that right?" Erin said and looked at Lizette for confirmation.

Lizette was clearly surprised to be called upon and sputtered, "Oh, right, yes, it's just as she said."

"We really should take better care of the Brownies, Mother. You should have a word with Millie about that."

"Brownies, eh? I reckon I *shall* speak to her about the matter," Annis said and then laughed. "Where'd yeh come up with that, then?"

"I found a little children's book on a shelf in Peter's room about Scottish creatures of lore. I wouldn't read it to a child, though, they'd have nightmares!"

"Ach, aye, though et could also be used as a device tae keep them in line. I reckon we should employ that for Daniel, don't you think?" she said with a twinkle in her eye.

"Not a bad idea, though he'd use it to frighten Rosie, I think," Erin said. "Too true, I'm afraid."

"It's a beautiful night, why don't we go for a walk?" Lizette said.

Erin smiled and looked at Annis. "I'm game, how about you, Mother?"

"Ach, I've a few things to do tonight," she said and stood. "You should go, it *is* a lovely evening."

The two younger women looked at each other. "Alright," Erin said and headed for the front door. They stepped outside and walked toward the narrow old road. She opened the sturdy wooden door next to one of the wrought iron gates and allowed her new friend to step through it first.

The evening sky was overcast, and the June air was cool, though not uncomfortable, as they headed toward the Sheep Heid Inn, commenting on the beautiful ironwork and fragrant roses in front of the many old houses on the street. "This is nice," Lizette said and linked her arm in Erin's.

"I agree. Let's go this way," Erin said and turned toward the ancient church, or kirk, as it was called in Scotland. "I've only been here once, at Easter this year. I noticed it has a lovely old cemetery! I *love* old cemeteries and thought we could explore it."

"I've never thought about them before, but I can see why you would, being a romantic person."

"Romantic, huh? I guess I am, aren't I?"

"Romantics and Goths love cemeteries," Lizette said as Erin let her arm go and headed toward one of the lichen-covered headstones.

"Don't forget historians." They laughed and spoke easily with each other as they took their time wandering through the ancient graveyard. Erin bent down to read the name on a particularly interesting headstone, and when she turned to tell Lizette what it said, she was gone.

She called her name, trying to find her, then saw the tall, slender woman as she rounded the far side of the kirk. Finding her bent over a clump of wild daisies, she went to her. "What gives? Why—"

"These are for you," Lizette said softly, holding out a small bouquet, her cheeks pink in the lowering sun.

"For me?"

"They're weeds, I know, but they're so pretty—I thought… hoped you'd like them," she said and smiled at her.

At that moment, Lizette looked so much like how she envisioned Anne Shirley that she was transported in her imagination to Edwardian era Prince Edward Island and its mahogany-red dirt roads. She took the bouquet and held them to her nose. They smelled like childhood summers, and she smiled wistfully.

"Thank you! That's so sweet of you to—" she began, but Lizette was standing inside her personal bubble, gazing at her in a way she couldn't read. The woman lifted one of her slender arms and placed her hand on Erin's shoulder, as gently as a feather might land after being carried on the wind.

Lizette grinned, then closed her eyes and turned away. "I'm glad you like them," she said softly. She took a few steps toward the kirk and Erin thought she seemed sad.

"What's wrong?" Erin asked, truly flummoxed by her change in behavior. It was as if a cloud had fallen over them and things were slightly less comfortable.

"Nothing is wrong, Erin. This is just such a lovely, romantic place, it has me… I don't know—" The cloud seemed to lift, and she turned back. "Listen to me, being foolish and sentimental! Never mind, let's explore the church before they lock it up for the night."

Her green eyes sparkled again as she took Erin's hand and pulled her toward the sturdy door. When they arrived, she pressed the latch, but it was locked tight. Erin was about to say something, but Lizette put her delicate finger onto her lips.

They held hands as they returned to the cemetery, then wandered around as the sky grew slowly darker. After a while, Erin asked, "I'm curious to know why you support Thistledown?" She watched as the beautiful and, for the most part, confident woman blushed and bowed her head as though she were ashamed. "Oh! I'm sorry if I said something wrong. You don't have to tell—"

"No, it's alright," she said and took a deep breath. "There was a time, when I was younger, that I had an eating disorder. Perhaps you think me thin now, but I assure you, I was a mere thirty kilos when I entered Thistledown.

"Oscar is a miracle-worker, you know? He found a way, the best way for me, to start healing. I wasn't as ill as other women I knew, Susannah Elliott being one of them. I don't know if you met her before she passed?" She looked at Erin, waiting for a response.

"Yes, I met her, and… well, I helped David give her CPR. I saw how thin she was." A shiver ran through her at the memory of that horrible day.

"I see, well, I didn't think I could respect you any more, but I was wrong." She smiled at Erin and squeezed her hand. "Like me, she allowed herself to follow those women into a lifestyle that ultimately killed her. Honestly, I've worried about you, that you might become their next target, though now that I've met you, I no longer see that happening."

"Oh, no, I love food too much for that," Erin said with a short laugh.

"I do as well. It's really not about whether or not you love to eat, it's about wanting to fit in or be accepted. A person like me makes a decision to trade health for appearance, convincing ourselves that we're ugly and worthless and that no one will love us if we don't conform to whatever standard we've chosen."

"I get that. Many years ago, I started losing weight. I set a goal of 130 pounds, which is a healthy weight for me, but the more I lost and the smaller size I could fit into, the more I kept trying to lose. I couldn't see it in the mirror like I thought I would. Finally, someone told me that I was starting to look sick. I think I was at about 125 then, so I stopped dieting.

"It was around that time that my Fertilis Defect symptoms began getting worse. They'd been pretty manageable up till then, but when I couldn't dance or exercise anymore, the pounds slowly came back. I met my first husband right around then, and once I was married, I guess I stopped trying, though I hated myself for it."

"Well, all of that is over now, and here we are, right?" Lizette said softly. "I honestly don't care what size you are, Erin, I think you're beautiful. I couldn't take my eyes off you at the gala, though I was careful not to allow you to notice."

Her pale ivory skin slowly bloomed pink, which Erin thought was extraordinarily attractive on her. That, in turn, caused her own cheeks to grow warm. She felt her hand getting sweaty, so she wanted to pull it away, but Lizette held it firmly and gently squeezed it as she began to lean in.

"Uh, thank you, that's very sweet—"

Time began to move slowly as their eyes locked, and she noticed tiny flecks of yellow and black in her dazzling green irises. Her face was getting closer, and Erin didn't know what to do. Then Lizette tilted her head and pressed her perfect, soft lips to hers.

She could feel her delicate hand move to her waist and thought she felt it trembling with excitement and anticipation, though she, herself, felt nothing. There was no spark, no excitement for her; it was just lips touching, no more. Lizette tried to pull her closer, but Erin gently pushed her away.

"I'm sorry, but I'm not—"

The lovely creature straightened her back and frowned. "I shouldn't have... I guess I just hoped... I mean—" she faltered, but Erin smiled at her.

"It's okay, I mean, I am married, so it probably wasn't the best form, but I'm not upset. It just proves that I'm straight, right? If someone as utterly breathtaking as you can kiss me and it does nothing, then... well, I'll never be into girls," she said and took Lizette's hand, which she'd dropped to her side.

"I'm sorry, Erin, I shouldn't have done that," she said, and it seemed like she might cry. "It was a moment of weakness, and it'll never happen again."

"Hey, it's okay. It was really nice, and I'm sure David would be excited beyond belief if I told him about it."

"Oh, please don't tell him!"

Erin laughed lightly and squeezed her hand. "Don't worry, I'm far too insecure to have him start thinking about you that way! I truly don't understand it. I mean, at home… er, America, no one looked at me twice unless I was wearing a low-cut top. No one ever showed the slightest interest in me there. Here, it seems every other man and the occasional woman," she said and smiled at her, "is enamored by me. It's not something I'm used to, but I like it."

The final twilight of the northern summer sky was upon them as they walked slowly and silently back to Owlgate. Though she tried to put her friend at ease, Lizette remained quiet and shy. When they got into the house, Lizette made her excuses about why she had to leave, so Annis said her farewells, and Erin walked her to her car.

"I'm sorry things are awkward between us now. I hope it doesn't stay that way," she said, feeling like she needed to fix it.

"Never mind, Erin, it's okay. I'll see you again soon, I hope." She stood with the car door open, and Erin leaned in to give her a hug, but the stately maiden slipped effortlessly into the driver's seat and pulled the door shut.

That night, Erin wrote a letter to David, then folded it up and put it into the lining of her travel bag. Though she wasn't planning to tell him, or anyone else for that matter, she simply had to write it down. In a way, she wished she *had* felt something from the kiss, though that would've made a mess of everything. She was more flattered than she could say, and it was a night she'd never forget, though the way it had ended had her feeling crestfallen and unsettled.

Chapter Thirty-Seven

THE OFFICE OF OSCAR

On Wednesday, Erin and Annis traveled to Thistledown with trepidation. They were led into Oscar's office by his secretary and told he'd be in shortly. Erin fidgeted as they sat in front of his large, old desk and waited for him to come in.

"Good afternoon, ladies," Oscar said as he stepped into the room. He shook their hands, then sat in his old-fashioned wooden chair.

It seemed to Erin that the furniture had been handed down for over a hundred years, and no one had ever bothered to replace it. "It's nice to see you again," she said.

"I will say, Oscar, we are verra curious as tae why ye've asked us here," Annis said frankly, and Erin nodded her agreement.

"Yes, I imagine you are. We've had a request from the patient to speak with you," he said.

Erin was shocked and stood. "I… don't want—" she began, feeling faint. The familiar spots were starting to appear in her eyes, so she sat again, looking at Annis and then at Oscar, wide-eyed and not knowing what to say.

"Don't worry, Erin. You don't have to agree, but I'd like to explain before you make your decision, if I may?" Oscar said gently.

Annis looked at him with a frown. "Explain, but I don't think et's a good idea," she said, and took hold of Erin's hand.

"I must admit that when Bran first came to us, we had little hope of any improvement. As you well know, he was wild and unruly, but then something happened. We aren't sure what it was; perhaps simply being off drugs and alcohol was the key, I don't know, but he started improving.

"It was a slow transformation, but it's been steady and has lasted this whole year. He wants to apologize to you both but especially to you, Erin. He seems to fully understand that what he did was wrong and feels true guilt.

"One of the things we stress here is to try to find forgiveness. To forgive yourself, forgive others, and to ask forgiveness of those you've wronged. He also wants to ask David's forgiveness, but he knows he'll have to wait to do that.

"He truly is a different person; helpful, considerate, and polite. Trust me when I say I am just as shocked as you, but I am obligated to try to help him. That is why I've asked you here today."

"But... what does it mean?" Erin said, feeling so much shock that she couldn't think clearly. "I mean, if you deem him 'corrected' or 'fixed,' what happens then? Is he released?

"I mean, I'm sure he's a smart person, could he be putting on an elaborate, long-term act in order to get released... and then come find me... and Juniper for revenge? I mean... David isn't... here to protect me... us, and... if he was released... I'd be afraid for—" Her voice was shaky, and she was trembling all over.

"Aye, I don't care what he's tryin' tae pull, Oscar, he's no' right in the heid, and I'll not allow you tae—" Annis began to say.

"No, no, that's not what I'm suggesting," Oscar interrupted. "Nothing of the sort; any talk of release wouldn't be for many, many years, even if we did suddenly trust him, which we don't. We are also keeping a close eye out for signs of an ulterior motive. You are safe, don't worry.

"All I'm asking for you to do is hear him out and then decide if you are willing to forgive him. He knows that it may take a long time for someone to forgive, and that you may not do it straight away. He also knows there's a possibility that you never will, but he's told me that he is determined to prove himself to you."

Erin closed her eyes, not knowing what to do. She'd been taught to forgive others if she ever wanted to be forgiven. *Would it hurt to just listen to him, or might he poison me with his words?* she thought. She was also afraid that if she saw him, the nightmares would start all over again, although they probably would anyway.

"Would it help for you to observe him without him knowing you were?" Oscar asked. "He's in the common room, and we have cameras in there. I could show you a live feed of him, and you wouldn't have to leave this room."

Erin looked at Annis. "I guess I could do that," she said, looking to her for approval.

Annis sighed and slowly nodded. "Aye, I reckon that would be a'right."

Oscar turned his computer screen to face them, and when he'd found Bran, he zoomed in slightly. Bran was sitting in an easy chair, reading a book. As he read, he smiled and laughed at whatever was on the page. Oscar picked up his phone and said something into the receiver.

A moment later, a male nurse approached Bran and said something they couldn't hear. Bran put his finger up, saying he wanted to finish what he was reading, then closed the book and stood. His face remained pleasant, without any hint of annoyance at being interrupted. He nodded to the nurse and put his book on the bookshelf.

Erin was struck, once again, by how much he looked like David, and it sent a shiver down her spine. Bran walked over to the ancient-looking piano and started playing it, though they couldn't hear anything. "He… can play the piano?" she asked, stunned.

"Aye, David had dance lessons, and Bran took piano, although I didn't know he'd absorbed any of et," Annis said and watched the screen.

"Well, I really need to hear that!" Erin said. "Is there sound?"

Oscar shook his head. "I'm afraid not, but I can take you to the room, and you'll be able to hear him through the doors."

Again, Erin looked at Annis for guidance. She nodded, and they stood, being led through halls that looked like something one would find in a nice, large home. As they approached the common room, they could already hear beautiful, complicated piano music that Erin didn't recognize.

"Who wrote this?" she asked, and Oscar shrugged.

"I believe he did, or more accurately, he's making it up as he plays. I've never heard him play anything familiar to me," he said, and both women's mouths dropped open.

"I can't believe et," Annis said. "He's always been so… difficult. I… didn't know—What've I done?" she whispered, and Erin took her hand. "I can't speak for Erin, but I'd like verra much tae speak with him." She seemed quite emotional, which was unlike anything Erin had seen from her before, except on very rare occasions.

"I'm… still thinking about it," Erin said.

Oscar asked them to wait there for a moment, then walked through the doors and spoke with one of the nurses. When he came back out, he led them to a small, cozy room with a table and chairs. There was a large mirror on one wall, and Annis was asked to take a seat.

Erin was led to a darkened room that looked into the one Annis was sitting in through the two-way mirror. "Please wait here. I'll be back shortly," Oscar said gently.

Chapter Thirty-Eight

THE PIECE OF BRAN

Annis was nervous and started wringing her hands, looking at her reflection in the mirror. After a few minutes, the door on the other side of the room opened, and Bran was led in, wearing soft restraints on his wrists and ankles. She was shocked, but, surprisingly, Bran smiled at her and shrugged.

"Et's a'right; ah understand why ah must wear et. Thank you for comin' tae see me, Auntie," he said, and sat on one of the chairs.

Annis stared at him in disbelief. "Yeh look good," she said, trying to stay neutral. "I… heard yeh playin' the piano; et was lovely. I didn't know you could do that."

Bran smiled at her. "Ah hated lessons because ah had tae play what was written on the sheet, when all ah wanted was tae play what was in ma heid. Ah'm glad yeh liked et, but there's somethin' more important ah'd like tae talk about, if yeh dinnae mind?"

"Aye, go on and say yer piece, then I've ma own tae say," Annis said.

"Auntie, ah was a holy terror for you and Uncle, and poor David, and ah, well, ah dinnae have an excuse. Ah was spoiled and felt ah didnae fit in with yer order and havin' things jest so. Mum and Da' weren't disciplined at all, and tha's all ah knew, sae tae move in wi' yeh, et was a great shock tae me, and ah didnae handle et well.

"Then, ah fell in with some rebellious lads, and after ma first shot of heroin, ah stopped carin'. Ah need, and desperately want, tae tell yeh jest how sorry ah am, and tha'… ah love yeh. Ah'd like tae ask yeh tae forgive me, please," he said, and bowed his head, as if waiting to find out if forgiveness would be granted or not.

Annis wiped an errant tear from her cheek and put her hand on the table, wanting to hold his. He placed his hands near hers, and she took them. "Ach, Bran, when I heard yeh playin' so beautifully, I was greatly moved. There was something tangible in the melody, so full of love and peace… and sorrow.

"I realized jest how I failed yeh. I should've tried tae help yeh, tae talk with yeh about how you were feelin' about yer mum and da', instead of tryin' tae beat yeh into submission. I reckon you were hurtin' verra badly, and we did nothin' for yeh… I couldn't see et till now. I was blind and stubborn… can you forgive me for that, Bran?" Tears were now running, unchecked, down her pale, soft face.

—

He was so polite and well-mannered, Erin found herself starting to like him and had to keep reminding herself of what he'd done. Oscar had come into the room to sit with her once Bran was led into the other room, and Erin looked at him. She just couldn't believe it, his transformation seemed outstanding, but she wasn't convinced.

When she saw Annis's tears, she stood. "I need to talk to him," she said suddenly. She didn't know what she would say or how to describe what she was feeling, but watching him and Annis like that was too much like watching the television. What she needed was to see him, to be face to face with him, looking him in those fucking hazel eyes which still haunted her in her dreams every once in a while. "Please," she added as an afterthought.

"Alright, are you sure? You don't have to, if you—" he began, but Erin was too worked up.

"I'm sure, absolutely sure. He needs to face me and give me answers," she said, feeling hot tears of anger rise up and threaten to fall at any moment.

Oscar left the room, then the door to Annis's room opened and he stepped in. In that time, Annis and Bran had forgiven each other and were smiling and talking freely. He whispered something into Annis's ear, and she looked into the mirror, causing Bran to do the same.

He didn't know it, but he looked straight into Erin's eyes. Hot, angry tears boiled over and ran down her crimson face as she trembled with rage. When Oscar returned and saw her, he seemed a bit hesitant as he led her out of the room.

"This isn't necess—"

"Yes, it is," she said firmly while they waited for Annis and Bran to say their goodbyes.

Annis's face was peaceful as she stepped into the hall, until she saw Erin, and her face fell. She looked at her with compassion and touched her arm. "I believe he's sincere, Daughter, jest hear him out."

Erin was vibrating; all the pent-up anger was tearing at her insides and demanded to be let out. She didn't say anything to her mother-in-law, she only nodded and waited for the door to be opened for her. When she walked in, she couldn't help herself, "FUCK!" she yelled and buried her face in her hands.

Bran stood and backed away from her, pressed against the wall since he could go no further. After a few minutes, Erin sighed, and sat on one of the chairs, taking a tissue from the box on the table, but Bran continued to stand. "Do you have ANY idea what I went through because of you?" she said and stood again.

She began pacing the floor of the miniscule room. "Do you even... can you even fathom what it did to David, and... to our... relationship? Now you stand here, all pie in the sky, 'please forgive me, Aunty,' and it's just supposed to be okay?

"And then! And then all those photos of you, with all those people doing all sorts of things to you... posing as David! Photographed being fucked by some guy... making him think he'd been drugged and then... raped! Do you have any idea of the hell you've put us both through this last year?"

Bran had looked fittingly contrite, humbled, and sorry, until she mentioned photos and being fucked by a man, then his eyes grew large, and he stepped forward, making Erin gasp and cry out, but he stopped and sat. "Ah... honestly dinnae ken what ye're talkin' about, Erin. Ah dinnae remember havin' ma photo taken, and ah didn't know about the... other—" he said 'other' very quietly.

Erin looked at him and saw the same disgust she'd seen on David's face when he'd shown her the hidden photo.

"Ye're right, ah've done naught but hurt you and David, and ah understand why ye're so angry. Ah deserve evera bit of yer anger and hatred, Erin. Ah'm ashamed of maself for doin' what ah did to yeh—" he said, but she was angry again.

"'What yeh did tae me?' That's a coward's admission! You need to name it, Bran, what did you do to me? Say it!" she yelled and slammed her palm onto the table.

Bran bowed his head and took a deep breath. "Ah… took advantage of yeh thinkin' ah was David, and… ah kent et was wrong tae do et, but… ah raped yeh, Erin. Ah forced maself on yeh, even though yeh told me, asked and begged me tae stop. Ah remember et, and et haunts me, though no' as much as et does you, ah reckon. Ah can only imagine what et did tae David, and ah'm truly ashamed."

Erin could see and sense that he was being sincere, but she wasn't ready to forgive just yet. "How could you not know about the photos and being… fucked by another man? Are you saying you don't know how you got to David's house in London? You did it for drugs and… money to finish your fucking tattoo, didn't you? She… Susannah… lured you into posing as David for a fix, right?"

"Aye… ah needed a fix, and ah knew Susannah would have somethin', even if et was just oxycodone. She'd given me drugs before, so ah went tae London, and this time she had cocaine, really good stuff, and ah went on a bender. Ah reckon tha's when she took the photos of me, but ah swear, she didn't tell me she was gonnae do et, and ah dinnae remember et at all."

'Jest wait till she's asleep, and she'll open her legs right up for yeh!' she heard David's voice in her memory and felt like she couldn't breathe. She put her hand on her chest, wishing she were being treated once a week instead of every fortnight. "I… can't do this. I… need… to go," she said, and pounded on the door.

"Ah'm sae sorry, Erin," she heard him say as the door was opened, and she stumbled out into the hall, leaning against the wall, trying to catch her breath.

Annis and Oscar were there in an instant, and Erin slid to the floor, wanting to scream and hit something. Seeing him, looking so much like David, made her miss him even more, and she didn't know how she'd live without him for so long. "I… need… my husband. What am I going to do?"

That night, back at Owlgate, Erin made her excuses and went to bed. She wasn't hungry and didn't want to talk to anyone. Bran's sincerity and genuine pleading rolled through her mind in a loop, along with the music he'd played on the piano. She lay in bed, tortured by a mixture of sadness, anger, compassion, and rage.

When she finally fell into a fitful sleep, she dreamed of David and Bran together, smiling and behaving like brothers. She was there, at her home, the one she'd dreamt of so often before moving to England, standing at the stove in her kitchen and laughing at something one of them said. Bran looked over at her, and she could sense that everything was healed between them as she smiled at him.

Chapter Thirty-Nine

A CHANGE OF POSITION

On Thursday morning, Roger drove Erin to the clinic in the Old Town. He pulled up to the building and got out, opening the door for her. "Are yeh sure yeh dinnae want me tae stay?" he asked.

Erin knew he felt protective of her now that David wasn't around. "I'm sure. I'd like to walk around a while. Maybe I'll stop by the curiosity shop we all went to last year on Victoria Street, but thank you, Roger," she said and smiled.

"A'right, but when yeh need me, I'll come for yeh. Be… careful, Erin." He got back into the driver's seat and pulled away, leaving her alone.

She took a deep breath and walked up to the door, feeling a bit nervous about the new location but also at peace with it. She would miss having Wendy there as a friendly face, but she was comfortable enough with Louis that she knew she'd be fine. A sign with an arrow pointed to the door for the clinic on the ground floor, so she followed it down a short hallway and went in.

The receptionist led her straight away to a room, where she was told that her appointed carer would be with her shortly. The room was much more like an exam room than the one in London, and it didn't quite have that home-like feel to it. She was glad she'd already had a few treatments before going there, as she might have changed her mind and walked out otherwise.

After about five minutes, there was a short knock, then a woman walked into the room, closing the door behind her. "Erin Elliott, es et?" she asked. The woman was much older than her and reminded her a bit of Millie with her no-nonsense way.

"Yes," she said.

"Alright, soo ye've doone thes b'fore, ah see." She had a nice thick accent, and Erin smiled at how delicious she thought it was.

"Yes, ma'am," she said, feeling as though the woman commanded respect.

The woman looked at her. "Ach, yeh needn't call me 'ma'am'," she said, and her face softened into a warm smile. "Ma name's Dorothy. I'll shoo yeh where ma call button es and answer ana questions yeh may have."

She walked over to the bed and lifted a handheld box with a thick cord, like Erin had seen in hospital rooms when she was younger. It had a small red button which read "CALL," and under it, side by side, were the light dimmer and the noise volume buttons. There was another button on the side of the box that worked the height adjustment of the bed itself, which was new for her.

"Oh, that's different. And where are the stirrups?" she asked, not seeing any out, or even a place for them.

"Ach, we dinnae have any on oor beds, dear. Ye've gottae doo et the old-fashioned way here, ah'm afraid."

Erin's face turned bright red. She hadn't thought about that and wasn't sure she liked the implications of it. "But how do things... remain... private, then?"

"Aye, et's a wee bet moore deffecult, but oor sheets are cut def'rently tae compensate," she said, then showed her what she meant. Instead of an overlapping slit, this one had a semicircular flap, like the hood on a sweater, though it had some kind of plastic tubing inserted around the edge to make it rigid. Dorothy stepped up to it and placed it on her stomach, showing how it would, hypothetically, obstruct the view of the man and prevent him from seeing anything.

"But he'll have to hold my legs up then," Erin said, not liking the idea of that at all.

"Aye, he will, ef yeh choose tha' position. Et works better ef yeh use the 'entry from behind position.'"

Erin frowned and closed her eyes. It was only two treatments, and she'd just have to deal with it. "Okay then, I guess that's what we'll do," she said, just wanting to get on with it at that point.

She was feeling uncomfortable with the amount of touching and feeling he would need to do, but it couldn't be helped. "So, I just hit the call button when I'm ready then?" She hoped Dorothy would get the hint and let her get undressed.

"Aye, ah'll jest step oot, then." Apparently, she got the hint loud and clear.

Erin sighed and took her bottoms off, leaving her socks on, as it was a bit chilly in the room. She got onto her hands and knees and pulled the curtain around her, then she pushed the call button and waited, feeling ridiculous. The door opened, and the nurse came back, speaking to someone she hoped was Louis.

"Ah'll show yeh where the call button es, dear," Dorothy said, and it sounded to Erin as though she was on the edge of flirting, the way her voice had even more of a sing-song tone to it with him. She showed him something Erin couldn't see, then carefully instructed him on how the curtain worked.

"Aye, I'm sure we'll figure et out," Louis said kindly but with the hint that he didn't need help.

"Well then, ef yeh need anathin', yeh ken what tae doo," she said and then left them alone.

"Erin?" he said timidly.

"Yes, it's me." She was glad to hear a familiar voice. "I guess we're changing positions while we're here." It was odd to be saying that to him.

"Right, I... see," he said, haltingly. "That's no' at'tall awkward, es et?"

Erin couldn't help but laugh. She liked his sense of humor and wished they could be friends, but after everything… it would be impossible. She heard him taking his clothes off, so she thought she'd give him the lowdown.

"I can... change the height... on the bed, so it's, umm, comfortable for you. Although I don't have a clue how we'll do anything without a lot of, umm... trial and error," she said, rolling her eyes at herself.

—

"Right... well, et's good tae try new things, eh? I'm ready, whenever… you... are," he said and walked to the end of the bed, which was quite high at the moment. He could see the outline of her rear end and legs against the cloth of the veil that separated them. "Uh, right, I reckon et's a wee bit too high."

The curtain started moving around, and he heard her trying to do something, but he didn't know what. Then, he heard her say *'shit'* twice. "Are yeh a'right?"

"I'm fine, just trying to get the handheld control box to unhook from the side of the bed. It's caught on something. Would you mind coming around and finding out what's the matter with it?"

Louis walked around to the side of the bed and lifted the sheet just enough to get a look at the control box. He lifted it out of the clamp it was attached with and then held it out under the fabric. "Here yeh are, love." Her hand touched his as she took it from him, and it sent shockwaves through his arm.

"Thanks."

He saw the bed start to move and went back to the end of it.

"How's that?" she said after she'd lowered it a bit.

He stepped closer and gently put his hands onto her hips, making them both shudder and start breathing heavily. "A bit… lower, please," he breathed, longing to touch her bonnie rear end and enter her right away. The bed continued to descend, but it still wasn't enough.

"More, please, jest… keep et goin'." He knew it would probably need to go all the way down to its lowest position and was embarrassed at how short he was. It finally made a grinding noise, indicating it couldn't go lower. "Aye, that'll do."

He lifted the hood, placed it on his belly, and tried to aim himself to enter her, but it was difficult in that position. He didn't want to start pushing in the wrong place, which was a real possibility, especially without being able to see or touch anything.

"Uh, please tell me… when I'm in the… right place," he said, wanting to spread her folds apart and feel his way with his fingers. He was having a difficult time; everything seemed to be getting in the way, obstructing him.

"Here," she said, and he felt her fingers brush against his cock as she spread herself open and then gently pressed on his head, causing him to slip easily inside her. He forgot himself with the excitement of her touch and thrust himself all the way in, making her flinch and pull her hips forward. "Oww!" she said, and he was mortified.

"Ach! God, Erin, I'm so sorry! Are yeh a'right? Did I hurt yeh?" *Of course yeh hurt her, otherwise she wouldn't have said 'oww', yeh numptie!* he chided himself.

"I'm fine, just try to ease into it, okay? I think… I… might be able to… take you all the way now, but you'll have to start out slowly."

He was shocked by that; he didn't know it was possible. "Right." He pushed himself into her slowly, feeling her body take him in and relax after each gentle thrust. Deeper and deeper he went each time, until he was completely sheathed by her.

Her skin was warm and smooth against the front of his thighs. He stood still, enjoying the feeling, until she started rocking, giving the hint that she wanted more. "God, tha'… feels so… good!" he said and thrust himself a bit harder, feeling her take him all the way in each time.

"Fuck!" she said as he continued to drive himself into her, using her hips to hold on to. "Oh!" she cried out, and he felt her, even stronger than he'd done before, clenching and releasing, over and over all around his cock.

"Christ!" he said, and he was there as well, filling her up and feeling her still tightening around him, which made each sensation feel more powerful. He stood still again, waiting for his sensitivity to die down before he slowly pulled out and stepped back, panting, not knowing what to say.

He saw her shadow collapse onto her side and was afraid she was hurt. "Erin? Oh God, what's the matter? Are yeh hurt?" he said, wanting to pull the curtain back and see to help her.

"I'm fine, Louis," she said weakly. "That was… just… so—I don't know the words… powerful… amazing."

Louis heard her breathing start to stagger, and then he could hear her crying. "Erin? Are yeh… cryin'?"

"I'm sorry, Louis, my body is just overwhelmed, I'll be okay in a bit."

Fuck! Yeh made her cry, he thought, not knowing how to react. "But are yeh hurt?" he asked, having never had anyone cry after sex with him before. He figured it wasn't due to guilt, as it had been during their second treatment, so concern and confusion gripped him equally.

"I'm not hurt," she said. "It was… it felt… so good that my body doesn't know how to process it, and this is what it does. I lose it for a bit, and then I'm okay. Please don't be worried."

"So… ye're cryin' b'cause et felt tha' good?" he said. He realized he should be getting dressed, but he was mystified, not knowing that was a thing. "I've never heard of tha'… but I reckon et **was** verra, verra good for me as well, so—"

Stop yer blatherin' yeh eejit, he chided himself. "Sorry, I'll stop talkin' now." He started getting dressed and heard a noise from behind the curtain that didn't sound like crying anymore. *Is… she laughin'?* "Right, then."

"I'm sorry, Louis, I'm not laughing at you, honestly."

"Right," he said again, not sure that he believed her. "I'll jest… go—" he began, but then she was sitting at the edge of the bed with her feet dangling off it. He noticed she was wearing short blue socks with sharks on them.

"Wait! Please… don't… don't be upset. I'm just… was just tickled by your reaction to… my reaction. I didn't mean to make you… I don't even know what… embarrassed, or wound your pride, maybe? Nothing like that."

Now *she* was rambling, and Louis smiled. "A'right, ma pride is intact. You are a rare woman, Erin—" He almost said 'Elliott' but caught himself just in time. "Thanks for yer consideration, and I'll see yeh in a fortnight," he said, and left the room, closing the door behind him.

—

Erin could tell he was confused, but then it seemed to become a kind of pride in him. She knew it would probably make a man feel pretty terrific to have made a woman so pleased during his lovemaking that she bawled like a baby. When he started rambling, it struck her as funny.

Then, she felt like she had to explain, which just made things awkward… and yet not. She hoped he believed her. *I wouldn't want him to be upset! I know what he said, but what if he's angry? If only I could explain it better… maybe I could find him and—*

Erin Elliott, you're a fool! Don't even start thinking— but she cut her own thoughts off.

He's going to be in town for the next two weeks! I could see him anywhere! She didn't know if she liked that idea, or not, though at that moment, she did like the thought very much. The thought even came to her that she would like to follow him through the old town to see where he went and find out what he looked like. *Holy Moses, this isn't good!* she thought as she got up, cleaned off, and got dressed.

<h1 style="text-align:center">Chapter Forty</h1>

LITTLE SHOP OF LETTERS

Erin wanted to see her friend Tim at the curiosity shop she'd visited several times the year before. Standing on the sidewalk outside the clinic, she tried to get her bearings and remember which way it was. She figured the best thing to do was start walking, so she made her way down the street and climbed the stairs of a narrow close.

The memory of the treatment made her pause and lean against the railing, gasping, as it nearly took her breath away. In the cool darkness, she closed her eyes, still feeling the phantom thrust of him inside her. As she reached the top of the close, she was more winded than she ought to be because of it.

Holy Moses, that was so intense and amazing, she thought.

No! Stop it, Erin! That's enough!

She found her way to the Royal Mile and was then able to find the little shop, where she opened the tall, wooden door and stepped inside. "Tim?" she said, only a little louder than she normally spoke, but the shop was empty, so it sounded like she'd shouted. A business-like woman came out from the back room and smiled at her.

"I'm sorry, but Tim is not here; may *I* help you?" she said with a gentle, slightly Indian accent.

Erin smiled back at her and thought she seemed friendly enough, as far as first impressions went. "No, that's okay," she said. "I was here last year and made fast friends with him. He's a really sweet guy." The woman looked at her with her head cocked to the side a bit. "Would you please tell him that—"

"Are you… Erin Elliott?" she asked, making Erin flinch. She must have seen the look on her face, because she stepped over to her. "I'm sorry, I didn't mean to startle you. I'm Rajani, the owner.

"Tim told me how… you… brought David Elliott here. He was thrilled that he signed the display to him. I don't think Tim would mind me saying how much he loves you and thinks the world of Mr. Elliott."

"But how did you… know it was me? I've never met you before, have I?" Erin asked, still a bit spooked.

An attractive man came into the shop, he was a bit older and bald, with salt and pepper facial hair. He smiled at the two women and then went to the other side of the room. The woman walked Erin over to the cash register and spoke much more quietly.

"My dear, poor Tim has been beside himself over your husband's… predicament, or more accurately, what *you* must be going through. Every week, he brings with him the newest tabloid, reading it with tears running down his face. Your picture is sometimes in them, and I recognized you from that, plus you're American, and you asked for Tim, so it made sense," she said.

Erin didn't know what to say. She felt sort of naked and wanted to cover her face, not wanting people to recognize her. "Well, uh, please tell him I was here—" she said and turned to leave.

"He'll be back in about ten minutes… probably less now, if you'd care to wait."

The older man walked over to the *Future Explorations* display, which was close to where they were standing, as Erin looked up at the display with David's signature and message to Tim. The part David signed had been removed and framed. She could see where countless hands had touched the words, smearing some of them and nearly rubbing others off the cardboard completely.

Rajani saw her and laughed. "It had to be done or it would've been ruined."

"I'm glad you saved it," Erin said and sighed. The man started picking up the items on the display shelf and turning them around in his hands. "Okay, I'll wait then." She felt like the man was standing a bit too close, so she walked away, trying to find something interesting to keep her occupied.

"Can I help you find anything?" the owner said to him, but he shook his head and put what he had back on the shelf.

Again, he moved near to where Erin was standing and started looking at the *Dr. Who* merchandise on the table next to her. She looked up at him, and he smiled. *What a handsome older man, and what an amazing smile!* she thought, and smiled back in spite of herself. She heard the shop door open, and there was Tim, eyes red and looking gutted.

"Tim! What's wrong?" she said, rushing to him and holding his shoulders so she could see his face. "You've been crying!" Tim made a noise of recognition and hugged her tightly. "Oh, Tim! My poor boy, talk to me."

Rubbing his back, she led him over to the large globe, which had been moved to the corner near the back room. She sat on the floor, pulling him down to sit with her, not caring who saw them. Her friend was hurting, and she was going to listen to him, that's all there was to it.

"Och, Erin!" he said. "Ah'm sae glad tae see yeh. Whit they ded tae David es jist terrible! Ah jist reid th' latest one frae heem!"

Erin gave him a look saying she hadn't quite understood all of what he'd said. "Alright, now slow down and repeat that last part; you just, what?"

He took a deep breath, clearly trying to speak in a way that she could understand, since his accent was really thick. He was also upset, which made him that much more difficult to understand. "Sorry," he said. "Ah jest read the latest letter from David."

"What letter from David?" she asked, not knowing what he was talking about. Everyone in the room looked at her with their mouths wide open in shock. Even the handsome older man, who was now looking at the rack of reels for the Viewfinder, was gaping at her, and she wished she could talk to Tim in private.

"Erin! Yeh dinnae ken about the letters?" he said, sounding utterly horrified. "How can yeh no' ken? In the tabloids… they're—"

"Oh, Tim, I'm sure it's all made up crap that someone is writing to sell papers," she said, interrupting him. She'd heard that there was something every so often in the tabloids claiming to be from David, but she believed nothing that came from them and had ignored it.

He frowned and shook his head. "Have yeh no' read any of them?" He opened the paper he had in his hand to the page the supposed newest one was on and handed it to her. "Read et and tell me if et's no' him… please."

Erin rolled her eyes and took the paper, reading it out in an impatient, mocking manner as though she were bored with it already.

> *Dear Erin,*
>
> *I dreamed we were dancing in #2, and you had your head on my chest. You looked up at me and held out your compass—*

Erin stopped talking; she had goosebumps all over, and her eyes filled with tears as she pulled out the compass pendant David had given to her in New Orleans. Tim took the paper to continue, but he couldn't read it either. The shop owner took it and continued where Erin had left off.

> *…but it had stopped working, and you were very sad. I looked at it, and it wasn't a compass any longer, it was an enormous pocket watch. It didn't show hours and minutes though, it showed the months, years, and days I'm meant to be stuck in here. The second hand showed days, the minute hand, months, and the hour hand, years.*
>
> *Erin, the 'minute' hand had only moved 3 ticks, as though, if it were a real watch, it was only 3 minutes past midnight. How can I live that long? How can I be away from you and our Junie for so long? Oh, God, Erin! Please don't forget me, and please tell Juniper how her da' loves her. Do the same for Peter, Charlie, Dan, and Rosie as well. I love you all!*
>
> *Please be patient and know that I love you more than I love myself.*
>
> *David x*

They had all watched Erin as Rajani read, and saw the tears run fast and steady down her face. "And… there are more… like this?" Erin said, trying with all her heart to not start bawling in front of them. She was breathing heavily and swallowing hard, then her chin started quivering and her breath became shaky.

"Aye!" Tim said. "There are at least half a dozen—I… have them… here, if Rajani hasn't binned them." He looked up at his employer, and she shook her head, plainly not wanting to start crying, too.

"In the back. I'll find them," she said softly.

The customer seemed to be trying to make himself scarce, clearly not wanting to seem too interested. He walked to another corner of the shop, where he tried to act preoccupied with a display of Anime stuff he probably knew nothing about. Soon, Rajani came back with a stack of newspapers and found the oldest one. She held it out to Erin and Tim, but they were in no shape to read it, so she found the page, and began.

Dear Erin,

She read them all, and by the time she was done, everyone in the store was in tears. Erin noticed the stranger come closer and watched as he handed her something white. As she was about to refuse it, she saw that it was a handkerchief, so she took it, looking into his kind, blue-grey eyes. He smiled at her and stepped away.

"Thank you," she said. He nodded, then turned and opened the shop door, leaving without saying a word. She wiped her eyes with it and looked at Tim. "That was interesting, wasn't it?"

She gave him a weak smile and looked at the corner of the old cotton fabric. There was a small, hand-stitched monogram, 'WM' it read, and she wondered what they stood for. "My rear end is asleep, would you mind giving me a hand?" she asked Rajani, who kindly helped her to her feet, then they both assisted Tim. Erin hugged him, then kissed his cheek.

"Ah was sae worried about yeh, Erin," he said. "May ah send yeh a text from time tae time, tae… check on yeh?"

"Aye, I'd like that. I'm only in Edinburgh for two more weeks, then I go back to London. It would be nice to hear from you. I'll have the children then, as well, so I can say 'hi' to them for you," she said, then looked at the stack of newspapers on the register counter and sighed. "I just can't believe they were all published! I haven't gotten a single one, you know."

Tim looked at the stack, then at her. "You can have mine," he said and picked them all up. "I've already read them, and you should be able tae go back tae them, yeh ken, when yeh need tae."

"Oh, Tim, you are the most sweet and thoughtful man, and truly a kindred spirit, but I'll try to find my own copies—" she began to say, but Rajani interrupted her.

"I've a photocopier in the stockroom. I could make copies of them for you, if you'd like?" she offered.

"Yes, please!" Erin said with a smile. "Thank you." Rajani took them and went into the back room. "That reminds me, here's your book." She took Tim's copy of Anne of Green Gables from her purse. "It was a hit, and now that my own copies have arrived from America, I've been using them. Thank you so much for loaning it to us, it means a lot to me."

"Ach, I'm glad yeh… got tae use it—" He hesitated, and Erin chuckled.

"Yes, Tim, he did," she said, knowing he'd want to know if David ever read out of it. "He often read the part of Gilbert."

"Goh!" Tim said and smiled brightly.

"You might want to have a peek at the inside front cover after I leave," she whispered as Rajani returned and two customers walked in from the street.

She took the papers and hugged Tim. "Keep in touch," she said, then kissed him once more on the cheek and left the building.

—

Tim went to the back room to put his things down and opened the book. On the inside front cover, there was an inscription.

Tim—

Thank you for the loan of your book, we've all loved hearing it read out by Erin. I now have a much better understanding of what a 'kindred spirit' is and can see that the two of you are most definitely that.

Your friend,
David Elliott

Tim closed the book and placed it over his heart. '*Your friend, David Elliott,*' he mused, then thought about Erin having to live without him for two whole years, and it broke his heart.

Erin was tired and really just wanted to go back to Owlgate and reread all the letters from David she suddenly had. She sent a message to Roger and asked him to pick her up by the Edinburgh Dungeons, then started walking in that direction. It wasn't long before Roger pulled up to the pavement and got out of the SUV to open the door for her.

She smiled, and he smiled back, though she thought he looked a bit awkward. "What's the matter?" she asked him as she got in. Roger frowned and closed the door.

An older man with a bald head and salt and pepper facial hair watched from a distance as Erin's driver got back into the vehicle and drove off. Louis thought about his encounter with her at the surgery and then at the curiosity shop. *She didn't know about the letters! How is et she didn't know?*

As a boy, his mother had always made sure he had a clean handkerchief with him. When he'd protested, his father took him aside, telling him that there might come a day when he'd meet a lass in distress, and then he'd be glad he had it. He'd kept up the habit, and his father had been right, he was *very* glad he had one *that* day.

He sighed, and walked over the bridge, making his way to his mate's flat near Abbeyhill.

—

"Come on, Roger, I can tell something's bothering you," Erin said from the back seat.

Roger shrugged as he navigated the streets of Edinburgh. "I was gonnae ask yeh how things went but then changed ma mind," he said and laughed, feeling his cheeks highlight his embarrassment at the thought.

Erin chuckled as well. "I see."

Because he was treating Tilly, who also had the Fertilis Defect, he knew how it worked. He also knew about the connection between matches. "Though—"

"It's complicated," she said softly. "It's so different from David… the connection, I mean. It's very powerful, but it's not the same. With David, there's something more, something deeper, and I'll never be able to live without him. I'm sure I'll be able to forget this other man once David comes home to us."

"Aye, I'm sure yeh will," Roger said. He'd often thought about whether he'd be able to give Erin her treatments if it worked that way. At the same time, knew he'd never be able to do it, even if it were possible. He would fall madly, deeply, and completely in love with her, and it would ruin everything in his life.

"I think Millie is preparin' a roast joint for supper, and et's drivin' me mad each time I set foot in the house, the way it smells," he said companionably, wanting to change the subject.

"Roger," Erin said, and he looked up at her in the rearview mirror. "I… I love you and… all of David's family. Thank you for being here for me and Junie, I couldn't make it without you." She turned her head, staring out the window as they rounded Holyrood Park and made their way back to Owlgate.

"We love yeh as well, Erin," he said softly, meaning 'I' when he said 'we.' A lump was forming in his throat, so he needed to change the subject again. "Tilly's gonnae be here at the weekend. I know she'll be glad tae see you, she asks about yeh often."

"Oh good! It'll be nice to catch up," she said and lifted the newspaper photocopies. "Did you know David's letters to me were being published in a tabloid?"

His face grew red again as he quickly glanced up at her. "Well, I'd heard they were, but I didn't believe et. However, I saw the latest one at the petrol today and finally took a look. Have yeh read et yet?" he asked.

"Aye."

"Et's him, isn't et?"

"Aye, it's him."

"Ma Losh, Erin! I hate tae read 'em, I mean, they're personal, and yet—"

"I know, Roger, you want to read them all, I understand. I didn't believe they were from him either, but Tim had them and… we read them out today. His boss made photocopies for me. I'll let everyone read them tonight.

"I just wonder where *my* letters are going. He isn't getting any of them, so are they also being published? But you know, I don't think I want to know that, because then I won't say what I really want to for fear of people's judgment."

"Aye, I reckon tha's wise," he said and pulled up to Owlgate.

—

"I'll get the gate this time, Roger, and I'll walk up the drive," she said as she got out of the SUV. "Thanks for the excellent limo service. Maybe next time you should use Neela, since David can't say no… and… she really needs to be driven."

Taking a step back, she turned away. Tears rained down her face as she stumbled toward the heavy iron gate that had little owls worked into it. She fumbled with the latch, but then Roger was behind her. She wheeled around and held him, shaking with the sobs that escaped her weary body.

"There, there, love," he said as he held her and stroked her hair gently. "You go on and let et all out. Ye've had a stressful mornin'." Cars overtook the idling SUV, the people in them staring at what looked like two lovers holding each other.

—

Roger had the most selfish feeling he'd ever felt wash over him just then. Being able to hold Erin like that was so blissful that for a split second he was glad David was in jail. Then he was ashamed of himself, both for Erin and David's sake but also for Tilly's.

—

Erin pulled away from him after a few minutes. "I'm sorry, Roger. Thank you for letting me cry on your shoulder, or, well, chest," she said and smiled. "You're right, I've had a stressful morning, and I need a nap, but I'll have to feed Junie and myself, I reckon, before I'll get one. I'll see you later." She managed to open the gate and walked through it, keeping to the side so Roger could pass her.

She went in through the side door and heard Junie crying, which, in turn, made her breasts begin to leak, drenching her front in seconds. *Damn!* she thought bitterly. "Kitty? Millie? Where are you?" she said as she roamed the main floor of the large, stately house.

"Oh, mum, you're 'ome! Junie's been in a right state, wantin' ta be fed, 'aven't ya?" Kitty said in baby talk as she bounced the baby on her hip. Her housekeeper then looked up at Erin and covered her mouth, seeing the state of her top. "Oh, dear! I'll bring 'er upstairs, you go on up and change."

"Thank you, Kitty," Erin said and trudged up the steps to her and David's room. The bed looked so inviting, and if she hadn't been sopping wet, she might've been foolish enough to climb in.

She took off her top, feeling the chill of the air on her skin, which made her already irritated and tender nipples hard and even more painful. She put on David's oversized terrycloth robe and sat in the rocking chair at the end of their bed. Kitty knocked on the door and entered, handing her the squirming and fussing four-and-a-half-month-old

Erin tried to start feeding her, but it wasn't working. "Come on, Junie, knock it off. If you'll just stop fussing, you'll latch on! Oww!" Erin pushed Junie away from her. She took hold of her leaking, now throbbing nipple and cupped it protectively, crying with the pain.

"What's 'appened?" Kitty said, rushing out of the bathroom, where she was rinsing out Erin's shirt in the sink.

"She scraped me with her razor blade fingernails. I can't tell if it's bleeding, but it feels like it should be," she said with staggered breaths. Then, because her meal source had been taken away, Junie began wailing. "I… can't do this! I… I'm ashamed that I want to throw her across the room right now!" she sobbed.

"Let's try the other side first, then. Let me 'elp ya, a'right?" Kitty said sweetly and with such tenderness and love that Erin began to cry about that.

"Thank you, Kitty. I thank God for you! I love you," she said as the young woman helped to hold the now screaming child until she finally latched on and began sucking hard, which hurt quite a lot. Erin allowed the tears to run down her face unchecked as Kitty examined her other side to see if she was bleeding.

"There's a slight scratch but no blood, mum."

"I feel so… I don't even know the word, weak and ridiculous, I guess. I know that so many people have things much worse than I do, and yet here I am crying and carrying on. Feeling sorry for myself as though—"

"Hush now, Erin. Whilst it may be true 'at overs 'ave fings worse than you, 'at don't mean ya can't cry or feel jilted, like. You're under a lot a stress just now, and ya don't need ta feel badly about bein' cross or aggrieved."

"I couldn't have said et better maself, Kitty. Once again, I'm glad our Erin has you tae care for her," Annis said from the doorway, making the younger woman blush. "I've some cream that will help yeh with the soreness, ma dear. I'll fetch et for yeh."

Once Erin was finally finished feeding Juniper, Kitty grew uneasy. She would act like she was going to speak and then seemed to change her mind. After the second time, Erin confronted her.

"Alright, Kitty, what's on your mind? I can tell you want to say something."

"Aww, mum, I hate ta ask, but me mum rang t'day while you was away, ya see, and, well, she's doin' poorly. It's only a virus, but I fink she's worse off 'an she lets on," she began, nervously wringing the washcloth she had in her hands.

"Of course you should go to her, Kitty! I've got Millie and Ann to help me while I'm here. Your mum is more important than, well, pretty much anything. I'll call Tina and have her arrange a flight for you, though it probably won't be until tomorrow morning or afternoon, I'm guessing."

"Oh, mum… Erin, I owe ya for it," she said, and Erin thought she seemed near tears.

"You don't owe me anything. Just do one… well, two things for me."

"Anyfing, mum!"

"First, give your mum a big hug for me and tell her I hope she's feeling better really soon, and please, Kitty, always come to me right away with things like this. The worst I'll say is that I want you to stay an extra day or something. I don't want you to ever feel like you're putting me out by having to leave or if you need a day off. I'll manage, and if I can't, I promise to tell you so, so we can work… suss out a plan," Erin said and hugged her.

"A'right, mum… Erin, I'll try ta remember it, and I'll tell me mum what ya said. She just loves you, so she'll be 'appy ta 'ere from ya."

Chapter Forty-One

THE THINGS YOU FIND HIDDEN

It was already twenty minutes past eleven on Thursday, and Ralph Reynolds needed to send his report to the office. If it wasn't sent by noon, he'd lose the contract he'd been vying for, but his blasted PC wouldn't boot properly, again. He knew his wife's laptop was rarely shut down, so he stepped into her office and logged into his email.

Thankfully, he'd sent himself a copy of the report, just in case, and managed to submit it to the office with only minutes to spare. Out of habit, he began to shut the laptop down, but a warning popped up on the screen, saying that something needed to be saved first. He saw the file open on the sidebar, clicked it, and nearly screamed.

The file was made up of images, dozens of pictures of David Elliott, with some of their friends, and other people he didn't recognize, doing obscene and indecent acts. There was something odd about them, though, as David appeared to be drugged. He was posed in uncomfortable and unnatural positions, seemingly oblivious to what was happening to him.

There were several with Susannah, and *Oh, God*, he thought, seeing his wife's dark hair and eyes looking out at him as she sat atop the man, both of them naked. He wasn't a fool; he knew his wife wasn't faithful. She'd made it perfectly clear from the start of their marriage that she would do what she wanted, and he'd have to accept it, so it didn't surprise him as much as it might have another man.

He knew there was something sinister about the whole thing, so he quickly sent a copy of the file to his inbox, then collapsed it, leaving her laptop just as he'd found it. A conversation he'd overheard with his wife and their friend, Detective Chief Superintendent Clive Dawson, came to his mind, regarding how to frame or blackmail someone. They'd come up with several ways to do it but had talked the longest about blackmail and planting evidence.

At the time, it had seemed like hypothetical blather. They'd been drinking, and he'd ignored it, laughing along with everyone else who'd been there. Some of them, he realized, were in the photographs with David.

*But why did David do it? Was he trying to frame the people he was posing with? It seems unlikely, as they seemed perfectly willing, whilst he was most definitely not a willing subject. Could it be that someone was trying to make it **appear** as though he were? But why? What might he have done for someone to do… that to him?*

It dawned on him that perhaps it had something to do with Susannah. He'd heard Clive compliment Susannah Elliott far more often than most other men, and now that he was thinking about it, he'd also noticed him watching her when they were at events together. Had he been naive to think that it was because he was a police officer, and it was in order to assure her safety? She was so slight, a breeze could've toppled her, but why frame her husband?

He shook his head, feeling like a right old git! *Erin Elliott, that's why.* They'd just met her at the gala, and he'd thought her lovely. He'd heard that she and David had met after he'd hosted the charity telethon for the Fertilis Defect. *Was that it? Was it revenge for his leaving Susannah?*

He didn't understand any of it, but he knew he had to tell someone, though he had no clue whom he could trust. Not Clive, or any of the people who worked for or with him, that was for certain. *Who do I know?* "Oscar!" he said out loud.

"What about Oscar?" his wife, Claudia, asked as she came into the room.

He jumped, and his face turned a vivid shade of pink, which wasn't abnormal for him. Claudia had a way of either evoking complete and total trust or putting the fear of God into a person. For him, it was the latter, especially after what he'd just found.

"Oh, nothing, thinking out loud. My PC wouldn't boot properly again, so I used your laptop to send a vital report. I hope you don't mind, love," he said, relying on the truth as his excuse for being in the room.

"I really don't care, Ralph, though do close the door on your way out, I've things to do and do *not* wish to be disturbed."

"Of course, darling," he said, thankful for the excuse to leave quickly.

He knew he wouldn't be able to ring Oscar whilst he was in the house, Claudia was always in his vicinity, ready to startle him at all hours. Thus, he took himself to the Harversham Club, where he knew he'd find some privacy, and lunch. From there, he made an appointment to see Oscar first thing the next morning. Perhaps he was being paranoid, but he didn't know how deep it all went, so that was the only way he felt safe communicating with him.

Chapter Forty-Two

BRAN LEARNS THE TRUTH

At first, Bran was upset that Erin wouldn't forgive him, but then he recalled being taught that it may take years for someone to forgive, and sometimes they never did. He couldn't control what other people did; he could only control himself. He'd never been taught that; his parents hadn't been much on discipline, and by the time anyone else got involved, he was already addicted to whatever his parents had left lying around the house for young fingers to find.

Convincing Erin to forgive him would be difficult, he knew, but persuading David seemed impossible. He'd have to prove himself somehow, though he had no idea how to do that. When he thought about her claim that he'd posed as David in photographs, his anger shifted to Susannah. It would be a long time before he'd be able to forgive her, even though she was dead.

That night, as he lay on his bed, he tried to remember the two weeks prior to him ending up at Owlgate the last time. It was a very low point in his life, and he didn't like to think about it. All he could remember was that Susannah had invited him to come to London, though he didn't know why she would.

He remembered arriving at David's house, being hurried inside, then taken directly into the kitchen, where he was given a small baggie of white powder. Clive, that fucking bawbag, was there, as well as one more person, a woman, but he didn't know her name. Everything else was foggy and disconnected, with only tiny snippets of clarity, making him think he'd been given more than just coke.

It must've been something strong if he couldn't remember being with… another man. Unless Erin was lying, trying to punish him, but she'd seemed far too angry to have made it up. He tried thinking of ways to convince David, and something occurred to him; he could prove that Clive was corrupt.

Being locked up at Thistledown, he was safe, at least Clive's henchmen wouldn't be able to get to him. Oscar was one of the few people he trusted, so he could tell him what he knew. Hope began creeping into his mind. *Maybe David and Erin will be able to forgive me, after all!* he thought.

First thing in the morning, he went straight to Oscar's office, but he was already in a meeting with someone else. He decided to wait for him, instead of going back to the common room, it was too important.

Oscar saw his secretary lead Ralph Reynolds into his office as he was headed toward the room. He stopped to tell her something, then turned toward the open door. "His office is threadbare! I simply *must* buy him some new furniture," he heard Ralph say under his breath as he stepped in.

"That won't be necessary, and in fact, I'd ask that the money you might spend on it be donated to the program." He smiled and shook the man's hand warmly. "Good morning, Ralph. Now, what is so urgent that you felt the need to come here this early?" he asked humorously, and then saw the look on his face.

"Honestly, you're the only person I can trust at the moment," Ralph said mysteriously.

Oscar raised an eyebrow, his curiosity piqued. "Well, you've got my attention, what can I do for you?" He walked around his desk and sat in his ancient wooden chair, which creaked and groaned in protest.

"I've found something disturbing, quite by accident, on Claudia's laptop, and you're the only trustworthy person with any authority I could think of to discuss it with. I don't know what to do with it. I need your help and advice." Ralph was sitting on the edge of the old chair he was on, his cheeks were red, and he was nervously drumming his fingers on the desk in front of him.

"What did you find that's got you so worked up? I've never seen you so agitated," Oscar asked, growing concerned.

"I… I will show you. I'd not do it justice if I tried to explain it. Do you have a—I'll just show you my mobile." He swiped his phone, and Oscar saw him wince at something on the screen. With a disgusted look on his face, Ralph handed him the phone. "Feel free to scroll through them all."

"Well," Oscar said when he was finished looking at them. "You may be surprised to learn that I'm able to offer you a clue as to at least a small portion of this. Give me one moment." He picked up his telephone handset and spoke with his secretary.

"Mary Claire, would you please have someone find Bran and—He is? Really? Well, I'll be out in a few moments, please make certain he doesn't leave. Thank you." He replaced the receiver and looked at Ralph. "Please tell me what you know and give me the names of everyone you recognize in the photos."

He listened as Ralph told him all about the conversation he'd overheard and how he'd noticed the extra attention Clive had given Susannah Elliott. Then, he gave him the names of everyone in the photos and told him he thought David Elliott was being framed, but he couldn't imagine how they'd managed it.

Oscar wrote everything down and had Ralph send a copy of the file to both his business and personal email accounts, just to be safe. "I'm going to introduce you to one of our residents who may be able to corroborate your story. Please excuse me for one moment."

He walked out of his office and stood before Bran, who was biting his nails, clearly impatient to speak with him but trying his best to overcome it. "How long have you been sitting here, Bran?" he asked.

"Ah wasnae lookin' at the clock, but I reckon at least half an hour. May I speak with yeh now? Et's verra important." He looked nearly as anxious as Ralph did.

"I'm going to introduce you to the man I've been speaking with. He has information regarding something Erin mentioned. He's safe, and you may speak openly with him."

Bran's whole forehead raised at the news. "A'right."

Oscar led him into his office, and as soon as Ralph saw Bran, he gasped. "Bloody hell! Who… how? Why do you… look so much like—" he stammered.

"Ralph Reynolds, I'd like to introduce you to Bran Elliott, David Elliott's cousin… and lookalike," Oscar said.

"Nice tae meet you, Ralph," he said, and then turned to Oscar. "Yeh said he has somethin' tae say about Erin?"

Oscar shook his head. "Please have a seat, Bran. I want to hear why you've been sitting out there waiting to speak with me, first," Bran told him everything he knew, what he remembered, and what he wanted to do with the information.

The two men sat and listened patiently, then Oscar rubbed his chin, and nodded slowly. "Why do you want to do this?" he asked.

Bran narrowed his eyes at him. "Ah reckon et's worth a go," he said.

Oscar wanted to help him, but he also needed to know that his motives were pure. "Alright, but I want you to have a good think about what it will mean if you aren't forgiven, even though you've done this selfless thing. I must be sure you can handle that. For instance, how did you feel yesterday when Annis forgave you but Erin couldn't?"

"Ah was gutted, but ah deserved et, and ah dinnae blame her. Frankly, ah'm surprised ma aunt was sae willin'. Ah thought she'd put up a bigger fight. Ye're leery of me and dinnae ken what's in ma mind, ah understand.

"Et's right tha' yeh should be, ah reckon. Ah've no' been trustworthy ma whole life, but ah willnae change ma mind, Oscar; ah must do right by ma family. Yeh ken ah've no' been sober since ah was ten years old, mebbe younger, but ah've never felt as good as ah do now, and ma mind has never been sae clear. Please, do et fer Erin and David if no' for me."

Oscar was actually impressed by his composure and honesty. "Alright, I will. I must say, Bran, you so often surprise me. Now, as for what Erin mentioned. Mr. Reynolds has something to show you."

He motioned for Ralph to hand Bran his mobile. As he did so, he stared at him, clearly trying to figure out what set him and David apart. "Et's the eyes," Bran offered, "His are brown, mine, hazel."

When he took the phone and saw the first image, he nearly dropped it. "Fuckin'… bloody—Oh ma God! Ach, poor David! He thought et was himself… Erin said as much. He—" When he got to the one where the man was having sex with him, he choked.

"Ah dinnae remember any of this, Oscar. God! Tae think David found these and thought et was him! Ah'd never have asked tae speak wi' Erin if ah'd known about this, yeh must believe me!" he said passionately, wiping away the one hot tear that had escaped his eyes.

Oscar looked at Ralph, who nodded, then turned to Bran. "I believe you, now to convince others to trust you as well. I know a Chief Inspector whom I would trust with my life. I will talk to him today and tell him the situation. Ralph, I'm afraid Claudia will be implicated in the crime as well," he said.

"I realize that, and I don't have a problem with it. She shouldn't be able to get away with this," he said.

—

Bran was angry—more than that, he was furious. He wanted to throw things and hit things and beg on his hands and knees for David and Erin to forgive him, now knowing they never would. He had only ever truly let loose and cried once in his life, at his parents' funeral as the caskets were lowered into the ground. That's when he'd bawled, wanting to stop them.

He knew they were faking it. If someone would just open the lids, they'd sit up and be their happy, carefree selves! Then he wouldn't have to go live with his goodie two-shoes, pampered cousin and his stuffy aunt and uncle, who looked exactly like his parents; a daily reminder that they were gone.

He wanted to cry just then. He wanted to bawl, knowing he'd fucked up so badly, he'd *never* be able to fix it. All the work he'd put into learning how to forgive and how to humble himself in order to ask for forgiveness… for what? It was a waste of time.

"May ah… go now?" he said quietly and stood. He wished he could erase from his mind the images of him with all those people, especially the man, but then he thought it only one part of a fitting punishment.

"Are you alright, Bran? You look… like you need help dealing with—" Oscar began.

"Ah'm fine! A'right, ah'm no' fine, but ah jest wannae be left alone now."

"Alright, but if you want to talk, come see me, and I'll make time for you," he said. Bran nodded and started for the door. "Bran, don't beat yourself up too badly, you obviously didn't know what you were doing."

"Aye, mebbe no' tha' time, but ah kent well enough what ah was doin' when ah wouldnae get off her, when ah let her struggle and cry, and when ah hit her. Ah knew it all too well. Ah most likely wouldnae cared if ah had known, ah reckon," he said hotly.

"Are you sure you're alright, Bran? I can—"

"Ah said ah was fine!" he yelled, with his fists balled up at his sides. He closed his eyes and took a deep breath. "Ah'm fine," he said evenly, "Now, may ah go."

—

"Yes, but I may need to speak with you later… if I need more details, or—" Oscar didn't get to finish his sentence, as Bran was already out the door.

"He's a hot one!" Ralph said once he was relatively sure he was out of earshot.

"He used to be, yes, but he's been doing so well. Listen, I have your information, and I'll be in touch as soon as there's any news. Thank you for your trust and for coming to me," he said, then ushered him to his office door. They shook hands, and Ralph left.

Oscar was feeling quite worried about Bran, so he went back to his desk and asked Mary Claire to make sure someone was watching him, just in case he tried to hurt himself.

—

Bran got back to his room and slammed the door behind him. He sat heavily on his mattress and lay back, shutting his eyes tightly against the emotional overload he was feeling. *Yeh never could get anathin' right, could yeh?* He thought to himself, bitterly.

Yeh also ken David's gonnae wannae kill yeh if yeh ever get out of here, and yeh cannae stay here forever. Living at Thistledown for the rest of his days wouldn't be a horrible existence. He knew he could be perfectly happy there until the day he died.

Oscar Lincoln had a reputation. He was someone not to be trifled with, tough and hard, demanding and commanding respect. Most people, those who didn't know him, thought of him that way. Although some people knew him to be an honest, kind-hearted man who helped people in need whenever and wherever he could, they also knew not to cross him.

Oscar had made quite a few connections over the years. He'd taken in many high-profile people's unruly family members, enough that all he had to do was ask one person for what he required, and it was done, no questions asked. One boy he'd helped to reform was Chief Inspector Halliday's son, who'd run away at thirteen and ended up hooked on Meth. Toby Halliday was now studying to become a barrister, making good grades, and able to function in society once again.

He rang C.I. Halliday's desk and heard the aging man's gruff answer, "Chief Inspector Halliday."

"Hello, Steven," he said, and the man's voice softened.

"Oscar! It's nice to hear your voice. What can I do for you?" he asked. Oscar told him what had just happened in his office and asked if there was anything he could do to help. C.I. Halliday told him he'd take care of it and not to worry, he had some connections of his own.

Chapter Forty-Three

A VERY TILLY WEEKEND

On Friday night, not long after Roger returned from the airport to drop Kitty off, he left the house again to pick Tilly up. They arrived at Owlgate and went directly up to his flat. Ten minutes before supper, they entered the dining room, faces flushed and smiling. Tilly went to Erin and gave her a hug.

They only had time for a quick greeting before it was time for Annis's prayer. While she prayed, Junie cooed and made lovely baby noises, making everyone smile. When she was finished, Tilly leaned over to get a good look at Juniper in her highchair.

She covered her mouth and squeed. "Oh, she's getting so big! She's adorable, and I just *love* her hair! I'm totally jelly!" she said passionately.

"Jelly, huh?" Erin said with an amused smile at her friend.

"I know," she said and laughed. "I heard a kid say that somewhere and, well, I guess I'm too old to use it, huh?"

"Nah, never too old! I'll just have to remember it and embarrass my kids by using it when we're with their friends."

They enjoyed their meal, Erin especially, since she hadn't gotten to eat Millie's meat pie the last time it had been offered to her. The cottage she was meant to cook it in had rudely burned down, the pie along with it. "Millie, this is scrummy!" she said, and the housekeeper smiled, her cheeks rosy.

After eating too much, she was sorry when Millie brought out cranachan for dessert. Fresh raspberries, toasted oats, and homemade whipped cream were layered in a large trifle dish, tempting her to really overdo it. Though, seeing she was breastfeeding Junie, and it had whiskey in it, she couldn't have eaten much anyway. She did have wee taste, and it was delicious.

After supper, Tilly and Erin helped Millie clear the table, then offered to help her wash the dishes, though as usual, she shooed them away. "Go on with yeh, and catch up," she said, so Erin kissed the mature woman's soft, age marked cheek. Juniper was being held by Annis, and would be for the foreseeable future, so Erin had some free time, which was nice.

The two women went out to the back patio and sat on the swing, talking about what had happened in their lives since they'd last seen each other. A while later, Roger came out of the garage, pulling the fire saucer with him, and went about starting a small fire. "We should make s'mores!" Erin said but then realized they probably wouldn't have the ingredients for it.

"Oh, yeah!" Tilly said longingly. "I haven't had one in years!" Being an American as well, Tilly knew the joy of roasting a marshmallow until it usually caught on fire. After blowing out the flames, it would be squished between two graham cracker squares with a piece of Hershey's chocolate on it. It was a messy affair but so worth it!

She started thinking and came up with an idea. "I don't suppose you two would like to run to the store and find some marshmallows, would you?" she said. "I saw some chocolate covered digestives in the kitchen, and I reckon they'd make a good substitute for graham crackers and chocolate."

Tilly got excited and nudged Roger with her foot. He smiled at her, then narrowed his eyes at Erin. "Aye, but dinnae allow the fire tae die out," he warned her in a teasingly harsh manner.

She laughed, then stood at attention, giving a salute with the back of her hand on her forehead. "Aye aye, cap'n," she said, and placed a twig on the flames to show her intent. The two lovebirds walked away to the garage, then she heard the SUV being backed out of the driveway.

She listened to the routine of Roger opening and closing the gate, then heard them drive off. Erin very nearly did allow the fire to burn out as she lay on the cushion next to her and nodded off. The sound of the car coming up the drive woke her, and she managed to add enough kindling and wood, to restart it just in time.

They enjoyed their mock s'mores while Erin and Tilly pretended to argue over how to roast the marshmallows. Tilly liked to burn them, and Erin preferred to take her time so they were brown and gooey all the way through. They joked and laughed, telling stories from the past and what they hoped for in the future.

"Oh my gosh! Remember the day I first came here?" Tilly said. "I thought… well, I don't know what I thought when I saw David coming at me like a steamroller! I nearly ran away screaming! I was sure you'd think I was a crazy fangirl who had enough balls to come into the yard to meet him."

Erin smiled, remembering it quite well. "The look of sheer terror in your eyes, and how you stared up at David as though he were some kind of alien, was too much! It was almost as priceless as the look of panic on Roger's face when David dragged him down here with his shirt buttoned wrong and his shaggy hair still wet!" she said, laughing till her side hurt.

"What? Ma shirt was buttoned wrong! Why'd yeh no' tell me?" he said, looking mortified.

"Tilly wasn't interested in your shirt, Roger, plus… I presumed it wouldn't be staying on you for long anyway," Erin said and began laughing again.

"Humph," Roger said, and then smiled warmly at them.

"No, I wasn't worried about your shirt, hon." Tilly patted his chest and kissed his cheek, then she looked at her friend, sitting alone. "You were so kind to me that day, Erin, bringing me back to sit with you, right here, actually. It did so much to calm me down. Thank you, retrospectively, for that." She then mouthed *Retrospectively?* "No clue where that came from!"

"Aye, you're welcome," Erin said. "I would've wanted someone to do the same for me." She heard Juniper start to cry in the house, so she stood. "I've got to feed Junie and put her to bed. I'll come back when I'm done if you're still awake," she said and went inside.

It was nearly a full hour later when she walked back onto the patio. Though she was very tired, she wanted to be with her friends more than she wanted to sleep. It didn't matter how much sleep she got anyway, since her latest treatment hadn't quite kicked in yet.

Chapter Forty-Four

A BAD START TO THE DAY

Since it didn't get dark until very late in Edinburgh at that time of the year, Erin and the others stayed up much too late, talking and laughing, then she slept in far too long the next morning. She dreamed she was visiting David at the prison. When she walked in and handed them her visiting orders, the officers shook their heads.

They told her they'd been forged, and that David didn't want to see her. She tried to fight her way in, but it was one of those dreams where you have no energy and can't manage to do what you want to do. Frustrated and upset, she woke up with a headache to Junie crying at the top of her lungs to be fed, which made her milk start flowing, drenching her in seconds.

"Okay, Junie, Mummy's coming," she said and rolled out of the comfortable bed. Not having a bassinet or crib, she'd taken out a dresser drawer and laid her in it on a blanket next to the bed. She lifted the baby and put her right back down.

Her diaper was full and had soiled the blanket and everything around her with urine and poo. "Oh, Junebug, I'm sorry. I shouldn't have overslept." Searching for the diaper bag, she walked around the bed but couldn't find it.

Junie was wailing, making Erin's head throb with each high-pitched scream, but the state of her diaper meant feeding her would have to wait. She then remembered that she'd brought the bag downstairs the day before and had forgotten to bring it back up. *Good night nurse! I can't go downstairs like this!* she thought, running into the bathroom to grab a towel, hoping to stop the milk from running down her front.

She began to cry, not knowing what to do, and grabbed the loo roll from the bathroom. Taking the nasty diaper off the screaming child, she used the toilet paper to wipe her the best she could. Then, she used the towel as a makeshift diaper and prayed she wouldn't wee in it.

There was a knock on the door just as she finally sat down to nurse Juniper, and she lost it. "What?" she yelled over the banshee-like screams of her baby daughter. "I can't hear you! Just come in already!"

The door opened and Millie stepped into the room. "Ach, Losh, what died in here?" she said in jest, referring to the stink of the soiled diaper, then she saw the state of the drawer, the soiled diaper, and the towel wrapped around Juniper. "Ach! Yeh poor thing! I've come tae tell yeh breakfast will be ready in twenty minutes, but I see tha' ye'll be a wee bit late. I'll bring yer nappy bag up, so dinnae worrit yerself."

She picked up the whole drawer and took it out of the room. Erin bawled and rocked her baby in the comfortable chair that Roger had put into her room earlier that year. Several minutes later, Millie knocked again and came in holding the diaper bag and a clean flannel washcloth.

"She's almost done with side one. Thank you for your help, Millie. I know you're busy with breakfast, and I'm sorry to put you out," she said, crying and rocking.

"Ach, et's a'right, love. I set everathin' out on the table, so there's nothin' tae fret over. I'll jest run a nice warm bath for yeh, and we'll clean up the wee bairn when she's through with her victuallin'," she said and noticed the questioning look on Erin's face. "Victualling, tae consume yer victuals?"

"Oh, right," Erin said without her usual cheerfulness. "Victuals makes me think of the way people talk in the Appalachian Mountains, but it makes sense. Most of them were from this area of the world."

"Tha's what ma gran used tae call nursin'. I haven't heard et used by anaone else, come tae think of et," she said and smiled at her.

She tried to smile at the housekeeper and, more importantly, her friend, but she couldn't fake it. Feeding Junie felt like a chore, without joy or peace. She just wanted it to be done, but she knew she still had a good fifteen minutes, at least. After burping her, she switched sides and sighed.

Millie went into the bathroom, and Erin heard her turn on the taps. A few minutes later, she returned to the bedroom. "I'll be back shortly," she said and stepped out of the room.

Tired of crying all the time, she was determined to change her mood, but she didn't know how she'd manage it. Junie was nearly finished eating when she heard another light knock, and Millie came in carrying a tray of food. "Oh Millie! Thank you so much, I'm so hungry!" she said, breaking down again.

Millie set the tray on the desk, then went to the tub to turn off the taps while Erin spoke to her. "I don't know what's wrong with me! I can't seem to stop crying this morning. I had a bad dream, and I feel like my day is ruined before it's even started."

Junie was done eating and was getting squirmy, so Millie picked her up and felt that in fact she had wet the towel. "A bath will have yeh feeling better in no time, dear. Go on and get yerself settled in et, and you can eat yer brekkie whilst I tend to our wee Juniper," she said. She quickly cleaned the baby with a few wipes, then put a diaper on her before laying her on the fluffy carpet.

Erin stripped out of her completely drenched nightgown, and Millie took the garment from her as if it had been clean and dry, though had it been her, *she* would've made a face after receiving something like that. "Millie, you're my favorite person today!" she said, and kissed her cheek, though she was standing there, naked and shameless, knowing Millie wouldn't judge her.

Millie's cheeks colored and she smiled. "I'm glad to have made yeh feel a bit better, love." She led her by the shoulders to the tub and helped Erin into it, then she brought the tray in and set it over her in the steaming water. "Now, take yer time and enjoy yer brekkie. I'll look in on yeh before long and remove yer tray, then you can relax and wash yerself."

"Okay, thank you," Erin said softly and watched her leave the room.

Half an hour later, Milly returned and took the tray away, then Erin washed her tear-soaked face with the soft, clean towel. When she was finished washing herself, she didn't feel like sitting in the bath any longer, so she got out and dried off. *Thank you, God, for the helpers You've placed in my life! I'm so grateful,* she prayed silently.

The rest of the day went much better. She sat on the back patio with Tilly, who doted over Junie as she held her, and they talked.

The next day, Erin joined Annis and Millie at the Kirk for Sunday service. The people she'd met at Easter were friendly, and the Minister's message was inspiring. It was a warm, cloudless day, and they had a pleasant walk back to Owlgate afterward, with lots of laughter and joy.

The next week flew by, and before she knew it, it was already Thursday morning, and Erin was getting ready to head into the Old Town for another treatment. As butterflies began filling her stomach, she tried to rein herself in, but it was proving difficult. She opened the photo album on her phone and gazed at her husband, feeling guilty again for her anticipation.

There was so much baggage to unpack every two weeks. The promise of at least a few days of relief from the exhaustion and a temporary end of the lead-ups. Then, of course, the encounter itself, both the pleasure and the guilt, immersing her mind and body.

It was the torture of intoxication, exhilaration, and energy, accompanied by a state of wretchedness, anguish, and sorrow, followed by both revitalization and distress simultaneously. The cycle seemed never-ending, bound to repeat itself for what felt like forever. That being said, she'd made it four whole months without David, and that gave her hope of coming out on the other side.

Chapter Forty-Five

A SECOND OLD TOWN TREATMENT

Louis arrived at the treatment surgery early, as usual. It was up to him to get there at least twenty minutes before or between five and ten minutes after the start of the scheduled appointment time for privacy to be retained. He parked and headed toward the door.

Thinking about the fortnight before, he recalled following her into the curiosity shop and witnessing her in her natural habitat, so to speak. She'd been lovely in every way; sweet and caring to her friend, and she'd even smiled at him, not knowing who he was at all. He knew he'd not be able to do that again, or she'd be suspicious of the old bald guy following her around, but he thought if he were careful, he might be able to watch her from a distance.

He knew David Elliott was a lucky man, just from spending a few minutes with her twice a month, and then the hour or so in that shop. *Ach! Tae be alone with her, without a curtain… tae be able tae make love to her the way I'd like tae, with kissin' and touchin'—Et would be heaven,* he thought.

His jeans were already tight in the front from thinking about her as he entered the reception area and greeted the woman at the front desk. He was told to walk down the hall, as Dorothy was on her way out to greet him. "Hello, Dorothy," he said, and she smiled at him.

"Hello, Louis. Erin's in room two today," she said brightly, too brightly.

He nodded and saw that he was in front of room one, so he kept going. Finding a card with the number two printed on it slipped into the small brass bracket on the wall to the left of the next door, he waited. When Erin pushed the call button, Dorothy gave him the okay, and he entered the room.

The curtain was wrapped all the way around the bed as usual, and she'd already put the bed to its lowest spot for him. "Good mornin', Erin," he said, then thought about her on her hands and knees, waiting for him, and hurried to take his clothes off.

"Good morning, Louis," she said.

The energy in the room had changed soon after he walked in. It was like a huge buildup of static electricity, and he imagined it might just raise his hair, if he'd had any. He was seriously ready for her, and stepped up to the bed, lifting the hood on the curtain.

He wanted to feel his way into her, helping himself to enter, unhindered, but he couldn't, so he took hold of his erection, and started trying to feel his way with it. As soon as his cock touched her, it seemed as though lightning shot from him to her, making her gasp and shiver.

"Well," he said, and pressed himself at the spot he thought was correct. She made a noise, indicating it wasn't the right place, and then spread her folds apart for him. This time, she took his cock in her hand and gently guided it into her, which caused both of them to moan.

He was careful to penetrate her slowly, not wanting to hurt her, thrusting slightly deeper each time. She had her first orgasm pretty quickly; he could feel her pulsing around him as she became wetter. That feeling was something he dreamed of often, and many times he'd wake after having a wet dream. It was intoxicating, and he wished he could tell her how it made him feel.

He could sense himself getting closer; his balls began constricting, and everything was tensing up, preparing to release. She suddenly began thrusting herself back toward him, making him go deeper still, until he had an amazingly powerful climax, the kind you might see people faking in a porn video.

Realizing they'd become quite loud; he hoped nobody could hear them outside the room. "Christ, Erin, tha' was fantastic!" he said, not able to keep from expressing himself. He didn't want to pull out, he wanted to stay there, feeling her warmth and continuing to feel the powerful energy between them, but he knew he must, so he started to back away.

"Wait!" she said softly but urgently. "Wait, one moment… stay right where you are, please." She backed into him, slowly plunging him deep inside her again. "That feels so good."

He didn't thrust or move at all, yet she was still breathing heavily, and he could tell she was building up once more.

"Oh! Oh, Louis!" Her body bucked in response to the powerful orgasm it was having. Standing still, he waited for her to finish, then, after a few moments, she started to relax, and her breathing began to slow. "I wish—" she began, then stopped. "Oh! I'm sorry… never mind, I shouldn't have said anything."

"I… do too," he said quietly, and slowly pulled out of her, watching the curtain move as she lay on her side, still panting and making little noises of pleasure. He cleaned himself off and started putting his clothes back on, wishing he didn't have to go, wishing he could hold her and talk to her.

"Louis?" she said, and he waited for her to continue, but she didn't.

"Aye?" he said and saw the small chair where she always folded her clothing. He lifted her things and placed them gently on the floor before he sat on it.

"Oh, Louis, I… I wish I had someone to talk to. I mean, I guess I do, but… I'm, well, her employer—I mean… my husband and I are. I… miss having a man's point of view. There are things that happen in my life that I'd like to talk to someone about who won't agree with me all the time with a 'Yes, mum,' you know?" she said, clearly flustered.

"Well, no. I reckon I dinnae ken what tha's like… no one says, 'Yes, mum' tae me," he said, and laughed. "Though I do ken what et's like tae be lonely and miss someone, wishin' tae have them with yeh… tae talk to. What's on yer mind?" he said, knowing they didn't need to rush out of the room.

"I… didn't mean you… really, I mean… I'm not sure why I'm even saying this to you. You're already giving me treatments, and now what, I want you to be my… counselor or something? Plus, I don't know you from Adam."

"Well, I'm much better lookin' than Adam!" he said with a laugh. "Besides that, we'll most likely never meet face to face, and… once yer… husband is available… once more, we'll never… meet… again." He didn't like the thought of that and was selfishly glad her husband would be gone for two years. "So, I reckon I'm a ruddy good choice tae talk to, innit?"

"I guess you have a point there," she said. "There are so many things! After our last treatment, I saw a friend at this lovely little shop. I found out something that made me so happy and yet so sad.

"I can't tell you what it was, it's too personal, but there was a man who showed up. He was quite a bit older than me, and… very good-looking, but… he was… listening to everything that was going on, and it was really awkward for me. Then he did the most extraordinary thing."

Louis's face was bright red as he waited for her to continue, but she didn't. "Aye? What… did he do?"

"He handed me his handkerchief, which had hand embroidered initials on it, then he smiled, not saying anything, and walked out the door. It was so strange! I thought… well, I thought it might be you, for about a second and a half, but the initials didn't start with an 'L', so I guess it wasn't.

"What do you think it means? I mean, I had a police officer give me one of his… in New Orleans… but we'd talked, and he knew what I was going through at the time. Why would someone give a stranger their hankie like that, not knowing anything about the person?

"This isn't the nineteenth century… I didn't know people still carried handkerchiefs. And don't get me wrong, it was sweet, and even romantic, like something you'd read in a romance novel, but I just don't understand it. I guess what I'm asking is, from a man's perspective, why do you think he did it?"

Louis swallowed hard, *she said I was good-looking… no, verra good-looking! That's nice,* he thought. "Right. Well, if you were cryin', I'd imagine he was jest tryin' tae be kind. If yeh weren't, then I've no idea," he said.

"I feel like I should return it to him somehow. It's odd, having someone's personal property… I mean someone I don't know. I guess he wouldn't want it back if he gave it to me and then walked away, right?" she said.

"Ach, he willnae want et back," he said. "He gave et to yeh… et wasn't a loan. Mebbe he… wanted you tae remember how someone did somethin' kind for yeh, when so often, people are rude and selfish, innit? Tha's ma best guess, anaway."

"I'm sure you're right, and I know I'm overthinking it. I just needed to hash it out… to… try and make sense of it. It's not that big of a deal, only…

I'm pretty sure he knew who I was at that point, and… I'm not… used to having people know who I am like that.

"I'm not used to getting attention from men, either. I'm not exactly what you'd call a looker," she said with a quiet laugh. "Sorry to ruin any imaginations you might have had to the contrary."

"I'm sure ye're lovely, Erin." *I think yeh are*, he thought.

"Humph. I like the thought of him doing it to be kind, rather than just because he found out who I am, and… I don't know," she said and sighed. "I'm sorry, here I am blathering on about things that I can't fully explain to you. Thanks for listening, and for your help, and… for… well, all of it."

"Aye, ye're welcome. I've nothin' tae do t'day, except sit in ma mate's flat, listenin' tae him complain about his job whilst tryin' tae keep his dug from pissin' on ma feet. I dinnae ken why he does tha', mebbe he smells ma cat?" he said.

"I dinnae mind talkin' with yeh, Erin, yeh seem… like a lovely person. If… things were… defferent, I'd… mebbe take yeh fer a coffee… or we could have a wee stravaig on an evening—But… well… I mean, would yeh… mebbe… no, of course not, what am I sayin'?

"Sorry, love; et's an odd thing… what we do. Hard tae remember boundaries, yeh ken? Et's too bad… I think we'd be mates… if—Ach! Tell me tae shut ma gob! I reckon I'll see yeh back in London in a fortnight. Take care."

"You too, Louis," she said, before he opened the door, stepped out, and closed it behind him. *Yeh numpty! Blatherin' on about things tha' cannae be! Foolish eejit!*

—

What's a wee stravaig? Erin thought as she heard the treatment room door close. Then, with a heavy heart, she got dressed and left the clinic. She decided to wander about the Old Town and perhaps have a bite to eat somewhere.

It was going to be a hectic afternoon of packing and preparing to return to London, so she wanted a bit of time to relax. Finding herself on the Royal Mile, she wandered in and out of the touristy gift shops, as she'd done when she'd first arrived in Edinburgh and David was gone doing a job in London.

Most of the things she saw were essentially junk that she didn't need, but in one higher-end shop, she saw something that caught her eye. Inside a glass case was a miniature claymore, the sword used by many Scottish warriors, including William Wallace, or at least that was the legend. *Ooh, that's pretty!* she thought and asked the saleswoman to allow her to see it up close.

"Aye, et's a beauty, innit? Et's our last one; the manufacturer stopped makin' them several years ago, now," she said as she handed her a small, flat, black box, opened to show off the item that was set into a red, velvet-lined tray.

"It's stunning," she said as she admired it.

"Tha' one's *sterling* silver. No' all of them were, yeh see. Some were pewter and more… affordable, yeh ken? They sold quickly, but tha' one's a bet more special."

"It's lovely. My… partner is away right now, and we weren't able to celebrate his birthday this year. I think he'd really like this," she said and lifted the small sword, which was weightier than she'd expected. "Yeah… I'll take it."

"A'right, shall I wrap it for yeh, then?"

"No, I'll do that, but thanks."

"I'll allow you tae continue browsing, then," she said, but Erin shook her head.

"No, I'm ready to go."

The woman rang it up and raised her eyebrows before resuming a look of being nonplussed. "Yer total is £295.00."

"Wow! And you're sure it's *real* silver, right?" she asked, suddenly fearing she was being bamboozled.

"I am, et has the hallmarks tae prove et." She took the box out of the bag and lifted the top. "Et's on the blade, here," she said, and held it up to the fluorescent light above them.

Erin could see the tiny symbols pressed into the metal and sighed. "Alright then," she said and handed her a credit card.

"Thank you… Erin Elliott?" she said after reading the name on her card. "Ye're not *the* Erin Elliott, are yeh, then?"

She wanted to lie and say that she wasn't, but she wasn't a liar by nature, so she nodded. "Yeah, but—" she began, but the woman covered her mouth with her hand and waved an associate over to them.

"This is *the* Erin Elliott! Can you believe et, Bridgette?" the woman said, far too loudly for Erin's liking.

"Well, I really should be—"

"Really? I've read all the letters! Truly heartbreaking, they are! May I have your autograph, please, Mrs. Elliott?" Bridgette said.

"I'd like one as well, please," the saleswoman said eagerly.

"Okay, but—" She wanted to explain that the letter had been stolen and the tabloids didn't have permission to print them, but she figured that would just take more time. "Never mind, what would you like me to sign?" When she was finally finished signing autographs and giving everyone in the shop a selfie, she rushed outside, flustered and out of breath.

"Mrs. Elliott? she heard behind her, and her heart sank as she turned around. "You've left yer purchase," the saleswoman said, waving it over her head.

Erin backtracked and took the bag from the woman's hand. "Thank you," she said gratefully.

"May I jest say tha' all my mates and me, we're on yer side, and we truly wish you and David the very best."

Erin bit her bottom lip and nodded slowly. "Thanks for that," she said and turned away, feeling both heartbroken and blessed. She walked all the way to Waverly Mall and went in, not realizing how many memories doing so would stir up.

She wandered through the many curtains of memories from the day she and David had taken the train to London. *That's where the mom and son waved to us. That's where David got his first proposal of the day. That's where we got coffee,* she thought at each turn.

Her head was abuzz with the events of her day as she stepped up to the coffee shop, joining the queue, and she needed a rest. She thanked the barista who handed her a hot paper cup, and as she left the café, she thought she saw a familiar face. It looked like the bald man with salt and pepper facial hair she'd seen in the curiosity shop.

He was moving fast, and though she tried to catch up to him, even following him out of the building onto Princes Street, he was gone, swallowed up by the pressing crowds of businessmen and tourists. *What would you have said to him, anyway?* she thought and took her phone out of her pocket. *I might have just said, 'thank you.'*

After a quick text to Roger, she waited, remembering the stranger who'd held her hand near the Balmoral Hotel during her honeymoon.

Chapter Forty-Six

It was the start of the children's summer break, and Tina had worked things out so that Erin would fly home on Thursday night. Then, on Friday morning, she picked the kids up at the train station and headed to her fifth visitation with David. It had been six weeks since her last visit, and she almost dreaded it after the way he'd behaved toward her the last time.

She decided to bring the kids, hoping it would help him cope and keep him from lashing out at her again. The whole ordeal was emotionally and physically difficult for her as she parked the SUV, and everyone got out. They huddled together and headed toward the building, Peter carrying the bag that held an expensive bottle of gin and a box of cigars.

Erin numbly carried Junie's car seat, covered with a blanket, bracing herself for the onslaught of questions the reporters would spew, like they always did. As soon as they were within earshot, it began.

"Mrs. Elliott! How are you coping?"

"Children! Do you miss your father?"

"Erin! This is your sixth visitation; how does it feel to know that you're less than a quarter into your husband's sentence?

She very nearly turned around and slapped the lady who'd said that, but she controlled herself and continued into the building. Once they were through security, she and the children waited to be let into the 'visits' room. All she wanted was to get through the visit and hoped it wouldn't hurt as much as it had the last time.

Ten minutes later, the officer opened the door, and they saw David sitting at a table wearing his grey sweats with his head down. Not bothering with coffee or snacks yet, they joined him. The atmosphere was odd, they could sense it, and the children were quiet, but she knew they wanted to hug him, so she stood and waited.

David crouched down to embrace his children, then he talked quietly with them, and they all sat at the table, waiting for something. "Here, Peter," she said, and handed him a ten pound note. "Help everyone get a snack, please."

"A'right, Mum," he said and then led his siblings away.

David approached her, but he didn't hug her that time, he just stood with his head down, not moving. "David? What's wrong?" *this time*, she thought. She wasn't in the mood for drama, so she set the car seat down and stood, waiting for him to say something.

He continued to look at the floor, and finally, she'd had enough. "Come on, David, what is it? Just cut out the drama, okay, I'm not in the mood. I'm tired, and I'm not looking forward to the third degree today, so spit it out already," she said, not speaking quietly.

The children looked back at her with wide eyes. They'd never heard her speak to their father that way before. He said something to her, but his words were muffled, and she couldn't hear him.

"What?" she said impatiently, wanting to leave.

"I'm sorry for how I behaved last month; I don't know what happened to me. I was so glad to be with you, but I started to panic, and then I was shoutin' at yeh and makin' yeh feel horrible. I've been sick over et for over a month, but I couldn't apologize until now. The fear that yeh might not come today haunted me, though I wouldn't have blamed yeh if yeh hadn't."

Erin's heart melted, and she began to relax, slowly letting out the breath she'd been holding for who knows how long. "Oh, darling, I love you. I'm sorry I was so short with you just now," she said, hugging him tightly. "Visitation days are so stressful, especially dealing with the press and everything."

"The press? What about the press?" he asked as they finished their hug and then sat at the table.

"You don't know about them?" she said as the children returned, and he shook his head slowly. She wished she hadn't said anything about it, since it would be one more thing to worry him.

"Reporters are camped outside the doors every time I visit you. I don't know how they know the schedule, but they're always here. I just ignore them, but they make it difficult to bring Junie when the children aren't here to help. Speaking of her, here," she said and handed the five-month-old child to him over the table.

"Oh, my darling girl! Look how you've grown!" he said, and just then Dan made a funny face that always made her laugh. She saw him and started to giggle, so he did it again and again. Pretty soon the whole room was at least smiling, and David was laughing so hard he had to wipe a few tears away.

"Alright, Dan, that's enough, now," Erin said gently after his next attempt. He shrugged and smiled at his dad and baby sister.

"Daddy, I have something for you," Rosie said and handed him a small envelope. He opened it and inside were a dozen pictures from the birthday party and of the family with Juniper. "Do you like them? It was my idea."

"They're beautiful, Rosebud, thank you for thinking of me. I'll treasure them!" he said and put his hand on her small face, running his thumb over her cheekbone.

"It wasn't *your* idea, it was Mum's," Dan said.

"Now, now, it doesn't matter whose idea it was," Erin said.

"Tell me about your month, Darling? How was the Gala?" David asked her.

"Well, it was a learning experience, that's for sure. Mother went with me as my date, so I wasn't fending for myself, and I think people respect her enough to not cause too much trouble for me. I met a few... people, I don't remember any names right now. Oh wait... Sandra and Déserée, maybe?"

She knew he'd know who they were, since Sandra, at least, had been in the photos. "There were others, but they were the most memorable, I guess. Nearly everyone *else* was nice, or pretended to be nice to me," she said vaguely.

"Tha's a relief. They can be... brutal."

"I sent you a letter, didn't you get it?" she asked, and he shook his head sadly. "Well, I danced with a lot of people, and we've been invited to Rome by someone named… Sabatini… his first name starts with an 'S', but I can't remember it. He's meant to be a really—"

"Silvano Sabatini? Really? He's invited us to be his guest, Erin?" David sat blinking in disbelief, shaking his head. "But how?"

She told him about their dance and the conversation, then about what Roger and his mother had said in the car on the way back to Owlgate, "I didn't know who he was, David, I was just—"

"Bein' yerself? Tha's enough, I reckon. Yeh never cease tae amaze me, ma love."

She didn't want to bring up what had happened at Thistledown with Bran unless she had to. He was having a hard enough time dealing with everything else, he didn't need to know too much about him. Just as she was about to change the subject, David spoke up.

"Did yeh speak tae Oscar? Did he… mention anathin' about Bran?" he asked, and she could've screamed.

"Aye, I spoke with Oscar. I danced with him, too, he was charming and kind. He sends you his best wishes." She purposely didn't add anything about Bran. "My dress was beautiful! Your mother and I had to—"

"And Bran? He's still locked away?" he asked, not giving up on his query.

"He's still… locked up and will be for the foreseeable future. Your… mother and I—" she began again, but he interrupted her a second time.

"Good! I'm so glad yeh went! Did yeh enjoy yer stay at Owlgate?" he asked, and she was glad he didn't want to hear anything more about the gala.

"It was so nice, David! I saw Tilly, and we ate s'mores using chocolate digestives instead of graham crackers."

"I'm glad you were able to enjoy yerself," he said. "Were the children with you?" he asked.

"No, I just picked them up from the train station this morning."

"Ach, I see," he said, and smiled sadly at his eldest son.

"What is it?" Peter asked.

"Ach, son, I'm jest sad tha' ye'll not be returnin' tae school, though I'm so proud of yeh," he said and put his head down again.

"But, Dad, I thought you understood! I changed my mind, I'm staying in school and will graduate as I was meant to," Peter said, and David beamed.

"Ach! Yeh did? But yeh said you were 'resolute in yer decision.'"

"Well, I was, but Erin and Dr. Dingledine helped me to see why it was more important to graduate," Peter said, smiling at her. "I'm starting a course in drama next term, and I was even allowed to observe several classes last month. I thought I could find out if it runs in the family."

"I'm glad tae hear et," he said quietly.

"I thought you'd be a bit more excited for him than that," Erin said.

"Ach, aye, I am, except I'll not be around tae…" His voice broke and she took his hand.

They were quiet for a while until Peter said, "Would you rather I waited until you're home?"

His dad's eyes were wet as he shook his head. "Not a chance! You have fun and learn all yeh can. I'm chuffed tae bits, and I can't wait for you tae tell me all about et," he said, and Peter's smile lit up his face. "And did yeh have any adventures besides s'mores in Edinburgh?"

"I saw Tim at the shop!" Erin said. "Oh, David, I read some of your letters to me! They're… being published in a tabloid. I know it's not ideal, but at least I'm able to read them now."

"A tabloid?" he said, visibly upset by the news.

"Tim has been following everything, he's been so worried about us. He's the one who told me about them. He's saved them and… had them at the shop. His boss read them out for us since we were too emotional to do it."

"Can't they jest leave us be? Isn't this enough torture, must they add to et?"

"I know, but it's helped me so much," she added, hoping he'd be able to see the bright side, but she could see he still wasn't happy about the news, so she stopped talking about it.

"I'm… glad to hear et," he said, but she knew he didn't mean it.

"I'll start making copies of my letters to you, so you'll be able to read them."

"In two years? Great. I look forward to it," he said sardonically.

"It's only a year and a half now, Dad," Charlie said, trying to be helpful without thinking it through, and it didn't work.

David closed his eyes and frowned. "Aye."

"Please, don't be moody. I want to enjoy this time with you," Erin said.

"Ach, ye're right, I'm sorry. I jest dinnae like the idea of other people readin' the things I've written for yer eyes only, yeh ken? I can't remember what I've… said, how much of et was… private."

"I don't like it either, but I've needed to read them so badly, and if it means sharing, I'll gladly do it instead of never seeing them. So far, none of them have been too private. I just wish I knew where mine were going—I am still writing to you, hoping you'll see them someday."

Just then, Junie grabbed David's sweatshirt and tried to put it into her mouth, but she couldn't manage it and started crying. He bounced her, but it didn't help, so Daniel stood and came over to his father and baby sister. He put his pinky knuckle into her mouth, and she started sucking on it, happy once more.

"She's teething Dad, and she wants something to chew on," he said, and started talking like a baby. "Isn't that right, baby Junie-Woonie? June-June-June…a…choo!" he said, pretending to sneeze, which made Juniper's arms flail out. She started laughing, which got them all going.

"Well done, Dan, thank you," David said. "I'm so happy to see how you're getting on with your new sister. I'm sorry I'm not there and that I'm missin' et."

—

All too soon, the officer was giving the five-minute warning. Dan took Junie after David kissed her and held her close to him, which she didn't much care for. The rest of the children came to him, and he held them as long as he was allowed. Finally, he held Erin tightly. He wanted to kiss her so badly, but he was still forbidden, though he heard and saw other couples doing it in the room.

"I love yeh all so much, and I think of yeh every day," he said, and then it was time for them to leave.

Chapter Forty-Seven

NO CONTEST

"Just leave it, Dan!" Erin heard Charlie say from up the stairs that night. "Sod off!" Dan yelled in reply, then she heard something that sounded like a tussle.

"What's going on up there?" she called up the stairs. There was a moment of silence that she hoped was the end of whatever the issue was, then she heard more yelling. Climbing the stairs, she saw Daniel and Charlie rolling around on the floor. Dan raised his fist as if to strike his brother, so she went to them and yelled, "That's enough! Daniel, get off of your brother, now!"

The boy, red in the face, stood, but not before she saw him pinch Charlie's arm, making him yelp in pain. "I can so!" he said, low and angry.

"Dan! Apologize to him!" she said and pointed to Charlie, who was now sitting up, clutching his arm protectively, clearly trying not to cry.

"But!" he protested.

"No buts! Do it now!"

"He should be the one apologizing to me, not—"

"I will not!" Charlie said.

"What's this about?" she asked, trying to keep her temper and wishing she had a chair to sit on.

"Doesn't matter!" Dan said and started to walk away, but Erin caught his sleeve and pulled him to her. She gave him a stern look, so he huffed and sat cross-legged on the floor with his arms crossed. "Fine!"

"He'd have me believe that he's able to… belch the entire alphabet, from A to Zed! He's a right plonker!" Charlie answered for him, clearly angry at first, then his face flushed, and he lowered his head.

"I can! I just need a fizzy drink to prove—"

"Seriously? Are you two kidding me? You made me come all the way up here because of that? Daniel Elliott, you will apologize to Charlie, both for being obstinate and for pinching him!"

"But I didn't—"

"I saw you do it! If I have to say it again, you won't be eating supper tonight!" Which was the only punishment she could come up with that might make a difference to him.

"But—" he began but saw the serious look she shot him and lowered his head. "Fine! Sorry!"

"Charlie, apologize for calling him names."

"What? But—Alright, sorry," he said, then he looked up at her. She could see something change in his expression, and tears began to form, pooling up in his long eyelashes. "I'm sorry, Mum. May I help you down the stairs, or… get you anything?"

Erin was stunned and accepted the warm hug he gave her. "Oh, Charlie, thank you. I'll be okay, just stop fighting, the both of you."

"Yes, Mum," he said and kissed her on the cheek.

Stubbornly, Dan stood with his arms crossed over his chest, stewing. "I can!" he said as she started down the stairs.

At supper, Daniel let out an enormous belch and laughed as he took another drink from his glass. "Dan! That's rude!" Rosie said, and Peter gave him a warning look.

The boy rolled his eyes and started swallowing air, trying to build up another one. "Listen to this!" he said and opened his mouth. "A-B-C—"

"Daniel!" Peter said, then Erin saw an odd look cross Dan's face. He stood and vomited all over his plate, shirt, and the floor in front of him.

There was complete pandemonium after that; Rosie screamed, Charlie fell over his chair trying to escape the mess, and Peter and Erin both stood, shocked and disgusted. As the boy heaved, Rosie's face began to look a bit green, and she also threw up, though she turned her head, so it ended up on the floor at Erin's feet, splashing onto her shoes.

The girl began crying loudly, and Erin wanted to cry as well, not knowing what to do. Luckily, Kitty came in and began clearing Dan's dishes. When she came back in, she had two plastic bowls and a bucket full of soapy water.

"Okay, everyone, let's leave the room," Erin said, beginning to feel a bit sick herself. "Thank you, Kitty."

"You're welcome, mum. Daniel, take your top off, an' leave it 'ere," Kitty said, and the boy obeyed promptly.

That night, Daniel was sent to bed early, and the rest of the kids sat in the media room, watching a movie. *I'm in over my head! I don't know what I'm doing at all!* Erin thought as she sat at the desk in David's office. Junie was swaddled in her bouncy chair, sleeping, and she was glad for a bit of peace and quiet.

Bedtime that night was a solemn affair, filled with tears and apologies. She told them everything was okay and that she wasn't angry, which was true, it was the self-doubt and frustration that made it hard to be herself with them. She read a chapter from *Anne of Avonlea,* the second book in the series, then kissed them and tucked them into bed.

Daniel cried and held her neck, telling her how really and truly sorry he was for trying to belch the whole alphabet but being sick all over the table instead. He'd apologized once already for his crimes, but he must've sensed that she was still upset about it. She thanked him for his apology and asked him to try to behave better next time, then she kissed his cheek and left the room.

Her best friend, Lily, was going to arrive the next day, and she should've been over the moon, but just then, she couldn't be. She still had to feed Junie and put her to bed, then she had to try not to overthink and worry herself into a fitful sleep filled with nightmares. She'd started having nightmares and strange, vivid dreams, usually sexual in nature.

She often dreamt of Louis, who frequently took the form of a floating spirit or the bald man who'd given her the hankie. Whatever form he took, it made her sexually frustrated. Then, one night, not long after she'd gone to Thistledown with Annis, she dreamt that she was at Owlgate.

There was an infestation of seahorses in the main house, but it was being taken care of by a pest control company. Then, she was alone in Roger's flat. There were a few dishes in the sink, so she washed them and set them on the tiny drying rack. Roger was helping in the house to clean up what had changed from seahorses into bats.

They had all been gathered into huge nets and looked like large, black, helium balloons as they were being taken out of the house. She decided to lie down for a while, as the sight wasn't pleasant from the sitting room window. She had just fallen asleep in Roger's spare room, when she saw the door open.

It was as though she were watching a film, not asleep in the bed, and she wanted to warn herself, but she couldn't speak. The tall, thin figure of Bran got into the bed with her while she watched, and her heart started racing. *Wake up! Get out of the bed!* she thought, trying to yell, trying to do something.

The man was clearly startled as her sleeping self rolled over and laid her hand across his chest. At first, he froze, then after a few seconds, he jumped and gasped. She noticed that her arm was moving downward under the covers, and she felt sick. *No! Stop! Don't do that!*

Bran rolled her over then, and she braced herself for the scene she expected to play out in front of her. However, instead of realizing that it wasn't David and trying to get him to stop, she watched as she allowed him to make love to her. She seemed to be enjoying it, and just as the Erin on the bed started to climax, her perspective changed again.

She was now lying under him, feeling her body release, sending waves of pleasure through her. "NO!" she cried out as she woke up in her bed, still feeling her body clenching from the very real orgasm she'd just had. She cried most of the day over that one, sickened by it and feeling guilty at the same time.

Another night, she dreamed she was in the treatment room in London. She was waiting for Louis to come in, but when the door opened and closed again, the curtain was gone, and David was standing there, naked. She reached out, took hold of his hard cock, and put her lips around his shaft, but then she felt someone enter her.

She knew it was Louis by the powerful energy she felt, and she was worried because David didn't seem to know it was happening. Trying to ignore Louis, she did all she could to concentrate on David, but it was impossible. He was thrusting so hard that she was having trouble keeping David in her mouth.

Suddenly, David looked over at Louis and smiled, then he looked back at her and lifted her head up to kiss her. As his lips touched hers, she woke from another powerful orgasm that had her breathing heavily and arching her back. She didn't know how to stop the dreams, though when it involved David, or even Louis, she honestly didn't want them to stop.

Her greatest fear was that she might have another dream about Bran, and it terrified her. The last thing on earth she wanted was to have sex dreams about him! To make it worse, she couldn't tell anyone about it; if she told David, he'd lose it, and to tell Louis would be completely inappropriate. She wasn't even sure she could tell Lily, but she planned to try.

Chapter Forty-Eight

LILY IN LONDON

Lily arrived at Heathrow Airport tired but looking forward to seeing her friend. She made it through immigration and waded through the sea of chauffeurs and drivers with names written on card stock and pieces of cardboard. She nearly walked past a tall man in an immaculate uniform with a placard that read 'Graves.' She did a double take and asked him if he was waiting for her.

When it was confirmed, he led her to a black 1959 Bentley Coupe. He opened the door for her to get into the spacious back seats, then he put her suitcase in the trunk. When he got into the driver's seat, he asked her if she was comfortable enough, which made her feel like someone *very* important. She only wished Erin was there to share it with her.

He dropped her off in front of the townhouse and took her suitcase out of the trunk. After he'd opened her door again and helped her out, she tried to give him a tip, but he refused it. "That's been taken care of for you, madam," he said with a lovely, formal English accent and a smile, then he got back into the car and drove off, leaving her impressed.

She had never been to Erin and David's house, only to Owlgate for the wedding, and was excited as she rang the doorbell. The door opened and a woman in a maid's costume, who was about her age, stood before her. "'Ello, 'ow may I 'elp ya, miss?" she said with an adorable London accent.

"I'm Lily Graves. I'm—Wait—Kitty? I know you! Don't you remember me?" she asked, and Kitty couldn't hold in her laughter.

"Aww ya got me, Mrs. Lily," Kitty said. "Erin and I fought it'd be fun ta play wif you a bit. Come in and I'll take your fings upstairs."

"Well, you had me for a second there," Lily said and hugged her.

"I'll be glad ta get 'is fancy dress costume off! It's not ruddy comfortable, I can tell you!"

Lily looked her over and shrugged. "I don't know, you look fantastic in it, you might wanna keep it in the back of a drawer. You never know when it might come in handy, if you know what I mean? Wink wink, nudge nudge."

"G'on! Yer as bad as Mrs. Erin, ya are! Speakin' of 'er, she's in the kitchen."

"Uh, okay—Where's the kitchen?" Lily asked.

"It's over here, Lil," Erin said, standing in the doorway. "Come and take a look at the ugliest kitchen that probably cost a quarter of a million pounds."

"Eeeee! It's so good to see you, Erin! You look really good! Where's—"

"Juniper? She's sleeping, but she'll be up soon. Seems like all we do is wake up, eat, sleep, wake up, eat, sleep, wake up," Erin said. My boobs are working overtime! We've started her on real food, so hopefully I won't have to be her cow as often.

"Her cow? You're silly! Oh!" she said as she looked around the dull, grey, lifeless, concrete kitchen. "You weren't kidding! This is—"

"Depressin'?" Francie piped up unexpectedly. "Tha's the word I'd use, maself, though I've been allowed tae add a bit of ma own… personality here and there," she added and pointed to the pretty Swiss dot curtains and vintage tablecloth. There were small paintings on the walls as well, which gave it some added charm.

"I think it helps a lot! Oh, look! Annis gave these to you at Christmas, didn't she?" Lily said, pointing to the small rowboat watercolors.

"Yeah, she painted them, aren't they pretty? I wish I could crawl into each one and see what's downstream a bit."

"Ye're hopeless, mum," Francie said, smiling and shaking her head.

Erin raised her eyebrows and took her cook by both shoulders, leading her to the little trio hanging on the wall. "Come now, Francie, just imagine a lovely, warm, June day… close your eyes," she said and waited for her to close them. "You and I are walking single file, down a well-beaten dirt path with tall, wild grass on either side. Oooh, it just became Victorian… no, Edwardian times, and we're young and thin—"

"Humph," Francie said but continued to close her eyes.

"We're wearing long, full skirts, gathered in the back in glorious bustles; mine is rust red, and yours is dusty blue. Our pure white blouses have puffed sleeves with long, buttoned cuffs that we have to have our lady's maids fasten for us every day. The front of our tops have panels of lace and hand embroidery, each of them one of a kind, of course."

"Oh! I want to come!" Lily said, playing along.

"Of course you do! You're already waiting at the small pier, where the boat is tied. Not only that, but you've brought a hamper full of food and cordial. You opened it when you got there and could smell the cold roast beef and custard tarts your cook made for us. Her name is… Katherine, with a 'K', and no one is allowed to shorten her name, but when you're really mad at her, you call her Cathy… always spelled with a 'C.' Where was I?"

"Custard tarts! I've never had a custard tart! They sound delicious, though," Lily said.

"Well, I happen to know someone who makes excellent tarts of all kinds. Perhaps I can persuade her to make some for us when we're back from our journey. Anyway, under our straw hats, our hair is piled up high on our heads, and we're each carrying a parasol to ensure our fair skin stays milky white.

"You, Francie, are carrying a blanket, in case we get chilled, and I'm carrying a book. I'm not sure what it is yet, as I was in a hurry and grabbed one at random from Daddy's bookcase. I'm not worried, though, father has excellent taste in books."

Erin looked at Francie's face and smiled. Her eyes were closed, and a slight smile revealed that she was enjoying the journey their imaginations were on. "Now, Francie, which boat would you like to use for our—"

"The yellow one," she said and smiled, showing her little off-white teeth. "Tha's ma favorite."

"Yellow it is then," Erin said and continued her tale.

"Wait, Erin, what color is my skirt?" Lily asked and smiled sheepishly at her best friend.

"Plum, yours is plum with tiny red and yellow flowers embroidered all over it. Your tall boots were shipped all the way from Italy, but you don't like them much because they're new and pinch your little toe. You'll take them off when we get to the narrow sandy island downstream.

"Oh! Can you feel that? The wind just picked up, and the tall grasses are singing to us. They want us to be still and quiet, so they're singing 'Shhhhh shhhhh, shushhh,' and the gulls are floating on the wind above our heads. We'd better get a move on, or we'll miss the tide and have to pull the boat whilst wading through the muck to get back."

"Oooh, I wouldn't like that! Let's get a move on! I want to eat everything in the picnic basket!" Lily said.

"Aye," Francie said as her cheeks turned rosy-pink.

"Well, we finally managed to get into the boat, even though that little rascal dog tried with all his might to trip us."

"I'm sorry, Erin, he followed me! What was I supposed to do?" Lily said.

"He is a dear wee thing," Francie added, shocking Erin completely.

"Wee, yes, sweet, we'll see. Now that we're as comfortable as we can be in our corsets, you two row, while I begin to read from… The Lady of the Lake—"

"Harp of the North! that mouldering long hast hung

On the wych-elm that shades Saint Fillan's spring

And down the fitful breeze thy numbers flung

Till envious ivy did around thee cling—" Francie quoted by heart.

"I clutch at my throat, as a bug flew into it, and I am unable to speak. Of course, I hand my book to you, dear sister, and take up your oar."

Francie smiled brightly and continued reciting 'Canto First, the Chase,' for a few more lines. "Ooch, I used tae ken et all by memory, but et's faded now. Et's a shame, really, as et's quite a lovely story."

"No matter, dear, as we are already at the island," Erin said. Kitty entered the room holding Junie. "Oh my! What do we have here, ladies? But a babe, left here by a forlorn mother who's not able to care for…" She pretended to look under an imaginary dress on Junie and nodded, "…the wee girl. We must raise her up and take over her care!"

"Here's a note!" Lily said and pretended to hand something to Erin.

"But I cannot read this, the bug has not yet flown away! Dear sister, please read it out for us?" Erin said, handing the phantom letter to Francie.

Kitty was clearly perplexed, though it seemed she knew Erin well enough to sit back and wait for an explanation. Francie blushed and was about to turn back to whatever she'd been doing before Erin had started her story but changed her mind. "If I must," she said, sounding exasperated.

"To whom et may concern: Ah am but a poor, widowed maid without a place tae lay ma heid. Ah cannae keep my Junie fair, and pray you take her from oot the weed; your daughter for you to be made."

"That was a poem! Did you just make that up?" Erin said, breaking character.

"Yeh asked me tae read the note, and ah have," she said, though her cheeks had become a much darker shade of rose.

"Well, the poor widowed maid is a fabulous poet, even if she can't keep the child. Hand her to me, please, oh… fairy queen," Erin said, reaching her arms out to Kitty.

"You're a born storyteller," she said and played at 'flying' Junie to her, which made the baby giggle.

"Look, miss Lily, this is Juniper! Isn't she divine?" Lily touched Junie's nose and then held out her arms, wanting to hold her. She was handed over, but Junie wasn't happy for long and started fussing.

"Well, it's a good thing I brought these two sacks of milk on the trip, or we'd have to turn back!" Erin said, making everyone laugh. "You two open the hamper and begin lunch while I feed the wee mongrel."

She sat at the breakfast table and began feeding the baby as she brought them all, once more into her tale. By the time Juniper was done eating, they were back on the boat, rowing toward the pier near the tall grasses. "Now we must walk back home. I don't know what we'll tell Mother about the baby."

"Tell her it's Cathy's baby and that she gave her to you," Lily said.

"Oh! That's a fabulous idea! Come now, Francie, dear, and don't forget the book! Father will give me the switch if it gets lost or damaged," Erin said.

"I'll give yeh the switch if yeh dinnae let me get back tae work, yeh raconteuse," Francie said.

"Ooo! That's a new word! You and your vocabulary! I take that as a compliment, though I'll have to look it up later," Erin said. "Ugg! Now I'm tired… and hungry! Francie?"

"Away with yeh!" she said and laughed. "There are grapes in the Frigidaire; you may eat those until yer supper es done."

"Yes, ma'am. Sheesh! What's got into her? You'd think she was just brought back into her harsh reality after a fantastical journey on a little yellow boat or something!" Erin took the bag of grapes and stood next to her cook as she washed them. "I love you, Francie," she said quietly.

"Ach, and ah love yeh as well, dearie."

Lily followed Erin up the two flights of stairs to Peter's room, where she'd be staying. While Erin helped her get settled, she explained that Peter would be sleeping in Dan and Charlie's room in a sleeping bag on the floor, so she'd allowed them to build blanket forts to make it more fun.

"That does sound like fun! We should do that too!" Lily said with a laugh. To her, Erin seemed happy, and things didn't appear all that bad, but she guessed it was because she'd just arrived, and the older children had been at the park the whole time she'd been there. "But seriously, how are you?"

"Follow me, and I'll give you the grand tour of the house," she said and led her down the hall to Dan and Charlie's room. "As for how I am, you caught me on a good day. I… just had a treatment on Thursday, so I'll be good until, say Tuesday or Wednesday.

"I might be okay until Friday, but by then I'm already tired. There's a window; a treatment takes a full day or two to kick in and only seems to last between four and seven days. Day four onward can be pretty rough, though, especially when the kids are here, because that's the most stressful time for me."

"I thought you said your treatments were every other week?" Lily said, realizing the math didn't add up.

"Yeah, once per fortnight, as I like to say, it's much more British," she said with a grin.

"But, Erin, that's not enough! What do you do for the rest of the second week?"

Erin shrugged and picked at an imaginary pull in her capris. "I… suffer. That sounds so dramatic, but it is what it is."

"But why don't you have them more often?"

"If you had to have sex with some other guy because Nick couldn't do it, would you tell him you needed it more often? David's under enough stress the way it is, I can't make it worse for him."

"You're the one under stress, Erin. I'm sure it's stressful for him too, but you've got five kids to care for, one of them needing those convenient bags of milk every few hours. I'm sure if you explained it to him, he'd—"

"No, Lily, he wouldn't. You haven't seen him… lately. He won't eat… maybe that's not fair, he *can't* eat, and he's driving himself… sometimes, I fear, literally crazy. He's terrified I'm gonna visit him one day just to let him know that I've decided to leave him for my temporary match. If I tell him that I need *more* sex from the man… he'll… break, I can feel it."

"God, Erin! That's horrible! So, you're both suffering without a choice. I'm so sorry, hun," she said.

"I'm going to confide in you, but you can't tell anyone, okay?"

"Of course! Never."

"I'm considering… just for August, that's all… just until the kids are back in school—I might change it to once a week. The thing is, I can't tell David, at least not until he's out of that place," Erin said and bowed her head in shame.

They had stopped to talk in the attic, where the old servants quarters had been. Lily took Erin's hand and led her to the stairs. They were narrow, so she stepped down a few and then sat, pulling Erin down to sit on the top step.

"I can't even imagine what you're really going through right now, Erin. You are Wonder Woman in my eyes. All I can tell you is that if you keep burning your candle at both ends, you're going to burn out, and it might just… I don't know, lead to something worse than what could happen if you just do what you need to do. I know that's sucky advice from someone who knows nothing about it, but—"

"No, I think you're right. I can feel it… like Bilbo said, I feel like 'butter scraped over too much bread.' I can't do this forever, and to be dreadfully honest, I wish… well, I wish it were every other day, then I might feel human again."

They sat quietly for a few minutes, then Erin stood and pulled Lily up, too. "Now, let me finish the tour, the kids should be home soon."

Chapter Forty-Nine

CLEAN UP BEFORE DINNER

When the children came home, they were filthy, at least for them, though the worst of them was Dan. He'd found something disgusting to roll around in; it was in his hair, all over his clothes, and he even had it in his ears. "Oh, Dan!" Erin said when she saw him, knowing he'd need a shower at least, though a bath would be better.

"Take everything off right here, and then put your filthy clothes in the laundry room. Make sure to take everything out of your pockets first! Then, I want you to go up and take a shower right away!"

"Here? In front of… her?" he protested, nodding his head toward Lily.

"If… you could just stay… even the slightest bit clean… you'd not… have to… worry about… that," she said, doing her best to keep calm. "You may keep your pants on, unless you've managed to get whatever that is on them as well."

Peter came back from the kitchen, where he'd gone to wash his hands and forearms. Erin made eye contact with him, and he came over to her. Daniel's face was set and angry, as if he were deciding whether to obey her or not, so Peter said, "Do what she told you already, Dan. It's your own fault, so stop arguing."

"I'll just go to the, umm, sunroom," Lily said, clearly not wanting to be in the middle of the war.

"Do as I say, Dan, or so help me… I'll—"

"What? What will you do, Erin, give me a smack? You just try it!" the boy said, and Erin saw Peter's face turn into his father's when he was furious.

"Daniel Lawrence! How dare you speak to her like that! If she doesn't give you a right smack, I will!" Peter said and came after him.

None of the children had ever spoken to her like that, not even close to it, and Erin was stunned. "I don't want to do this," she said and put her hand out to stop Peter's advance, "but, Francie made you and Charlie a cake for your birthdays, and…" Tears of anguish over her dear son's punishment ran down her face. "… and you will not have any of it tonight, and… maybe not at all if—"

"Wait! Mummy, no! But… that's what I was—I was sore that Peter and Rosie had a cracking party… I'm sorry! I really am, Mummy! I thought you'd forgotten about us… again! Please forgive me, please!" he wailed, hanging on to her with his arms wrapped around her waist.

Erin looked at Lily then Peter, wanting them to be the parents for a while. She knew there was no winning; if she gave in, the next battle would be worse, and if she held her ground, he'd hate her for who knew how long. Lily shrugged, and Peter shook his head.

It broke her heart, but she pushed him away and calmly asked him to do what he'd been told. He backed away from her, not knowing whether she was giving in or not. Lily and Peter both gasped when they saw that whatever had been all over Dan was now all over Erin.

"Go… to the bloody laundry room, Daniel, and take off your—"

"I'm sorry—"

"GO!" Erin screamed, which made Junie start to wail, and that made Erin's milk start to flow. "ARRRR!" she yelled in frustration and ran up the stairs, bawling.

—

"*I hear you, Junie! Just stop!*" Lily and Peter heard from the bottom of the stairs. Peter turned and walked toward the laundry room, barking insults at Dan, trying to hurry him up. Lily didn't know where to go or what to do, so she started climbing the steps.

"What happened, Mrs. Graves," Rosie and Charlie said from the top of the stairs, above her. They had changed out of their play clothes and were clean.

"Dan—" she started.

"Oh, that explains it," Charlie said, his brother's name clearly being enough of an answer. "Is our mum a'right? I've never heard her yell like that before!"

"I don't know, Charlie," she said, and they all watched as Daniel ran up the stairs as fast as he could in nothing but his birthday suit.

"Ewww!" Rosie said, and Lily thought she saw him give her the British equivalent of 'fuck off' with his first two fingers, but she wasn't going to say anything.

Peter came running after him, yelling, "And you'd better wash your ears as well, or I'll be twisting them until you cry, you... muppet!"

Lily turned and sat on the nearest step, not knowing where to go. Charlie and Rosie each found steps and sat with her, heads propped up on their palms. "How are you two doing? It must be hard to have your dad gone... like this," she asked, hoping she wasn't making things worse.

"We're used to Dad being away. We've been in boarding school for a while," Charlie said. "Well, Rosie hasn't, but it's not so new for us. Thank you for asking."

"You're so polite! Adults really appreciate that, you know?"

"Yes, Mrs. Graves, we're taught that in school. What... did Dan do?" Rosie asked timidly.

"Rosie!" Charlie scolded.

"It's okay, you can call me Lily, or miss Lily. He wouldn't obey Erin and then talked back to her. She had to punish him, and I know she doesn't... didn't want to. Oh, and then he hugged her and got whatever that stuff all over him was all over her."

"Poor Mummy!" Rosie said. "Dan's an obnoxious twit sometimes. Mummy is so good at being... our mummy," she said with the hint of a grin. "But she's never been a mum before, and it must be hard work, because she gets really tired at times."

"Dan should try to help her," Charlie said.

"Our real mum didn't like us and sent us away to the bad school. I don't want Erin to do that as well," Rosie said and buried her face in Charlie's shirt.

"Oh, baby girl," they heard Erin say at the top of the stairs. "That'll never, ever happen. I will love you forever and ever and ever, no matter what."

She sat on the top step and took her daughter onto her lap, cradling her and allowing her to cry. Lily saw Peter, and Dan, who was now clean and dressed, standing in the hall behind her, but Erin didn't know they were there.

"Lily's right, I didn't want to punish your brother; it breaks my heart to do it, actually, but… it's up to me to do what's right for you. If I allow Dan to challenge me and disrespect me and my authority, how will that help him to learn that it's not okay to do that to me or his teachers, or perhaps a police officer someday?

"I know he's going to… hate me for a while, and I really, really don't want that," she said as tears rolled down her face. "But it's better for him to hate me and grow up to be respectful, knowing that there are consequences for his actions. I was really looking forward to what he's being denied tonight. It gives me no joy to keep him from it, and I wish he could understand that," she said and held Rosie close, rocking her as she cried.

"I do understand it, Mummy!" Dan said. "I don't like it, but I'm angry at myself now and not at you. I'm very sorry for my behavior, will you please forgive me, and will you still… want me to be your son?"

Erin turned and looked at the boy who was growing up before her eyes. "Oh, Dan, I forgive you, and I love you. I will always want you to be my son!" Rosie got off her lap and Dan came to sit next to her, allowing her to put her arm across his shoulders and squeeze him a little bit. "I… still need to punish you, but I'm not angry anymore, okay?"

"Supper is—" Francie said as she entered the foyer, expecting to see just Erin and Lily, or Kitty, on the stairs. Instead, the whole household, except Kitty, were sitting there, and Erin was crying. "…ready, mum. Are yeh a'right?"

"I'll be fine, Francie, just… setting boundaries and getting to know my family. We'll be down in a few minutes," Erin said and turned to Charlie and Rosie. "Now, help your old mum up!"

For supper, they had lamb chops, with all the fixings, and for dessert, they had a beautiful cake, two cakes, actually. One was a pirate ship with edible sails and several licorice cannons poking out the sides. The second one was a treasure chest with edible pearl necklaces, chocolate coins, and ring pops. Both of them were so amazing, Erin had a hard time not giving Dan a piece, even though, or especially because, he didn't ask or look forlorn.

"You may have a slice with supper tomorrow, Dan. Thank you for changing your attitude," she said.

They sang "Happy Birthday," and "For They Are Jolly Good Fellows," then they each blew out twelve candles, making it twenty-four, in total. There were a few gifts to open, too. Erin got them a game called "Zombie Dice" and a redesigned "Capture the Flag" game, where instead of fabric flags, they had to get a glowing orb. Teams were identified through glowing bracelets, which meant that the game could be played in the dark.

Francie bought each boy a jumbo box of Celebrations chocolates, which made Dan blush and thank her meekly, remembering the ones of hers he'd taken. Kitty handed Dan a wrapped box and told him to open it. He tore into the wrapping like a Tasmanian Devil, and inside, was a Lego Creator three-in-one astronaut to space dog to Viper jet kit. He was about to tear the box open, but Erin advised that he wait until it was in his room, and he hesitantly agreed.

Kitty then handed Charlie a letter-sized envelope with his name written on it and said, "Read the letter before ya say what it is."

He frowned, clearly confused that he'd not gotten a toy, but he did as he was told. It took him a few moments to read it, though as he did, his face grew more and more excited. "Goh, Kitty, that's bloody brilliant!" He handed the letter to Erin and hugged Kitty. "Thanks ever so much!"

Erin read the letter, which said,

Dear Charlie,

I found what you left in the garret and thought you might enjoy a few lessons with me mum. She is a seamstress and made your mum, Erin's, bridal gown. She should be able to teach you how to make things such as pillows and curtains, as well as your own clothing, if you'd like. I know she'd enjoy the company of a bright young man such as yourself as well.

I weren't sure if you'd be embarrassed over what I found, so I figured you could keep it to yourself if you wanted and tell them whatever you fancied. I hope I were right in thinking you'd fancy this more than a toy. Oh, and you might want to show this to your mum, as well.

Happy Birthday,

Kitty

"Oh, Kitty, that's perfect! How thoughtful of you," she said and smiled at Charlie.

"I agree and can't wait," he said.

"Well, what is it?" Dan asked.

"It's nothing you'd appreciate," he said, and his brother shrugged.

"May I be excused, please?" Dan said, holding the Lego set tight to his chest.

"Yes, you may," Erin said, and the boy ran out of the room with a 'hurrah.'

"Will you tell me?" Rosie asked her brother hopefully.

Charlie told everyone in the room what the gift was, and they all agreed it was perfect.

Erin and Kitty watched as Charlie stood with Peter and Rosie, discussing what he hoped he might learn from Kitty's mom. "Me mum wanted me ta thank you for allowin' me ta come back early from Scotland, so's I could tend ta her. She also asked that I tell ya how much bet'er she's feeling." Kitty said.

"Please tell her that it was the least I could do, and that I'm chuffed to bits, knowing that she's doing well."

All in all, they ate more cake than they should have, since it was so light and fine and delicious. It was difficult to control themselves, and they practically had to roll themselves out of the dining room after the meal.

Erin went into the kitchen and gave Francie a hug and a kiss on both cheeks. "Francie! That was scrummy, as always! You help me so much! I'd never make it if it weren't for you and Kitty. Thank you for… just everything," she said and tried not to cry again.

"Ach, Erin, dear, thank you for the holiday thes afternoon. Ah didnae realize how much ah needed a wee bit of imagination. Yeh spun yer tale and took us with yeh, effortlessly! Et was magical, and ah hope ye'll do et again someday," she said.

"It's a deal! I think we should have a family talent show, or maybe an entertainment night. I can try to take everyone on an adventure, the children can show us a few things they're good at, and you can read 'The Lady of the Loch.' Then, when… David comes home… we can… have another one, and… I'll make him sing for us! Yes, that'll be perfect," she said. "Good night, Francie, sweet dreams!"

"Alright everyone, I'll read to you in a few minutes, then I'd like for you to play quietly in your rooms until bedtime," Erin said when she found everyone but Dan in the sunroom.

"A'right, Mum," Peter replied.

"Thank you, my dears. Oh, and please tell Dan." They ran up the stairs, saying 'goodnight' to Lily as they passed.

"You're a really good mom, Erin," Lily said, and Erin shrugged.

"I'm trying."

"You're succeeding! They really love and respect you."

Erin led the way to the staircase and sighed, not looking forward to the climb. "When I was pregnant, David used to push me up the stairs," she said and laughed, starting her ascension.

"You mean like this?" Lily said, and began pushing her rear end, which made them laugh the whole way up to the third floor.

"Just like that! That was great, I think I'll keep you here!"

They joined the children, who were waiting in Charlie and Dan's room. There were Lego pieces all over the floor on Dan's side of the room, so they mostly kept to Charlie's side. "Do you mind if I join you?" Lily asked, and everyone agreed that she was welcome.

Erin read two chapters in "Anne of Avonlea," then she asked Dan to move his mess to the edge of the room. After a bit of complaining and prodding, he obeyed, so she tucked them all into their beds and kissed them goodnight. As the two women descended the stairs, they could hear Junie beginning to fuss in the nursery, where Kitty was changing her diaper.

"'Ello, mum, Miss Lily; our Junie is all ready for ya," she said and handed the baby to her.

"Thank you, Kitty, you're such a big help to me! What did you find in the attic?" Erin asked as she sat in her nursing chair to feed the baby.

Kitty smiled and looked over her shoulder as if she didn't want to be overheard. "Well, mum, 'ee 'ad a spool of 'fred, a needle, shears, and… one of Rosie's dolls dresses, along wif a few bits and bobs of lace and trims, like."

"Really?" Erin said, her eyes wide.

"Yes, mum, seems 'ee were tryin' ta tart it up," she said with a grin.

"Tart it up?" Lily said.

"Right, ta make it prettier, like," Kitty translated.

"Well, who knew," Erin said.

<h1 style="text-align:center">Chapter Fifty</h1>

SECRETS BETWEEN FRIENDS

Once Junie was fed and placed in her crib for the night, Lily was tired, but it didn't seem like Erin wanted to go to bed yet. Her eyes were a bit droopy, but she was acting like she had all kinds of energy, talking about going downstairs and watching a movie or playing a game. Trying to give her friend an obvious hint, she yawned and said, "Oh, I'm so tired!"

"The truth is… I am afraid to go to sleep," Erin admitted bluntly.

"But why?" Lily asked, looking concerned at the apprehensiveness she saw on her best friend's face.

"Never mind," she said, "it's nothing. I'll just read or something." Lily gave her a look, so Erin sighed in resignation. "Okay, I'll tell you when we get to your room." They walked up the stairs to Peter's room, and Erin closed the door behind her.

"Now tell me," Lily said and sat on the edge of the bed, giving her full attention to Erin.

"Nightmares," she said quietly, and started pacing. "Well, sometimes it's nightmares, and sometimes it's… well… it sounds ridiculous, but wet dreams."

Lily couldn't help herself and began laughing. "I'm sorry… really, I am. It's not really funny, but it kind of is," she said, trying to keep a straight face but failing miserably. "I'm a terrible friend!" she said as she doubled over with the giggles.

—

Erin watched her and shook her head. She could see how it would be funny to hear, but it was serious to her. She decided to let her find it funny and deal with it some other way.

"Okay, okay, yeah, it's funny," she said, not wanting her to think she was upset. "Well, I'll let you—" she began, but somehow, Lily managed to sober up.

"Oh, Erin, I'm so sorry! I'll listen now. It just struck me as funny, but I see now that it isn't. Please tell me about it," she said. "Wait, let me get into my pajamas. Why don't you do that too, and it'll feel like a slumber party?"

Erin smiled at her. "Okay, I'll be right back." She went to her room and quickly changed, then she padded barefoot down the hallway and back up the stairs, before slipping quietly into Lily's room again. They sat on the bed against the headboard, with the covers up over their crossed legs.

"Now, tell me," Lily said, "I want to hear it all!"

Erin stalled, she knew she'd have to explain some things about Bran and Louis to her, and she knew it would be a long night, filled with tears, shock, and laughter. She told her about being raped by Bran and they both cried, then she told her the dream she had about it and then the one about David and Lewis. Then, she explained that she hadn't actually seen Louis's face because of how the clinic worked.

Lily sat with her mouth open in disbelief. "Do you have... feelings for him... like you did for David when that whole thing was going on... with Todd?"

"No, thank God! I'll tell you, Lil, it's been some of the best sex I've ever had, and from what I know of him, behind the curtain, anyway, he's a really sweet and caring man. I'd love to be friends with him, but I could forget all about him if David came back tomorrow.

"The thing is, I keep having these vivid dreams with both him and David making love to me, and it's so powerful that it's hard to forget. I end up daydreaming about it all the time, not realizing I'm even doing it until someone interrupts my thoughts, and then I'm mortified! I don't know what to do. That dream about Bran was so horrible, and I *never* want to have another one!" she said and shivered.

"This might sound insensitive, but I wouldn't mind having an honest to goodness wet dream about… well, I was going to say David, but that's just really, really wrong now. But Louis seems like a good, safe person to have one about. Maybe, if you accept the ones with David and/or Louis, the ones about Bran might go away. Your body craves sex with your husband, that's natural, and maybe if you stop fighting it, it will be him more often?" Lily said.

"That sounds reasonable. Yeah, maybe you're right. I'll just invite those with David and Louis and not stress about it so much. I am only human, right?" she said with a soft laugh.

"I'm sure David has dreams as well," Lily said, and Erin felt sick to her stomach. She didn't want to think about David having dreams, especially wet dreams, about anyone but her. She must've seen the look on her face, and gasped. "Oh, Erin! I didn't mean it like that! I just meant about you… I should just shut up!"

"It's okay, I know what you meant. Let's just hope they *are* only about me, right?" She was suddenly very tired, and she just wanted to go to bed and hold David's pillow close to her. "Well, thanks for listening and for being here for me. I'm beat, so I'll let you get some sleep," she said and got out of the bed.

Lily got up and came around the bed to hug her. "Goodnight, Erin, I hope you have peaceful, good dreams about David."

"Me too, thanks. See ya in the morning."

Erin went straight to her room and climbed into bed. She grabbed David's pillow and held it to her face, trying, once again, to get a whiff of his scent. In desperation, she took the duvet off the bed, grabbed both pillows, and went into his closet. She pulled one of his dress shirts off its hanger and laid it over his pillow, then curled up under the blanket and fell asleep.

In the morning, she woke, not remembering any of her dreams, which was a true blessing. Actually, the whole week Lily stayed with them, she couldn't remember her dreams, which was very peculiar. She chalked it up to perhaps feeling a bit safer with her friend there and tried not to overthink it.

After a truly lovely week together, it was hard for Erin to say goodbye to her best friend when Lily left that Sunday morning. It was nice to have someone there who really knew her, and they both cried when she left for the airport. Erin could feel depression creeping ever closer as the hired car drove away.

On Monday morning, as she sat in her chair feeding Juniper, her mind was muddled and foggy, and her body ached. This was her new normal, starting a week or less after a treatment. She couldn't function, though she didn't want anyone to know it. Kitty knew she wasn't her normal self, but Erin hid most of the pain and exhaustion from her.

Depression knocked at her door all day, every day. Early on, she could find ways to keep herself preoccupied and still found moments of joy in living. Those moments had become fewer and fewer over the weeks then months of suffering, until she knew the door to depression was open a crack.

She was well aware that she was also feeling sorry for herself, but it didn't seem like the treatments with Louis were helping as much as David's did. It was hard to tell, as she and David tried to have sex every day, not once every two weeks. She felt like she was just barely staying afloat and knew she needed more.

Being pregnant wasn't an excuse any longer, but she did have massive amounts of unavoidable stress. The next course of action would be to increase her treatments to once per week, but it broke her heart to do so, knowing David wouldn't deal with it well. *Why can't things just be easy now? Is this some kind of punishment for leaving Todd?* "I just need a break," she whispered as she sat, feeding Junie.

The children were still home on their summer break and would be for another six weeks. She loved them with her whole heart, and they were so well-behaved for her, but it was still so stressful. She'd never been a mom before and didn't know if she was doing it right or what to do most of the time. Just thinking about it was stressing her out.

Junie stirred, letting her know it was time to change sides, so Erin put her over her shoulder and patted her back like always, waiting for the burp that was stuck in her little belly. She finally let out a loud belch, and Erin moved her to the left side to finish her two-course meal. *Oh, David, I miss you! I need your help! I can't do this alone for another year and a half.*

Erin didn't know that David had just had his room searched again. They took the letter he'd just finished for her, as well as the photos he'd been given by her at her last visit. She also wasn't aware of the perils in his life.

He'd managed to keep away from the men he knew were trouble. The most outwardly aggressive one was Sullivan "Sully" Spencer, whom everyone referred to as "Sally" because he could be quite flamboyant and camp at times. He knew Sally wanted to 'score' him as his next conquest, but thanks to the 'gifts' of fine whisky, cartons of cigarettes, and the occasional box of cigars, the officers were never far away. They often threatened him, saying that a 'meeting' with Sally was imminent if he didn't cow down to them, and/or if Erin stopped bringing them gifts.

He was feeling jealous and sorry for himself, wishing for help as well. *I can't do this for another year and a half! I need your help, Erin,* he thought that night as he held his pillow tightly, hoping he'd wake up with her next to him in the morning, all of it having been a bad dream.

On his most selfish days, he thought that he'd even settle for waking up next to Susannah, but then he'd hate himself for thinking it. Not only had she not loved him, but it was essentially because of her that he was there in the first place, not to mention all the evil things she'd done to the children and to him. The very thought of being with her made him feel physically ill.

Then there was the thought of Erin having treatments from another man, which was never far from his mind. Though he tried to push it back and remember how much she loved him, it didn't always work. Some nights he would lie in bed dwelling on it, making himself so sick and angry he thought he'd go insane. He wanted to kill the man who was allowed to make love to his sweet, bonnie wife, while he was locked up for something as ridiculous as his charges had been.

Chapter Fifty-One

INVITATION

Erin heard the mail drop on Tuesday afternoon. Francie had the day off, Kitty was running errands, the children were at the park, and Junie was asleep. It had been a week and a half since her last treatment, so she was tired and feeling a bit sorry for herself as she trudged to the front door.

Bending to pick the scattered pile off the floor, she had to fight the very real urge to continue her journey and take a nap right there. *Why don't we have a wire cage attached to the mail slot?* she thought. There was an ad for Domino's delivery, a solicitation from a lawn care service they didn't need, and a heavy, expensive-looking envelope that was handwritten in a lovely script. There was no return address, so she turned it over and saw the embossed initials, BTV. *BTV?* she thought but couldn't come up with anyone who had a name that fit.

Inside David's office, she sat on his soft, leather office chair and opened the top middle desk drawer. She saw the box she'd bought him with the silver letter opener, shaped like a claymore sword, and picked it up. Though it was meant to be a belated birthday gift, she decided to put it to use until he came home and took it out of the box.

She slipped the blade of the sword under the flap, and it sliced the top fold effortlessly. Inside the outer white envelope was a black one with shining gold lettering. "Wow! That's fancy!" she said out loud as she pulled it out and ran her fingers over the words, 'Mrs Erin Elliott.'

That envelope wasn't sealed, so she lifted the flap and gasped. The inside lining was the night sky; darkest blue with stars that shimmered like diamonds. She found a magnifying glass in the drawer to get a closer look. "I think those are real!" she said and again ran her fingers over them. "Who on earth—Baz! It has to be Baz!"

Smiling, she pulled out the card, the outside of which was the color of twilight, noticing that there were diamond stars on it too, though not as many. It read, 'Please Join Us,' in polished silver letters. The inside of the card was the color of dusk, just before the sun had completely faded. The only star was a slightly larger diamond she presumed to be the north star.

In shimmering pinkish-orange, it read:

You are most cordially invited to the home of

Barry and Vincent Thompson

to celebrate Future Explorations in the grand,

extravagant way it was meant to be done.

Then, in very tidy, handwritten penmanship, it continued:

Dearest Erin,

Do join us for a night of elegance and showmanship to rival any 'do' you've ever attended! With utter devotion, we promise you shall be treated as royalty ~ pampered and spoiled beyond your wildest dreams.

We are both beside ourselves, devastated that our David cannot join you; however, to us that means you simply MUST attend! It shall be an escape from your solitude and a short respite from your daily life. On second thought, we shall hear no arguments on the subject and will send a car to deliver you to us the day previous to the party! This will allow you to acclimate to our abode and rest beforehand.

*Vincent would like for me to add that you shall be
our 'especial guest of honour' and that he truly wishes for
you to come to us.*

Sincerely, your humble and obedient servants,

Baz and Vincent

Erin laughed and held the card to her heart. *They're so sweet!* she thought,
but she wasn't sure she really wanted to go. She felt fat and didn't want anyone
to feel sorry for her. Plus, there'd be far too many unknown people there. *I
don't think I'll go.*

The next unsealed envelope was a gradient of medium pink, orange, and
dark rose, like the sky as the sun is setting. Presuming it would be the RSVP,
she lifted the flap, noticing that the envelope lining was just a bit paler than
the outside. She then pulled out a pale blue card embossed with shiny clouds
of the same color.

When she opened the flap, she laughed. The inside was the perfect sky
blue and had the shadows of birds gliding on an imagined breeze. Handwritten
on this one was,

*Please do come! Vincent says that you will be unsure
and perhaps will not wish to attend alone, fearing image
or meeting new people. This is something I am entirely
unfamiliar with, but I trust my darling to understand. He
would like to write something now, so please turn this card
over. Baz x*

She flipped it over and saw a lovely, flowing, feminine script.

Bellesa estimada, Erin,

*My poor heart will be breaking if you are refusing
us! I am being ill in my heart for you, my amiga! I am
pleading to you on my knees and hands for this to come to*

pass! Permit Vincent to cover and shield you from every anxiety, bellesa! V. xx

Below that, in Baz's handwriting, was added,

P.S. If you require childcare, our nanny is at your disposal.

Her heart melted, and she knew she had to go, if only for Vincent's sake. *Don't be a ninny, Erin! They aren't going to ostracize you! They're your friends!*

The next envelope was preaddressed and stamped; it was pale blue with embossed, iridescent dewdrops on it. The inner paper of the envelope was blazing yellow and reddish-orange, like a magnificent sunrise. Inside was a dark blue card, with just a few tiny diamond stars.

It read, *RSVP* in raised yellow-pink letters, along with a line to fill in how many guests would be attending. Below that, it read,

Please include your email and mobile number.

Having to open several drawers, she finally found some fine linen paper and took out several sheets. Then, she found a luxurious, antique-looking fountain pen in what appeared to be scrimshawed ivory. As she wrote the date at the top of the page, she saw that the ink was reddish-purple, which delighted her.

My dearest friends,

Your invitation is superb! It's something plucked from my wildest dreams! I will keep and treasure it for always! I adore that it was as if time were going backward, nightfall to sunrise, since Joe could only travel into the past! It's genius, and I say bravissimo to the whole idea! I can't wait to show it to David when he comes home!

You were correct, Vincent, I was thinking about sending my regrets, but because of your sweet words, I have

changed my mind. I shall be prepared and waiting for your car the day before the event, as you said. I must admit that I am still a bit nervous to be around new people; nevertheless, you have promised your protection, so I will do my best to not think about it- too much.

Thank you for thinking of me and for being so sweet and generous! You are both kindred spirits, and I love you very much.

Your friend,

Erin Elliott

P.S. Your handwriting is beautiful, both of you! xx

She placed the letter in a matching envelope, along with the RSVP card, addressed it, and applied two stamps, just to be sure. Then, as soon as Kitty returned home, she went outside and placed the letter in one of the red Royal Mail postboxes a few doors down from her house.

That evening, she received a message from Tim.

Tim: *Hello Erin, it's Tim. I was wondering how you are?*

Erin: *Hiya, Tim. Thanks for asking. I'm okay, but my friend from America just left and I'm feeling a bit down. Your message has cheered me up a bit, though.*

T: *Aye, it's hard to say goodbye to a good friend. And speaking of friends, the message inside my book is a belter! I wish I could thank David for it.*

T: *Seeing you at the shop was Fantastic! I hope you're able to come again soon.*

E: *We'll come back soon, I'm sure, and I agree, seeing you was some thing I didn't know I needed, but I really did.*

E: *Oh, Junie is fussing and needs to be fed. I have to go for now, but take care of yourself and give yourself a big hug from me!*

T: *Alright. Sweet dreams! x*

Chapter Fifty-Two

A FAMILIAR TREATMENT

Erin was exhausted as she entered the clinic, more tired than she'd been in a long time. It had taken all her energy to get herself up and ready to leave the house that morning. If it weren't for Kitty's help every day, she'd be flat on her back, sleeping all the time.

The receptionist remembered her when she stepped into the clinic, and asked her to have a seat, as Wendy was with another client. She sat in the more-comfortable-than-you-might-think upholstered chairs and woke with a start when Wendy entered the waiting room. "Erin! It's good to see you!" she'd said brightly, then, realizing she'd woken her, put her hand over her mouth. "I'm so sorry."

Erin smiled up at her. "It's fine, I needed to wake up anyway," she said. "Are we all set?"

Wendy looked somewhat uneasy. "I'm afraid Louis has just rung here saying he had a minor emergency and hopes to be able to reschedule," she said.

She frowned, then tried to act like it wasn't a big deal, though she knew she was failing. The symptoms were creeping up on her again, and she really needed that treatment. "When?" was all she could say without crying. She sat on the chair again and put her head in her hands, resting her elbows on her knees.

Wendy squatted in front of her, her face full of concern. "Are you quite alright, Erin? You seem knackered, more so than usual," she said. "Maybe you should come in once per week for a while?"

She sat there, breathing hard and willing herself not to cry. "How long will I need to wait?" she said softly.

Wendy looked at the receptionist, who could hear the conversation, but the phone rang, so she couldn't respond right away. "Oh, yes! Yes, I am sure that would be much appreciated. I'll tell her. Yes, see you then," the receptionist said excitedly, and the two women looked up at her.

"That was your match, Mrs. Elliott. He said he's fixed the problem and can be here in about thirty minutes."

Erin's eyes filled with tears. She swallowed hard and had to take several deep breaths to keep from sobbing. It took a moment to collect herself, then she smiled at Wendy and nodded to the receptionist.

"Good, that's good, I can wait, and I think... maybe I should start coming here once a week, like you said. I... I don't want to, and it'll only be until the children go to their grandmother's house at the end of August. After that, if I need more appointments, I'll set them up then," she said, thinking a month was a good trial.

She really hoped it would take her past that hurdle. After that, she would resume their usual schedule. "I hope Louis is available that often."

"I'll have a talk with him and find out. Now, let's get you into your room," Wendy said, and Erin smiled. She stood with effort, then they walked into the familiar room and Wendy closed the door. "Did you have a good experience in Edinburgh?" she asked.

"Yes, it was fine, though they don't have beds with stirrups there! Can you believe that?"

Wendy looked at her the same way she'd looked at Dorothy after being given the same news. She explained how it all worked, and Wendy listened with her eyebrows raised, occasionally shaking her head or laughing. "Well, I imagine you're glad to be back here, then?" she said, and Erin cocked her head to the side.

"Yes, I am, except—" she began, and Wendy gave her a questioning look.

"Except—what?

"Well, I hate to admit it, but... well, I liked the other position better," she said, and they both chuckled.

"Alright, I'll make a note of it and change your preference in your chart. Now, I'll leave you to get yourself ready and comfortable. Push the call button, as usual, and I'll send him in when he gets here."

Erin sighed deeply. "Okay, and thank you, Wendy, for being such a help to me. I'm glad I got you for my… what is your title?" she asked, and Wendy shrugged.

"I don't really have an official title, but I think of myself as a care assistant. I'm pleased that you're comfortable with me, and I know you'll get through this, Erin. Mr—Oh, dear, I almost gave away his surname!" She turned bright red, plainly flustered. "What I mean is, Louis is a really kind man, and I think… well, I don't know what I was going to say actually, but I'm glad you have a man like him for your temporary match," Wendy said, then rolled her eyes and left the room.

Erin got undressed and folded her clothes neatly, laying them, as usual, on the chair near the door. She wished she'd asked Wendy how to lower the bed, just in case she needed to, though that bed was already much lower than the other one. There was also the issue of how to use the curtain, since there wasn't a hood to protect her privacy, and her ass would be up in the air.

Maybe this wasn't such a good idea after all, she thought.

Sitting on the bed, she pulled the curtain around it, leaving only her feet and ankles sticking out. She didn't want to assume a kneeling position too soon, as she might have to wait a long time, and she thought it would be exhausting. After pushing the call button, she pulled her feet up onto the bed and curled up, making herself comfortable.

—

Louis arrived just a bit later than he thought he would, as he'd had to stop for pedestrians and then slow down for a minor accident on his way there. Thus, he was a bit flustered when he walked in and spoke to the receptionist. "I'm sae sorry et took sae long, I hope Erin is… no' in a hurry," he said as he ran his hand over his scalp, truly anxious about holding her up.

"I wouldn't worry; I reckon she's just grateful you're here," the young woman said with a smile.

"Ach, good. May I go through now?" he asked but heard Wendy's greeting before she could answer him.

"Hello, Louis, I'm glad you were able to come. I believe Erin is having a rough time of things at the moment. I've spoken with her about changing the treatment schedule to once per week, just for the month of August, if you're available?" she said as they walked to the door of the treatment room.

He was surprised, he might have expected for her to change them to once every three weeks, but to increase them was not something he would have predicted. "Right, aye, I can do tha'. Ah hope everathin' is… I dinnae ken… a'right with her. Do yeh think she needs… help?" he said, not knowing why he was even asking; he wouldn't be able to do anything to help her, anyway. "Ach, tha's a daft question, I reckon."

Wendy smiled at him and touched his arm. "Not daft, Louis, you're a caring man. I don't imagine you'll be able to help, except with this. The treatments are what she requires help with most of all, I think," she said. "She's already pushed the button, so you may go in now."

He nodded, then turned the doorknob and stepped into the familiar room. "Hello, Erin," he said but was met with silence. "Erin?" Still nothing. *Did she go to use the loo or something?* Not sure what to do, he said it again, "Erin?"

Starting to feel a bit silly, especially if she wasn't even in the room, he gently moved the curtain to see if there was anything on the bed at all. He saw the slightest shape of what was most likely a knee. It didn't take long for him to figure out what was going on when he heard a light whiffling noise as she breathed. *She's asleep!* he thought.

Though he didn't want to wake her, he figured she wouldn't want him to sit there and listen to her snoring either, so he touched her knee gently. "Erin? It's Louis," he said a bit more loudly than he had when he'd come in. He heard her take in a deep breath and saw the curtain move as she sat up.

"Oh, Louis… I'm sorry, I… fell asleep," she said drowsily, with a light laugh. "I've been burning my candle at both ends lately, and it's catching up to me, I guess."

Louis smiled, liking her American accent and glad she had a sense of humor. He began to undress, but when he didn't see the curtain moving, he paused to listen. Just as he was about to say something, he heard the gentle whiffle of air as she slept once more, sitting upright.

"Erin… are yeh… a'right?" he asked and gently touched her knee again. He felt the current flow between them, and she drew in a long, deep breath.

"Good night nurse! I'm so sorry! It's so hard to keep my eyes open. Okay, up I go," she said.

He saw the curtain moving as she got into position. "Don't worry, I only listened to yeh snore for a few minutes," he said as he finished getting undressed, laying his jeans and pants over the back of the chair.

"Ha ha—" she said and then stopped, "Wait, I wasn't really snoring, was I?" she asked, and Louis laughed.

"Only a wee bit, love. Et was endearin'," he said and stepped up to the end of the bed. "And… how… shall we be… positioned this time?" he asked, not seeing the stirrups out, as they usually were.

"Yes, well, I thought we… could continue with the… uh, rear… entry, if you're okay with it, but I don't know how to work that… I mean, with the… way things are here," she said, clearly flustered. "I'm not sure if this bed is… adjustable, like the other one… and, well, I'm not sure about not having a hood on the curtain. I can't remember what I was told on my first visit about that."

"Right, allow me. There's a button on my end—" he said and laughed at how odd that sounded.

"Ooh, nifty," she said as the bed began to descend.

"As for the hood, I'm afraid ye'll jest have tae trust me no' tae… uh… look," he said, not trusting himself at the moment, as he could see the outline of her plump, round bottom getting closer to his rock-hard cock. He'd gone mostly limp waiting for her, but he was quite ready for her after that and took a half-step forward. "I'm sorry, though… if I end up touchin' yer… skin… on your legs—" he said with a slight cough and swallowed hard at the thought.

He heard her swallow hard as well. "O-kay," she breathed.

When the bed was at the correct height, he parted the curtain slightly, trying not to look at her. "Ready?" he asked quietly.

"Ready," she whispered.

He took hold of his penis and aimed it between her legs, which was difficult, as the gap in the sheet kept closing. Not looking wasn't going to work, so he parted the curtain again. He saw her pale skin and just the slightest bit of pubic hair, making him shudder.

"Sorry," he said. "Just tryin' tae figure everathin' out. I'm no' as ambidextrous as I imagined I was." He was having trouble, so, once again, Erin had to help him by taking hold of his cock, putting it in the right spot, and then gently pushing his head into her.

"Christ," he whispered, as he felt himself slide inside her. He pushed against her but didn't have anything to hold on to. With the hood, he could hold on to her with the sheet wrapped protectively around her legs. However, now he knew if he tried to do that, the curtain would part, and he'd be faced with her lily-white ass, and she might not appreciate that. "Erin," he said, "I… need tae… take hold of yeh—"

"Yes, please… do what you need to," she said, sounding desperate.

He carefully spread the curtain so that it lay over her back, revealing her beautiful rear end and pale legs. She had a small scar on her back, just above her right cheek, and he wondered how she'd gotten it. He could see himself inside her, and grabbed her legs greedily, needing to thrust into her yet going as slow as he could until her body relaxed, yielding to his length.

"Okay—" she said, and he knew what she meant.

He thrust, all the way in, feeling the soft skin of her bottom against the hairy skin of his lower abdomen. Moving his hands up to the indents at the top of her pelvis, on her hips, he continued driving himself into her, making her moan. She pressed herself back against him, propelling him further, deeper into her.

He felt her climax at least twice before he felt himself ready, wanting to release but also wanting to continue giving her pleasure. He held off as long as he could, which he knew was probably against the rules, and more than likely immoral as well. Finally, he shuddered and let out a deep, satisfying moan, grunting as he felt his semen leave him, which he'd never actually felt in that way before.

"Christ, Erin, I… wish I could… tell yeh—" he didn't finish his thought. "Et's… so… amazin' with you. I'm sorry… I ken I shouldnae say anathin' but I… cannae keep et in."

"Thank you," was all she said.

He pulled out of her and backed away but not before taking one last, selfish glance. He wanted to tell her how bonnie, at least that part of her, was to him, but he wouldn't dare, that would be going way too far. Instead, he started to clean himself off, as usual.

"Louis? I need to apologize to you about our last treatment. I shouldn't have asked you to listen to my problems and concerns. It wasn't a good thing to do, and I… won't—"

"Shush now. Ye're welcome tae say whatever you want tae me. I'm all ears, and I dinnae mind. As I said last time, I enjoy talkin' with yeh, so dinnae worry about it. And if yeh need someone tae listen to yeh again, or help you tae figure somethin' out tha's puzzlin' yeh, dinnae hesitate tae ask me," he said gently. "But et's my turn this week tae ask you somethin', if yeh dinnae mind."

"I don't mind, what is it?"

He hadn't planned on saying anything, but he had to know. "Are yeh… doin' a'right, Erin? Wendy said ye'd like tae increase yer treatments, and I'm more than willin' tae do tha', but I need tae know if ye're… okay," he asked, hoping she wouldn't brush it off and answer him with a lie. He waited for her to say something, but she didn't. He still waited, but silence. "I'm—"

"I… don't know," she finally said. "Our kids… are home on their summer holiday, and we have such good times. I want to make a million memories with them. Their… birth mum wasn't a good person, and I want them to know what real motherly love is like, so I feel like I need to be 'on' for them all the time while they're home.

"But without David… my husband… home to help with them, and with the baby, I'm starting to feel worn out. I have our housekeeper, who's brilliant and takes so much of the load, but it's still so much more than I'm used to, or… apparently equipped for.

"The thing is, stress can make this fucking disease do crazy shit, and I've got more stress than I know what to do with at the moment. Wendy suggested we meet once a week for a while, and I think she's right, at least until the children go to their gran's in Edinburgh."

"Ach, Erin," he said, and stood next to the bed, wishing he could see her face. "May I… take yer hand?" he asked, assuming she'd say 'no.' Instead, she lifted the curtain, just enough to stick her hand out from under it.

Holding it with both hands, he saw her wedding ring on her unmanicured fingers. He took the opportunity to gently kiss her knuckles, feeling a jolt of electricity flow from her hand to his lips. "Et must be so verra hard tae be without yer husband, especially with children and a house tae run.

"Even with help from yer housekeeper, there must be a million decisions tae make evera week." He could hear her start to cry softly and squeezed her hand. "I wish with all ma heart I could help you. Tha' I could take some of the burden, but the only thing I know tae do tae help is tae be here, tae listen, and… tae… care about yeh. I hope that'll help a wee bit until yer husband comes back from… wherever he is… that… he's no' available now," he said, trying to cover his near admission to knowing who she was.

Erin didn't say anything for a while; he heard her taking great gulps of air, clearly trying to compose herself. She squeezed his hand, and after a few moments let out a long breath.

"I almost wish it had been you with the ready hankie in the shop in Edinburgh, that way we could drop the whole curtain thing, but," she said, before he could say anything, "I'm also… glad it wasn't, cuz that would mean you… followed me, and… that would make me uncomfortable. Being here for our treatments and listening, are actually the best things you can do for me, Louis. That does show me you care."

"Aye, about tha'… today… I'm really sorry—"

"It doesn't matter, I'm sure it was important. I don't see you as the type of guy to… how would you put it… skive off… something that feels like this," she said and laughed.

"Ye'd be correct in yer assessment of ma type," he said, glad she didn't actually ask if it had been him in the shop, as he couldn't have lied to her about it. "Right, I'll be here next week without fail," he said and reluctantly let go of her hand. "Take care of yerself, Erin."

Later that day, Erin got a call from the clinic. Louis had asked them to ring her and find out if they could move all of August's appointments to Mondays, as he had to attend all-day meetings every Thursday that month.

Erin didn't mind, as it would actually give her one extra week before they went back to bi-weekly sessions, and because of the change, the first treatment in August was only four days after the most recent one.

Chapter Fifty-Three

SIXTH VISITATION-JULY THIRTY-FIRST

After struggling through the reporters again, this time in the pouring rain, Erin stood and ignored the stares from the other visitors while they waited to be let into the 'visits' room. Most of the time, she liked being left alone, but sometimes she wished they'd just ask their questions instead of whispering behind her back. She'd worn a raincoat, or Macintosh, as Kitty had called it, but her hair was drenched, and she was a bit chilly.

Depression was still sidling up, wanting her to embrace it, and the weather wasn't helping much, but she was strong. She knew she'd pull through once she got past that part of her life. Also, talking to a counselor took too much work, and she didn't want an antidepressant pill forced on her, plus she didn't think it would really help her, anyway.

They were finally allowed in, and her heart skipped a beat as she saw David sitting in one of the chairs that was bolted to the floor. He stood, and she hugged him for as long as they would allow, which was never long enough. Though he still couldn't kiss her, she could feel his breath on her ear as he bent over, and it was almost good enough, almost.

"Ma darling! Oh God, how I've missed you!" he said and smoothed her hair with his hand, looking into her eyes.

"I've missed you, too." When she'd first started visiting him, it was hard not to cry, whine, and complain. At that point, though, she was starting to feel numb and just wanted to get off the emotional roller coaster she was on. She didn't want him to see her suffering or make the visits all about her. Sometimes she succeeded.

"You look so sick, David," she said as they sat with the table between them. "I'm worried about you. Have you stopped eating altogether? Are you trying to kill yourself, because you'll never live out your sentence at this rate."

She was so angry that it seemed like he wasn't even trying to live. "You promised you'd try to stay healthy for us! God, David, don't you care about us? Don't you want to live for us? I can't stand seeing you wasting away like this!"

She put her head on her arms, which were crossed on the table in front of her and cried. Huge sobs filled the room. They echoed off the gymnasium-like walls, and she couldn't stop gasping and wailing with grief.

"I'm sorry, darling. I'll try harder tae eat, but et's difficult," he said softly. "Please… dinnae cry—I promise I'll—"

She shook her head and sat up. "I'm afraid you're going to die in here, and I can't live without you. And not just because of the treatments, fuck the treatments! I need you. I… know you're upset about what I'm having to do, but I'd rather have you a million times more than… him. Please… please try to stay healthy and… alive for me!"

"I'm… afraid of that sometimes as well, darling, but… I'll try harder—"

A thought occurred to her just then, and her eyes grew wide, making him stop talking. "David!" she whispered and glanced around them, not wanting to be overheard, which probably just made her look suspicious. "Are you… safe… in here? Have you been… taken against your will? If you have, I'll still love you, but… is that why you're not… eating? Please tell me the truth." She was breathing heavily and blinking furiously, scared of his answer.

He took her hands in his and shook his head. "No, ma love, though I've heard things in the night… things that sound like someone begging for mercy from what everaone knows is forced sodomy. Et chills me to the bone, but I've been spared thus far. I believe yer gifts are savin' me from that. Yeh brought more today, I hope?"

"Aye, a box of cigars and a bottle of bourbon from the cellar. I looked it up, it was valuable, but not priceless," she said and gave him a slight grin.

"I dinnae care if et was worth millions, darling, as long as it gives me a few more weeks of relative safety. They sometimes threaten me with a visit from Sally, but so far et's been just tha'."

"Sally, huh? So, there *is* a threat in here for you. I'll try to up my game. I'm glad you have a wine cellar; I'd hate to have to go shopping for things every fortnight."

"*We* have a wine cellar, darling. Are you… doing okay? How're the children? I think about you all the time, truly, and I worry that ye're overdoing it," he said.

"I've been better, to be honest. Your… treatments seem to last longer, or maybe it's just because we had them more often, I don't know, but… it's a struggle sometimes… often. The children are so dear, David. Peter makes sure to keep them out of my hair as much as he can, taking them to the park, and they watch far too many movies in the media room, though he always comes to me to make sure I approve them first."

"I'm glad ye're gettin' on together so well, I worry about that sometimes."

"It hasn't always been sunshine and roses, but we're managing," she said, and David gave her a 'tell me more' look, so she sighed. "Did I tell you that Lily was gonna visit me? Well, she got here the day after our last visitation and stayed the whole week. I had Tina arrange everything. I… hope you don't mind paying for… it… I should've asked you, but—"

"I dinnae mind at all, ma love. I'm glad tae hear she was there for yeh, but dinnae change the subject," he said.

"I'm not changing it, exactly." She told him about what had happened with Dan and about the cake Francie had made. "It broke my heart to punish him, David! I wanted to give in with everything inside me, especially when he hugged me so tightly! Parenting is the hardest thing ever!"

"What did yeh do? Did yeh give in?"

"No, I didn't. I was talking to Rosie and Charlie about how hard it was to follow through but why I had to, and he overheard me. His attitude impressed me. I was afraid he'd be mad at me, and I think he would've been if he hadn't heard what I said. He said that he was mad at himself and that he understood. I hope Junie grows up to be like they are."

"Well, parenting hasn't been ma greatest strength, as yeh well ken. I'm proud of you for standin' yer ground, love. Thank you for…" he began, and then got choked up, "…bein' a mother tae our bairns, as yeh are.

"You didn't ask tae be a single mum tae five children, four of whom yeh hardly ken at all. This shouldn't have been put upon yeh sae… early in our relationship, or ever, actually. Ye're sae strong, and… ye're ma hero, Erin. I need for you tae know tha'."

Erin sat still with her eyes closed, wanting to soak up his words so she could remember them when she felt like a failure. "I don't always feel strong, and I don't feel like a hero," she whispered.

The officer's boots squeaked on the floor as they monitored the inmates. She could hear snippets of other conversations in the room, as well as her own breath as it exited through her nose. Everything was suddenly sharpened and focused.

She didn't know why, she didn't have any kind of epiphany, but for that moment, she was existing in the present, and when she looked up at her husband, she felt love. Not generic love or desire but a feeling of real, full, complete love.

His scent, pheromones, or whatever they were, began to crowd out everything else; she felt at peace, and David seemed to relax along with her. They had spent every visitation trying to cram in fourteen days' worth of fears or events or information, but just then, they could live and love in the time they had. It felt almost like a religious experience, or as if they were both on a mind-altering drug.

Their elbows were resting on the table, and when David opened his hand, she rested her cheek in his palm. They didn't speak or rush, they didn't need to. His energy began to flow through his hand into her and tears began to flow, but she didn't feel sad or angry. She felt whole and as though they were one.

She'd never felt anything like it before and didn't want it to end, but she wasn't afraid of that happening. Time really felt like it wasn't moving, like they were in a bubble that time forgot. Then, just as suddenly as it had begun, it ended.

"Five minutes," one of the officers said.

"Erin, darling, et's nearly time tae say goodbye again," he spoke softly, just above a whisper, calm and even. "I dinnae ken what that was jest now, love, but I could live there. I… feel at peace and in control, and I've no' felt tha' way in longer than I can remember. Right now, I'm actually hungry," he said and gave her an honest to goodness, genuine smile.

"I felt like I could… like I was inside you and could feel… you… like we were one person, like there was no hiding or fear. God, David, it was almost better than sex," she said and laughed lightly. "I also feel better, like I can make it at least another two weeks, and it's been hard to think that far ahead lately."

The officers were standing at the doors, ready to open them, so they stood, but Erin didn't feel panicked. "I love you, David, and we'll get through this. Be safe, and take care of yourself, my love."

"I will, darling. I love you as well, give Junie a kiss for me," he said and hugged her until an officer opened the doors and she had to leave.

Chapter Fifty-Four

BEGINNING OF AUGUST

That Monday, she waited in the treatment room as usual, and he was right on time, as usual. She'd been calm that whole weekend, ruminating over her shared experience with David. However, when Louis entered the room, a sense of wild abandon threatened to overcome her.

Out of nowhere, she had this crazy idea to throw the curtain back and allow him to make love to her. She wanted to watch him, to see his face and the expressions he made, but she managed to control herself. There seemed to be a similar fight going on in his mind as well, she could feel it, though she didn't say anything for fear that speaking the idea would somehow make it easier to give in to.

"Thank you, Louis," she said when he was finished and getting dressed again.

"Ye're welcome, love," he said. "See yeh next week."

"Aye, next week," she said, and he left the room. *How am I gonna do this for another year and a half and not give in?* she thought again as she got up and put herself together. *Please, send David home early,* she prayed silently as she left the clinic.

"I'm bored!" Daniel whined for the third time that afternoon.

"Yeah, I know... so am I, actually," Erin said just before her phone dinged. It was a message from Lily, so she opened it and saw a video from a social media site. She sighed and touched the link, hoping it wasn't something that would make her cry.

After watching it twice, she stood and smiled at the kids. "Let's go on an adventure!" She held out her hand to help Peter off the sofa.

"What sort of adventure?" he said after a long stretch.

"A surprise adventure, but first we have to go to ASDA or maybe the Pound Saver. Get your shoes and sweaters on."

"Sweaters? Do you mean jumpers?" Dan asked.

"Ugg, yes, I mean jumpers, now hop to it, time's a wastin'. Meet me at the front door," she said, and hurried to find Kitty. She found her in the study, dusting. After explaining her plan and showing her the video, Kitty insisted on watching Juniper so it would be easier on them.

"All I ask, mum, is 'at ya take loads of photos, so as I can 'ave a laugh at what you've done," she said with a smile.

"It's a deal!" Erin grabbed her sweater, purse, keys, and phone, then hurried to the door, where her four kids were waiting.

"Arts and crafts department," Erin said as they stepped into the nearest ASDA, which was like a small version of Walmart. She asked an associate to help her find what she was looking for and was led there. She thanked her and the woman nodded but stood there, staring at Peter oddly.

"Aren't you… I mean… you look like that man… John Thomas—" she sputtered before Peter turned to Erin, looking uncomfortable.

"I'm sorry, Kimberly," Erin said, reading her name badge, "but it's not him. Thanks for showing us—"

"Never mind, but he sure does look like 'im!" the girl said with a shrug and then walked away.

"Thanks, Mum," Peter said softly. "I hate when that happens."

"No worries, darling. Now, let's see," she said, scanning the shelves and pegs in front of her. "Aha! Here we go, and they're sticky back too! Awesome!"

She took five packages of googly eyes off a peg and then saw another package that had a variety of different sizes. Grabbing four of them, she smiled at the children's confused expressions. "You'll see, now let's get going."

She paid for their things, and they stepped out into the dreary, foggy, chilly afternoon. "I'm hungry!" Dan exclaimed.

"Shut it, Dan!" Peter said. "We've just finished lunch an hour ago."

"But I didn't eat enough!" the boy whined.

"You can each pick out a snack at Tesco, alright?" Erin said and hailed a taxi.

When they arrived at Tesco, a store that sold mostly food products, Erin handed each child a page of googly eyes. "What are we meant to do with these?" Charlie asked, looking amused but unsure.

"I'll show you," she said, and went to the produce section. Finding a red apple, she peeled two eyes off the plastic sheet and stuck them to it. When she stepped away, Peter laughed so hard, he snorted.

"You're bloody brilliant!" he croaked and picked up a bunch of mostly green bananas. He picked off two eyes and stuck them on the center two adjoining bananas, making the whole bunch look like a face.

Rosie gasped, her eyes wide. "But, Mummy, isn't that vandalism?" she whispered, looking anxiously around them.

"Naw, they're easily removed, and it'll give the next person a smile. It might just brighten their day, right?"

They proceeded to the dairy section and Erin saw a large cart that held eggs. She lifted the lid on a carton, checked that none were broken, then placed one eye on each of the two eggs in the center front. After spending a good forty-five minutes there, she bought them a snack, and they left the store, laughing as they recounted the items they'd given faces to.

When they got home, a large package was waiting for Erin, but she didn't remember ordering anything. She and the children dragged it inside, and she used a key to break the tape. Inside, she saw the canvas prints she'd ordered quite a while ago. The first one brought tears to her eyes.

It was an image of her and David sitting on a fallen tree at Cave Point in Door County, taken the year before. The kids smiled at her and watched as she unwrapped the rest of them. The next image was taken on the Eagle Bluff tower in Peninsula Park, then the romantic dinner in New Orleans.

She told them about when they'd met and all about the place where it had been taken. The next two were wedding photos, one of the wedding party, including the parents, then one taken when she and David had sung together. "Oh, that was lovely," Rosie said.

"Yeah, I had no idea he'd planned it, either," Erin said.

There was one of their first kiss as husband and wife, and the selfie from the day he'd proposed to her in his office. The last one was of the whole family, including Juniper, at Owlgate, not long before David had been arrested. Charlie and Rosie helped her decide where to hang the photos, while Peter got to hammer the nails into the walls. Daniel wasn't really interested, so he went up to his room.

That night, after having a laugh with Kitty and Francie over the photos she'd taken of the googly eye adventure, they had a lovely, animated supper. At bedtime, she read to them, as usual, and tucked them into bed. The children were happy and so was she. She left their rooms feeling like, as long as she continued doing things like that, David's time in jail wouldn't seem as long.

"Mummy?" Rosie called out from the bottom of the stairs. It was a Tuesday, which meant Kitty and Francie had the day off, so Peter had taken her and her brothers to the park while Junie was napping. She'd found a beautiful, sparkling, pink rock and an old coin and wanted to share it with Erin, so she got permission from her brother to come home.

There was no reply, so she began her search in her father's study, as that's where she usually was. The study was empty, so she went into every room on the ground floor and then through every floor above, but there was no sign of her. The only place left to search was the lower level, so she opened the stairway door and, though it was faint, heard someone talking.

She crept slowly down the stairs to the media room, where the voices were coming from. The door was open a crack, so she gently put her eye up to it and watched on the projector screen as her father ran around the old farmhouse in *Future Explorations*. She'd never watched past that point in the series before.

As her father searched for his family, looking so upset, she couldn't take her eyes off him and began to cry. A noise startled her, and she wondered what it was, until she realized it was the sound of Erin crying as well. She didn't know if she'd be in trouble for it, but she pushed the door open and tiptoed up to the overstuffed sofa her new mother was sitting on.

She was holding a box of tissues and jumped when Rosie sniffled, but then she pulled a tissue out of the box and handed it to her. Setting the box aside, she opened her arms. Rosie crawled onto her lap and the two female Elliotts cried together for a while.

"I miss my daddy," Rosie said quietly.

"I do too, baby girl," Erin said and blew her nose. "I'll turn this off, and we can—"

"Actually, I'd like to watch it, if that's alright?" Rosie said. "I've never seen the whole program, and I think I'd like to now."

"Alright, sweetheart, you can watch it with me. Are your brothers upstairs?"

"No, they're still at the park, but Peter knows I'm here. I wanted to show you something I found, but I'll do it later," she said and snuggled up with her new mum.

A quarter of the way through the fourth episode, there was a light knock on the door. Peter poked his head in and asked if he and Charlie could join them. Erin paused her copy of the DVD she'd brought with her from America and waved them in. "Sorry about the tissues," she said, and began picking up the ones that had missed the bin.

They joined her on the sofa and didn't say anything for a while. Finally, Erin pressed play, and they sat watching John Thomas of Fife trying to 'do good and help people' as best he could. When they finished the eighth and final episode of season one, she stopped the disk.

"Well, that was nice," she said and stood to take the disk out of the player.

"May we watch more, please?" Charlie asked, and the others nodded and looked at her.

"Oh, I didn't think you'd want to, but sure, though I have to feed Juniper, so you'll either have to watch without me or wait until I get back down here with her."

They decided that they'd wait, so she inserted the disk for season two and paused it. Suddenly, Dan ran in, out of breath and yelling, "Erin? Junie's in a real state!"

"Okay, I'm on my way," she said and hurried out of the room.

The 'state' Juniper was in meant she'd just begun to fuss a wee bit, not that she was wailing, so she changed her diaper and carried her and the nursing pillow back down to the media room. After asking the children, Daniel included, to turn away, she got the baby to latch on, and they were able to watch one episode of season two. They were asked to look away again when she changed sides, and they watched episode two.

"I think that's quite enough for today," she said after Juniper was burped.

Peter carried the pillow, and Erin carried the baby up to the sunroom, where they played with her while she babbled and giggled, filling them all with joy.

After finding the boxes of costumes while searching for hidden photographs earlier that year, she'd written out a few basic ideas for skits they could perform for each other. Now that David was gone, she thought she could ask them what they thought of preparing a few of them for their father when he returned. She just hoped they wouldn't be tired of playing by then; two years was a long time for a child.

That night after supper, they went through the costumes and began trying them on. Their excitement over the idea thrilled her, and she had to write as fast as she could to get all their ideas on paper. The rest of the week was filled with joy and laughter, along with plans, scripts, and even a song or two.

Chapter Fifty-Five

AUGUST TREATMENT NO. TWO AND A MUCH-NEEDED JAB

On the second Monday in August, Erin was just beginning to feel better, so much so, that she wanted to ask Louis to give her treatments twice per week, but she didn't. That session started off no different than the others. It seemed that no matter how much she tried to harden herself against going too far, as soon as he touched her, she was suddenly weak again.

That day, she longed for ex-ray eyes so she'd be able to see him. She listened to each of his noises, a small moan as his cock slipped into her, then his breathing as it changed from excited panting and deepened with each level of exertion. Then, she paid attention to what happened if *she* made noise.

A small gasp or a moan of pleasure from her caused a reaction in him, and she tried to guess what it might be. *Will he speed up or slow down? Will this make him gasp, moan, grunt, or say something, like, 'Oh,' 'Christ,' or 'Fuck?'*

It hadn't occurred to her until then that, being on her knees, she could look between her legs. She could see his grey leg hair and his balls as they hung down, slapping against her with each thrust. Her mind began to wander, and her imagination took control.

She'd had vivid dreams about Louis being with her and David quite a few times. As she knelt there, she thought about what it would be like to have one of them making love to her while she gave the other a blow job. The mere thought made her have a delightful orgasm.

She didn't have to concentrate with Louis, she could orgasm from just a touch, and she did, regularly. His very presence in the room was sometimes enough to bring her to the edge, and she often wondered if it would be as good with David when they were together again. The thought of her husband usually brought back the guilt, and she'd cried herself to sleep more than once after the particularly good sessions.

That day, however, she pretended he was there, in the room with them, and it filled her with a longing she was both excited by and afraid of. *If David knew her thoughts, what would he think?* she wondered.

I'll tell you what he'd think! He'd be furious!

You don't think he'd be turned on, even a little?

Are you kidding me? It'll NEVER happen, so you will NEVER bring it up!

"Thank you, Erin," Louis was saying. He'd just finished and was pulling out of her.

"You're welcome. I hope you have a good week," she said and laid on her side.

"Is everathin' a'right? Yeh seem distracted."

She could hear him getting dressed and couldn't help but laugh softly. "All is well, Louis. I'm just in my head today."

"Ach, I see. Well, I'll see yeh next Monday, then," he said, and she heard him open the door, though it seemed to her as though he stood there for a moment before stepping out and shutting it behind him.

After her treatment that day, Erin had to go to the clinic, or surgery, as they called it, for her next Birconti shot. When she got there, she gave the receptionist her name and then took a seat. Her mind began to drift back to her fantasy in the treatment room while she waited to be called.

"Erin?" a nurse said, startling her.

She stood and walked back to an exam room with the woman. "Hello, I'm Lena," she said and asked her to verify her name and birthday. "Our records indicate that you had your first jab on the twelfth of May, correct?"

"Yes, and I chose to come back a few days early just to be sure there was no chance of this one being late. The last thing I need is to get pregnant again," *especially from my temporary match!* she thought, and a shiver ran down her spine at the thought of the chaos *that* would cause.

"Understandable, I'd say. Now, did you notice any side effects from the medication, at all?"

"I don't think I did."

"Good, then let's just get this over with, shall we? Are you adversely affected by needles?" she asked.

"Adversely affected?" Erin said, not understanding. "I mean, I don't get a rash or… Oh, wait, you mean do I faint? No, it's all good."

"Yes, that's what I meant," Lena said as she wiped Erin's arm with an alcohol pad. She then prepped the shot and gently pinched the skin on her upper arm. "You'll feel a slight jab—There we are, all sorted." She dropped the syringe into a sharps container, then returned with a small, round band-aid. "And now, the plaster, I hope you like cats?"

Erin looked at the bandage and smiled at the image of a fluffy, ginger kitten. "I do, actually."

Chapter Fifty-Six

SEVENTH VISITATION-AUGUST FOURTEENTH

On Friday, Erin clutched a bag which concealed an expensive bottle of whisky and two cartons of cigarettes, while Peter carried Juniper in her car seat as they approached the prison building. Rosie had drawn a picture for her daddy and held it out carefully, not wanting it to get damaged. Charlie walked next to his sister, keeping his head down, and Dan glared at the reporters who were blocking the entrance.

"Erin! May we see the baby today?"

"Erin! How are you feeling?"

"Children! Are you glad to be seeing your dad?"

"What's that? Did you draw a picture for your dad? May we see it?" The reporters called out, and it took every ounce of self-control Erin had not to engage them. She wanted to tell them to shut up and leave them alone, but that would only give them something to print.

They made it into the building and went through all the usual security measures, including drug-sniffing dogs, then stood at the doors to wait. The other visitors stared at them, and she heard one woman whisper her name, which made her even more self-conscious. The announcement was given, and when the doors were opened, everyone went in, searching for their loved one.

Erin gave the children money to buy a small snack once they'd greeted their dad, and asked Peter to bring her a cup of tea. When Rosie saw David, she called out to him, saying, "Daddy!" which broke both her and David's hearts. When they got closer to the table, they could see his face was sunken in, skeletal looking, and he had large, dark rings under his eyes.

The ugly grey sweatsuit he wore just hung on him, and the children stared at him, wide-eyed, clearly frightened. He frowned, not understanding, and looked at Erin. "It's okay, he's not sick, don't be afraid," Erin assured them. "Go on, say hello to your father."

Peter gave him a tentative hug. "Sorry, Dad, but you're so… thin, it's scary," he said, speaking for them all. The children nodded and tried not to stare.

"So yer mum has said. I'm eatin' more, I promise. Rosie, what's that ye've got there?" He pointed to her drawing, and the young girl knit her brows. She then looked at Erin, who nudged her, and handed it to him.

David took the paper and looked at it. It was a stick figure man standing behind bars with a tear on his face. There were six more stick figures, standing on the other side of the bars, all of them also having a tear on their faces.

"This shows how very much we miss you, Daddy," Rosie said, and David didn't look up. He stared at it until a tear fell and hit the paper. "Daddy! You're going to ruin it!" She looked anxiously at Erin for help.

"It's okay, Rosebud, it won't be ruined for him."

"Come here, darling," David said and set the paper on the table. "Et's lovely, thank you." He held her for a few moments, until an officer barked his name, then he set her down. "I'll think of you all when I look at it."

Charlie stood and hugged his dad, while Dan just waved. "I expect ye're bein' helpful and behavin' for yer mum, Kitty, and Francie?" he said. They nodded and then sat awkwardly for a few moments.

"Why don't you go get something at the concessions," Erin said to the kids, then turned to David. "Do you want anything?"

"No—" he began and then changed his mind. "Aye, a bag of crisps, please, any flavor'll do."

The children stood and joined the queue. Erin watched as a woman approached Rosie. Instantly, the three boys surrounded her until the lady walked away, and she was so proud of her brood.

She took the receiving blanket off of Junie, who was sleeping. She'd brought a bottle with her breast milk in it in case Juniper got hungry, and hoped she wouldn't start crying. The last thing she needed was for her damned boobs to start leaking.

The six-month-old woke when she started to undo her harness and smiled at her. "Gah!" she said.

"Well, gah, right back. I'm glad you're a happy girl today. Look who's here, it's Daddy," Erin said.

Junie looked at David and began babbling. "Gah! Ba-ba-eeeeeh gah," she said. Erin sat her up on the table just as the children came back. Charlie handed his dad the bag of chips, and Peter handed Erin her tea. When she let go of Junie, she sat up by herself.

"Juniper," Dan said, and she looked at him. He pulled his best 'make Junie giggle' face, which didn't disappoint.

"Da-da da-da."

"Ach, ma wee girl! How ye've grown!" David said and picked her up. She saw the zipper pull on his sweatshirt and squeed. She tried to put it into her mouth, but David stopped her and attempted to put his knuckle in her mouth. At first, she sucked on it, but then she bit down, and he pulled it out, shaking it. "Oww!"

Rosie grabbed her pacifier out of the car seat and tried giving it to her, but she was getting upset. "Oh dear, Mummy, where's the bottle?" she asked.

"Right here," Erin said and took it out of the seat as well, since she didn't bother bringing in the diaper bag. "Here you are, June Bug." She handed the bottle to David, who tried to get her to drink, but she began to cry.

Erin quickly snatched her out of his arms and nearly forced the clear nipple onto her mouth. "Please stop crying, baby, please!" Erin said, obviously beginning to panic.

"Erin?" David said, plainly not understanding what the problem was. Finally, Junie began to drink, but Erin was still really tense. "What's the matter—"

"If Junie cries, Mum's tits leak and her front becomes all wet," Dan said loudly enough that several people at nearby tables looked at them. Some seemed shocked, while others laughed.

"Daniel, please keep your mouth shut!" Erin hissed at him, and David seemed livid.

"Daniel Lawrence! Where did you hear that? I can't believe you'd say something like that!"

"But… it's the truth, Dad. I… was just trying to answer you for her. I… didn't mean—" he said and put his head down on his arms. Soon his body was shaking with small sobs.

"Oh, Dan, I don't know where you learned that word, but that's not a nice term for… them, okay? I believe that you didn't mean to say the wrong thing, but it's better to not say anything about… them… in public, alright?" Erin said and rubbed his back since Juniper was holding the bottle to her mouth.

"He wasn't wrong, actually. All she has to do is start crying, or even if I hear a baby crying on the TV, I'm suddenly drenched. It's not like I can turn it off, like a f— stinking spigot, either, and it's just… awful and embarrassing."

"Oh, I didn't know about… that… I mean—" David said, a bit flustered.

"Yes, I know, I'm sure Susannah's… never once did anything she didn't approve of. She was perfect, wasn't she?" she said out of frustration and jealousy, then regretted it. She didn't want to look at her dear family after her outburst and closed her eyes, ashamed of herself. "I'm sorry, everyone. That wasn't—"

"Et's a'right, darling, jest relax and hold ma hand," David said.

"Dad? Did Erin… I mean, Mum tell you it was me and Charlie's birthday two weeks ago? And… did she tell you… what happened, and about the cake?" Dan said.

"I knew et was yer birthday, and yes, she told me all of it," David replied.

"Oh, are you very disappointed with me?" he asked with his head down.

David looked at Erin, and she could see the compassion for his son on his face. "No, Dan, not very. I was at first, but then she told me what yeh said after you heard her reasons for the punishment and how you behaved when the cake was brought out, and I wasn't anamore. She said the cakes were brilliant."

"They were crackin', Dad!" Charlie said.

"Pure ledge!" Peter said.

"The chest was filled with candy treasure, Daddy! Necklaces and coins, and I got a ring pop, as well!" Rosie said excitedly.

"Ma Losh, that sounds fantastic. I'll have tae thank Francie… when I see her," he said and cleared his throat. "Yer mum's told me how good you've been for her, especially you, Peter. Thank you for stepping up and being so helpful with the others, I'm so verra proud of you, son."

Peter blushed and beamed. "It's the least, Dad. She's so tired sometimes, and I know we're a lot to deal with. We've actually had a laugh, trying to think of things to do together. Erin—Mum suggested we each take up a musical instrument and start a band. We did learn that Charlie and Rosie are rather brilliant singers," he said, nearly letting slip the skits and talent night they'd been planning.

"Peter!" Rosie scolded him under her breath.

"Ach, ye're growin' up b'fore ma eyes… the lot of you, and—" David said, sounding gutted.

"I grew two inches over the—" Dan began, but Peter shot him a warning look, so he stopped talking.

"Da, da, da, da da!" Junie said, and David picked her up. She was glad for the attention for only a moment, then she reached for her brother, Daniel. "Da! Da…da! Da!" It was suddenly clear that she was trying to say 'Dan,' not dad, and Erin's heart ached for her husband.

David gasped and tears began to well up in his eyes. He handed his daughter to his youngest son, and the family watched the excited six-month-old smile and wrap her arms around Dan's neck. "Hiya, Junie!"

"Da!" she repeated, joyously. "Da!" He booped her nose and made her giggle, causing the whole room to smile and look at them. She laid her little head on his shoulder, sucking on her two middle fingers, while he bounced her gently and patted her back. *'Braaap.'* A long, loud burp came out of her tiny frame, and everyone laughed or smiled at the scene.

Some people commented, 'Well done!' or, 'Good on you!'

The rest of the visit was strained. David put on a brave face, but Erin could feel his anguish and pain. The chance to finally bond with his children had been waved in front of his face, only to have it ripped away from him. She knew it was his worst nightmare and that it was breaking his heart and spirit.

The five-minute warning came too soon, as always, and everyone rushed to get in their final goodbyes and words of love. The children each hugged their dad and told him how much they'd miss him. He held them and told them how he loved them dearly and couldn't wait to see them again.

Erin held her husband and wished she knew what to say to help him feel at least a bit better, but there wasn't anything to say. "I love you, David," she whispered.

"I love you as well, darling. I think of you all the time, and I… I long for you. Please… don't—Never mind," he said and stroked her hair.

"Please take care of yourself and try to eat. We need you to be healthy and—"

"Time's up!" one of the officers said.

"I will. I love you! I love you all," he said, turning to his family.

"We love you too, Dad!" the children said, and then they had to leave.

Chapter Fifty-Seven

AUGUST TREATMENTS NUMBERS THREE AND FOUR

The third Monday treatment in August was very much the same as the rest, though Erin noticed that Louis seemed to last longer and lingered inside her awhile after he was done. It felt so good that she didn't say anything or stop him, which she felt guilty about afterward. The session ended, as usual, with him saying he'd see her on Monday.

That week flew by, and before she knew it, she was back at the treatment surgery, waiting for her fourth Monday treatment. She was finally starting to feel better; she had a bit more energy, and really felt like she was improving. For a bit of variety that time, she decided to return to the missionary position, and as he entered her, the desire to pull the whole curtain system down nearly consumed her.

"Louis!" she gasped when he was finished. "I… want to—"

"Aye? Yeh wannae, what?" he asked breathlessly.

"I… want to… thank you—" she came up with, when what she really wanted to say was, 'I want you to crawl underneath the curtain, lay on top of me, and kiss me.' The treatments helped her fight the disease, but she craved the touch of a man on her body, to feel his hand on her breast and his breath on her neck.

—

"Ach, ye're… welcome, love. Thank you, as well. I'm… ashamed tae tell yeh tha' I dinnae want tae… leave yeh. I wannae stand here and feel maself in yeh… for as long as I can. Et makes me feel sae selfish, but I just—" he said and touched her thigh, pushing his still slightly erect cock into her again, which made her moan.

"Please… dinnae be… upset. If yeh want me… tae… stop—" He couldn't finish and felt himself getting hard again. He'd only ever been able to go twice in a row once before in his life, but at that moment he felt like he'd be able to do it a dozen times. As he started moving slowly, he waited for her to tell him to stop and that she wanted him to leave, but she was silent, so he sped up.

"Oh! Yes! Yes! Just like that!" she gasped, followed by a powerful orgasm he could feel all the way through his shaft and into his body, deep within him. He parted the curtain so that her legs were exposed and gently lifted one leg over his shoulder, causing him to go deeper into her than he'd ever done before. One of his hands held her soft, plump thigh, while the other took hold of her waist.

His hand moved slowly over her belly, until he felt the indent of her bellybutton, and he stopped. He didn't know whether to move his hand up toward her breasts or down to touch her clitoris with his fingers. Instead, he turned his head and kissed the inside of her leg at the knee.

"Christ, Erin, if yeh dinnae tell me tae stop, I willnae be able… and I dinnae ken what I'll do to yeh. I… feel sae out of control right now. Do yeh want me tae—" he said, using all his willpower not to pull out of her and touch her with his tongue.

"Finish again, if you can, but… put the curtain back," Erin said, sounding a bit faint.

He continued making love to her until he had his second climax, which wasn't nearly as strong as the first, then he pulled out and stepped back. She pulled her legs in, and he saw her shadow curl up into a ball on the bed. Next, he thought he heard her sniffle as he got dressed.

"Erin? Oh, God, Erin. I'm sorry. I shouldn't have done tha'. Are yeh hurt, or—"

"I'm not hurt," she said with staggered breath. "I'm… ashamed of myself for wanting you to do that so badly. It… well, it was… nice to be touched— Never mind, I should have told you to stop. I was wrong, and—I don't know… we can't keep doing that, or it will only cause trouble. I can't… I just can't…

crave that from you… only David. I love David. God, Erin, what are you thinking? Please, Louis, just… go now. I'm sorry, but I need to—"

"Aye, I'm sorry. I'll see yeh next week. Take care," he said.

—

Erin heard the door close behind him. It had taken every ounce of willpower she had after he ran his hand over her stomach not to beg him to pull out and touch her with his tongue. She cried and cried, still craving his touch, replaying it in her mind over and over, already longing for the next visit so she might feel it again.

Chapter Fifty-Eight

WEYMOUTH BEACH AND THE DÉJÀ VU

"I feel like taking a drive," Erin said on the fourth Tuesday in August. She thought she'd surprise them with a day at Weymouth Beach, so she and Kitty had searched the house high and low for large beach towels and swimming suits the day before. The children had grown so much she figured they'd need new ones anyway, so she packed what she found and planned a trip to ASDA for sunscreen, then to wherever rich people shopped for things like swimsuits.

She asked Kitty if she wanted to come along, as a treat for her day off. Kitty said she was sorry, but she needed to check in on her mum, as she'd missed her last day off because Junie had been sick, and she hadn't wanted to leave Erin alone with a sick baby.

Somehow, she managed to convince the kids to gather at the SUV, and Peter attached the car seat to its base for her. Once everyone was settled in, she smiled at their wondering faces and said, "Who wants to go to the beach?" The back two rows exploded in excitement, which startled Juniper and made her cry. Dan started making faces at her, though, and she quieted down right away.

"Yes, please!" Peter said.

"May we please go to the arcade?" Dan said.

"I wish we had our trunks!" Charlie said.

"I don't have my costume!" Rosie said, sounding distressed. It took Erin a few seconds to translate that one. *Swimming costume, right!* she thought, and smiled.

"Don't worry, between Kitty and me, we've found what we hope will still fit you, after all, we just bought some of them last year. Anyway, if they don't, we can go to ASDA or somewhere and get you whatever you need." *I can't forget the sunscreen!* she thought.

"Peter, I couldn't find yours, so I brought a pair of your father's trunks for you, but we can buy something if you'd rather—"

"They'll work brilliantly, I'm sure," he said and smiled broadly at her.

She figured he'd get a kick out of being grown enough to wear something of his father's. Not to mention it would be something of David's nearby since he couldn't be with them. Erin typed 'Weymouth' into the Sat Nav, and they followed the directions that the pleasant RP lady's voice gave them.

Soon, they were out of London and on the M3, headed South. The Sat Nav lady continued her directions, saying things like, *"At the so-and-so roundabout, take the second exit."*

Charlie was really excited and copied her, sounding very much like her indeed, so he got teased that he could get a job as a computer voice when he was out of school, since he had no other talents. "I have talents!" he said defensively. "I just haven't found out what they are yet."

"We don't need talents!" Dan said. "Dad's got loads of money."

Erin had to stifle a laugh.

"Dad isn't going to support us! I don't want him to anyway," Peter responded to his brother irately.

"Well, we all know what Peter's passion is, and I'm sure he'll do very well at it, but what about Dan?" Erin asked. "Who knows Dan's talents? He likes dogs—" she began.

"Yes, and getting into trouble!" Rosie interrupted under her breath, making Dan try to hit her over the seat.

"Now, now, none of that," Erin said, laughing while still trying to keep order as she watched them laughing and teasing each other in the rearview mirror. "Can he earn a living from that? Maybe he could study to be a veterinarian?"

"You mean as Dad was in that program?" Dan asked, not sounding enthused at the idea.

"What's wrong with that?" she said, then turned her attention to his brother.

"Charlie," she said, "perhaps you'll be a famous writer when you grow up. If you keep reading like you do, you'll have so many words inside you, you'll be able to make up your own stories. Or… maybe you can write about your life experiences. They *have* been rather extraordinary so far, haven't they?"

"Have they? Why, because Dad's famous?" he said, obviously not counting that as being extraordinary.

"Oh, well, I hadn't thought of that, I meant that you **have** met me after all. I reckon that would fill up a whole book in and of itself," she said, laughing.

"Maybe you're right, Erin… I mean Mum," he said, smiling at her in the rearview mirror.

Two and a half hours later, they arrived in Weymouth and pulled into the ASDA parking lot. "Now, before we go on a wild goose chase, let's see what we've got already," Erin said, walking around to the back of the SUV and grabbing her tote bag. She took out two swimming trunks and a swimming suit that was far too small for Rosie. "Well, I reckon you've grown a bit, haven't you?" They both laughed as she held it up to her.

"That was from two years ago," Rosie said.

The twins took theirs and held them up, shaking their heads. "These are too small, Mum," Charlie said and handed his and Dan's back to her

She looked at Peter, who was holding up his father's trunks, which were a bit too large for him, she could tell. "They're ace," Peter said, smiling.

Erin knew he wasn't going to pass up the opportunity to wear his dad's clothes, she only hoped he didn't get pantsed by one of his brothers or by a strong wave. "Alright, just be sure to tie the strings tightly, please. No one wants to see your birthday suit today!" she said, teasing.

Peter smiled and blushed slightly. "A'right, Mum."

"We'll donate these, then. Now, Peter, would you please help get Junie's car seat out for me and then put it into a cart… I mean trolley." She knew

America and England were two countries separated by a common language, but she'd had no idea how different it was until living there.

"Okay," he said and went about doing as she asked. She watched him do all the heavy lifting and carrying, as Charlie ran to get them a trolley. "She's getting so heavy!" he said, smiling at the little girl, who was sleeping peacefully.

"Thank you, Peter, you're such a great help to me!" Erin said and put her hand on his shoulder.

When Charlie returned, they installed Junie in the cart and made their way into the store. The ASDA was crowded with tourists and packed with merchandise. Thus, it was hard to maneuver the cart and watch out for her four children, the third eldest of them either running around the racks or singing loudly, without a care of who was around them.

Erin found the sunscreen first, then they went upstairs to the clothing section, but their selection of swimwear was not very good, so they decided to try someplace else instead. She allowed each of them to pick out a snack and drink, then stood at the check-out, looking at the tabloids and magazines set there for impulse purchases.

"Mummy!" Rosie said and pointed to one of the tabloids near the bottom, which Erin hadn't noticed.

Squatting down to Rosie's level, she saw David's face looking sad, with a caption that read:

THE LATEST LETTER FROM PRISON IS HERE!

Erin sighed, having mixed emotions. She was glad to be able to read his letters but sad that his children had to deal with the shit they dealt with so brilliantly.

She kissed Rosie's cheek and reluctantly took one off the shelf. It was placed on the conveyor, along with three bottles of sunscreen, four packages of underwater goggles, and a blow-up beach ball. Next came four bottles of disgusting looking sweet drinks, a package each of Jammie Dodgers, Custard Creams, a Mars Bar, a bag of salt and vinegar crisps, and a Curly Wurly for her.

When everything was paid for, they left the store, then had to reverse the order of operations. Once Junie was back in the vehicle and the trolley was returned, the kids piled into the SUV, and Erin drove around to the Debenhams and TK Maxx buildings. She parked in the nearby parking garage, figuring they could use the stroller and leave the SUV there for the day.

She loved walking around Weymouth, and it helped that she'd had her latest treatment the day before, so her energy level was pretty high. They managed to get Juniper into her stroller, not without much crying and fussing from the aforementioned infant; however, Dan made her laugh while she held onto Charlie's pinky.

They went into Debenhams, and found trunks for the twins, then Erin pulled out a swimming 'costume' for Rosie. On the front it had two large pink flamingo heads, facing each other, with little, green lace ruffles at the top of the leg. It reminded her of The Little Mermaid, and she thought Rosie would love it. Instead, she turned her nose up.

"Oh, no! That's so gaudy!" she said, sounding exactly like her mother. "I wouldn't be caught dead in something so garish! Honestly!"

Erin raised her eyebrows in shock. She'd never seen her do anything quite so Susannah-like, and it stunned her.

Rosie must have seen the look on her face, because she put her head down and looked up at Erin with only her eyes. "I'm sorry, Mummy, I didn't mean to hurt your feelings," the young girl said, and Erin could feel tears prickle in her eyes at the sweetness of it.

"You didn't hurt my feelings, darling," she said. "This one reminded me of—"

"The Little Mermaid?" Rosie said. "Me too, but I'm too old for it now," the ten-year-old said sadly. "I like this one better." She held out a two-piece red suit that read 'I OWN THE OCEAN' in shiny gold letters.

To be honest, Erin liked that one better too, so she smiled and said, "Go try it on." It fit her well, so they headed to the checkout.

"Aren't you going to get one?" Charlie said to Erin, who laughed, not wanting any of them to see her in a bathing suit.

"No, Charlie, I've got Juniper to watch, so I won't be swimming today. I may dip my feet into the water, but I can wear my clothes if I do," she said, thankful for a good excuse. They paid, then headed out the door. "Now, do you want to change in the car or find a water closet?"

The boys said the car would be fine, but Rosie wanted to find someplace more private, so Erin handed Peter the keys to the SUV. She then tasked him with helping the boys, while she took Rosie back into the store to use the ladies room.

"Dan," she said before they split up. "I expect you to do as Peter, or even as Charlie says while I'm not there, or no arcade, alright?" She looked him in the eye, and he nodded. "And Charlie, I expect you to not get carried away with it." She kissed his forehead, then walked away.

Ten minutes later, Erin and Rosie were back at the SUV, and Peter was just emerging from it wearing David's trunks. She smiled at him, seeing in her mind's eye a very young David. "Oh, Peter, you look so much like him," she said, then had to turn away to hide the tear that had escaped and was rolling down her cheek.

She took a deep breath and turned back to them, having composed herself. Peter and the boys put their tops on, using the trunks as shorts, and were ready to go, except Erin noticed that Dan still had the tags dangling off the side of his. "Oh, Dan, come here," she said, and carefully pulled them off, managing not to rip the fabric. "Did he listen to you?" she asked Peter and Charlie, and they nodded to say he had, so Erin decided to take them to the arcade first.

They made sure everything was out of the SUV, packing everything into the stroller or carrying it in the tote, then headed down New Bond Street. Peter thought that because of their recent media attention, that way might be too crowded, so he suggested they use a quieter path. She hadn't thought of that, so they doubled back and walked down to Lower St. Alban Street, which turned into St. Alban's Street, which became a narrow walkway with shops.

Being a Tuesday afternoon, it wasn't busy, and they made it through without incident. His suggestion turned out to be perfect, though, because it gave them a straight shot to the arcade. It was actually a small amusement park, called Alexandra Gardens, which also had a few rides and a carousel.

Erin spent way too much money on rides, and even went on the carousel with Rosie, sitting on one of the bench seats while holding Junie on her lap.

She looked up, and though it wasn't as grand, she remembered sitting with David at the Carousel Bar in the Hotel Monteleone in New Orleans. She had to fight back the sobs she felt wanting to escape, though a few tears did succeed in breaking free before the ride ended.

Erin gave each child ten pounds to do whatever they wanted, and before long, Dan came back with a huge pile of white tickets, while Rosie, Peter, and Charlie only had a few each. "I know how to win tickets," Dan said simply when everyone started commenting. "And I'm not telling you lot how, either."

"Alright, let's cash them in," Erin said and followed them into the noisy building where the arcade games were. They fed the tickets into a machine, which tallied them up and gave them a printed receipt. Daniel had over six hundred tickets, so he walked up to the desk and put his slip on the counter. Erin scanned the wall of prizes and pointed out everything he could 'afford'.

The other children's tickets were only twelve, put together. They laid the short stack of slips on the counter and the attendant said, "You may choose a lolly, two boiled sweets, or a rubber."

Erin smiled at the use of that word; at home it meant condom, but there it meant eraser. Each child pointed to the one they wanted, but the young woman shook her head. "Not each of yous, just one, if you combine them."

Erin raised her eyebrows at them, as they were looking slightly disappointed. "Why don't you give them to Dan, and we'll get something in one of the shops along the street, maybe a 99 or gelato, alright?"

They agreed, and what they gave him allowed him to go up a tier in the prizes. He got a box of make your own bright neon slime and then got each of them a roll of swizzles, which were similar to smarties. Erin was proud of him for that.

"Hold up!" The woman at the counter said. "I know who yous are! I seen yous in the papers! You're that actor's wife, the one what supposedly attacked the po-leece—The one what's in jail now, ain't ya? I'm real sorry for ya. Are these 'is kids, then? Aww! Tha's Junie, ain't she?" she said, pointing to Juniper and smiling.

How on earth, she thought, gobsmacked, and not knowing how to respond. She stood there, blushing and trying to think of what to say, until

Peter stepped up. "Thank you... for... your concern," he said, pulling Erin gently by the arm. "I'm empty, Mum, let's get something to eat."

Before she knew it, they were outside again, and the children were gazing up at her. She looked at Peter and put her hand on his shoulder. "I don't like that, it's too surreal."

Trying to snap back into reality, she shook herself. "Let's get some fish and chips," she said as they walked along the Esplanade, past the tall, stately houses that had been turned into inns and apartments.

They passed under the bust of Queen Victoria mounted on the front of the Fairhaven Hotel, which reads, 'Jubilee 1887-1897.' Dan made a face, trying to imitate the bust, and made everyone laugh. *A comedian, that's what he'll end up being,* she thought.

She asked Peter to mind everyone while she stepped into a small charity shop that helped the elderly. It had a placard outside the door that read, 'Accepting Donations.' She grabbed the children's outgrown clothes out of the stroller and brought them inside with her.

"Hiya, ya a'right?" she heard a woman's voice say from somewhere in the shop.

"Hiya, I'm well, thank you. I'd like to donate these," she said and handed the swimming suits to the diminutive old woman who stepped out from behind a clothing rack and smiled at her.

"Oh, thank you! They're ever so lovely," she said as she took them out of Erin's hand, genuinely thrilled about the gift. She then noticed the herd of children clustered together, waiting for her outside the door. "They grow far too quickly, don't they?"

"You're welcome, and to be honest, I really don't know yet. They're my new family, and I've got a lot to learn."

"Well! That's quite a lot of new family then! I wish ya luck!" the woman said and smiled genuinely at her.

"Thanks, I'm sure I'll need it. Well, cheers and have a lovely day," Erin said and opened the door with a smile.

"But I'm hungry!" she heard Dan whining loudly when she stepped outside.

Chapter Fifty-Nine

DÉJÀ VU

Erin got takeaway fish and chips at a shop called, creatively enough, 'The Fish Place,' then they crossed the Esplanade. She found a seat under one of the beautiful Victorian canopy benches. They looked to her like an old-fashioned bus stop, facing out across the dark blue waters of Weymouth Bay.

"Okay, while we let the food cool down, I'm going to put sunscreen on you lot, so take off your clothes and stand in line. Peter, you may apply your own, and I'll help you with your back and any other places you can't reach."

Rosie took off her clothes, revealing her adorable new swimming costume, and Erin slathered her down with thick, white lotion, which made her hands feel gross. Next, she helped Dan and Charlie with theirs, then Peter came up to her, needing help with his back. After she spread the lotion on him, she asked if he'd gotten his ears, which he hadn't.

She applied it to both sides, remembering how David had put up with her doing the very same thing in New Orleans. When she was finished with them, she applied some to her face, neck, and the bit of her feet and ankles that stuck out of her capris, and then got out the baby version, bathing Juniper in it as well.

She asked Rosie to find the baby wipes and used them to clean her hands the best she could, then she opened the bag of deep-fried fish; the smell made her mouth water. She gave Peter one of the paper trays with a piece of fish and a few chips in it, telling him to come back for more if he was still hungry when he was done.

"Thanks, Mum," he said and smiled David's brilliant smile at her.

He sat next to her on the bench, and she continued doling out the rest of the food, bit by bit. Daniel scarfed down two large fillets of fish and a whole tray of chips, while Charlie and Rosie took a bit here and there, but they wanted to play. She didn't mind and enjoyed watching them run around.

It was a perfect day to be at the beach; she could smell the salty, seaside air and feel the cool breeze coming from the water. "Thank you for coming to my rescue at the arcade," she said to Peter. "I didn't know what to do."

"No worries, I'm used to it. Happens quite a lot, actually, though it's usually Dad who's the center of attention, not us," he said.

A seagull had smelled the food and was inching closer and closer, trying to find a moment when no one was paying attention to fly up and take its own portion. However, Dan and Rosie were on to it and kept shooing it away, making a game of it. Out of nowhere, Erin had a strange sensation.

"I've done this before," she said, mostly to herself, and then everything became focused and intense. She looked around her, having the feeling of déjà vu so strongly, she wanted to stand up, but there were too many things on her lap. Rosie ran up to her, looking exhilarated.

"Mummy! Look what Charlie found!" she said, and Erin nearly fainted.

Charlie came up to her with a diamond tennis bracelet, excited to show their new mum his treasure, but when he saw her reaction, he seemed worried about her. "Mum? Erin? Are you a'right?" he asked her, and she figured he still had the slight fear that she might die, just as his real mother had done nearly a year earlier.

Erin shook her head, and smiled at her brood, all standing around her. They all looked worried, and she wanted to ease their minds. "Hush now, I'm fine. I just had the most powerful déjà vu, and it shocked me, that's all."

"What's 'dey-vha you'?" Rosie asked.

"It's 'déjà vu,' Rosie, and it's French, it means something like 'already seen.' It's when you're living your normal life, and you suddenly feel like whatever is happening around you at that moment has happened to you before, like in a dream or something; it's a strange feeling.

"I think I had a dream, long before I met your dad, when I wanted lots of children who called me mummy," she said and smiled at Rosie. "I dreamed of you all, and everything that just happened over the last few minutes was in that dream. I saw the pram next to me, and I noticed that you were all older children.

"I was feeding you fish and chips out of a bag, just as I have been, and Rosie, you ran up to tell me what Charlie had found, but I couldn't hear his name. I woke up before I found out what it was, and I was so upset. I wanted to know what the boy had found."

"I found a beautiful bracelet, and I'd like to give it to you!" Charlie said, handing over the shimmering, obviously real, diamond tennis bracelet. The sunlight danced over the facets, dazzling their eyes.

"Oh, Charlie! It is stunning, but we can't keep it. We need to try to find the owner and report it to the police if we can't," she said, seeing the disappointment on his face.

"Finders keepers!" Dan said and ran over to look at it.

Erin shook her head, understanding but not accepting his attitude. "Come here, everyone," she said, and pulled out the little compass charm David had gotten her a few days after they'd met in New Orleans.

"Do you see this charm? It doesn't look like much, but to me, it's priceless. Your father bought it for me on the weekend we first met. I would be very, very upset if I lost it and someone just took it and didn't try to get it back to me."

The children looked at it closely, watching the hand spin as she moved it. "This bracelet doesn't mean anything to you, but it might mean something special to the person who lost it. I think you should try to find her.

"Ask some of the people near where you found it if they've lost a bracelet, but don't mention that it's diamond, or they might lie. If someone says they have, ask them to describe it, and bring them to me. It will be like the opposite of a treasure hunt!" she said, trying to make it sound like a game.

The boys looked at her as if she'd gone mad but walked away to do as they'd been told anyway. She watched them go along the beach, asking strangers if they'd lost anything. Although she knew their British upbringing would make talking to strangers a difficult task, she wanted to teach them the value of honesty and integrity. Being the children of a celebrity would make it that much more difficult, but it was the right thing to do.

She had just looked away from Rosie, who was standing near one of the souvenir huts on the beach, trying to locate one of the boys in the crowd, when she heard a commotion where Rosie had been standing. She couldn't hear what was being said, but she saw Peter, tall and lean, running toward his sister. A woman was holding Rosie by the arm, and when Peter got to her, he began pulling the woman's hand off her.

Erin wanted to run to them, but she had all sorts of things on her lap and the bench all around her, not to mention the stroller, which she doubted would go anywhere on the sand. All she could do was watch, hoping Peter could get things under control. He kept pointing to her, motioning for the lady to follow him, and as they got closer, she heard the woman talking to him and Rosie.

"I'll have you know that *my* bracelet is worth more…" she paused and looked at Erin the way Susannah had the few times they'd met, "…than anyone *you* know has ever seen in their lives!" she said and held out her hand, expecting the bracelet to be placed into it. A girl who looked to be about Peter's age finally caught up with them, panting and trying to catch her breath.

"Grandma!" The girl said, but the woman ignored her, ranting about giving her her property, and such. Junie started wailing with the commotion, and it looked as if Rosie wanted to do the same, but she went over and tried to calm the baby down instead.

"It's okay, Junie," she said.

The teenage girl looked from Rosie to the baby, then Erin, and finally Peter, who was visibly angry but still so much like his father. The older woman was shaking her hand and saying rude things to them about taking things that didn't belong to them. "Grandma!" The girl repeated, and the older woman snapped at her.

"What *is* it, Elizabeth?"

"I think you should show more respect to these people. They might have just kept it and not tried to find you," she said with a slight Australian accent. She smiled at the family, clearly hoping her grandma would stop her insults.

Erin smiled back at the young woman and scowled at the old one. "I think this might be a matter for the police. Perhaps you'd like to file a complaint? Tell them you dropped your bracelet and didn't even know it was missing.

Then, be sure you mention how these hoodlum children were so rude as to try to find its owner and actually give it back," she said loudly.

By now, Charlie and Dan were back and seemed excited to find out what was happening. They'd only ever seen Erin as angry as she was once before then. There was also a crowd gathering near the covered bench to find out what the fuss was all about.

"I'm sorry for my grandmother's rudeness, Mrs. Elliott, but well—" The girl paused and looked at her grandmother. "Actually, I can't think of any excuse at all. Perhaps you *should* take the bracelet to the police and force her to get it back from them," she said, and her Grandmother looked at her as though she'd gone mad.

"Do you know this woman?" her grandmother demanded, and the young woman sighed.

"No, but I worked it out," she said, rolling her eyes. The girl whispered something into her ear, and the older woman's eyes grew large, then her eyebrows shot up, making her look like someone who'd had a botched facelift.

She looked Erin over again. "*You're* Erin Elliott? *You...* are married to David Elliott?" she asked rudely. "But you're—"

Peter and Charlie had clearly had enough of the lady and stepped in front of her. "What of it?" Charlie said.

"What are you getting at?" Peter said, and Erin saw that his face was red and a blue vein was now sticking prominently out of his forehead the same way David's did when he was furious.

Erin handed what was in her lap to Daniel and stood. She put her hand on Peter's shoulder and turned him away from the woman. "Alright, now. No need to get that upset, it's okay," she said, but it was plain Peter wasn't going to give up that easily.

"No, Erin, it's not alright. My... our mum was just like this woman, and I hated her for it. She was hateful and rude, and I don't want her to have the bloody thing back," he said, and Erin could see tears of rage building up in his eyes.

Charlie looked as though he felt the same way, and neither of them wanted to back off. Elizabeth looked at Erin, clearly not knowing what to do,

Junie was now wailing, and Erin had had it with the whole situation. She grabbed the woman's hand and dropped the bracelet into it.

"This is what I get for trying to show my new family the value of integrity and honesty! You… are a horrible person, and I want you to walk away now," she said and then picked Juniper up, bouncing her and saying soothing words into her ear.

The woman huffed and walked away, muttering something about gold digging, but the girl named Elizabeth stayed. "I really am sorry for this, and you're right, my grandmother is a really horrible person." She then turned around.

"I'm glad you stood up for your stepmum, she seems like a lovely person," she said to the boys, but mostly to Peter, who had turned away and was standing with his arms crossed, staring at the ocean. Junie was happy now that the attention was back on her and started cooing.

Elizabeth looked at her. "May I please see your baby?" she asked sweetly, so Erin turned her around. "Oh! She's ever so lovely. How old is she?"

Erin smiled at the pretty girl and motioned for her to sit next to her. "She's six months old, aren't you now, you big girl!" she said, mostly to Junie, and Elizabeth laughed.

"Do you… mind if I sit with you for a bit? My grandmother will be doing nothing but whining and complaining, and I'd rather not hear it," she said. Charlie came up, now that he'd calmed down a bit and was playing with Junie, trying to ignore the girl with the rude grandma. "My name is Elizabeth, what's yours?" she asked him sweetly.

Charlie looked at her and then at Erin, shaking his head. Erin sighed and said, "I'm sorry, Elizabeth, but the whole fame thing is tricky. It's not usually a good idea to give out personal information to strangers, as I'm still learning."

"Oh, I understand!" Elizabeth said passionately. "My parents are both actors in Australia. Well, my father's an actor, and my mother is a 'television personality,'" she said with air quotes.

At that, Peter turned around and started paying attention. Erin could almost hear him thinking, '*She's like us?*'

"I spend my school holidays here with my Gran, but it's not something I look forward to."

They sat watching people walk along the paved path that was the transition between the road and the beach, listening to the gulls and the waves. Children laughed and played, and parents walked past with prams. A black crow sat atop a flagpole, squawking and making the hairs rise on the back of Erin's neck.

Someone on a bench nearby was speaking in Polish, and cars passed continuously on the road behind them, occasionally honking at someone who hesitated too long in turning. The air smelled of fried fish and seawater, mixed with the overly strong cologne on some of the people passing by.

The black pavement of the promenade radiated heat, but a fresh breeze would occasionally come off the water, cooling them before they couldn't take it any longer. Erin wanted the children to have plenty of time to play and swim and be kids, and she wasn't going to let a little midday heat ruin it for them.

Peter was sitting on the far end of the blue painted benches, and after a long stretch of companionable silence, Elizabeth stood. "Well, I should—" she began, but Peter was also standing, and approached her.

"Would you like to… uh… go for a walk with me?" he asked nervously, making Erin say *aww* internally.

Elizabeth smiled a brilliant smile at him, and Erin thought it looked as though she was thinking, *I thought you'd never ask.* They both looked at Erin for permission.

"Alright, but please be back in about half an hour," she said, and noticed Peter's face, both thrilled and scared at the same time.

"Yes, Mum," he said, throwing in a light peck on the cheek for extra points.

Chapter Sixty

A TIMELY MESSAGE

Erin watched Peter and Elizabeth walk away in the opposite direction from where her grandmother was sitting and sighed. Junie was sitting up, playing with the mobile that hung over her head and pounding her rattle on her lap. She took out the tabloid she'd bought and stared at the sad photo of David on the cover, which made her heart ache. Finding the page she was looking for, she read:

> *Dear Erin,*
>
> *'Let me not, to the marriage of true minds admit impediment. Love is not love, which alters, when it alteration finds, or bends with the remover to remove. Ah no! It is an ever fix-ed mark, that looks on tempests and is never shaken…*
>
> *Love's not Time's fool, though rosy lips and cheeks within his bending sickle's compass come; Love alters not with his brief hours and weeks, but bears it out even to the edge of doom.'*
>
> *Our love IS an ever fix-ed mark, my love, and will never be shaken. Please think of me when you have your treatments. I think of you always and hope you… remember us. Oh God, Erin! The thought of you needing to go through what you have got to do makes my blood*

boil. I sometimes lay on my bed, not able to get the thought of it out of my head, and I feel as though I'll go mad!

Juniper is six months old today, please kiss our darling bairn for me, and tell the children, when you see them, how very much I love and miss them all. I pray for your safety and peace all the time, and I long, with my whole heart, to hold them and you again.

Please be patient and remember that I love you more than my own life,

David x

Erin closed and folded the paper and held it to her heart, then she put it in the tote bag and picked up Junie. It was time to feed her, so she placed a light blanket over her shoulder and the baby, then lifted one side of her shirt. She unclasped the little hook at the top of her nursing bra with one hand, then helped Juniper latch on, feeling the pull of liquid being sucked from her body.

It was a strange sensation, not unpleasant, but nothing you could really describe to someone who'd never breastfed a baby before. Rereading Shakespeare's 116th sonnet in her mind, she closed her eyes and allowed the tears to fall. She'd asked David once if he thought their love was an ever fix-ed mark, always in the same spot, reliable, and he'd said it was.

To hear it from him again gave her comfort. She knew people were staring at her, a lady breastfeeding and crying at the beach; she must've looked a sight, but it didn't matter. That letter had brought David back to her for a moment, and nothing was going to bother her.

Hearing the children coming closer, she wiped her face with the blanket, and pinned up the panel on her bra. Once the children had run off again, she would put Junie on the other side, though she felt a bit lopsided. One breast was nearly empty and one full to bursting, but she didn't want to make them uncomfortable with her manipulating things under her top.

"Mum! Peter is walking with that girl!" Charlie said.

It was just too uncomfortable, so she interrupted. "I'm sorry, but would you lot please turn around while I switch sides?" she said, and they were happy to do so. After repositioning the blanket, then unpinning the other side of her bra, she sighed, finally getting the relief she needed when Junie latched on and settled in. "Okay, continue."

"He's holding her hand!" Rosie said, sounding shocked and making a face that made Erin laugh.

"Yes, I know he's with Elizabeth, and I'm not surprised that they're holding hands," she said. Then she saw Elizabeth's grandmother coming her way, but she was pinned again, unable to stand because of the bundle in her arms. The woman looked disgusted that she was actually feeding her child in public and started yelling at her.

"Are you aware that my granddaughter is off with David Elliott's boy!" she barked.

"He's my child as well," Erin said, feeling a rage toward her that was unlike her usual nature. "And yes, I do know they went for a walk together. You should be thrilled, I mean, someone who knows someone who's seen the amount of money your precious bracelet is worth… you should be jumping up and down for joy that she's met a boy like him." She could feel her face getting red with anger.

"That may be, but the son of someone who's been sent to prison for beating a police officer! That is simply *out* of the question!" she said, and Erin stood.

"I'll tell you what's not going to happen," she said, and her blanket fell down, revealing Junie, happily drinking her milk. "You are not going to speak to me or my children anymore. You are going to return to your little world of elitist snobs and fuck off!" Rosie picked up the blanket and handed it to her. She took it, covered herself back up, and then resumed her seat, feeling the prick of angry tears smarting her eyes.

Peter and Elizabeth were now back, and Peter looked mad. He stepped up to the immaculately dressed woman, who was at least seventy though trying to look thirty. Something in his expression stopped her from the tirade she was about to begin, and she started walking away.

"Come with me, Elizabeth," she demanded.

Peter looked at the young woman and smiled David's smile. Erin could see the girl melting as she smiled back at him, "I'm glad I met you, Peter. Text me," she said and reluctantly turned away.

"A'right, I will," he said and stood, watching her get farther away from them. He was clearly smitten by her but also furious at her grandmother, and he looked completely conflicted. "Are you a'right?" he said to Erin and sat next to her on the bench.

"She didn't like that look you gave her, did she?" Erin said, glad for the distraction from the rage that had built up in her.

Peter laughed, and she saw a hint of color bloom in his cheeks. "Do you remember the movie Dad was in, *Lost in Vengeance*, where he was stuck in the transition between being mortal and being a vampire?" he asked.

"Oh, yes, I do!" Erin said, shivering slightly. "That movie gave me nightmares! Your father was the epitome of terrifying in that one!"

"Yeah, it frightened me to shreds when I was finally allowed to watch it last year. Well, I took a notion to practice the face he pulls in it… in the mirror… and well, I let that witch have it," he said and laughed at the look on Erin's face.

"Peter! You didn't? Oh, that's… that's the best thing ever! I'm afraid to ask, but… would you—" she didn't need to finish, as he turned away, and when he looked back at her, her heart skipped a beat. His face was completely unnerving to behold.

"Okay! Alright, you can put it away now," she said, having turned her head. "Thank you for sticking up for me, it really means everything, you know."

Her children were gathered around her once more, and she was tired, ready to think about heading home. "Alright, everyone, make sure you have everything, and brush the sand off your legs and arms," she said. When they were distracted, she pinned up her bra and pulled her shirt back down.

She removed the blanket, laid Junie on her shoulder, and started patting her back until a nice big belch came out of her, making the younger children laugh. Erin asked Charlie to throw the garbage away, then they were ready to go. "Who wants a 99?" she asked.

They all said 'yes,' so they crossed the Esplanade and went into one of the tourist shops, with their sunglasses and fridge magnets, postcards, straw mats, and stuffed crabs that had *Weymouth* embroidered on them. While they waited for their soft serve ice cream with the Flake to be prepared, she looked through the postcards and found a few to send to Lily. She paid for their items, then they trooped back to the car.

Chapter Sixty-One

RETURNING HOME

Everyone was tired after a long day in the sun, and Erin knew they would most likely sleep on the way home. They piled into the SUV, and Peter again helped to put Junie into the permanent frame that her car seat clicked into. Once all the seatbelts were buckled, she touched 'Home' on the Sat Nav, and they were off.

It was nearly three hours on the M3 to get back to London, and Peter spent most of that time on his phone. She presumed he was talking to Elizabeth, as he would occasionally laugh or sigh. At about an hour and a half, she pulled into a motorway break to fuel up and allow them to use the loo.

Peter stayed in the car with Junie, then ran inside to use the WC when Erin returned. They had a really good system, the two of them, and she was thankful for an older child to help out.

When they finally made it home, they were worn out and hungry. It was Francie's day off, so they would have to fend for themselves. Erin was tired and didn't really want to cook, but she also didn't want to get takeaway again. She changed into some comfortable clothes and put Junie in her highchair with some dry cereal, then she scoured the kitchen to see what they had on hand.

They had eggs and milk, a bit of ham, and some cheese, so she decided to make a quick quiche. She made a simple crust and lined the bottom of a pie plate with it, then she chopped some onions, sautéing them in butter. While they cooled, she mixed the eggs, shredded cheese and bits of ham in a bowl, then combined it all in the crust.

It took longer than she thought it would to cook, and the children were getting cranky, so she had them make a big salad with the odds and ends she found in the fridge. By the time the salad was done, the quiche was nearly ready, so they ate the salad in the dining room, and when they were done, the quiche was cooked but still needed to set for about ten minutes.

She asked them to help her bring the salad dishes to the kitchen and then washed them quickly while they waited, which made the time fly by. The quiche was really good, if she did say so herself, and everyone stuffed themselves, finally satiated and ready to relax. Erin told them they could leave, but Peter stayed behind to help her clear the table and anything else she might need.

"Thank you, darling. You are such a help to me, truly," she said, then Junie started to fuss, needing to be fed. "Okay, Junie, Mummy will be right there," she said, knowing she had no concept of time, only of 'I'm hungry now!' and to make matters worse, hearing her cry had made her milk start to flow and the front of her top was now soaked. "Shit!" she said, forgetting herself.

—

Peter saw her wet top and looked away. "Why don't you feed her, Mum, and I'll take care of this," he said, not looking back at her.

"Are you sure? I—" she began.

"I'm sure; I'll be fine," he said, though he'd never actually cleared the table or done any washing up on his own before, but he thought it couldn't be that difficult.

"Thank you… again. I'll come back down when Junie's finished, to help you," she said and picked up the wailing six-month-old. "Alright! Supper is on its way, calm down."

As she left the room, Peter sighed. It made him uncomfortable sometimes, knowing how his infant sister was primarily fed. He tried not to think of it, but Erin's wet shirt made him feel grossed out.

He started carrying the dishes into the kitchen and set them on the countertop. Then he put the stopper into the sink, as he'd seen Erin do earlier, but he didn't know how much washing up soap to use. After reading the back of the bottle, he was still unsure about measurements, so he opened the tap and squirted quite a lot into the rising water, hoping that too much was better than not enough.

The suds rose faster than the water, and he started putting the dishes in before realizing he was using cold water. He turned the tap to hot and waited until it was full, then he put a stack of plates into the now lukewarm water, and it overflowed everywhere. The polished concrete floor became slippery with the soapy water, and his feet flew out from under him, causing him to fall hard on his tailbone.

He crawled to the range, where there was a small towel, and laid it on the floor, but it wasn't enough. Soaked from top to bottom, he would've thought it was funny, except that his backside hurt pretty badly. Giving up was not an option, so he stood tentatively back at the sink, plunged his hand in, and felt something slice his finger. When he pulled it out, it was dripping with blood.

Erin took Junie to the nursery and laid her in her crib. By now, the baby was furious. Her little face was red with anger and hunger, but she needed to at least find a new shirt to put on after she was done feeding her. She quickly ran to her bedroom and found one of her nightgowns, grabbed it, and then headed back to the baby.

It was useless to try to change clothes until she was drained, but she was also uncomfortably wet, so she closed the nursery door and peeled her shirt off. She laid it over the end of the crib and then lifted Juniper, only to see that her diaper was also soaking wet. "Oh Junebug, I think I'm officially failing at this tonight," she said and quickly changed her diaper.

She sat in only her soaked bra and got comfortable in her chair with the pillow under her arm. She tried to relax, but the infant was so upset, she didn't want to latch on. "Come on, sweetie! You're not gonna feel better until you cooperate!" she said, wanting to get angry.

Finally, she got her to start drinking, but it was stop and start with the shuddering breaths and then the biting, as she was teething as well. "Owww!" she said loudly, as Junie bit her hard. She was glad she didn't actually have teeth yet, or she knew she'd have drawn blood.

Erin was getting frustrated, and Juniper already was, fussing and crying and then suckling for a few seconds, just for it to start all over again. Meanwhile, her breasts were still flowing; milk was running down her front on the other side, and she needed help. She sat there and wailed, just like her baby, not knowing what to do.

Eventually the task was completed on both sides, and both of them were worn out, so she took off her bra, laid her nightgown over the top of them like a blanket, and fell asleep.

"Bloody hell!" Peter said. He didn't know where anything was in the kitchen and looked around frantically for something to stop the bleeding. He knew he shouldn't use the towel he was standing on, but there wasn't anything else that he could see.

He looked down and saw that his shirt was already covered in blood, so he took it off, one-handed, and wrapped it around his now throbbing finger. *Now what do I do?* he thought. He didn't want to put his hand back into the dangerous water, but he'd told Erin that he could take care of it.

His finger hurt really badly, but he was afraid to take his shirt off to look at it, so he carefully made his way to the breakfast table. Sitting on one of the chairs, he put his head down on his arms, not knowing what to do. He must've fallen asleep, because he woke sometime later to an angry sounding Scotswoman.

"Ach! Fer the love of—" Francie said as she walked into the room and saw the mess of water, the small towel on the floor, and the dishes still sitting on the countertop.

Peter stood, causing his finger to throb again. "I'm sorry Francie! I was trying to help Erin. She had to feed Junie, and her front was all wet, and she was crying, so I offered to do the washing up, but I used too much Fairie, and then it was cold water, and then it was too full and went everywhere, and then I fell on my tailbone, and it hurt, and then I put a sharp knife in the water and cut myself, see?"

He spoke very quickly, wanting her to understand before she got angrier, and held out his t-shirt wrapped hand. "I… told her I could… manage it, but… I—" he said and had to turn around so she wouldn't see him crying like a child.

"Ach! Yeh poor wee thing. Set yerself doon where yeh were and ah'll take a look-see," she said gently.

He did as he was told, relieved that she didn't yell at him. She opened a cupboard and took down a first-aid kit that was attached to the inside of the door, then she pulled out one of the other chairs and sat in front of him. When she unwrapped the wound, her eyebrows shot up.

"Ach, ma boy! Tha's a mighty deep cut ye've go' there. Yeh did well tae wrap et up as yeh did."

Peter felt a bit better and watched her put some antiseptic cream, then a plaster on it. "Thank you, Francie. I'm really sorry for the mess," he said sincerely. She smiled at him then, and he realized that he'd rarely seen her smile before and smiled back at her.

"Dinnae worrit yerself, laddie. Ah'll finish et fer yeh, and Mrs. Erin doesnae need tae know et wasnae you who done it. Ye're a good lad fer helpin' yer poor mum. She's sae strong, but she needs all the help she can get, yeh ken?"

Peter nodded. He could've hugged and kissed her at that moment. He was so happy to know that under her gruff exterior, she felt the same way he did about Erin. "Be careful of the knife!" he said and watched her moving around swiftly and economically, not wasting a single step.

She picked up the towel and wrung it out, then she went to the small closet and took out the mop and bucket to soak up all the water and wrung it out, as well. Then she put on her rubber gloves and carefully started taking things out of the sink. Finding the knife, she laid it on the counter.

"Ah'll shew yeh what tae do in case ye're ever gallant enough tae offer yer help again, a'right?" Francie said.

"A'right, should I be taking notes, do you think?" he asked seriously.

"I dinnae think ye'll need tae do all tha', love." She showed him the proper amount of washing up soap to use and what temperature the water should be.

Next, she made sure to stress the importance of keeping anything sharp out of the water until it was time to wash them.

She also showed him where the towels were, in case he ever needed them, as well. "The way tae a woman's heart, Peter, is by showin' her ye're willin' tae wash a few dishes and help oot around the hoose. Tha's a thing, at yer age, yeh may wannae keep in mind, yeh ken?"

Peter smiled and blushed. "I reckon so," he said.

Erin woke to Kitty lifting the nightgown and taking Juniper out of her arms. "Oh, thank you, Kit—Peter! Oh, no!" She stood and began putting her nightgown on, but Kitty placed her hand on her shoulder.

"Tha's all been sorted, and he's already in bed. Now it's your turn, mum." She led her to the bedroom and lifted the covers.

Erin turned and hugged her friend. "Parenting is hard work, and I'd never be able to manage it without you. I know I say it a lot, but I mean it every time. I love you, and I'm so thankful you're here to help me."

She then got into bed, and Kitty covered her up. "I love ya too, Erin, and I'm blessed to be able ta help you. Sweet dreams."

On Wednesday morning, when Erin came downstairs, she saw the bandage on Peter's hand and gasped. "What happened?" she said and went to him.

He shrugged, and his cheeks turned pink. "It wasn't anything, really. Just a little cut, no big deal," he said and accepted her hug.

"Well, at least let me kiss it and make it all better," she said and laughed at the look he gave her. "That's what my mom did if I hurt myself."

"Uh, a'right," he said and lifted his hand.

"Aww, you poor thing!" She touched her lips gently to the bandage and said, "There, now it'll feel better sooner."

His smile was bright, and his eyes were just a bit misty. "Already does, Mum."

"You're such a good sport."

"You're such a good Mum, actually. I've never had anyone… care enough to do something like that. It's rather nice."

She hugged him again, then took a big breath, fighting the urge to cry. "Well now, we've got a lot of work to do to get you lot ready to visit your grandma. A whole week in Edinburgh sounds lovely."

The rest of the day was spent packing, and even Daniel behaved himself. They practiced some of their skits—she taught them some songs she knew, and they taught her some of their favorites. At bedtime, she decided to have them read to her for a change.

She started with Peter, who read a whole chapter, then Charlie read one. Next, Daniel read four paragraphs, but he was having difficulty pronouncing some of the words, so Rosie finished the chapter. "Well done, all of you! I won't make you do this every time, but I really enjoyed it, thanks," she said, feeling such love for her new family.

On Thursday afternoon, Erin drove the children to the airport, while Kitty watched Juniper. Though she was now eating solid foods, she made sure to pump enough breast milk for her next feeding, just in case she was detained for some reason. The ride there was a quiet one, the mood a bit sad and depressed.

When she had to leave the children, they all hugged her, and Rosie cried, making her want to as well, but she held it in until she could let it out on her way home. "I'll see you in a few days," she said. They had gotten so much closer and had learned to lean on each other since David was gone. It was hard to say goodbye, even if it was only for a week.

As she walked away from them, she waved, then headed back to the car. She got home feeling exhausted. The weekly treatments had been helping to keep her stable, but it still wasn't enough, and she wished she'd included September in her weekly treatments.

Kitty met her at the door with a crying Junie, who was hungry and demanding to be fed. After thanking Kitty for watching her, she climbed the stairs, laid Junie on the bed, then put on her pajamas, not caring if that's what she was wearing at the supper table. There wasn't anyone to see her, except Francie and Kitty, anyway.

She took Juniper to the nursery, then sat in the big, comfortable chair David had bought her, and started to feed her. It actually helped her relax, since she could doze, until Junie stopped getting any milk and started crying again. "Oh, aren't you just a hungry little hippo?" she said as she moved the pillow and switched sides.

She drifted off again until Kitty gently knocked on the door frame, letting her know that supper was almost ready. Being comfortable, she didn't really care about eating just then. She could've laid Junie down and gone right back to sleep in the chair, as she'd often done, since she started missing David next to her in the bed more and more each night.

"Okay, Kitty, would you mind—" she asked, but Kitty had already come in and was taking the baby from her before she could finish. She put Junie over her shoulder, and out came a nice, big burp, then she laid her down. Erin followed her sleepily down the stairs and into the dining room.

She dozed on and off during the meal, hardly able to stay sitting up, and was glad when Kitty brought out the pudding. "I'm going to bed now," she said drowsily to her housekeeper and friend. "I'll see you in the morning."

Though she felt like she could've simply put her head down and slept right where she sat, she made the effort to stand and trudge up the stairs. Not bothering to unmake the big bed, she sat in her nursing chair, reclined it, then pulled a light blanket over her and fell asleep.

Chapter Sixty-Two

EIGHTH VISIT-AUGUST TWENTY-EIGHTH

Erin almost dreaded visitations now, not that she didn't want to see him, but all it did was make her miss David more. She was finally beginning to find ways of coping with his absence. It was really difficult, but she was managing. To see him in the visitor's room, wearing a sweatsuit and looking subjugated and weary, was emotionally taxing.

The media were still at it as well, perched like vultures by the door with their ridiculous questions at every visit. She couldn't understand why they bothered, she'd never said anything to them, so what did they hope to gain from it?

Standing and waiting as usual, she was thinking about how she'd have to wait until Monday for her next treatment, wishing they were more often, and knowing that after that one, they would go back to twice per month. The doors were opened, and as soon as she saw David, she blushed such a deep red that her whole face burned.

"Oh, David! I'm sorry." She was ashamed for allowing herself to daydream about Louis while visiting her husband.

"Sorry for what?" he said, looking confused.

"Oh, just, I don't know, I'm tired, and my mind isn't all the way here."

"Where's the rest of your thoughts, then?" he said with a smile as he hugged her.

Her neck was now red, and she began to sweat. "I missed you!" she said, avoiding the question. "How are you being treated? You… still don't look well. Are you eating?"

"Everything is fine, darling. Yes, I'm eating, I promise. How are you? Yeh look bonnie! How's Junie and the children?"

"We're all okay. The children send their love, they're in Edinburgh for the week. Kitty asked me to say hello for her as well. Have you gotten any of my letters yet?" she asked, already knowing what he'd say.

"No, darling. Have you gotten any of mine?"

"No, well, not in the post, only in the tabloids."

"Humph," he said. "Yeh look tired, love, are yeh feelin' a'right?"

She shook her head, wanting to lie and say she was doing great, but he'd see right through it. It was impossible to tell him that she was having weekly treatments and it still wasn't enough. "I don't know what to tell you. I'm… between treatments… and with the children being home, it's stressful."

"And they're behaving for yeh?"

"They've been amazing, David. I can't believe how sweet and thoughtful they are! Even Dan is more willing to give me a hug and has been trying to be on his best behavior.

"It's still exhausting having to keep up with Junie, but she's a sweet girl. I'm afraid everyone is spoiling her, especially since you aren't home. I think they take their sorry feelings about it and dote on her more than they should."

"Aye, et makes sense, but yeh should try tae keep them from et. Et won't do her any good," he said, and Erin's face fell. "What is et?"

"I'll try, but that's just one more thing I need to be on top of, and my list is already longer than Santa's," she said and smiled. "Speaking of Santa, I don't know what we'll do about Christmas."

"Et's August, darling—"

"And now is the time I should start thinking about what to get people. I'm not a Black Friday shopper."

"Can yeh no' ask Kitty tae help yeh?"

"No, I can't. She's been amazing, being housekeeper and nanny, and I can't ask any more from her. I'd hire someone else to help out, but I have no idea how to go about that. I guess Christmas will be hit or miss this year. We can go to Owlgate, and it will feel like… a real holiday there, at least."

"Aye. I wish I could help yeh. If yeh need et, ask Kitty tae tell yeh how tae hire someone. Et's a'right by me if you do." He was suddenly very serious.

"I'm still havin' dreams, Erin, dreams where yeh… stop visitin' me, and I find out ye're seein'… yer other match. I dreamed I came home, and he was sleepin' in our bed. Et's almost more than I can bear. Please… darling, put my mind at ease… again."

"I know it's hard for you to deal with me having treatments, but you must believe me, David, I love only you, and I'm not going to leave you for him. It's… not like that with me and him, you just have to believe me. Our love is an ever fix-ed mark, remember?

"This is a tempest, darling, but nonetheless, it is never shaken. Love's not time's fool, David. I would love you the same, even if you were in here for life. Someday, we'll look back on this time, and it will all seem like a bad dream. If I could, I'd swear in my own blood that I'll not leave you for him, or anyone else," she said, looking him in the eyes.

He sighed and smiled at her. "I love yeh, Erin Elliott, and knowin' yeh love me is the only thing tha' keeps me sane in this place, yeh ken? If you… were waverin' in tha' love, I dinnae ken what I'd do. Thank you for remindin' me, and I'm sorry if I need yeh tae do et again at yer next visit. There's no love in here, and et's hard tae hold onto and remember et."

"I understand. I wish we could do that zen, mind-meld thing again. I felt so relaxed after that. Oh, by the way, Baz's party is this weekend, and I'm a bit stressed about it. "I'm sure I'll have fun, and Vincent did promise to shelter me from ALL anxiety," she said with a smile. "I admit that a week at Owlgate sounds like a better time, but I don't want to miss another visit, plus, I promised Vincent—"

"If et'll help yeh tae go to Mother's, even after the party, you should do et. I'll… be a'right."

"I won't be."

"Well, whatever yeh choose, remember everathin' and tell me all about et at yer next visit, a'right?"

"A'right, I promise. What I wouldn't give for a kiss right now," she said, holding his hand to her cheek.

"Aye, it'd be heaven. Do you—No, don't tell me, I don't want to know," he said and shook his head.

"Whatever it is, I'm sure you don't need to worry." She could feel his energy through her cheek and wanted to tell him how badly she wished he could just take her over the table, right there in front of everyone, but it wouldn't be fair to do that.

"Penny for your thoughts?" he said.

"Oh, I don't think you wanna know that," she said and saw his face grow hard. "No! It's not anything… that should make you angry. Fine, I'll tell you, but I think you'll regret it."

"Go on," he said, sounding leery.

"I was just… well, I was imagining you… well," she lowered her voice and leaned in close to him, "bending me over this table and having your way with me, right here, while everybody watched us."

David's eyes grew wide, and he cleared his throat. They were both breathing hard and staring into each other's eyes. The electricity was almost palpable between them, and she wished she hadn't said it.

"Ma Losh, Erin! Ma Losh! Aye, perhaps you were right. Perhaps it would've been best to keep that to yourself. On the other hand, et's good tae feel something other than fear, ya ken?" he said and gave her a smile that melted her heart.

"Good night nurse, it's gonna be hard to recover from that one. It's like when we were on the bluff in Port Washington, and you pinned me up against the back of the bathroom building. I wanted you so badly, I fainted," she said and laughed lightly.

"Ach, aye. Yeh make me so radge, I can hardly control maself. As soon as they let me out of this hell, I'll be takin' yeh everawhere I can, hen, just you wait," he said, panting.

"Good!" They sat for a few minutes, trying to calm down, until Erin finally asked, "Tea, do you want some… tea?"

"Aye, that'd be good," he said.

She managed to get her legs to move her toward the refreshment counter, though it was difficult to stop panting. "Two teas, please," she said to the young man, who took her two pound coins and handed her two paper cups with the brown liquid about three-quarters full. She quickly added milk and sugar to their taste, then turned and saw her husband waiting for her.

Her knees grew weak again, and it took real effort to perambulate back to him. He smiled and stood as she approached the table, and she could see the bulge in his sweatpants, which made her gasp. "Holy Moses, David, we need to calm down, but… I just wanna crawl under the table, you know?"

"Oh!"

She could see the tea sloshing in the cup as his hand trembled. "I'm sorry, I shouldn't have said that. It wasn't fair," she said, as what felt like heat lightning passed between them, back and forth.

"No, love, perhaps not, but I'm glad yeh did. I'm chuffed tae know you're still thinking of me in that way, yeh ken? Ma mind sometimes has me doubting, now that you're… with—"

"No, darling, I want you, and love you and… need you. That'll never change, ever."

"And yeh don't—" he said, trembling again, though the mood had seemed to change. "Ach, I dinnae want tae know!" he said and put his palms on his temples, as if trying to push the horrible thoughts and fears back.

"Whatever it is, I don't."

Before they knew it, the officer was calling out the five-minute warning, and they had to say goodbye, dreading the two long weeks before they'd see each other again. They stood, and Erin wrapped her arms around him, listening to him breathe. "I love you, David."

"I love yeh as well, Erin. Please… dinnae forget me. I'm terrified—"

"Shh, don't think about things like that, because it's a lie. I will love you forever plus one, okay? I pinky promise!" she said and held out her pinky.

He grasped it with his as his chin quivered, then he drew her in for another hug. "Ach, thank you, ma love. Kiss our Junie for me and say hello to Baz and Vincent if you go."

"I will, and take care of yourself for us," she said and then had to leave.

Chapter Sixty-Three

NO PARTY POOPERS

Erin had a million butterflies in her stomach as the classic Rolls-Royce pulled up to Baz and Vincent's house the next morning, though mansion was a better term for it. The suntan-colored gravel crunched under the tires and then under the polished leather shoes of the uniformed driver as he walked around the car to open the door for her. She took his hand and allowed him to help her out of the dark back seat and into the sunshine of a nearly cloudless day.

"Thank you," she said and made eye contact with the man who'd driven hours to deliver her out of London and then west to the Lake District.

"It was my pleasure, madam," he said and touched the brim of his flat, black chauffeur's hat. She held out a folded ten pound note, but he put his hand up. "Thank you, but that won't be necessary. The Thompson's are generous, though I do appreciate the offer."

"You're welcome, it was a treat to ride in such a beauty!" she said, laying her hand on the gleaming pale yellow and pea-green paintwork. "How old is she?"

"She is a 1931 Rolls-Royce Phantom II Continental Sports Saloon, and I assure you, madam, she is also a treat to drive," he said with a grin and a wink.

She turned to gaze at the façade of the white lime-rendered building, which had many bits and pieces of additions around the main structure. "This place is magnificent," she said.

"Yes, the Thompson's have done many improvements."

"Oh, so do you live here?" she asked, having thought he was just hired for the event.

"Yes, I'm their full-time driver and live in the gamekeeper's cottage. If you enjoy the car, I reckon you'll enjoy the cottage. Please feel welcome to come 'round for a cuppa and a tour of the property before you leave. They've done it up brilliantly, and she's a treat to lodge in, actually."

"I love old things… I mean, antiques and architecture, and… so on. I'd be honored to come by for a visit, thrilled, actually, thank you. Being Baz and Vincent's full-time driver must be… well, fun," she said with a smile. "I imagine they're full of surprises."

The white-haired man laughed, his brown eyes crinkling up, revealing his crow's feet, and nodded emphatically. "Fun is a well-chosen word for it."

The two of them stood for a moment, looking at the house and stunning landscaping. Work had already begun on the party decor, which Erin could tell was going to be extravagant. She watched a man carrying a ladder walk past them, absorbed in his task.

"Would you like for me to escort you to the door?" he asked, presumably because she hadn't moved since he'd helped her out of the car.

"Oh… no, that's okay. Honestly, I'm a bit nervous and not sure what to expect."

"Expect the unexpected with Baz, especially, though I've never known him to be unkind. Allow me to walk with you," he said, and held out his arm for her to take. "I'll deliver your luggage to your rooms as soon as I am able."

"Rooms… plural? Well then," she said and raised her eyebrows. "Thank you—Good night nurse, I never asked your name! That's not like me, but I suppose I haven't been myself for a while."

"My name is Philip, madam, and don't you fret about it. Most people don't bother to talk to me at all. Now, shall we go?"

She linked her arm in his and walked with him toward the front door. "Thank you, Philip, I guess I just need a bit of a push."

The curtains moved in one of the windows, then the large, solid wooden door swung open. "*Bon dia, bellesa*! My dear friend, welcome to our home… and yours! Is she not *perfecta*, Philip!

"Come, *Bellesa*, come! We are waiting for you all the day! Do you have hunger or do you thirst? We shall bring you a feast," Vincent said, waving his arms about, then he took her hands with both of his and kissed her on the lips.

Erin couldn't help but laugh at his excitement as he led her into the grand foyer, talking non-stop, sometimes in English and sometimes in his native tongue. "We are living *a la quinta forca*, I know, but this is good, *bellesa*, as we are not disturbing those around us. Are you wanting *un got d'aigua o de vi?* Anything you are wanting, I will be giving to you!"

"I'm afraid I missed some of that, but I thought I heard something that might've been water, but I didn't recognize the other word," she said.

"*Ho sento*—I am meaning to forgive me. I am not being so fluent with the English. Yes, *bellesa*, do you wish for water or wine?"

"Actually, a cuppa would be lovely, and you don't have to apologize to me for not knowing English very well. I'm sure I would have a really hard time learning Andorran if I were to go there."

The strikingly handsome, younger man smiled at her and kissed her mouth again. "You are too good! Catalan is the language of my country. I am teaching it to you while you are staying."

"Good, I look forward to it."

"Erin! You're here! Welcome to our home, my friend!" Baz said as he entered the room and saw her. "Can we tempt you with a glass of champagne, my dear?"

"I'd prefer a cuppa, if that's not too much trouble?" she said, and then accepted air kisses on both cheeks.

"There is nothing you could ask for that would be too much trouble, we shall offer you the whole world," he said as he stepped up to a long, embroidered cord that hung against the wall near the door. He gave it a smart tug, then returned to her, smiling broadly.

A few moments later, a young man of about twenty-five appeared and stood a yard or so away from Baz. "Claude, this is our…" he paused and smiled at his husband. "…*especial* guest, Mrs. Elliott—"

"Please, I'd rather be called Erin," she inserted.

"As you please," Baz said. "Please make sure she wants for nothing."

"Yes, sir," the blonde haired, blue-eyed man said with a slight accent she couldn't place, and turned to her, bowing slightly. "It's a pleasure to meet you, Mrs. Erin. If you need anything, please pull any of the cords throughout the house and I will come to you as soon as I am able." He then turned to Baz again. "Will there be anything else?"

"Yes, please prepare tea in the conservatory for us and Caroline. Also tell Yonnie to impress our esteemed guest."

"Oh, Baz! I don't want to put anyone out! I don't need to be impressed, really—" she began, but he took her hand and kissed it, then he nodded at Claude, who returned the nod and walked briskly away.

"The more you protest, my dear, the more deserving I know you to be. Please trust that I will not overexert my staff; however, you shall still be pampered and looked after whilst you're here. If anyone in the household gives you even the slightest sniff, I ask that you inform me. I pay them far too much for any of that. Now, would you care to rest in your chamber until tea, or would you rather we give you a tour of our *wee* cottage?"

Erin could tell in his eager expression what he hoped she'd say, and she couldn't disappoint him. "You're like an excited pony, champing at the bit, so I'll give you full rein to do with me as you will," she said and then cocked her head to the side. "That sounded better in my head. Give me the tour."

"I am liking you very much, *bellesa*! You will be loving our home, I am knowing this!" Vincent said and took her hand like a child would his best friend.

"And I like you very much as well, Vincent. Wait, Caroline! That's right, you have a new family member, don't you? I can't wait to meet her!"

"You are going to be loving her, Erin! She is our *princesa*, our song of happiness!"

"Oh, that's a lovely thing to say about her. And I love the name Caroline," she said.

"This is what her name is meaning: song of happiness," Vincent said and led her by the hand to a nearby credenza, where he lifted a photograph of a smiling baby.

"She's delicious! Look at those ringlets... she has your hair, Vincent... but how is that... oh, did you... she have a surrogate mother?"

"I am not understanding," Vincent said and looked at Baz.

"She means substitute, darling. Yes, my dear, and thankfully it went off without a hitch. One does hear nightmarish stories involving such things. Her name is Petunia, and she is very pretty and sweet, thus our beautiful Caroline. Who knows, we may decide to try again with her," Baz said.

"Oh yes, Petunia is a dear flower. We are very happy to be knowing her, and I do hope we are trying again someday soon, my Bazzy," Vincent said, looking very hopeful.

He handed the photo to her and by the weight of the frame, it had to be solid gold. "She really *is* delicious," she said again and gave the frame back to Vincent, who had an odd expression on his face.

"Why are you saying this word, delicious? Does this not mean… ah, tasting good?" he asked, and Baz let out a joyful laugh.

Erin blushed and shrugged. "Well, technically it does, but… well—"

"It's a compliment, my love, and let's leave it at that," Baz said and leaned over to kiss his husband's cheek.

They began the tour by climbing the grand, curved staircase. Baz rattled on about this piece of furniture and that, how old they were and who had owned them before they acquired them. He listed which auction they were won at and how much they'd paid for many of them.

Soon, his mobile started chiming like Big Ben, and Erin giggled. "I guess you can take the boy out of London, but you can't take London out of the boy."

"Quite right and well said. That was Claude, our tea is served," he said and took Vincent's other hand.

Erin was led into a large sunroom the size of her whole house in Wisconsin, made wholly of glass and elaborate white ironworks that were clearly from the turn of the twentieth century or earlier. There were plants and trees everywhere, and beautiful ceiling fans spun noiselessly over their heads, creating a perfect atmosphere that wasn't too hot and not at all chilly.

She could hear birds, but she couldn't see any. The table was laid out with perfectly pressed linens and the most delicate, striking china she'd ever seen in dark red and gilded with gold. Garlands and bouquets of fresh, fragrant, tropical flowers covered the table and the surrounding furniture.

"I've died and gone to Heaven!" she exclaimed as she closed her eyes and breathed deeply. "It's utterly delicious!"

"Delicious… again you are saying this word," Vincent said and frowned.

"How can I explain it to you?" Erin said and pursed her mouth as she considered it. "Yes, most often, the word delicious *is* given to food or drink, and I guess it's a colloquialism or something, but when I say it, I mean delicious for my eyes or ears… my senses, you know?

"For instance, your hair, Vincent, is *utterly* delicious, and I find myself wanting to run my fingers through it. I don't know what products you use, but it just looks delicious to me. This whole room is delicious, and so is the smell of the flowers."

"My hairs?" he said and laughed in a way that was quite contagious. "*Sí, bellesa*, perhaps I am understanding now, though I am not using any products into my hair. I am bathing it with *oli d'oliva* only."

"*D'oliva*… oh, olive oil? Well, that explains it. It's intoxicating… oh, there's another one, ugg. Well, just know that I love it, and it's very *especial*, like you," she said with rosy cheeks.

Again, the beautiful man laughed and went to her. "You may be running your finger throughout my hairs at any time you are wishing it, *bellesa*!" He took her hand and lifted it up to the top of his head, making her cheeks blaze.

She touched several curls and sighed. "Yes, just as I imagined it would feel, and I stand by my adjective… delicious." Just then, a small woman entered the room carrying a baby dressed in white from head to toe. *Junie would ruin that in a matter of minutes*, she thought as the child was placed into Vincent's arms.

"*Moltes gràcies*, Helga," he said, then she nodded and left the room without making a sound. He turned to Erin. "This is our Caroline, *bellesa*. I am believing she is most delicious."

"Oh, yes, I am agreeing with… I mean, I agree! As delicious as a crème brûlée, I'd say! She's truly one of the most beautiful babies I've ever seen, and I've seen photos of *me* when I was her age," Erin said and laughed.

Baz stepped up to his child and ran his finger over her downy nose, then gently touched the tip of it and said, "Boop."

She lifted her arms to him, squealing with laughter. "Da! Da da da… da!" she almost sang with joy.

Vincent handed her to him, and he held her in the air while spinning slowly. "Hello, my darling! Did you have a pleasant slumber? Daddy missed you terribly!" He then cradled her and looked at Erin, his face glowing. "This is our Caroline."

Erin smiled at the little girl, but she was too engrossed in her daddy's face to pay any attention to her. Vincent stood next to her and beamed, gazing lovingly at his daughter. "*Mare!*" she said and squirmed in Baz's arms, trying to get to Vincent.

"*Mare?*" Erin said. "Isn't that the sea?"

The two men laughed heartily. "*Sí*, in Italian, this is the meaning, but in my language, it means the mother," Vincent said, still chuckling lightly as he took the girl and accepted the wet kiss on his mouth.

"Oh, I was thinking of the French song, "*La Mar*," she said, feeling a bit dumb as they took their seats at the table.

"Ah, yes, well, it's a matter of spelling. *La Mar*, no 'e' is the sea, in *Français*, and *mare*, with an 'e' is both the sea, in *Italiano*, and mother in Catalan. It's an easy mistake," Baz said with a kind smile.

"Well, I don't know any language other than English, though I really wish I did! Oh! I do know Pig Latin, but that doesn't count," she said and laughed.

"What is this Pig Latin? I am not ever hearing of this language," Vincent said while getting Caroline settled into her highchair.

"*Jar, jar!*" the baby said, beginning to sound upset.

"*Sí, sí, nena,*" he said and took the plain digestive biscuit Baz handed him.

"Jarjar, nena? Jarjar is a character in Star Wars," Erin said and smiled, figuring it had nothing to do with that.

Baz laughed and shook his head. "Thank you, now I will never get the image out of my head!" he said. "*Jar* is short for *menjar*, which means eat or food in Catalan, and *nena* means baby girl." He pulled out a chair and motioned for her to have a seat.

Erin waited for a young, handsome man to pour out the tea, then she began fixing it the way she liked. When she looked up, Vincent was regarding her as if waiting for something. "Hmm? Did I miss something?" she asked, worried that she'd been too greedy with the sugar.

"What is the Pig Latin?" he asked again.

"Oh! Sorry, it's nothing, really, just a silly way to speak English by moving some of the letters around a bit. Haven't you heard of it, Baz, the man of the world that you are?"

"I must say I haven't, but I would be thrilled to hear you speak it, if you wouldn't mind?" he said.

"Good night nurse, I don't know what I'd say! Let me think." She felt a bit ridiculous speaking such a fake language in front of them, but she decided to say something anyway, knowing they'd catch on immediately and think she was making it up.

"*Ellohay! Imay aimnay isyay Oejay Itehallwhay, andyay Iyay omecay omfray ethay uturefray–*" she began, her face burning.

"My word!" Baz said, seemingly mesmerized. "Whatever did you say?"

"Really? You didn't recognize it?" The two men shook their heads and she smiled. "Well then, I don't feel like such a fraud! I can't believe you didn't get *Oejay Itehallwhay*, Baz! I almost split it up into *Oejay Itewhay Allhay*, thinking it would be too obvious." She looked at their blank faces and said, "Joe Whitehall, of course. Hello… *ellohay*. My name is… *Imay aimnay isyay*– I'm just taking the first one or two letters of the word, moving them to the end and adding ay, yay, or hay."

Vincent looked at Baz and shrugged. "I am still not understanding," he said, and then picked up the sippy cup Caroline had dropped on the floor.

"Well, I guess it would be more difficult for you since English isn't your first language. Your name would be *Incentvay Ompsonthay*, which is kinda odd because the th in Thompson just sounds like a 't', but in Pig Latin you'd really need to say 'th' instead."

"What is Bazzy's name being?" Vincent said with an amused grin.

"I guess it depends on what form you're using. Bazzy would be *Azzybay*; Baz would be *Azbay*, and Barry would be *Arrybay*." She glanced at the baby, and in a kind of baby-talk said, "And widdle Caroline would be…"

She had to think for a moment to get it right. "*Arolinekay*, or your *Ongsay Ofyay Appinesshay*," she said and chuckled at the confusion on both their faces. "That's song of happiness, of course."

"*Molt bé, bellesa!*" Vincent said.

Erin spent the next half hour or so trying to teach them how to speak it, but in the end, it seemed to be a losing battle. They did have a lot of laughs, and Caroline learned how to say, 'Erin,' though it sounded like, 'Urn.'

"I hope you don't mind, Erin, but I've invited some of my friends to join us early. Think of it as a pre-party party," Baz said with a smile.

"Why should I mind? It's not my shindig, it's yours. Invite whomever you want, whenever you want, silly boy," she said.

"See, darling, I knew she wouldn't mind," he said to his husband as if gloating.

"Perhaps, this is *perquè*… because she is being a *bona dona, sense voler decebre*—" Vincent shook his head. "She is not wanting to disappoint, although I am standing on my words. It is being rude, Bazzy," he said. "She will be wanting relaxation, not a… party of the before—Well, you are knowing what I am meaning."

"Pish posh, I disagree," Baz countered.

"Now, now, boys, I'll not have any arguing whilst I'm here. Thank you, Vincent, for thinking about me and wanting to make sure that I'm comfortable and can rest. You are so thoughtful, but I'm not upset… unless you've invited my ex-husband or… an enemy of mine, I suppose," she said, looking at Baz with her eyebrows raised.

The flamboyant, aging man laughed heartily and kissed her cheek. "None of that, I promise. Well, not unless you are in some way feuding with the Joplin Brothers?"

"Joe and Billy Joplin? Really?" she said, her eyes wide.

"Really and truly, my dear, in the flesh."

"Oh, I love their music! They were at my birthday party, but I didn't get a chance to talk to them. They're coming here tonight? When?"

This time both Baz and Vincent laughed. "Alright, Bazzy, you are winning," Vincent said.

Baz looked at his watch and grinned. "I'd say in half an hour, perhaps an hour if Phillip finds himself suffering through heavy traffic."

Her eyes grew even wider and she squeed in excitement. "I have to get ready!" she said, then stood and kissed them both on the cheek before rushing out of the room.

Chapter Sixty-Four

AN UNEXPECTED SING-ALONG

An hour later, Erin was pacing the hall in front of her room, trying to be patient and fearing that if she went downstairs early, she'd seem far too eager. She didn't know when she'd begun wringing her hands, but when she heard footsteps behind her, she dropped them and felt her cheeks begin to burn.

"*Bellesa*? What is troubling you? Why are you doing this twisting of your hands? Are you unwell? Tell Vincent everything," he said and held out his arms as if knowing she needed a hug.

"I'm not unwell," she said after embracing him. "I'm, well… I'm nervous. It's stupid, I know! They're no different than Baz or David or the dozens of other celebrities I've met over the last year, but I've gotten myself all worked up and don't know how to stop freaking out."

"This is not being stupid, *bellesa*, this is natural. May I confess to you something?" he said and led her to a small sitting room filled with extraordinary decor.

"Of course you can! Anything to get my mind off this," she said and smiled at him.

"I am doing very much the same whilst waiting for you to arrive, *bellesa*. I am wanting everything being *perfecte* and the excitement was overflowing. When I see Philip arriving, I am saying to myself to behave as I wasn't caring, but I am not able. I failed and went to you, are you remembering?" he said, and Erin noticed his cheeks blooming pink.

"Really? That just makes me feel so… I don't know, honored and, well, not stupid."

"This is true, my friend."

"Oh, Vincent, thank you for telling me that. I feel a bit less frantic now."

"Come with me, and we will make our guests very welcome."

"Sounds good," she said and took his outstretched hand.

Vincent and Erin came down the grand staircase, holding hands and laughing. It took a moment for them to notice that both Joplin brothers were standing just inside the door with Baz and Claude. She squeezed his hand and took a slow breath in, then let it out even slower.

"Aha, Vincent, Erin, I'm glad you're here! Come say hello to our esteemed guests," Baz said.

Billy Joplin, who was the younger of the two, met them at the bottom of the stairs and held out his hand for Erin, helping her down the last step. "Mrs. Elliott, I'm chuffed ta meet you! I was gutted that we weren't able to speak at your birthday party."

"Yes, he was near tears, I can tell you," Joe Joplin said with the same easy British accent as Billy, and stood next to his brother, who looked mortified. "He's a true fan of both you and your husband, as am I, but I reckon he's especially enamored with you—"

"Joe! Brown bread, remember?" Billy interrupted in a harsh whisper. "Ignore him. I just feel devastated for you and your situation! I can't imagine—"

"He cries himself ta sleep every week after reading the tabs," Joe said, clearly for the entertainment of Baz and whomever else was listening.

Billy gave his brother a sharp jab in the side and began to lead Erin away from the other people in the room. "Is there anything I can do ta—" he was saying when Joe cleared his throat and laid his hand on Billy's shoulder.

"Are you going to deny me the honor of an introduction, brother?" he said with a genuine smile.

Baz came to the rescue, saying, "Come, let us sit in the solarium and get to know one another better."

Vincent raised his eyebrows at him and nodded his head toward Erin. "Introductions first, I think, Bazzy," he said and went to her like a mother hen.

"Right, Erin Elliott, allow me the honor of introducing Joe and Billy Joplin," Baz said.

Erin was trying not to laugh at the clear sibling rivalry and enjoying the attention of Billy. Joe stepped up to her and took her hand, bowing quite formally as he kissed it. "Mrs. Elliott, I apologize for our display. It's just… difficult for me ta keep from winding my baby brother up. I do hope you'll forgive me? I hope he'll forgive me as well," he said quietly, as an aside.

She looked over at Billy, who seemed a bit sullen. "It's a pleasure to make your acquaintance, and I will do my best to put in a good word for you with your baby brother. You really should be nicer to him, after all, he's the one with the most talent," she said and laughed at the look on Joe's face.

Billy perked up when he heard that, and Baz laughed heartily. "Perhaps it's a bit late in the day for the solarium, what say you to sitting in the library with a drink and perhaps a song? Don't think I'm unaware of how much you've wanted to get your hands on my grand piano, Joe Joplin."

"I've not kept it a secret," he said and put his arm around Billy's shoulders as they were led through the house to the two-story, opulent library. "Bloody— Oh, sorry, Mrs.—"

"I was just about to say the same, and please call me Erin. Baz, why didn't you tell me this work of art existed? That's it! I call dibs on this as my bedroom for the remainder of my stay!" she said and felt her neck begin to cramp because she couldn't stop looking up at the hundreds or maybe thousands of shelves, filled with ancient books.

"You are liking this room, *bellesa*? This is being my favorite as well. Bazzy, tell them about this," Vincent said proudly.

"My pleasure, darling," he said, and then led them around the room, showing off his treasures. "When we had our first viewing with the estate agent, this room was very nearly complete, though it lacked any flair or theatrics."

"Yes, it was being very ugly, but I am in love with it, even so. Thus, at the time, I am telling this to my Bazzy," Vincent interjected.

"What's not to love?" Erin said.

"Quite right. Naturally, I asked if the books were included in the sale," Baz began, but it seemed Billy couldn't wait.

"Were they?" he asked like a child, listening to a bedtime story.

"Alas, the agent said they were not."

"Oh no!" Erin said, in spite of herself, and laughed with Vincent. "Sorry, Bazzy, please continue."

"I simply *had* to have them, so we asked him to make an offer, far above the asking price, with the condition that the books stayed."

"Really? And they agreed?" Joe said.

"They were allowed to take a dozen or so that were special to them, but yes, they agreed," Baz said and smiled at his husband, who was gazing at him lovingly.

"My Bazzy is a most generous man. This is why I am loving him so very much," Vincent said and went to him, planting a kiss on his cheek.

"You, my love, are worth every penny," Baz said, revealing a moment of tenderness that was usually covered with flamboyance.

"Aww, you two are so sweet together! You make me miss… David," Erin said, losing a bit of steam.

"Let's not get misty! Come, Joe, play us something to raise our mood a bit," Baz said and stood in front of a magnificent, gilded grand piano.

The sides, keyboard cover, and music stand were adorned with exquisite paintings, inlay, and marquetry of mother-of-pearl, ivory, precious stones, ebony, and other exotic woods. He lifted the long, curvy top, revealing not only the strings and inner workings of the instrument but a pastoral scene of nymphs and shepherds on the underside of the lid.

The tall man in his late thirties gasped and actually took a step back.

"It's too… much! I can't touch it, Barry!" Joe said.

"May I?" Erin said.

"Be my guest," Baz said and opened the golden keyboard cover. On the underside of it was a continuation of the scene under the lid, complete with exposed breasts and male genitals. It resembled an orgy, and she couldn't help but laugh.

"Wow, Baz, that's… graphic," she said. "I bet you love the toilets at… what was the restaurant… Sarastro, don't you?"

"You know me too well, my friend!"

"It was definitely a shock to my Puritanical American sensibilities!" she said as she sat gingerly on the small gilded, ornate bench and pretended to crack her knuckles. "Any requests? I know 'Chopsticks' and 'Heart and Soul.'" She placed her fingers on the ivory keys and gently played a C scale. The instrument came alive and filled the room with a kind of magic.

"A'right, Erin, get on with your "Chopsticks." I'd like to try my hand at it now, if ya don't mind?" Joe said.

"Ha ha! My plan worked like a charm!" she said and stood. "Do *you* take requests?"

"Perhaps, but my first choice will be my very favorite," he said and sat on the bench after moving it to accommodate his long legs. He placed his fingers over the keys and began playing a familiar song.

"Moonlight Sonata," she whispered, and allowed the haunting melody to fill her with wonder. After a while, she glanced at Vincent, who was wiping tears off his face with a handkerchief. She went to him, took his hand in hers, and leaned against his arm, then closed her eyes.

The melody came to an end, and everyone stood silent, allowing the memory to sink in. Finally, Baz said, "Please, do continue. She rarely has any exercise, and you have us all enchanted."

"Yes, please!" Erin said.

Joe played one of the songs they were famous for, then Claude was summoned to bring refreshments and Billy retrieved his guitar from the foyer. After a few more of their popular hits, they played one of Erin's favorites, and she was encouraged to sing along. She closed her eyes, forgetting where she was and who she was with.

It was a beautiful song, the lyrics were lovely, and she knew them by heart. Suddenly, she realized she was the only one singing, so she stopped and opened her eyes. "What?"

"Please continue, *bellesa*! You are singing with such beauty!" Vincent said, and she could feel her cheeks burning.

"I'd like to hear more as well," Joe said, and his brother smiled, nodding his head in agreement.

"Oh, uh, well—Now I'm self-conscious!" She laughed nervously until Billy began strumming, "Something in the Way She Moves," by the Beatles. She sang all the words she could remember and allowed Joe to fill in what she didn't.

When the song was done, she sighed. "I love that song! I'm really glad you thought of it! I also love 'I Will,' sung by Paul. Do you—" before she could finish her sentence, Billy began playing it. The words of longing, telling the yet unknown person it had been written for that he'd wait for them as long as they had to, caught Erin off guard.

"I forgot that's how it started," she whispered and stepped away from the piano to hide her tears. When the song was done, Vincent went to her with a few tissues, and she hugged him.

"I'm sorry, it's just that… David's afraid I won't be able to wait for him and… that I'll find someone else. I wish I could sing that song for him every day… so he'd know that I will also wait a lonely lifetime for him if I have to." The room was silent until they heard Billy softly playing the opening bars of a song she didn't recognize. "That's pretty, did you write it?"

"I've… I mean, *we've* been working on a new song, would you like to hear it?" Billy said and looked at Erin hopefully. "It's not finished, it needs something else, but maybe I'll find inspiration here."

"Are you kidding? Of course I wanna hear it, finished or not!" she said and wiped her wet face with one of the tissues.

"It's called, 'Again,' and I hope you like it," Joe said and began playing a simple melody, then Billy started singing the words of the first verse.

Away from you… I'm nothing much… a shell of a man.
Away from you… our memories I touch… the best I can.
Don't stay away… I need you today.
I'm chilled to the bone… I can't live alone…

"Here's the chorus," Billy inserted.

You are mine… I am yours.
We're better together, now and forever.
You are mine… I am yours.
We'll soon be together, and life will be better
Again… woah… again.

"Verse two," Billy said.

Together we're better than a symphony, apart, a mere cacophony.
The song of us will never fade. Our melody is worth the pain.
Apart we are, for now tonight. Though soon, I vow we'll reunite.

"Then the chorus again," Billy supplied, and they sang it for her. "So, that's essentially what we've got… so far." He stood before them all as if waiting for a reaction, but the room was silent.

He frowned, clearly confused, until he saw Erin, tears running down her face. "Erin? Are you alright?" he said and stepped up to her. "As I said, it's not finished, so it'll be more polished and—"

"I'm fine, Billy. That was beautiful! Truly stunning. It reminds me… again… of… David, and everything we're going through, that's all."

Joe and Billy exchanged a glance, then Billy hugged her. "I'm glad you like it. I'll work on it more tomorrow and sing it at the party," he said, but Joe rolled his eyes.

"Come now, Billy, tell her the truth," he said, and Erin watched as his brother's face turned an uncomfortable-looking shade of red.

"Tell me what?"

"If you don't, I will," Joe threatened, while Billy shook his head emphatically. "Fine then, the truth is—"

"I was inspired by your story and… well, I wrote it for you. In truth, we wrote this song as a duet and weren't planning to record it ourselves. Here, listen to how it's meant to sound," Billy said and joined his brother after picking up his guitar again.

The two men sang the now familiar words, harmonizing and singing different parts alone and together. Erin thought it was even more beautiful that way. "That was stunning and actually made more sense. Some of the words were a bit confusing sung by one person, but as a duet it's perfect!" she said.

Joe glared at Billy again. The young man shook his head until Joe opened his mouth like he was going to speak, and he sighed. "Okay," he said defensively. "There's more to it than that. I simply didn't want you to be… upset, that's all."

"Upset? Why would I be upset?"

"Well, listen, this is the bridge and the end tag," he said, and Joe sang,

> J: *Don't lose heart, my love, and light, With*
> *all that's within me, your loving wife.*

> B: *I love you more than life itself. You're the*
> *only one who can mend me… Again*

They sang the chorus again, then Billy said, "Here's the end tag, though I wish it were better.

> J: *I sit in the darkness… alone in our*
> *room… not crying is a losing fight.*

> B: *I gaze through the bars… on my thick*
> *ugly door… glowing with fluorescent light.*

> T: *Wishing you were with me, of all nights,*
> *tonight. Again.*

Erin felt a bit light-headed and didn't know what to say. "I don't—"

"I'm sorry, Erin, I know it's too much," Billy said.

Vincent came to her and took her hand. He led her to an age softened leather chair, where she sat, confused and a bit overwhelmed. "What are you feeling, *bellesa*?" he said softly.

"I'm blown away! It's one of the most beautiful… I wish… David could hear it."

"We can make that happen if our friends are willing," Baz said, raising his eyebrows toward the brothers, who nodded and smiled.

"Absolutely!" they said in unison, though they didn't seem to know what he was talking about.

"That would be amazing!" she said. "But how?"

"Come with me and bring that guitar," Baz said, then stood before her.

"What? I'm confused. We can't go to the prison now," she said, shocked as she took his outstretched hand.

"Perhaps not, but there are other ways for a person to hear a song, aren't there?" he said a bit cryptically.

"I feel a bit dense right now, please spell it out for me," she said as he led her out of the room by the hand.

Chapter Sixty-Five

A DREAM COME TRUE

Baz was talking non-stop, saying something about dabbling in mixing and singing, and she didn't hear all of it. He led Erin, Vincent, and the Joplin brothers outside after grabbing a large iron keychain filled with bulky skeleton keys. They stopped in front of a small, picturesque stone building with a thatched roof and a wooden door that was decorated with black, iron nailheads.

He unlocked it and opened the door, which swung silently on its hinges. Erin didn't know what to expect, but what she saw was nothing she could have imagined. Instead of being filled with hay or farming implements, the interior was brand new and filled with musical instruments, microphones on stands, mixing boards, earphones, music stands, and lots of sound-proofing materials.

"Good night nurse!" she exclaimed.

"What she said," Billy said as he examined the room with his eyes.

"Now, now, it's nothing much," Baz said, though it was clear to Erin that he was proud of the space. "I don't often reveal this… side of me, but I've been known to sing when the mood strikes; however, I will *not* be persuaded tonight. Tonight, I would be honored if you'd allow me to record that lovely new song of yours."

"You mean now?" Erin said, utterly flabbergasted, and noticed that Billy had a similar look on his face.

"No time like the present," Baz quipped.

She looked at the Joplin brothers, unsure if they were really that keen, but they were both smiling and seemed excited. "Well then, I can't wait to watch this!"

Once the brothers were on board, the technical stuff was set up relatively quickly. They sang through it a few times, and Erin couldn't help but sing along with the chorus. She was talking to Vincent while levels were being adjusted and such, so she didn't notice Joe and Billy standing in front of her until one of them cleared his throat and said, "Erin?"

She looked up, surprised to see them. "Yes?"

Billy nudged Joe, so he began with, "We've heard you singing along, and, well, we agree that the song needs a female voice, at least it was written for—"

"Please sing the female part, Erin," Billy interrupted.

"Me? But… you've worked with some of the greats, I'll never live up to them!" she said.

"It's not a competition, and besides, it's *our* song, and we agree that you'd be brilliant," Joe said passionately, then cleared his throat.

Billy smiled at his brother's enthusiasm. "Just try it, okay? If it doesn't sound as good as I *know* it will, then we'll find someone else, a'right?"

"But I don't know the words and—"

"Not an issue," Billy said and went to his guitar case. A moment later, he returned with a notebook that had the words written out.

She looked at the brothers, then at Vincent, who was smiling proudly. "Should I?" she asked him, and he gave her a sideways hug.

"This is for you to decide, *bellesa*, though I am thinking you are not losing anything if you are trying it, *sí*?"

"Yeah, I guess so, but I'm nervous," she said and held out her trembling hand.

"What's there ta be nervous about? You're only faffing about with your mates, right?" Joe said, taking her hand and leading her toward a black foam-covered microphone.

"This is crazy!" she said and allowed Billy to place the headphones over her ears. She repositioned them a bit, then gently cleared her throat.

Billy ripped several pages from his notebook and laid them out on the music stand. "Don't want ta hear them being turned over," he explained.

She heard the piano in her ears and looked at Joe, who was sitting at an electric keyboard. He played a scale and said, "Sing this with me."

He went through a few vocal warm-ups, nothing fancy, then Billy joined them, holding his guitar. They traveled together up and down the major scales once, then the minor ones. The brothers were all smiles when they were finished.

"Let's just sing it through once, for practice, a'right?" Joe said and began playing the intro, then Billy joined with the guitar and sang the first line:

Away from you, I'm nothing much; a shell of a man.

Erin couldn't remember when she was supposed to sing or which lines were hers, so there was silence for a moment. "Sorry, was I supposed to—"

"Bugger, that's my fault," Billy said and leaned down to reach a pencil in his guitar case. He then stretched his headphone cord all the way to where she was standing and made a few notes on her lyric sheets. "There, now it should be clearer, and remember, this is just practice, so don't worry if ya mess up, just keep singing, and we'll do it again. No one will be hacked off at you, okay?"

"Okay," she said, smiling sheepishly at him, and he began again.

Away from you… I'm nothing much; a shell of a man.

She sang the next line, which echoed his:

Away from you… our memories I touch… the best I can.

Then they sang together, Billy singing the harmony. It was difficult to keep her composure, remembering David's fear that she'd leave him for Louis. She couldn't dwell on it, though, as Billy was singing his part of the chorus:

He sang, *You are mine…*

She sang, *I am yours.*

They both sang, *We're better together, now and forever.*

The chorus repeated once and ended the second time with,

…again.

Billy began the second verse, then she echoed, same as the chorus. They sang the chorus again, then came to the bridge, where Erin started first:

Don't lose heart… my love and light.
With all that's within me, your loving wife.

Then Billy sang:

I love you more than life itself.
You're the only one who can mend me…
Again

The chorus repeated, then they sang the end tag, Erin starting, then Billy, then both of them together:

I sit in the darkness…
alone in our room…
not crying, a losing fight.
I gaze through the bars…
on my thick, ugly door…
glowing with fluorescent light.
Wishing you were with me,
of all nights, tonight…
Again

Erin swallowed the lump in her throat and waited to say anything, just in case there was more. The room was silent, and when she looked at Vincent, he had his hand over his mouth. "What? Did I do something wrong?" she asked, terror filling her heart at the thought that she might've ruined their beautiful song.

Vincent shook his head and looked at Baz. Erin followed his gaze and saw that the man who was usually full of mirth and fun was now in tears. "Baz!" she exclaimed and took off her headphones, thinking she'd go to him, but then Billy was hugging her, and Joe was wiping his eyes with his sleeve.

"If you didn't record that, Barry, I'll throttle you," Joe said, then stood and joined the hug.

"Do you think me an amateur?" Baz said and smiled. "Of course I did."

"Let's hear it, then," Joe said, but Erin shook her head.

"Um, no, thank you! My self-esteem does not need to be any lower!" she said emphatically.

"Don't be absurd, Erin, that was beautiful!" Billy said and gestured to Baz to play it anyway.

Baz looked at Vincent, who was shaking his head, then he looked at Erin. "I'll not play it if you're serious, but I must agree with Billy; it was fabulous, my dear, truly."

She rolled her eyes and sighed. "Fine, but if it's garbage, you have to promise to turn it off, okay?"

"Agreed," he said, grinning, and began looking at the mixing board in front of him. "Now, I've not adjusted it a'tall; I don't claim to know anything about that, but here it is in its raw form."

They all listened to the piano, then Billy's familiar voice filled the room. Erin screwed up her face, waiting to be disgusted, but surprisingly, when her part began, she didn't hate it. She didn't love it, really, but she could hear something in her voice that blended well with Billy's. When it was finished, everyone in the room looked at her, clearly waiting for her verdict.

"It's okay, I mean, I don't hate it," she said, feeling her cheeks get warm again. "I just hate hearing my own voice."

"You'll get used ta that," Billy said, grinning from ear to ear, almost comically. "I think it's stonking, and it'll be a real success, Erin."

"You mean you wanna play that... I mean... put it on the radio or whatever?"

"Why not? It just needs a bit of work on the soundboard, and it's just as good as anything else we've recorded," he said.

"I don't know—"

"Alright, let's not get worked up or ahead of ourselves, here," Joe said. "Give her a minute ta absorb it, Billy. I agree with him, Erin, but ultimately, it's up ta you, and I, for one, am not gonna push you."

"Uh, I'm a bit tired now. It's a lot to take in, you know?" she said and stood. "I should really talk to David about it, too, before any decisions are made."

"*Sí, bellesa*, you are being very wise. There is no cause for rushing. Come, and Vincent will be helping you to your bed."

"Thanks. Goodnight, guys, thanks for this amazing experience," she said and followed Vincent back to the house.

Chapter Sixty-Six

THE BIG DAY

In the morning, Erin woke feeling refreshed and well-rested, the events of the previous night not yet recalled. There was a knock on her door, so she sat up and told whomever it was that they could come in. Vincent popped his head into the room and smiled at her.

"*Bon dia, bellesa, com estàs?*"

Erin smiled when she saw her friend, who was wearing a flowing, cream-colored, silk dressing gown and carrying a tray with a steaming cup of tea and little cream and sugar bowls. "Good morning," she said and began to get up so she could take the tray from him.

"Do not rise, I will be serving you," he said and carried it to her.

"Thank you, and did you ask how I'm doing? Is that what *com estàs* means?"

"*Sí, bellesa, molt bé!*"

"I feel great this morning, thanks. I like it here, I might just move in," she said with a laugh.

"And you are being always welcomed!" he said and sat on the side of the bed. "Today is being very full, and I am being *molt emocionat!*"

"Emo… I don't know that word," Erin said.

"Oh… allow Vincent to—"

"It sounded like emotional, but that doesn't seem to fit."

"*Sí, bellesa,* happy… *anticipacio.* Are you knowing what I am meaning?"

"Anticipation?"

"*Sí!*"

"Oh! You're very excited?"

"*Sí, bellesa, molt bé! Gràcies,* because you are thinking how to be understanding Vincent. I am loving you too much!" He leaned over and kissed her cheek.

"That should be 'I love you very much,' but I like the way you said it better!" She drank down her tea and sighed. "That's really good tea! Thank you."

"*De res,* though, you are seeming to me troubled," he said.

"I'm nervous. First of all, I don't know what to wear or what to expect. And I really don't want anyone to, I don't know, feel sorry for me or have to talk about how awful it is that David is… where he is, all night. I guess that makes me self-absorbed or something, but I feel a bit lost without David here, you know?"

"*Sí,* I am knowing this feeling," he said and held her hand. "The modeling of pants is not much glamorous; not that only, but I was being much younger when I was doing this. Bazzy is very much famous, more than I, *bellesa.* He is being very much more *còmode en una multitud.*"

"Commode? Uh, to me, that means… toilet," Erin said with a grin.

Vincent laughed and covered his mouth. "He is being a more sociable person than I am being; are you understanding?"

"*Sí,* I understand. And it's funny because I think I'm more outgoing than David, but not when I'm uncomfortable."

"*Sí, ets una persona extrovertida*—Pardon… you are—"

"Extroverted… Yes, that's a good word for it. Will you help me decide what to wear?"

"*Sí.* Come show to me what you've brought."

Erin got out of bed, then she and Vincent went to the large, walk-in closet together. After about half an hour, her stomach began to grumble, so they decided to go down to breakfast and think about the party later.

After breakfast, Vincent excused himself in order to get dressed, so Erin decided to sit in the solarium alone. The guests were meant to start arriving at about four o'clock, so she had time to relax. The day didn't seem overly promising, as thick dark clouds covered the morning sun, threatening rain.

As she sat with a Vogue magazine, sipping a perfect cup of tea, she scanned the room. Green palm trees, tall ferns, and glorious hibiscus flowers in all colors surrounded her, making her feel calm. *It's probably all the extra oxygen in here,* she thought and opened to a random page. She was greeted with two bare breasted girls who were far too young and thin, so she returned it to the table she'd gotten it from.

"Peek-a-boo" she heard nearby, then, *"Hiya, ya a'right?"*

Intrigued, she went in search of the voice. "Hiya, ya a'right?" she repeated and was rewarded with a noise that sounded like a kiss.

"Muah!" the voice said as Erin rounded a large group of shrubs with dark purple flowers on it. Behind a rather dense arrangement of ferns and such, she saw an enormous birdcage, which took up three quarters of the two-story wall on that side of the room. Inside it, she saw at least three parrots, one that was mostly red, one that was a rich, cobalt blue, and one large, white macaw, crowned with a glorious mohawk of yellow feathers atop its head.

"Well, aren't you guys beautiful! Hello," she said, but none of them replied or did much of anything. "Which one of you was just talking to me?" She took a step closer to the white bird, noticing that it was in a part of the cage that was sectioned off from the others.

"Be nice, Paco!" she heard, though it hadn't come from any of the ones she could see. *"Hello! My name is Joe Whitehall, and I'm from the future."*

"Hello, Joe Whitehall," Erin said, thoroughly amused. "Where are you?" She still couldn't see where the voice was coming from.

"Le' me help yeh intae ma home," the voice said, mimicking John Thomas's thick Scottish accent perfectly.

"No, it's too late for me. What's your name?" she asked, playing along.

"Ma name's John Thomas of Fife."

"Ah dinnae understand what ye're tellin' me!" she said and smiled when a small, green and white parrot hopped over to a little perch near her.

"Just do good and help people."

"Joe? Joe—What shall ah do wi' thes?" she finished the dialog from season one, episode two of *Future Explorations*. "Well, aren't you just a clever little thing!"

"Hiya, ya a'right?" it asked.

"I'm very well, thanks. What's your name?"

"Ma name's John Thomas of Fife," it said, and Erin laughed out loud.

"You're adorable!"

The small bird turned all the way around on the perch, then lifted each foot, like it was marching or dancing. It then began whistling the theme song to FE and nodding its head. "Be nice, Paco!" it said, and Erin noticed that the white bird had moved closer to them and was sticking its beak out of the bars on the cage.

The red bird then spoke up, saying, "Peek-a-boo!"

"*Bellesa?*" she heard Vincent call out.

"I'm over here, with the birds."

"*Ooh la la!*" the cobalt blue parrot said. "*Un coup de foudre!*" When Vincent appeared, the bird fluffed up and whistled a cat call. "*Bonjour, mi amor!*"

"*Silenci!*" he said, blushing.

"What was all that?" Erin said, trying to hold back a laugh.

"It is from an advertisement," Baz said as he joined the group.

"*Un coup de foudre!*" the bird said again.

"What does that mean?" Erin asked.

"It is meaning 'a bolt of lightning,'" Vincent said, clearly exasperated.

"It's a way to say, 'love at first sight,'" Baz added. "The advert—Allow me to show you." He took his mobile out of his pocket, but Erin saw how uncomfortable Vincent was, so she placed her hand over the phone.

"That's okay, Baz, maybe another time. I'll just use my imagination," she said.

"*Moltes gràcies, bellesa!*" he said.

"Very well," Baz said and scanned the birdcage. "I see you've found our menagerie."

"Peek-a-boo!" the red bird said.

"Be nice, Paco!" The little green one said, and Baz stepped swiftly away from the cage, just as the white bird stuck its beak out, trying to bite him.

"Thank you, Baby," he said, and went up to a small door in the cage. He put his hand out, and the green parrot hopped lithely onto his first finger.

"Ma name's John Thomas of Fife. Le' me help yeh intae ma home. Just do good and help people," it said, and Erin laughed.

"You've trained him well," she said, and Baz held out his hand toward her. She raised her eyebrows, then held out her finger, allowing the bird to hop onto it. "Its name is Baby?"

"Yes."

"Hello, Baby," she said. "You *really* are adorable!"

Once again, the little bird spun in a circle on her finger, then began nodding its head and whistling the FE theme song. "Joe? Joe—What shall ah do wi' thes?"

"I think I'm going to take you home with me! He sounds just like him!" she said and petted its head with her other hand.

"He is a *she*, and she is a dear!" Baz said, and suddenly it flew off her finger and landed on a high tree branch.

"Oh, no! I'm sorry, Baz! I didn't know—"

"Never mind, dear. She knows how to open the door and will return to her home before long. Now, Paco, on the other hand—"

"Be nice, Paco!" Baby said from above their heads.

"He would peck your eyes out if given the chance. We're in the process of finding a more suitable home for him. I reckon he's jealous of the others, and perhaps a cage doesn't suit him.

"He was rescued in the wild, a broken wing, from what I was told. We've tried to give him love and a good home, but he needs his freedom. A sanctuary may have a place for him soon," Baz explained.

"Ach, yeh poor wee thing!" Erin said.

"*Le potage*, yeh poor wee thing!" Baby said, quoting one of David's lines in season two.

"Muah!" the blue parrot said and giggled like a little girl.

"Aww! Is she mimicking Caroline?"

"*Sí, bellesa*; the most beautiful sound, no?"

"Yes, it's delicious!" she said.

"Indeed," Baz said and took Vincent's hand. "Come, allow us to finish our tour, and then we'll have lunch."

"Oh! I almost forgot; Philip invited me to stop by to see his... I mean your... well, the cottage he's living in," she said and rolled her eyes at herself.

Baz laughed and nodded his approval. "Then you must go to him. This is a good time for it, I'd say."

"Okay, good. I won't be gone long," she said and left the room.

Chapter Sixty-Seven

COTTAGE PIE

Erin headed outside and stood for a moment in the warm sunshine before deciding which direction to go. There were people scurrying around assembling, unpacking, and unloading lorries throughout the gardens. *I should've asked someone where the gamekeeper's cottage was,* she thought after searching for half an hour.

"May I help you, madam?" she heard Philip's voice behind her.

"Well, that depends," she said with a smile as he approached her. "I heard from a pretty reliable source that there was a gamekeeper's cottage on the property. I, in fact, was invited for a visit by the current resident, but I seem to be lost."

"You don't say? I've heard the man's an old curmudgeon, though some say he's a wizard who brews potions that persuade his unsuspecting guests to do his bidding." He looked at her with his eyebrows raised. "Mind you, that's just the local gossip, and I rarely take heed of that sort of chatter."

"A wise man," she said with a grin and fell into step with him. "All the same, I do think it would be rude of me not to stop for a short visit, at least, don't you? I mean, what harm can be done in a half hour or so?"

He stopped and looked at her as if mulling it over. "I've a mind to agree with you, Mrs. Elliott, but for safety's sake, I would recommend a chaperone, someone such as myself, if you're inclined toward my company."

Erin slipped her arm through his, thankful to have found a kindred spirit. "I thought you'd never ask. Lead on, sir."

In a matter of minutes, they were standing outside a picturesque stone cottage, quite similar to the camouflaged recording studio. "Welcome to my home," Philip said with a short bow.

"It's lovely, and your garden is delightful!" she said and stepped up to a rose bush that had more thorns, it seemed, than roses. "This smells like heaven!"

"Thank you, I'm rather proud of it as well, though I admit it was here long before I arrived. And yes, it smells like heaven, but hurts like…"

"H-E- double hockey sticks?" Erin supplied.

Philip chuckled. "I reckon that's one way to say it. Do come inside and have a cuppa with me? I may even have a pork pie, if you'd care for a nibble?"

"I'll give you a solid yes for the cuppa and a tentative maybe on the pie. I don't think I've ever had one, so I'll have to decide once I've seen it, if that's acceptable?"

"Quite so. Come, and I'll give you a tour," he said. He approached the old wooden door and opened it, then stepped aside, allowing her to enter first.

The first thing she noticed was the smell, like the attic in an old house where the wood had been too hot and too cold for many years. She closed her eyes, took a deep breath, and sighed. "Yes, I could live here, though I'd probably get used to it and wouldn't notice it anymore, which would be a shame." When she opened her eyes, he was looking at her, clearly amused. "Sorry, it's the smell."

"I thought as much, and I had the very same reaction when I first came here. The trick is to spend a lot of time out of doors, that way, when you return, the scent is still there to greet you. You see, I knew you'd be enchanted with her, and you've hardly even opened your eyes to see her. Now, I'll put the kettle on, and you may explore."

"Okay, thanks," she said and watched him step up to an enormous stone fireplace, which took up at least a third of the small building. It had a small pile of coals smoldering at the back, and he lifted a black iron tool with a long handle to stir it up. He added a few rough, black lumps of coal, and a lively little fire blazed before them.

On a swinging hook, there was a blackened kettle, which he lifted and then went to the small sink under a lovely old window with the waviest glass panes she'd ever seen on the outer wall of the cottage. He filled the kettle with tap water, then turned, clearly surprised she was still standing in the same spot. "Go on… explore," he said, and it seemed he flushed a bit under her gaze.

"Oh, I will, but it's a small house, and I'd like to watch you for a moment. It's a bit like stepping back in time, you know?"

"Yes, I do know," he said as he replaced the kettle onto the hook and swung it over the flames. "Ah, perhaps you'd prefer a tour?"

"Perhaps. May I help you set up the table? Where do you keep your mugs?" She turned and saw them set out on a small shelf next to the sink. There were only two of them, so she went to retrieve them while he filled a small pitcher with cream that he'd taken from a tiny refrigerator camouflaged to look like a lower cabinet.

"I feel like I'm a small child, delighted to be having a 'real' tea party!" she exclaimed, then felt her cheeks grow warm.

"I am a bit mad, like the hatter, some might say," he said and set the cream and sugar on the small wooden table, which seemed as though it was also original to the cottage. He then returned to the refrigerator, took out a plate covered with a tea towel, and set it on the table.

"I wish David were here to see this," she said as she took a step back to admire the setting.

Philip had just begun filling a well-used, plain brown teapot with hot tap water. He turned to her and set it on the counter. "I've not seen much coverage of the trial, but I have noticed many headlines in the shops over the past few months.

"I've also watched Vincent…er, Mr. Thompson, in tears over the whole affair. There were nefarious workings behind the scenes, I reckon, and things simply *must* come right for you!" he said passionately. "There's nothing else for it! If not, then I've lost faith in the whole legal system."

"Yeah," she said simply. "Thanks."

He turned back to the sink and opened a cupboard, lifting a tin off a lower shelf. The kettle began to whistle, so he poured out the hot tap water from the teapot, opened the tin, and began spooning the tea into it.

"Loose leaf tea? Well, that's a nice touch."

"Yes, that is why I employ them; supermarket tea bags just don't have the same charm. I'm sure you've noticed I prefer the old-fashioned ways. Perhaps I'll even read your tea leaves when we're through," he said and laughed at her wide eyes. Then, he went to the kettle, where he used a small, thick cloth to remove it and began filling the teapot with boiling water.

Erin lifted the corner of the tea towel and saw two small, round pastries sitting on a plate. "Oh, these look nice," she said and took the towel off them. "Other than pork, what's in them?"

"Hmm, I'll look at the label," he said and pulled a box from the recycling bin under the sink. "Fortified wheat flour, water, pork lard, potato starch, salt, pork fat, pasteurized free-range egg, pork gelatin, white pepper, and black pepper."

"Pork gelatin? That doesn't sound very appetizing," she said and couldn't help but scrunch up her nose. "And you say it's good?"

Philip laughed and shrugged. "Now, I'm from Melton Mowbray, where they know how to make a pie, but these'll do in a pinch. However, if you don't fancy them, you may decline to clean your plate without any sore feelings on my part."

"Okay then, it's a deal," she said and shook the man's hand. "So, tell me about living here… what's Claude like? He seems a bit… formal, I'd say."

"Oh, he's a'right. He's not a—"

"Kindred spirit?" she suggested.

Philip laughed. "Precisely."

A few minutes later, the tea was ready, so they sat, and he poured out. They talked and ate and drank their tea. Erin liked the pie, though she scraped the gelatin off the best she could. When they were done, she insisted on helping clear the table and do the washing up.

When that was sorted, she asked for the grand tour and wasn't disappointed. The house was charming and had several quirks that delighted her. As they returned to the kitchen, there was a scratching at the door. Philip opened it, and a beautiful grey and ginger cat pranced into the house, as if it was the master of the estate.

"Mrs. Elliott, it is my great pleasure to introduce you to Churchill, our resident mouse hunter."

Erin smiled and bent to pet it. "Hello, Churchill," she said, admiring the feline's long, pure white whiskers. Clearly, he wasn't shy and purred loudly as she scratched behind his ears. She stood, and Churchill wound himself around her legs, rubbing his face against them. "Oh, I like you!" The cat looked up at her when she addressed him and meowed as if to say, 'What's not to love?'

"He's a… what word is it you used? Kindred spirit? Yes, he is that for me. We often sit of an evening, watching the fire. He listens to all my complaints and never speaks a word of it to anybody."

"Meow!" Churchill said rather loudly.

"Ah, he's hungry. I reckon he smells our pies and wants one of his own." Philip went to a cupboard and took out two small dishes. One, he filled with tap water, and the other was filled with dry cat food from a box he took from under the sink.

"Meow-ow."

"You're quite welcome, my friend," Philip said.

The two adults stood, watching the cat eat for a moment, and smiled at each other. "Will you be attending the party?" Erin asked.

"No, it isn't really my sort of thing," he said and glanced at his watch. "As a matter of fact, I really should be preparing to fetch the guests who are staying at the local inns and hotels. I'm ever so glad you've come to see this old man; you've truly brightened my day." His smile was warm and sincere.

"Truthfully, I'm not looking forward to the party. This visit has helped take my mind off it, and I can't thank you enough."

"I'm glad of that, now please allow me to see you out." Two steps later, he was opening the door and warm afternoon sunlight was streaming into the small cottage. She stepped outside and waved before heading back to the house.

Erin stepped into the house and headed to the library. She'd only been there about half an hour when Vincent entered the room carrying a long mass of what appeared to be clothes covered with dry cleaning bags. "Come, *bellesa*, let us find Bazzy," he said and took her by the hand.

They traveled through the house, Vincent pulling her up stairs and down hallways. Finally, they reached his bedroom. "Bazzy, darling, come, I am wishing to show to you—"

"I'm in my dressing room; help me decide what to wear," Baz said, so Vincent pulled her into the large closet filled with clothing and costumes both hung and displayed on the walls and shelves.

"Good night nurse!" Erin said when she saw huge, framed portraits… nudes… of Vincent scattered around the walls of the room and then Baz, only half dressed in a plain white t-shirt, black socks pulled up to his knees, and tighty-whities. She turned on her heels, feeling the heat of her embarrassment overwhelming her. "I'm sorry!"

"Never mind, Erin, I reckon you've seen men in their pants before, no need to be ashamed," Baz said kindly.

"Uh, yeah, I have, but I've not seen Vincent naked before!"

"Now, now, there is nothing shameful about a naked body. Come and look at my specimen!" he said and took her by the shoulders, turning her around to gaze at the photos.

"Bazzy! She is not wishing to—"

Erin looked at the images, blushing horribly, though she could see the beauty of his form, so she tried to relax. "It's okay. You are a very beautiful man, Vincent, I must say," she said and smiled at him. "Baz is right, you are an especial specimen."

The younger man waved his hand in much the same way she'd seen David do to dismiss something. "*Anat l'olla!*"

Erin looked at him sideways. "What does that mean?"

"You are being insane," he said, though he was smiling.

"Ah, you're being humble, I see… *bell-esa*," she said teasingly, and hugged him. "Speaking of beauty, I'm gonna find Caroline!"

"You'll not find her, I'm afraid," Baz said. "She has been taken to my parents' for the event."

"Bummer! Oh well, I guess I'll go back to my room and get dressed."

"I am joining you soon," Vincent said.

"Okay," she said and left the room.

"*Oh, Bazzy! I am loving her too much!*" she heard him say.

Chapter Sixty-Eight

MEETING HUGH

Just over an hour later, Erin was dressed, her hair was styled, and her makeup was done, with Vincent's help of course. It was then time for him to get ready, so he left the room after a kiss on both cheeks. As the time grew nearer, she began to seriously dread the party, so she dawdled and took her time, putting away her makeup and the clothing that had been tossed here and there.

She began to read the book she'd had in her hand when Vincent pulled her away from the library, thus borrowing it. It was too hard to concentrate, so after she realized she'd stopped reading and was staring across the room at the dressing table, she put it down and began pacing. Eventually, there was nothing left to do, and it was time for her to leave the sanctuary of her bedroom to join the party.

She checked her hair and makeup in the mirror again, then reluctantly stepped out into the hallway. As she approached the stairs, she met Claude coming up. "Hello, Claude," she said.

"Oh, Mrs. Erin, I've been sent to find you," he said.

"Congratulations, here I am. Are there a lot of people here yet?"

"Oh, yes, quite a few guests have arrived. Mr. Thompson has been waiting for you, he is quite eager to introduce you to his friends. Please, allow me to lead you outside."

"Hmm, yes, and that's what I'm *not* looking forward to. Isn't there a secret room somewhere in this great big house where I could hide?" she said, only half kidding.

"Telling the truth, I know of two, but the garden is so lovely, Mrs. Erin! I am sure you will love it. I should not say this, but I overheard Mr. Vincent and Mr. Thompson as they were preparing for the event. They chose many of the decorations expressly for you and are hoping you will be delighted. If you do not come, Mr. Vincent will be heartbroken. Please, do reconsider and do not ask me to hide you," he said, sounding serious, though there was a gleam in his eyes.

Erin considered him for a moment, then sighed dramatically. "Well, if you put it that way. The very last thing I would want to do is break Vincent's heart. I suppose you may lead me to my host, and I'll just have to suffer through it."

Claude's face lit up in a stunning smile that made her do a double take. "I am pleased to hear it, Mrs. Erin."

"Why, Claude, where have you been hiding that smile all this time! You should bring it out and wear it more often," she said and then covered her mouth. "Oh, that might have sounded rude, I didn't mean it that way."

"I understand, but I try to remain professional at all times. You could say that I reserve it for special occasions. However, I shall wear it especially for you whilst you are a guest, if that would please you?" he said as they arrived at the door that led to the side garden.

"It would please me very much, thank you. Now, what would please me even more is if you could somehow give me a pep talk. I'm a bundle of nerves."

"I am not aware of anything *I* could say to help you, I'm afraid," he said with his brows knit.

"Well, then how about showing me that smile again. I think that could make the meekest person brave."

The young man's eyes gleamed again, and he gave her a short bow. "As you wish, Mrs. Erin." His face then lit up as his lips parted and turned upward, revealing a neat row of straight white teeth. He opened the door for her and motioned for her to go ahead of him.

"Thank you, Claude, I am—" she began as she turned back to speak to him, but the door was now closed, and Claude was nowhere to be seen. "Sneaky!"

"I've been called worse," said a familiar voice to her right.

She turned and saw Hugh Jackman smiling at her. Her face began to burn, and she didn't know what to say, but she couldn't just stand there like an idiot. "Uh… I doubt that," she managed, though it made her cheeks so warm they hurt.

His smile was disarming as he held out his hand. "I don't believe we've met, have we?"

Erin lifted her hand, expecting him to shake it, but he lifted it and lightly kissed it instead. "Uh… thank you, I mean, damn, now I'm all flustered. That's no fair! Sometimes I think you guys do that on purpose to gain the advantage. I'm Erin Elliott, and you are?" she said, then laughed, unable to follow through.

"I… am delighted to meet you, Mrs. Elliott. Hugh Jackman, at your service." He still held her hand as he bowed slightly.

"Oh, you're charming, aren't you? But I like it. It's a pleasure to meet you, Mr. Jackman, and you may call me Erin if you wish."

"Then I shall. I presume you're David Elliott's wife, then?" he asked.

Just hearing his name made her want to cry, wishing he were with her. "Yes," she said softly.

"I've not had the pleasure of meeting him, but I would like to one day. Oh, I hope talking about him doesn't upset you," he said, looking uneasy.

"No, not upset. I just wish he was here, that's all. I'm sure he'd be chuffed to bits to meet you, *Mr. Jackman*," she said, smiling.

"Yes, well, you may call me Hugh, if you please," he said.

"Then I shall. Have you seen Baz? I guess he's looking for me."

"Truthfully, I've only just arrived, but if you don't mind my company, we could search for him together."

"How could I refuse," she said, not believing her luck. "We should make that happen, by the way."

"If I knew what you were referring to, I'm sure I would agree," he said as he held out his arm for her to take.

She linked her arm in his, and they began walking toward the stage and the enormous screen that was halfway through showing season one, episode one of *Future Explorations*. "You said you'd like to meet David. It might be a while, but I'm sure we could squeeze you into his schedule… eventually," she said and couldn't fake a real smile. It was then she noticed that the crowds of people were turning and staring as they passed by.

"Good, I'll have my people contact your people. Well, look at that," he said and nodded toward the al fresco dining area. Long rows of tables stood under canopies of gossamer thin mosquito netting woven with twinkling fairy lights.

Each table was draped with black tablecloths that reached to the ground, then again by sparkling fabrics of iridescent blue, rose gold, and finally, pale yellow. The centers of each table were covered with vases and arrangements of exotic flowers that ranged in color from white, sky blue, yellow, blazing orange and red, and dark blue and purple, surrounded by sumptuous, shimmering netting and luxurious, extravagantly beautiful fabrics.

The trees above stretched out their branches and held gleaming orbs that dangled at varying heights through holes in the gossamer ceiling. Each fixture was radiating with just enough light to keep things intimate and still see everything clearly. "Oh, wow! That's stunning! I've never seen anything like it before!" she said, wanting to get closer, though she knew she'd have to wait.

"Neither have I," Hugh said.

"Aww, come on! You want me to believe that you don't dine like that every night?"

He laughed and raised an eyebrow. "Not that I wouldn't enjoy it, but it would be a lot of work and upkeep, don't you agree?"

"Yeah, I guess so. The delight of it would wear off eventually, too." She sighed, wishing she could take a million photos so she could show David someday. "They would never do it justice," she said under her breath.

"What was that?" Hugh asked as they continued toward Baz, who had a throng of people surrounding him.

"Oh, nothing, just talking to myself." It was then she finally perceived the theme of the surrounding decor. The garden was transformed into a scene from her wildest imagination. It took a moment, but as they walked, she noticed that it was changing, slowly transitioning from darkness to bright... almost daylight before her eyes.

"Sunset to sunrise in reverse!" she said, and Hugh looked at her questioningly again. "The theme of the party... just like the invitations.

They… made us travel backward in time, from midnight, to sunrise. Each envelope and card got brighter and—Didn't you notice?"

"Oh, well, I guess that escaped me. You're right, though, it seems to be getting closer to daylight, even as we speak! Oh, my," he said, pointing toward the stage. "It seems there's a photo op over there."

Erin gazed in the direction he was pointing and gasped. She saw two large cut-outs, one of Baz as Joe Whitehall, and one of David as John Thomas Fife. A man and woman were posing next to them, and someone was taking their photo. "Wow, that's surreal!" she said, not having any other words for it.

"Erin! Hugh! I'm so pleased to see you! Please, come closer!" Baz said, waving his hands about as he spoke.

Hugh smiled at her, and she shrugged. "I guess there's nothing for it," she said as the crowd seemed to envelop them.

Erin couldn't really get a word in edgewise while Barry gushed over her, even mentioning that he had recently learned of her 'exceptional' singing voice, which annoyed her a bit. Finally, after nearly an hour of standing there, she noticed Vincent speaking to someone by what appeared to be a refreshment table. She was forced to excuse herself twice, since Baz continued to pull her into his conversation.

"Listen, Baz, I'm parched. I need a cuppa and a hug from your husband. Please excuse me… for real this time," she said, to much laughter.

"If I must," he said as she made her way out of the throng surrounding him.

When she was free, she took a deep breath and checked herself over to make sure she was still in one piece. "Well, I'm glad that's over," Hugh said from behind her.

"You can say that again! I'm happy to see you've escaped as well."

"I saw my chance and took it. Now, I'm truly not trying to follow you, but it appears we are, once more, headed in the same direction. Mind if I join you?"

"Don't mind at all, and I'm glad for the company," she said and took his offered arm. *Good night nurse! I can't believe I'm here* and *on the arm of Hugh Jackman! This is insane! I'd never have believed it a few years ago!*

"Vincent! It's so good to see you again!" Hugh said as they approached.

"I am very much pleased to see you have met our especial guest!" Vincent said and accepted the air kisses on both cheeks from the tall, handsome man before him.

"I have, and she's been good company," he said, sounding sincere.

"Hugh!" an older man who had a long beard, a bushy mustache, and scraggly eyebrows, all in pure white said.

"Walter!" he said to the man, then turned back to them. "Please excuse me for a moment."

They watched him walk away, then Erin turned to Vincent. "You look stunning!" He was wearing white linen gauchos and a flowing silk blouse that made him look like a real-life angel.

He blushed and waved his hand dismissively. "*Moltes gràcies, bellesa*, as do you."

"Now, do you need anything, Vincent? Is there any way I can help you? I don't really feel much like mingling, and though there is nothing I love more than seeing my dear husband's face, it's bittersweet now, you know?"

"*Bellesa*, you are *amable, amic meu… perdona'm…* I am meaning you are kind of heart, my friend, but the party is being for yourself, and you should not be *preocupat…* in concern because of me. Are you understanding?"

"Yes, I understand," Erin said, though she thought having something to do might help her get through the night.

"You are feeling lonely, yes? But you are finding a friend, no?" Vincent said and smiled at Hugh, who was laughing with the man named Walter.

"Yes, I have, but… I'm not going to burden him with my company all night. He didn't come here to babysit a fat, middle-aged—"

"Nonsense! Do not be giving to yourself so little value!"

Hugh returned to them and said, "So sorry. I haven't seen old Walter since he had dark hair! What did I miss?" He smiled at them, and Erin shook her head.

"Nothing much. I was just going to find something to nibble, though I still haven't quenched my need of a cuppa," she said. "Please excuse me."

Vincent put his finger up, then turned and beckoned to someone Erin couldn't see. Within moments, a young man with a boyish face, who was wearing a kilt in John Thomas's tartan pattern, appeared, holding on one hand a gleaming etched silver tray with a full tea set atop it, complete with two delicate china cups and saucers, linen napkins with thread crochet around the edges, and silver utensils. A small china plate held several chocolate digestive biscuits, as well.

"Please follow Leandro, and he will be pouring out for you both," Vincent said in a way that seemed to defy any arguments.

"Wow, he's perfected his mother voice, hasn't he?" she said to Hugh, just loud enough for Vincent to hear her as they fell in behind Leandro.

"I'd say he has, though a cup of tea would hit the spot," Hugh said.

They were led to a round bistro table with a bright white tablecloth covered with silk chiffon the color of sunset. Hugh pulled out Erin's chair and then sat across from her while Leandro wordlessly laid everything out, then poured. The tea was dark and steaming as it filled each cup.

The fragrance of the fine English brew filled the air, and Erin's mouth began to water. She received the offered cream and sugar, then waited for Hugh to be served. "Thank you, Leandro. I really appreciate your good service," she said sincerely, making the boy's cheeks flush, then he nodded and walked away.

Hugh grinned and used the small, polished silver teaspoon to stir his tea. "Well done, remembering his name. I try, but sometimes it's beyond me."

"I was a waitress when I was a teenager, and my supervisor's name was Leandro. Funny how things stick, isn't it?" she said while stirring her tea, then she lifted it to her lips and couldn't contain the soft moan that escaped her. "Oh, this is good! I'm going to have to find out the brand so I can have it at home."

"Would you like one?" he said and used the silver serving tongs to point to the plate of biscuits.

"Yes, please." He lifted one and was about to set it on her saucer, but she held out her hand, and he placed it on her palm. "Thank you, Hugh… oh dear, that's a tough one, isn't it?" *Kind of like Huge Ackman*, she thought.

"Yes, similar to Huge Ackman, right?" he said, and she nearly choked on the bite of digestive she'd just bitten off. They sat for quite a while, laughing and being comfortable together. It turned out they had a similar sense of humor and talked easily with one another.

Erin excused herself to use the ladies and headed to the house. At the side door, she heard Vincent and he sounded quite upset. "I am still not approving, Bazzy!"

"I don't understand why you're so upset, darling. My scheme has come together quite nicely, I'd say," Baz said.

"This is a deception of our especial friend, and—"

"It's not deception, and we've already been over this. I want our friend to have a smashing good time, and I'm sure that if she were expected to stand around... twiddling her thumbs, she would be quite miserable. There is no harm in asking him to—"

Erin stepped around the back of a tall fountain made with large stones. "Okay, what's going on?" she said before it dawned on her. "Actually, I can guess what it is... it's Hugh, isn't it? Holy Moses, you asked him to befriend me, didn't you? Oh... this is not good! I've been talking away like an idiot, and he's sat there the whole time having to entertain me! Good night nurse, that's just—"

"*Deu meu, bellesa*!" Vincent said, taking her hand and kissing it gently.

Baz stood behind him, looking contrite. "It wasn't meant—"

"I... have to go," Erin said, feeling betrayed. She turned and walked away, wanting to escape. As she neared the house, she stopped, having to catch her breath, and placed her fist over her heart, which was beating fast.

"Erin? Are you alright?" Hugh said from behind her.

She stopped and stood for a moment, not sure if she wanted to run away or turn and either confront him or apologize for what he'd had to put up with all night. A warm hand rested on her shoulder, and she closed her eyes. "I'm so embarrassed. I found out about what Baz asked you to do, and I'm really sorry you had to—"

"Ah, I see. Please, listen to me." He took his hand off her shoulder and stood in front of her. She shook her head but didn't say anything. "Yes, perhaps Baz's plan wasn't very well thought out, but he was only trying to be helpful. Anyway, it's not what you're most likely thinking; he didn't ask that I watch over you or keep you entertained."

Erin looked at him sideways and raised her eyebrow. "I'm not sure I believe you," she said softly, then hung her head and stared at the dark green grass at her feet. "I feel so foolish to think that *you* would just decide to hang out with *me*."

"The plan was for us to be introduced and then, if I saw you looking glum, I was encouraged to approach you, that's all, I promise," he said. "I wasn't expecting to meet as we did, but I'm glad it worked out that way. I've enjoyed spending the evening with you. You're smart and funny and at no time have I wished to be elsewhere. David is a lucky man," he continued and waited for her to look up at him.

"How do I know you're not just saying that because you're a nice guy and to spare your friend my wrath?" she said, though he was so sincere it was difficult not to believe him.

"Honestly, I think he deserves a bit of your wrath. I told him it was a bad idea, but you know Baz, he wouldn't be dissuaded."

"Yeah, I do know that about him, but, honestly, you don't have to keep an eye out for me. You are hereby relieved of your mission," she said.

"Eh, I'll keep that in mind, but what do you say we get our photos taken with John Thomas and Joe?"

Erin laughed and looked up into his smiling face. He raised his eyebrows as if asking again and nodded his head in the direction of the cut-outs. "Thanks, I'd love to," she said, and accepted the hug he offered.

Crossing the expansive lawn, they began to see several more *Future Explorations* photo ops and games. There was a cut-out of John Thomas as he held a dying Joe that you could put your head through. Erin was Joe, of course, since Hugh was taller.

One of the best games was a bean bag toss shaped like the time travel device with a tall screen that wrapped around the back of it. Each hole the bag landed in caused a different place in time, in the form of scenes from the show, to show up on the screen. If it landed in a blue hole, you went forward, and in a green one, you traveled back.

Chapter Sixty-Nine

TIME TO EAT

Erin and Hugh shared a lot of laughs but weren't tied to each other, often parting for this reason or that, though they did spend much of the evening together. Hugh had just excused himself to use the loo, when on one end of the garden, the sunrise side, with its decor in shades of misty blue-white, pale yellow, and sand, a cock began to crow.

She was standing toward the center, or midday, which was a mixture of several shades of blue, though there were smatterings of white, seeming to indicate clouds. There, she heard something similar to a cartoon-like whistle that reminded her of an old-fashioned way to signal lunchtime in a factory. Finally, on the other end, the sunset side, where everything faded from blue, pink, salmon, and rose, then climaxed into red, orange, dark, dusky purple and blue, she heard a triangle, the kind used to call cowboys in for their grub.

She was then herded, as were the other guests, toward the dining tables by the handsome, young, barely clothed, male staff. More staff held the mosquito netting aside while the guests entered the dream-like bower. To her delight, her name card was in the purple and orange place settings of sunset.

She didn't see Hugh anywhere, but the seat next to her was empty, so she figured he'd be arriving soon, if Baz had anything to do with it. Trying not to be too obvious, she eyed the name card on the adjacent plate and, as she expected, his name was on it. Before long, he and a few other stragglers arrived, and that's when the fun began.

Those already in their seats watched the show, while the latecomers went from seat to seat, trying to locate their names. It didn't take any time at all for

Hugh to spot her and approach the empty chair, then he played at reading the card and turned away as if his name wasn't there. "Well then, if you'd rather sit by old Walter, I guess I can't blame you," she said with mock diffidence.

"Not a chance," he said and returned to his place.

When everyone was seated, Baz stood, and the crowd grew quiet. "I'd like to welcome everyone to our little soirée and thank you for coming. I do hope you are enjoying yourselves," he said and waited for a response. He was not disappointed, as a cheer arose from his guests to the affirmative.

"I won't bore you with a long, drawn-out oration, but suffice it to say, I'm thankful for another year in which to celebrate the masterpiece that is *Future Explorations*. Now, as the staff begin to serve you, our Vincent would like to say a few words." He took Vincent's hand and held it as the tall, stately, handsome man, who still had his boyish, chiseled looks, stood. He kissed him gently on the cheek, then took his seat.

"*Bona nit*, my friends!" he began.

Everyone responded with, "Good evening," as if it had been planned.

"*El temps és or.*"

"Your time is worth our money!" the crowd said in unison, making Erin glance around her as if she'd missed the memo.

Hugh looked at her and laughed at her bewilderment. "I'll explain it to you as we go," he whispered. "That one meant, 'time is money.'"

"Right," she said.

"*L'àguila no caça mosques.*"

"None of us are eagles, we are all flies," was the response from the congregation.

"Eagles don't catch flies," he said, but she shook her head. "Means something like the rich, don't bother with the poor."

"O—kay," she said, but Vincent was talking again. He said a few more things she didn't understand, but the guests laughed and responded to each. Hugh didn't even bother to explain and shrugged his shoulders when she looked at him.

Finally, he said, "*La burla deixar-la quan més plau,*" and everyone clapped, including Hugh.

"It means, 'leave them wanting more.' He's nearly finished."

Vincent then raised his glass and his other hand, signaling everyone to stand. The guests stood, raised their glasses, and said in unison, *"Dei memor, gratus amicis* – Mindful of God, grateful to friends. Salut!"

"Wow, that was something, wasn't it?" she said softly, and Hugh laughed.

"That's precisely what I thought the first time I attended one of these. I reckon after a few years of having to explain himself, people began to remember what he was trying to say. It was also a way to make him feel better about not being able to communicate very well in English."

"That's really nice. I hope I'm able to attend often enough that I'll remember how to respond."

"I hope so, too, and soon David will be able to join you."

"Yeah, that'll be nice. You know, he never even knew about this. All those years of invitations, and Susannah never told him," she said, her heart aching.

"Really? That's incredible! Every year, at the end of the night, Baz got into the habit of giving a final toast, saying, 'To all of you, and perhaps next year, to David as well.'"

Erin had to swallow a sob at the thought of their friend's persistence. "Tell me something else… please, or I'll—" she said panic-stricken, knowing she was a millimeter away from breaking down.

"Oh, yes, alright. Did you know that they have a trivia contest?" he said.

"They do? That sounds like fun," she said, already feeling a bit further from the edge.

"It is. Actually, it should be starting soon."

Indeed, about halfway through the meal, the guests were entertained with *Future Explorations* trivia. Erin felt as though she shouldn't be allowed to participate since people might think she had an unfair advantage. Baz seemed to anticipate her thoughts and called her out, telling her he'd better see her hand raised just as often as everyone else's.

For each correct answer, the person's name was added to a large, fancy goldfish bowl. At the end of five rounds, Vincent drew three names. The winners were directed to a large table, piled high with wrapped gifts.

Erin's name was picked, so she chose a small flat package and went back to her seat blushing. Baz made everyone open their prize, though she would rather have waited. A woman named Jade won a scarf in the same tartan as John Thomas.

A man named Carl won soap on a rope with an image of Joe Whitehall dying in John Thomas's arms. The tag revealed that as it was used, the soap turned red, like poor Joe's blood. There was a consensus in the crowd of being grossed out, but Carl seemed good-humored about it.

Erin felt her face burn as she unwrapped hers and found a full-length satin body pillowcase. It had an image of David as John Thomas on it, shirtless and kilted. Everyone laughed and applauded, even Erin, though crawling under the table had never been more tempting.

Hugh was kind enough not to tease her, and she put the thing under her chair, wanting to forget about it. They were served limoncello soaked pound cake with lemon and lavender flavored gelato for dessert, which was stunning.

After such a lovely meal, she was feeling a bit tired. "Listen, I'm going to rest here for a while, why don't you go ahead and mingle. People are going to talk if you never leave my side—Well, they probably already are, but I think you should do your own thing for a while. I'll be sure to find you if I'm feeling forlorn," she said to Hugh with a laugh.

"Well, if I'm such poor company, I suppose—"

"Ha ha ha. You know that's not what I'm saying."

His face lit up with a sweet smile, and he stood, laying his napkin over his empty dish. "Okay then, I will see you later," he said and walked away, scanning the crowds.

"Later," she said softly and sat under the canopy of sparkling lights, trying to absorb the atmosphere. The party was a hit, and she was having a really great time, but what she'd hoped would be a respite from constantly missing David turned into an ever-present reminder of his absence. She took out her phone and wrote an email to David, telling him all the things that had happened that night, knowing he wouldn't get to read it for a year and a half.

Dear David,

I'm at Baz and Vincent's party. We've just finished the most amazing dinner, and I am missing you desperately! I've met a new friend; someone who says he'd love to meet you someday. I can't believe that I am able to call Hugh Jackman my friend!

Baz had this dumb idea that he should befriend me and then, if it looked like I was feeling forlorn, he was meant to come cheer me up. It didn't work that way, and I found out about it, but Hugh said he was enjoying my company. I don't know, I feel like a fish out of water, you know? I'm having a good time, and I guess I wouldn't be if it weren't for Hugh, but I miss you and I feel like everyone is staring at me. They probably aren't, but it just feels that way.

I met Caroline, their daughter, and she's one of the most beautiful humans I've ever seen! Oh, and they have parrots that quote the show! It's a hoot! I can't wait until you can join me, I'll have so much more fun with you here!

Anyway, I just wanted to share this with you. I love you!

Your loving wife,

Erin

Your loving wife... those words were in the song, weren't they? Was that a coincidence, she thought.

Chapter Seventy

UNWELCOME ATTENTION

Erin was about to stand and quietly head to her room when she felt a warm hand on her shoulder. Turning, she saw Billy Joplin smiling at her.

His smile faded when he saw her face. "Are ya okay, Erin? You seem so sad," he said and took the now vacant seat beside her.

She was taken aback by his comment and tears sprang, unwelcome to her eyes. "I'm okay. I just can't seem to get away from… everything, you know?"

Billy took her hand in his and squeezed it gently. "Yeah, I can see how this party might do that to ya, but I've come ta help distract you." Erin dabbed her eyes with her napkin, then looked at him and cocked her head to the side, waiting for him to continue.

Clearly, he thought she would say something, so he floundered. "Ah, well, Baz asked Joe ta have me…"

"You had me at 'distract you,' Billy," she said with a grin. "What did Baz ask Joe to have you say to me, then?"

"Nothing."

"Nothing? Well then, you've done a good job, though, technically you did ask me if I was alright… no, you said 'okay,' didn't you?" She raised her eyebrows as if she'd caught him doing something wrong, but she couldn't hold it and laughed.

"Ha! The joke's on you, as I wasn't meant ta *tell* you anything!" He stuck out his tongue at her and stood. "Baz asked Joe ta have me bring you to the stage. Now, if you'd be so kind as to permit me ta do so—"

"Uh, why do they want me at the stage?" she asked warily.

Billy rolled his eyes and held out his hand to help her up. "I reckon you'll find out once you're there. My instructions were clear and didn't involve explanations."

Erin sighed, and though the privacy of her room and softness of her bed were calling to her, she stood and allowed him to lead her toward the stage, which was beside the enormous movie screen. Season three, episode five was halfway over, which was the second to last in the series. It was clear Baz had chosen to skip any episodes he didn't deem adequate for the occasion.

"Erin, darling!" Baz said dramatically when he saw her. "I hope you're having a pleasant night?"

"Of course I am, the party is amazing," she said, though she knew she didn't sound convincing.

"You're fooling nobody, my dear, but that's about to change. Billy, please find—Ah, Joe, you've returned just in time," he said to the tall, slender man who'd just stepped onto the low stage which held a grand piano, guitar, and loads of things like monitors, microphones, music stands, and speakers. He jumped down and joined them.

"Uh, what's this about?" Erin asked, suddenly realizing why she'd been summoned. "If you think I'm gonna... sing for these people—"

"Now, Erin, you and your lovely voice rose to the occasion last night—" Baz began as she shook her head vehemently in protest.

"But Erin—" Billy began, then Joe put his hand on his brother's shoulder.

"A'right, now, there's no way we're gonna be able to convince her unless..." he said and acted as though he were thinking hard.

After a long moment of waiting, Erin rolled her eyes and crossed her arms. "Alright you, out with it," she said, crossing her arms and tapping her first finger on her bicep impatiently. A wily grin spread across the handsome man's face, and before she could protest, he hopped back onto the stage, went to the piano, and sat on the bench.

He tapped the microphone gently to see if it was live. "Joe Joplin, you come back—" she began, but he'd already started talking.

"Excuse me, everyone..." he began.

"Joe! Joe, don't," Billy said to deaf ears.

"We have a special guest here with us tonight…"

Erin felt her stomach drop and looked at Billy in disbelief as Joe continued talking to any guest who would listen. "I'm sorry, Erin," Billy said, also clearly shocked. "I didn't know he was gonna do this."

Baz stepped up to her and turned her toward his guests. "These people are your friends, Erin. What I heard last night should be shared, don't you agree? You said yourself that you didn't hate it, remember? Now, it's just you, Billy, and Joe, and I'm asking you to share your talent with my friends and yours. Won't you agree to it, please?"

She felt cornered and coerced and was about to tell him she wouldn't, when Joe turned to her and began playing the melody to the song they'd written for her. "She has a truly amazing voice, and we've written this for her and her husband, David, who couldn't be here. Please give a warm welcome to Mrs. Erin Elliott!"

Her face was hot as she stood there, all eyes on her. *You used to want to be a famous singer, didn't you? Just do it!* she thought. Baz took her hand as he stepped up on the stage and gently pulled it toward him.

She pulled her hand away and instead, went around to the small set of stairs toward the back of the structure. When she stepped toward him, he had a microphone in his hand and gave it to her. "Oh, uh, hi," she said, as it was all she could think of to say.

The guests laughed and most returned the greeting. Someone near the back whistled loudly and a few people cheered, making her laugh in spite of herself. A chant began and swiftly grew, 'Er-in, Er-in, Er-in,' until Billy stood beside her and put his hands up to stop them. He then pulled a tall stool up to the far side of the piano and motioned for her to sit.

"I'm so sorry," he whispered. "Thank you!"

"Let's sing one we all know," Joe said, easily changing the tune and began playing one of their best-known songs.

Erin sang along, though she didn't use the microphone. As that song ended, he played another, and Billy convinced her to sing into the mic. She did it, though her hand trembled and her voice shook. It helped that the crowd was also singing along.

Finally, Joe nodded to Billy and stopped playing as his brother began the song he'd written for her and David. Joe reached a sheet of paper to her with the words, color coded in dark pink and blue. "Yours is in pink," he whispered with a grin.

Erin shook her head, though she couldn't help but smile at him. Billy sang the first part of the first verse and Erin's mouth became so dry she thought she wouldn't be able to open it at all. Somehow, she managed to sing her part, then the chorus.

He started the second verse, and before she knew it, it was over. The crowd roared with applause and cheers, then began saying, "Again," over and over until Joe motioned for Billy to restart it. That time, Erin was better able to relax and actually enjoyed it.

Joe began a popular duet of theirs, then Billy joined in. Erin noticed that Baz was back, and she saw Hugh on the stage next to him. Hugh said something to him and was then, it seemed, gently pushed forward. He smiled at her as the crowd began cheering and joined her behind the piano.

"He just won't take no for an answer, will he?" he said softly in her ear.

"Did you say no?" she asked, knowing what a showman he was.

"Well, no, but I didn't make it easy for him, either," he said with a laugh.

"Good! I'm glad you're here, now I can leave!"

"I'll not do this without you," he said, raising his eyebrows at her.

She was about to stand when Hugh shook his head and turned away from her as if to leave the stage. "Wait," she said, and after a well-timed pause, he smiled and turned back to her. "Meanie!" she whispered.

"No, I believe the word you're looking for is 'sneaky,' remember?" he said under his breath and waited for her to recall his reference.

"No, you said you've been called *worse*, remember?"

"*Is* 'meanie' worse than 'sneaky,' though?"

"I'd say it is… maybe… it depends on the circumstances."

By now the Joplin's had stopped and were watching the apparent argument along with the rest of the guests. "Don't mind us," Hugh said and gently nudged her arm, making her laugh.

After that, Joe and Billy took a few requests, which included some traditional songs, such as "Danny Boy," "The Girl I Left Behind Me," then, in honor of the party's theme, they sang, "Here Comes the Sun," "Good Day Sunshine," and "A Hard Day's Night." Erin and Hugh sang along until it was time for the festivities to wind down.

When they were done, she was glad she'd joined them, though all the compliments afterward embarrassed her. So many people she hadn't met shook her hand or told her how amazing her voice was as she and Hugh rejoined the crowd. The words 'thank you' were said so many times they started to lose their meaning.

Finally, Baz took the stage. He was in his element as he addressed his guests. "Again, I'd like to thank you for coming. If you have a glass, please raise it. To all of you, and perhaps next year, to David as well." Everyone's eyes turned to her, and her face burned.

There was an awkward silence, so Erin lifted her bottle of water and said, "Perhaps next year… to David's early release." She closed her eyes, wanting to flee, but knew she was surrounded. A warm hand touched her shoulder, and she turned, burying her face in Hugh's shirt.

Baz finished his speech and told them to stay as long as they wished but to be sure to take a parting gift from the table before they left. Hugh led her out from the middle of the crowd as the large screen began playing the last episode of season three. It began with a long recap of everything that had happened beforehand.

Finally, David is seen standing on a hill holding the time travel device, the strong wind blowing his hair. He looks tired and weary, sick of being torn through time. Lifting his hand, he stares at the thing with hatred.

Erin watched her husband close his eyes and hold it out as though he would drop it. That scene made her catch her breath every time she saw it, including then. The show's fans knew that if he let it go, the show would be over, and nobody wanted that; she even heard a woman nearby whisper, "Don't do it!" and she couldn't help but smile.

Instead of letting it go, John Thomas clutches it, his knuckles white, as a tear rolls down his cheek. His struggle is heartbreaking. Then, with a wild look, he raises the device and throws it like a baseball with all his strength.

The screen goes black, and it's as if the audience is experiencing what he does. Birds are twittering, and the wind is heard moving the tall grasses as he opens his eyes and turns around. Before him, just at the bottom of the berm he's standing on, is his small farmhouse.

Gasping, he begins to run toward it, falling and tumbling, just as Joe had done before him. When he stands to his feet, it's clear that the farm hasn't been lived in since he disappeared. Weeds and vines have engulfed most of the house, and the land has become overgrown, covered with brambles and trees.

John Thomas approaches the door and tries the handle. It is unlocked, though it takes a bit of effort to free the rusty hinges. His home is unchanged as he slowly steps inside.

At ten o'clock, Erin began yawning so hard her eyes would water, so she knew it was time for her to head back to the house and turn in for the night. She said goodnight to Baz and Vincent, then found Hugh, sitting with a smartly dressed gentleman who seemed only a few years older than her. "Erin! I'd like to introduce you to Nicholas James Heenan, the—"

"Director of *Future Explorations*, I know! Oh, it's so nice to meet you, Mr. Heenan!" she said, her sleepiness forgotten for the moment. The two men stood, and Erin shook his outstretched hand.

"Everyone calls me Heenan—"

"And the *ladies* call him 'He-man,'" Hugh said and laughed, while the greying ginger Irishman rolled his eyes.

"I think I'll stick to Heenan, thank you," Erin said. "I'm Erin Elliott, Da—"

"David Elliott's wife, yes, I know. Hugh has been tellin' me what good company you've been tonight," he said with a delightful Irish accent.

"Has he? Well, I've been telling everyone what a pain in the rear end he's been," she said and played at punching his arm.

"I'm glad the two of you've been gettin' along so well," he said, his blue eyes twinkling before they suddenly turned to her and became serious. "I must say, it's nonsense, this whole mess with David! He's the last person who'd do such a thing, and anyone who knows him would agree."

"And most who don't," Hugh added.

"Yeah, it's not been fun. And *I* must say that what you did with *Future Explorations* was amazing! I wish they'd do a spin-off or something."

"Ach, well," he said and looked around them before leaning in closer to her. "You didn't hear it from me, but conversations are bein' had about that very thing." He then put his finger up to his lips.

"Wow! If I *had* heard what you'd just said, I'd be freaking out right now, but since I couldn't hear you, and as I don't speak Irish and never would've understood you anyway, the secret is safe with me. May I tell David what I didn't hear?"

"I like her," he said, turning to Hugh. "I'd hold off just for now, if you're able. It may take several years to have somethin' worth producin', and he'll be hearin' about it soon enough if anythin' comes of it… once he's home, that is."

"I can't tell you how much I hope that happens… the show and him coming home… soon. Oh, and our son, Peter, will be starting drama classes next term. He and David look so much alike, perhaps he could stand in for a younger John Thomas," she said and laughed. "I know, wishful thinking."

"Food for thought," Heenan said with a smile.

The tiredness was back, and she yawned, causing a chain reaction. "Well, I'm off to get some beauty sleep, I need all I can get. Have a nice night, and it was so good to meet you, Heenan." She accepted an air kiss on each cheek and then hugged Hugh.

"Please excuse me for a moment," he said, and then led her a few feet away. "I truly am glad we met, Erin. I've had a much better night in your company than I would've had alone."

"Yeah, me too. You're alright for an actor," she said and hugged him again.

"I don't know when I'll see you again, but take care of yourself and, give David my regards the next time you see him, alright?" he said, still embracing her.

Erin smiled at the way he said 'alright' with his gentle Australian accent. "Okay, I will. I hope it's not too long till I see you again! You're like the Aussie big brother I didn't know I had," she said, then let go of him and turned toward the house.

"Erin?"

"Yeah?" she said and turned back to him.

"It's gonna to be alright, you'll see," he said and smiled warmly at her.

"Yeah, I know. Thanks."

Chapter Seventy-One

AFTER PARTY

In the morning, Erin got out of bed feeling like the night before had been a dream, though she could still remember snippets from the ones she'd actually had. In them, David was home, and Hugh knocked on the door unexpectedly. Kitty led him to David's office to wait for them.

She entered the room, so he stood and hugged her. Suddenly, David came in, saw them, and began trying to beat Hugh up. She was trying to keep them apart and explain that nothing had happened and that she only thought of him as a brother. However, David wouldn't listen and hit Hugh, breaking his nose.

She sighed at the memory, wishing life wasn't so complicated, and trying to decide whether she wanted to tell David about what happened at the party or not. *Damn! I already sent him an email. Oh well, I'm sure someone who was there will sell the story and the tabloids will have a field day with it, so it doesn't matter.*

Her body ached as she stood, and though she felt like she'd slept well, she was still tired. *Thank God I have a treatment tomorrow!* she thought and headed to the bathroom.

Too tired to get dressed, she went to breakfast in her pajamas and robe, desperate for a cup of strong tea or coffee. She didn't say much, though Vincent was bubbly and talked non-stop about the events of the night. "Oh, *Bellesa,* you were having a good night with Hugh?"

"Yeah, it was really nice. I guess I should thank you, Baz, for trying to bring us together," she said.

"I am only glad you've forgiven me for doing so without your knowledge. I'm pleased to hear you enjoyed yourself," he said.

"How soon do you think Philip could be ready to take me home?"

"There's no need to rush—"

"Something is not right, *Bellesa?*" Vincent said, interrupting Baz.

"I'm fine, I just need to get back to Juniper," she said, but Vincent cocked his head to the side as if he didn't believe her. "I guess it's just that I had such a good time… with adults, and it's not going to be like that again for a while. It's a bit sobering, but I really do need to get home."

"*Sí, bellesa*, perhaps this is being so. I will be sending to your home with you some of the cakes of the party. I will not be eating all of it!" he said and laughed lightly.

"Good, it was scrummy! Please tell Yonnie that it was delicious!"

"He is knowing this, *bellesa*. He is very much not modest of his ability, but I will be telling him for you anyway."

"Thank you," she said and tried to relax while she ate her breakfast. Though there wasn't any reason she could think of for it, her nerves were on edge, and she couldn't finish her food. Finally, she couldn't sit there any longer. "I need to get dressed and packed," she said, though she wasn't looking forward to the chore.

After a long goodbye, several bags of party favors, cake, and many hugs and kisses, Erin was in the back seat of the Rolls-Royce. Philip smiled at her in the rearview mirror, and she tried to smile back. "I'm sorry, Philip, I'm just really tired and maybe a bit melancholy today," she said.

"That's quite alright, and most understandable," he said kindly, and began rolling slowly down the crunchy gravel driveway. "If you'd like a chat, I'll be here."

She smiled in spite of herself. "Good to know you won't be going anywhere," she said, and settled into her seat, longing for a short nap.

"Here we are, Erin," Philip said and turned the ignition off.

"Here? What do you—" She woke with her seatbelt still fastened, lying awkwardly on the seat, her purse and some of the gift bags under her head like pillows. Sitting up with a groan, she looked out the window and saw they were parked outside her home. "I… slept the whole way here?"

"You did," he said, and got out to open the door for her.

He took her hand to help her out, and she felt dazed. "I'm sorry, Philip, I didn't expect to sleep that long."

"Nothing to apologize for, my dear. I had a comfortable, quiet drive, though it seems you didn't," he said, seeing her trying to stretch out all the kinks and cricks from sleeping in such an awkward position. "You go on inside, I'll open the boot."

"I'll be alright," she said and bent back into the car to grab her purse. On the seat, she saw the pillowcase she'd won the night before had fallen out of a gift bag. *Holy Moses!* she thought and quickly stuffed it back into the bag.

"Never mind that, Erin, I'll gather your things for you," Philip said, coming around from the trunk.

"Thanks," she said and stepped through the iron gate, then up the five steps to her door while reaching into her purse for her keys. Not finding them, and being too tired to keep searching, she rang the doorbell. Philip joined her, carrying her suitcase and her many bags while she waited.

Finally, Kitty opened the door, smiling, but clearly surprised to see them. "Aww, 'ello, mum, I weren't expectin' ta see ya 'ome so early," she said as Erin stepped inside, and Kitty took the things from Philip.

She was closing the door and Erin said, "Wait!" She flung open the heavy wooden door and ran down the stairs.

Philip stopped, looking a bit perplexed, and smiled at her. "Have I forgotten anything?"

Erin shook her head and wrapped her arms around him, unable to keep from crying. After a while, she could finally speak. "Thank you for everything you've done for me this weekend. It just means the world to me!"

"But I've done nawt, really."

"Oh, but you have! I had an unforgettable tea with you, and I got to meet Churchill. You have been a kindred spirit to me, and I'll never forget it!" she said and covered her face.

"Now, now, you speak as though you'll never see me again! I'll be here next year and the year after to deliver you to the Thompson's, and I'll expect you to find time to join me and Churchill again for a proper tea party each year. Now, dry your tears, love… chin up!" he said.

"Okay, that sounds nice, something to look forward to. I'll miss you," she said.

"I'll miss you as well, Erin." He touched the brim of his black flat cap and nodded his head, then he got back into the car and drove away.

Chapter Seventy-Two

Erin was having a hard time concentrating on anything Monday morning except the promise of another treatment. What made it worse was that it had become forbidden fruit because she wanted him to touch her body and enjoy it while she enjoyed his. She was trembling as she sat on the bed in the clinic, waiting for Louis to come in.

The anticipation was almost overwhelming, and she jumped with every noise she heard, wanting it to be the door opening. Her breath was coming out in a short, staccato rhythm, steady and strong and getting faster as the minutes dragged on, until she finally heard Wendy greet him.

The door opened, and the room filled with their energy, making her ears ring. "Good... morning... Louis, how—" she began, short of breath, but he didn't allow her to finish.

"I... need tae tell yeh... before we start... before I'm tempted again... tae— I dinnae wannae cause yeh any more heartache, sae... I—I... Please stop pantin', Erin! I cannae stand et!" he said, also breathing hard.

"I don't think... I can," she said, longing so badly to reveal herself to him yet knowing it was wrong, and also not wanting him to see her fat, naked body.

"I dinnae ken if I can control maself today. Ma heart wants tae resist the temptation, and no' make yeh cry again, but ma body wants tae... do sae much more. Even now I'm fightin' the desire tae pull the curtain away and... well, I'll no' do et, but et's almost more than I can stand at the moment. How will we make et... another year without... givin' in to these desires, Erin? And then what?"

Erin's heart sank. "Oh God, you're right. I don't know what to do. My heart is sick over it, but my body... longs to be held and touched by a man's hands. That fucking judge!" she said.

"Aye," he said, and then remembered he wasn't meant to know who she was. "Tell me about yer husband, his personality, for example? What's he look like... where's he from? Yeh mentioned a judge, so I reckon he's... in jail?"

"Oh, shit! Did I? Yeah, he's in jail, but I don't want to talk about it. He's tall, thin... Scottish. He's patient and gentle and loves me. He's terrified that I'm going to leave him for you, and if he knew about... this, he'd be beside himself.

"Dammit, Louis! This is too hard! How did I let it get so out of control? Okay... let's just... get the treatment over with, and... would you please hand me my phone? It's under my things on the chair."

"Aye," he said and lifted the curtain just enough to hand it to her. She opened her phone's photo album, seeing David's face smiling at her, then she relaxed and allowed herself the pleasure of *his* imagined touch.

—

Louis took his clothing off and braced himself, knowing it would take all his waning willpower to keep it 'business only' that time. He approached the bed and touched her leg, which made him become so hard it throbbed. "Oh!" she moaned as an exhalation when he entered her.

He could hardly stand the conflict he was faced with. He had started dreaming about her nearly every night, waking to an ache and longing in his heart for her company and her touch on his body. Though he knew it was wrong and dangerous to dwell on it, it was so powerful, and he was so... alone, that he often indulged in fantasies about her.

He hated the thought of going back to bimonthly treatments and was more tempted to touch her and even to try to win her love for himself than he'd ever been about anything in his life. But... to hear her cry again, as she'd done the week before, would rip his heart out once more, and the last thing he wanted to do was hurt her. She'd admitted to wanting his touch but hated herself for it.

He wanted her love but only if it was freely given, without regret or filled with guilt, and he knew he'd never have that from her. She had already climaxed twice for him, and she seemed calm and relaxed. He'd gotten that far without giving in to the temptation, but when he looked down and saw himself sliding into her, he was overcome with desire.

—

Erin suddenly thought she felt the bed begin to move. Louis pulled out of her, and then she knew the bed *was* moving upward. "Louis! What are you doing?" she exclaimed. There was no answer. "Louis?" She felt his hands on the insides of her thighs, moving toward her pubic area, and she didn't know what to do.

It was clear to her what he was setting himself up to do, and she longed for him to touch her and taste her, but she also wanted him to stop. "Louis, please!" She could feel his hand trembling as he lay it over her vulva, and his first two fingers gently touched her clitoris. Panic was setting in, and she was frozen, wanting it both ways, not able to make up her mind.

His fingers moved slowly down to the opening of her vagina. Panting, she shook with desire and fear, but didn't… couldn't tell him to stop. He pressed his fingers into her and fluttered them together as they penetrated her deeply.

When he plunged them into her further, he began kissing the insides of her thighs, and she knew she needed to stop him or they'd both lose control completely. His lips were getting closer; she could feel his breath and facial hair tickling her skin. It was suddenly too much, way too much.

"No! Stop! Louis, stop!" she cried.

He stopped, but he didn't back away. "God, Erin! I want tae… please allow me tae—I wannae taste yeh. I wannae touch yeh with ma tongue!" he begged and continued pressing his fingers into her.

"Stop! Please stop! Please back away and put the bed back down or… or I'll have to press the call button. I can't do this with you! Please… finish the treatment and… leave." He removed his fingers, and she felt the bed begin to descend.

—

"A'right. You're right, I'm sorry. I... lost ma resolve for a moment. I'm a'right now," he breathed. He entered her once more and didn't waste any time. She was right, he'd crossed the line again, and it was time to get going. He'd have to rein himself in and stop the fantasies between treatments, as it was making it so much more difficult to control himself.

He finished and pulled out of her, feeling ashamed. She didn't say anything, she just pulled her legs in and lay silently on the bed. He wanted to apologize and try to fix what he'd done, but he could sense a slight hostility coming from her, so he cleaned off and got dressed without a sound.

"I'm sorry, Erin. I'll see yeh in two weeks," he said and left the room.

—

Fuck! FUCK FUCK FUCK! That was too close! she thought as she laid on her side and trembled.

It's not all his fault, you know? You wanted him to do it! You desire him and his touch even more now, and you'll let him do it next time.

You're such a fool, Erin!

Chapter Seventy-Three

YOUTUBE SURPRISE

E rin's phone rang on Monday afternoon as she was trying to forget about what had happened with Louis that morning. She was surprised to see it was Lily. "Did you leave something here?" she said when she answered.

"Huh? What? Uh, no," Lily floundered, clearly not expecting the greeting.

"Oh, well then, what's up?"

"It's simply gorgeous, Erin! I bawled my eyes out the first time I heard it, truly!" her friend gushed, utterly confusing her.

"Well, that's nice… I think, but what are you talking about?"

There was another moment of silence before Lily began laughing. "You had me going there! You know perfectly well what I'm talking about."

"Maybe we should start over. Hello, Elliott residence, this is Mrs. Elliott… Oh, hi, Lil, it's so good to hear from you! To what do I owe the pleasure of hearing your lovely voice?"

"Come on, Erin, the song! I can't believe the Joplin brothers wrote a song for you and that you did a duet with Billy and—"

"What? How'd you hear about that?" Erin said, interrupting her.

"It's everywhere, silly! Everyone wants to know who the female singer is, but I know it's you! They're just lazy anyway, your name is in the description."

"I assume there's something on YouTube, then?" Erin said, her cheeks growing warmer by the second.

477

"You mean you really don't know about it? That's crazy! Just search Billy Joplin… or I'll send it to you, hang on."

"Wait, Lily, this is long distance. I'll look it up and call you back, okay?"

"Oh, okay. I'm sorry, Erin, I didn't know you hadn't—"

"Don't be silly, Lil, you didn't post it, so don't worry. I'll call you right back, bye." Erin hung up and groaned. *Of course someone posted it! Great, this is just what I need, more attention and more questions,* she thought.

She opened YouTube and the very first suggestion was called, '*Billy Joplin Performs New Song With Unknown…*' Her name wasn't on that one, which made her feel a bit better. She tapped on it and braced herself, then noticed how many views it had.

"Ten million views? Good night nurse!" she said out loud and stood. Next, she heard footsteps approaching quickly toward David's study, where she was at the time.

Kitty poked her head through the open door, out of breath and panting. "What is it, mum? Are ya a'right?"

"Sorry, but I just got some crazy news, and I'm a bit stunned," she said and beckoned her into the room.

"Cor blimey, mum, ya gave me a fright," she said with her hand pressed to her heart. "What'd ya learn, then, if ya don't mind my askin'?"

She held up her phone and touched play. They listened together, Kitty watching the screen closely, while Erin looked away. "That's what I learned. Lily called me all excited about it."

"I reckon I'd 'ave done the same, mum! That were stonkin'! You've a lovely voice, truly," she said, beaming. "Did ya sing more than one?"

"What do you mean?"

"This one 'ere says—"

Erin looked at the screen and her heart jumped. "Oh no!"

"I fink we should at least listen to it, mum, wou'n't you agree?" she said slyly, but Erin knew her motives.

"You're fooling nobody, but go on, just don't laugh at me."

Kitty's mouth opened wide with shock, then she knit her brows. "I fought ya knew me bet'er 'an 'at, mum," she said, sounding wounded.

Erin sighed and touched the woman's hand tenderly. "Yes, I do, and I'm sorry. I'm just afraid it'll be… bad, I guess."

"G'on now, I've never known anyfing you've done to be bad. And beggin' your pardon, but if it's at all like the o'ver one, it'll be brilliant!"

"Well, I'm glad you have so much faith in me," Erin said and touched the play button.

The next song began, and she smiled from the memory of singing with the Joplin brothers. It was one of their best loved songs called, "Out of the Wilderness," and it usually made her get choked up. The night of the party, she'd gotten through most of it before having to stop and let Billy finish without her.

When the video reached that point, Kitty covered her mouth. "Blimey, 'at were lovely, truly!" she said when the song ended, and they could hear the guest's applause in the background.

Erin shrugged. "It helps to be singing with Billy! He was so sweet when we met. He was nervous and a bit shy, while Joe was full of beans, goading him and trying to tease his little brother. We got on right away," she said.

"Mum? Does 'at say 'Hugh Jackman?'"

She watched the words scroll when she hovered over the next video, and sure enough it did. "Wow! Yeah, it does." Kitty raised her eyebrows and gave her a look that seemed to say both, 'You didn't tell me?' and, 'Are you going to play it or not?'

"Fine," Erin said and rolled her eyes as she touched it. It began with Joe singing, until Billy joined in. There was a commotion on the side of the stage, then the crowd began going wild when Hugh stepped into view, though it seemed as though he'd been given a slight push.

Erin was sitting behind the piano, and Hugh approached her. The video showed him lean in toward her ear, and Kitty gasped. "Mum! What'd 'ee say?"

Erin paused it and laughed. "Amongst other things, he said, and I quote, 'I'll not do this without you.'" She'd forgotten about that and felt her cheeks get warmer still at the memory. "That was really sweet of him, wasn't it?"

"I'd say so! I can 'ardly 'b'leave it! Now, don't keep me in s'pence!"

She touched the screen again, and the two women watched as Erin's eyes grew wide. It seemed like she was about to get up, but Hugh shook his head and turned away from her as if to leave the stage. "Wait," they could just barely hear her say, then Hugh smiled and turned back to her.

By now the Joplin's had stopped and were watching the apparent argument along with the rest of the guests. They watched one more video, then Erin gasped, "Oh, shoot, I have to call Lily!"

"And I've laundry ta get back to."

"Have fun with that," Erin said with a smile as she opened her phone app. Kitty left the room, already humming the songs softly to herself.

"Well? Isn't it wonderful?" Lily said when she answered.

"You're asking the wrong person. *Billy* was fantastic, at least," she said, knowing her friend would disagree.

"Are you kidding, Erin… *over ten million views*? Come on, everyone loves it! Nick has been gushing over it, and my mom messaged me to say she had it and the others on a playlist she's been listening to on repeat! I even called the radio station and requested it, but they told me that they don't have them yet. You do know there's more than one, right?"

"I noticed, yes, and okay, they aren't horrible, but I didn't know they'd be shared with the world! It's an odd feeling that I don't know how to process. Usually, it's David's fame that gets me any attention, but this seems to be for me… though maybe it's mostly Billy who people are watching—"

"No, Erin—Well, maybe that's why they're clicking on it at first, but they are watching it multiple times because you and him… he… Well, whatever the proper word is, they love your voice too," Lily said passionately.

"Thanks, Lil," Erin said softly. "It's 'he,' I think."

"Huh?"

"You and he, not you and him."

"Uhggg, whatever," she said with exasperation, then giggled. "Now I can say I knew her when!"

Erin couldn't help but laugh with her best friend. "I miss you so much!"

"I miss you the most! Oh, wait! And Hugh Jackman? Are you kidding me? I need details! Damn, the bus is here to drop off Ariana, It's an early release today, so I gotta go. Details later, okay? Love you!"

"Okay, I promise. I love you too, kiss her for me!"

"Will do, bye!"

The line went dead, and Erin sighed. Almost immediately, her phone began to ring again. "Hello?" she said, not recognizing the number.

"Hello, Erin, ya a'right?" Billy's friendly voice said.

"Billy! Wow, it's good to hear your voice. What's up?"

"Have you been on YouTube today?" he asked.

"Hmm, yeah," she said grimly.

"Aww, come on, Erin, have you seen the view counts?"

"Yes, I have, but—"

"People love it, and so do I. Joe's mobile hasn't been off his ear all day," he said with a joyful laugh. "We've not had this much attention since 'Plum Crazy' came out three years ago!"

"I'm so happy for you, Billy! I hope—"

"No, it's not us, Erin, it's you. That's part of the reason I've rung you, actually."

"Oh boy, go ahead," she said, not liking the thought of what might come next.

"Well, Joe wants to have the recording we made remastered and released as a single. Our manager is on him to have you sign a contract. We're not allowed to release it until we have that. You'd be entitled to a percentage of the—"

"Okay, stop," she said, her head still spinning. "What do you mean, a single?"

"Oh, right, well, a single is a song that's released separately from an album, though it may also be on an album at some point. The radio stations and streaming services are going mental, wanting to play it. It's being requested—"

"Billy, I just don't know. What will David say? Give me a minute to think." *You know he'd be chuffed! This is something you've always wanted, so just do it.* "Billy?"

"Yes, I'm here," he said, the excitement in his voice overflowing.

"Okay, I'll do it, but I'll have to talk to David's... people and have... other people look it over... I guess I'll have to figure out who, before I sign anything," she said and laughed.

"You're aces, Erin! I'm chuffed to bits, aren't you?"

"Not yet, but if I keep talking to you, I'm sure I will be soon enough. Now go on and tell your brother that you wore me down, and I'll wait for the paperwork."

"Alright, and you take care of yourself, okay?" he said sincerely.

"I will, bye."

"Bye… bye… bye…" he said until she ended the call.

Dang, now I've gotta find out who to call! she thought, and decided to start with David's assistant, Becky. When she opened her phone, she saw that she had a new message. It was from Joe Joplin, asking for her email to send to their manager, so she sent it quickly and then called Becky.

A few minutes into the call, she heard a notification that she'd gotten a new email. She was able to look at it while on the phone, and learned it was the contract; clearly, they'd been working on it beforehand. Once it was sent to Becky, who said she'd send it to someone else, Erin thought she could relax; however, she then heard Junie fussing and Kitty trying to console her, so she got up, knowing she'd want to be fed.

That night, Erin saw her gift bags from the party sitting neatly on her bed. She opened the one she'd stuffed the pillowcase into and took it out. It was wrapped in a heavy plastic sheath that snapped at the top.

After moving the bags to the floor, she sat on the edge of her bed and stared at the image of John Thomas Fife, smiling at her. He was so young and beautiful, and even then, living in the house she shared with him, it was difficult to believe that *he* was her husband. She unsnapped the top, pulled the soft satin fabric out of the bag, and unfolded it.

Through the creased and wrinkled fabric, she saw David, nearly life-sized, his legs pooled up on the floor. When she'd unwrapped it at the party, her plan had been to chuck it when she got home, but in the dark privacy of her bedroom, she changed her mind. She stood and laid it on the bed, then she opened her closet and found several extra pillows.

Feeling utterly embarrassed, she stuffed them into the body-length pillowcase and stared at it. *This is ridiculous, Erin! You're not a teenager or an obsessed fan! What if someone finds out?* she thought as she got undressed and into her pajamas.

"I don't care," she said softly as she laid it in David's spot, the image's head on his pillow. She pulled it close to her, lay her arm across the chest, and snuggled up to it. *This isn't* my *David; this one doesn't know I exist. This one is married to Susannah.*

That night, Erin dreamed that she sat up during a treatment and began kissing Louis through the sheet while he cupped her breast through the thin fabric. She was so turned on when she woke in the middle of the night, that she masturbated, wishing she had her vibrator. Feeling guilty, she went back to sleep, mentally beating herself up.

When she woke again at midnight, the pillow unchanged and lying next to her, she shuddered, remembering how foolish she'd been. She sat up, pulled all the pillows out of it, and replaced them in the closet as neatly as she could, hoping Kitty wouldn't notice they'd been moved. The pillowcase was then balled up and thrown in the small garbage next to her bed.

It was then she remembered what she'd dreamed earlier that night, and what she'd done. She pulled the pillowcase out of the garbage, found David's smiling face, and held it, asking him to forgive her. Finally, she threw on her robe and padded down to the basement, tiptoeing past Kitty and Francie's bedrooms.

She sat in the media room, a tissue box on her lap. The large screen, sound muted, showed David standing in his kilt and jacket, waiting for her. He was clearly nervous and excited as he checked that his tie was straight and his cuffs were positioned correctly several times.

Roger leaned over and said something into his ear that made him smile and turn toward him. After a short nod, the music changed to what she walked down the aisle to, and David's face blanched a bit, then lit up. His smile was unguarded as he turned and watched the scene behind him.

The camera then panned over to her as she stood waiting for her musical cue. Her cheeks were rosy with her increased activity and preparation, as well as excitement and nerves. Her dad was beaming and resplendent as he stood next to her in his full Highland Dress.

Erin paused the recording and closed her eyes, remembering her wedding day. She pulled a tissue out of the box and wiped her eyes, then sighed. It was a dangerous thing, sitting in the dark, feeding her loneliness and knowing it would make her depressed, but she needed to see her husband smiling at her.

It wasn't as though she did it often. Tuesday was normally the only day she allowed herself to dwell on it. She was alone, then, and could cry all she wanted without worrying anyone. On the days Kitty and Francie were there, she managed to keep it together… mostly.

When she finally returned to bed, she stuffed the John Thomas pillowcase again. Like before, she snuggled up to it and told him how she missed him. No matter how silly it was, she did feel a bit better and slept peacefully through the rest of the night.

Chapter Seventy-Four

NIGHT GUARD

On Monday night, David lay on the bed in his cell, wanting time to go faster, but it went slower and slower every day. It was only five months into his two-year sentence, and he didn't know how he'd ever make it that long. He wondered if Erin was asleep, *and is she alone in our bed?* his mind slipped into his thoughts, though he tried not to think that way.

Too often, his mind was obsessed with the man allowed to give her treatments, while he was stuck in his worst nightmare, though he knew if he didn't keep his thoughts in check, he'd drive himself mad. He was already usually paralyzed with the fear that she'd choose the man she could be with over him, that two years would be too long to wait.

David fell asleep that night imagining he was holding Erin in the bed next to him. He woke sometime later, hearing an unfamiliar noise nearby, too nearby, and realized in an instant there was someone in his cell with him. The blood froze in his veins, and he broke out in a cold sweat, not knowing what to do.

"Mornin', Elliott," he heard Officer Guthmann say. "Get up!" he barked and ripped the bedding violently off the bed. "You should know, Elliott, Sally's paid me all his personal cash for the last two weeks so I'd set up a tryst with you." He sounded almost giddy at what he knew would be going through David's mind at that moment.

David took a deep, cautious breath, trying to keep from showing his terror. "Aye? And how much will et take tae keep him away?" He hoped there was a price and that he'd be able to pay it.

"Unfortunately, you'll not be able to pay it, Elliott," Guthmann said, building the suspense and making David want to vomit.

Everything in him wanted to run or fight, but he knew better. If he even tried to resist, he'd get a true beating, plus whatever Sally had planned for him. He rolled over and sat up on the edge of his mattress, starting to tremble despite his efforts not to.

"You know what to do!" He was obviously enjoying his power. "Up against the wall." This was asked of him often when they did a search of his cell, but that was usually done during the day, not the middle of the night.

"Listen," David said, hoping against all hope to sway him somehow.

"Shut up and *relax*." There was a sinister edge to his voice, so David stood, facing the wall opposite his bed, and put his hands, palms flat, against the cold concrete. "Now drop em," he whispered, putting his face up close to his ear.

He could feel the man's hot breath on his cheek and a shiver ran through him. Panic was building inside him, so he closed his eyes, thinking about how Erin had looked just after Juniper was born. Her hair wet and her face red with exertion, holding their newborn daughter and smiling at him.

He pulled his boxers down, then heard his room being torn apart, and everything went flying. Seeing one of his shoes come flying toward him out of the corner of his eye, he ducked and let out a short yelp of fear. Officer Guthmann seemed to be amused by it and laughed.

He took his baton and touched it to the inside of David's leg, "Now spread 'em." He was right next to his face, running the baton up and down the inside of his leg, bringing the bile up to his throat.

"Please," David said, desperate and not knowing what to do.

"Oh! So now you're askin' for it?" Guthmann teased and watched him shaking in fear. "DO IT!" he yelled, still with his head right next to David's.

"A'right!" He lifted his foot out of the leg of his shorts, moved it over about eight inches, and set it back down.

"More, Elliott," he said calmly and quietly, with a foul, nauseating tone. David thought he truly might be sick as he stood naked, legs spread before the man, waiting for what he just knew was coming next. "Don't move an inch!"

Officer Guthmann stepped out of the cell, and David started to shiver with adrenaline and the cold air hitting the sweat he was covered in. After a few long, terrifying minutes, he heard someone step quietly into the cell. He heard something being placed onto his bed, and then someone was again, too close behind him.

"Pack up, Elliott," Guthmann whispered into his ear. "You've been exonerated and will be released before lunch." The man walked out of the room, closing the door behind him with a bang and the sound of the lock engaging.

David stood frozen in place for a few seconds, trying to catch his breath and keep from bawling like his infant daughter. When he regained his composure, he got dressed in the clothes he'd been wearing when he'd been arrested, which were lying on his bed next to an empty copy paper box. He then put the few items he possessed into the box, wondering what had just happened.

His head was swimming, and he thought he remembered Guthmann say he'd been exonerated. He sat on his unmade bed, allowing his body to decompress. *Exonerated?* he thought, *but how and why?* Though he assumed he'd be told eventually, his mind kept going round and round with unanswered questions.

If he were released, *released!* he thought, wanting to cry at the word in itself, where would he go? Where would Erin be? She'd mentioned at her last visit that she'd been thinking of staying with his mother in Scotland but didn't want to do that because she'd be further away from the prison.

He skipped breakfast, not wanting to deal with the rest of the inmates, and he wasn't hungry anyway. At eleven o'clock, he was brought to the governor's office and told to sit on one of the chairs placed in front of a large, imposing, wooden desk. The governor came in, and David felt as though he were sitting before his old headmaster at the boarding school he'd attended, so long ago. The man put a manila folder on his desk and sat in his high-backed leather chair.

"Well, it seems you've been wrongly accused, and as of 11:55 today you will be exonerated. You may use the telephone once your paperwork is signed and in order. You will then be given any personal belongings that were confiscated at your arrival, as well as £40.00 for a taxi before you leave the building. Your barrister has been made aware of this and should be in contact with you before too long, I expect."

He was asked to sign quite a few pages and then given several pamphlets and booklets on his rights. Once that was done, he was led to a room where the contents of the box were inspected, and he was given the opportunity to use the telephone. He didn't know Erin's mobile number, so he tried his landline in London, which rang and rang without answer.

"May I have my personal effects now, please?" he asked the woman behind the thick glass near the row of telephones. She nodded, pointed to a door, and continued typing on an unseen computer. David knew his mobile would be dead by then, so he went back to the telephone he had just used and saw the number for several taxi companies.

He chose one at random, called them, and then went to the door, which the woman had to unlock for him. There was a loud buzz before he was allowed to push it open and walk through. Standing at a high counter, he gave the man behind it his prisoner number and waited while someone went to wherever the items were stored.

A clear plastic bag was handed to him, which contained his mobile, billfold, and keys, along with the odds and ends that had been in his pockets when he was arrested. A few quid in change and a pink stone which shimmered in the light that Erin had found whilst on a walk they'd taken with Junie on that strangely warm March day nearly six months earlier.

The last thing he took from the bag was his daughter's dummy, although Erin called it a nukie, and smiled, though what he really wanted to do was cry. It had fallen on the ground, and he'd slipped it into his pocket to be washed later. He put it back into the pocket it had been in when he'd been booked and held it tight as he was led to a heavy metal door.

The man behind the counter pushed a button and there was another loud buzz. When he went through that door, there was another one ahead of him. He was in a vestibule and waited while the same man stepped into a room adjacent to the one he'd just been in, with thick, bulletproof, security glass.

There was another loud buzz, and David was then able to push open the thick, heavy door, letting bright, midday light into the room, which caused him to have to shield his eyes as he stepped out into his newfound freedom.

ACKNOWLEDGEMENTS

Thank you to Scott, my dear husband, who has been my rock and helper throughout this whole ordeal. I couldn't have done this without him!

Thank you to Mr. Alan Povey, who has been a Godsend regarding British boarding schools and has written the part of Dr. Dingledine, brilliantly!

Thank you to Karen Rathburn, my friend and best beta reader, ever! Your keen eye and comments have helped me so much with this book, and I appreciate it so very much!

Thank you to my family and friends for being there for me and supporting me!